TALES

OF THE

CARAVAN, INN, AND PALACE.

TALES

OF THE

CARAVAN, INN, AND PALACE.

BY

WILLIAM HAUFF.

WITH THE ORIGINAL ILLUSTRATIONS.

TRANSLATED FROM THE GERMAN
BY
EDWARD L. STOWELL.

Fredonia Books
Amsterdam, The Netherlands

Tales of the Caravan, Inn, and Palace

by
William Hauff

ISBN: 1-58963-837-9

Reprinted from the 1882 edition

Fredonia Books
Amsterdam, The Netherlands
http://www.fredoniabooks.com

TRANSLATOR'S PREFACE.

In introducing to American readers these charming and unique Tales, a few details may properly be given of their author's life and literary work. The record, though brief, is one of unusual interest.

Wilhelm Hauff was born at Stuttgart, Germany, in 1802, and received his education at Tuebingen. He graduated from the University, in 1824, with the degree of Doctor of Philosophy; and for the following two years filled the position of tutor in a nobleman's family. It was during the leisure hours afforded by this occupation that he composed the greater part of the works upon which his fame rests. In 1826 he published his "*Maerchenalmanach auf das Jahr* 1826, *fuer Soehne und Toechter gebildeter Staende,*" a translation of which is herewith tendered the American public, under the changed and abbreviated title of: "Tales of the Caravan, Inn, and Palace." In the same year, and closely following the "Fairy Tales," came "*Mittheilungen aus den Memoiren des Satan,*" "*Der Mann im Monde,*" a second volume of "Satan's Memoirs," and a collection of short tales. These volumes appeared in such rapid succession as to obscure for a time the brilliancy of the "Fairy Tales;" but later editions of them acquired a widespread circulation, while their popularity is so constantly on the increase as to suggest the thought that in time they may prove a formidable rival of the "Arabian Nights," in the regards of the young, the world over.

The publication of "The Man in the Moon" gave Hauff a national reputation; but when his "*Lichtenstein, eine romantische Sage*" appeared, shortly afterward, the Wuertembergers hailed him as the coming Walter Scott of Germany. Whether he would have merited this fond and proud prediction of his countrymen, can not now be told. We only know that he seemed to recognize in the historical novel his true field of labor, and that he had already begun a second work of this nature, when he sickened and died, in the Fall of 1827, before he had reached his twenty-fifth birthday.

Hauff stood on the threshold of his career as an author, in the dawning glory of his brilliant talents, when he was stricken down; yet his writings betray no sign of immaturity, and his collected works assure him a niche, high in the temple of literature. The art of investing localities with ideal characters who, in the reader's imagination, haunt the spot forever after, was a gift Hauff shared alike with his English brothers, Scott and Dickens. On crossing the Bridge of Arts, in Paris, at night, one familiar with his works is apt to look about for the tall and graceful form of the "Beggar Girl," with her lantern, and the plate held out so reluctantly for coins. Or, if he wander through the rugged Suabian Alps, Hauff's "*Lichtenstein*" will be the guide-book he consults; and through the valleys and over the hills to the *Nebelhoehle* he will trace the flight of the stern Duke Ulerich, pausing maybe at the little village of Hardt to pick out if possible the piper's home, and to look sharply at every village maid, lest the kind-hearted little "Baerbele" should pass him unawares.

Some of Hauff's poems became quite popular in Germany, and several of his songs may be heard to-day rising on the evening air from out the beautiful valleys he loved so well.

Because of his genius and his early death, Hauff becomes associated in our mind with the English poets, Chatterton, Keats and Shelley; and in thinking of him we recall his own sad words—

> "Oh, how soon
> Vanish grace and beauty's bloom;
> Dost thou boast of cheeks ne'er paling,
> Glowing red and white unfailing?
> See! the roses wither all!"

CHICAGO, *October*, 1881.   E. L. S.

CONTENTS.

Part I.

Tales of the Caravan.

Part II.

Tales of the Inn.

Part III.

Tales of the Palace.

CONTENTS

PART I.

TALES OF THE CARAVAN.

THE CARAVAN.

ONCE upon a time, a large **caravan** moved slowly over the desert. On the vast plain, where nothing was to be seen but sand and sky, might have been heard in the far distance the tinkling bells of the camels and the ringing hoof beats of horses. A thick cloud of dust that moved before it indicated the approach of the caravan; and when a breeze parted this cloud, gleaming weapons and brilliantly colored garments dazzled the eye.

Thus was the caravan revealed to a man who galloped towards it from one side. He rode a fine Arabian horse, covered with a tiger skin; from the deep-red trappings depended little silver bells, while on the horse's head waved a plume of heron feathers. The horseman was of stately bearing, and his attire corresponded in richness with that of his horse. A white turban, richly embroidered with gold, covered his head; his coat and Turkish trousers were of scarlet; while a curved sword, with a rich hilt, hung at his side. He had pulled the turban down well over his face; and this, with the black eyes that flashed from beneath the bushy brows, together with the long beard that hung straight down from his Roman nose, gave him a fierce and uncouth appearance.

When the rider had approached to within about fifty paces of the vanguard of the caravan, he spurred his horse forward, and in a few moments reached the head of the procession. It was such an unusual occurrence to see a single horseman riding over the desert that the escort of the train, fearing an attack, thrust out their spears.

"What do you mean?" cried the horseman, as he saw this warlike reception. "Do you, then, believe a single man would attack your caravan?"

Ashamed of their momentary alarm, the escort dropped their lances; while their leader rode up to the stranger and asked what he wanted.

"Who is the master of this caravan?" inquired the horseman.

"It does not belong to one man," replied the guide; "but to several merchants who are returning from Mecca to their homes, and whom we escort across the desert, as it often happens that travelers are annoyed by robbers."

"Then lead me to these merchants," requested the stranger.

"That may not be done now," replied the guide, "as we must proceed farther on before coming to a halt, and the merchants are at least a quarter of an hour behind us; but if you will ride on with me until we encamp for our mid-day rest, I will then comply with your wish."

The stranger made no reply, but produced a pipe that was fastened to his saddle-bow, and began to smoke, meanwhile riding near the leader of the vanguard. The guide knew not what to make of the stranger; he hardly dared to question him directly as to his name, and no matter how skillfully he sought to draw him into conversation, the stranger would only reply to such attempts as: "You smoke a fine quality of tobacco," or, "Your horse has a splendid pace," with a short "Yes, certainly."

Finally they reached the spot where they were to camp for the noon. The guide posted the guards, but remained himself with the stranger until the caravan should come up. Thirty camels, heavily laden, and attended by armed guards, passed by. After these came the four merchants to whom the caravan belonged, mounted on fine horses. They were mostly men of advanced age, of sober and staid appearance. Only one seemed much younger than the others, and of more cheerful countenance and vivacious spirits. A large number of camels and pack-horses completed the caravan.

The tents were pitched, and the horses and camels ranged around them in a circle. In the centre stood a tent of blue silk cloth. To this tent the leader of the guard led the stranger. As they entered through the curtain, they saw the four merchants sitting on gold embroidered cushions, while black slaves handed them food and drink.

"Who is it you bring to us?" cried the young merchant to the guide. Before the guide could reply, the stranger said—

"My name is Selim Baruch, of Bagdad. On my way to Mecca I was captured by a robber band, and three days ago I succeeded in making my escape from them. The great Prophet permitted me to hear the bells of your camels in the distance, and thus directed me to you. Allow me to journey in your company. Your protection would not be extended to one unworthy of it;

and when you reach Bagdad, I will richly reward your kindness, as I am the nephew of the Grand Vizier."

The oldest merchant made reply: "Selim Baruch, you are welcome to our shelter. It gives us pleasure to assist you. But first of all, sit down and eat and drink with us."

Selim Baruch accepted this invitation. On the conclusion of the repast, the slaves cleared away the dishes, and brought long pipes and Turkish sherbet. The merchants sat silently watching the blue clouds of smoke as they formed into rings and finally vanished in the air.

The young merchant at length broke the silence by saying —

"For three days we have sat thus on horseback and at table without making any attempt to while away the time. To me this is very wearisome, as I have always been accustomed after dinner to see a dancer or to hear music and singing. Can you think of nothing, my friends, to pass away the time?"

The three older merchants continued to smoke, seemingly lost in meditation, but the stranger said —

"Permit me to make a proposition. It is that at every camping-place one of us shall relate a story to the others. This might serve to make the time pass pleasantly."

"You are right, Selim Baruch," said one of the merchants, "let us act on the proposal."

"I am glad the suggestion meets with your approval," said Selim; "but that you may see I ask nothing unfair, I will be the first to begin."

The merchants drew nearer together in pleased anticipation, and had the stranger sit in the centre. The slaves replenished the cups and filled the pipes of their masters, and brought glowing coals to light them. Then Selim cleared his voice with a generous glass of sherbet, stroked the long beard away from his mouth, and said —

"Listen, then, to the story of the Caliph Stork."

THE CALIPH STORK.

I.

NE fine afternoon, Chasid, Caliph of Bagdad, reclined on his divan. Owing to the heat of the day he had fallen asleep, and was now but just awakened, feeling much refreshed by his nap. He puffed at a long-stemmed rosewood pipe, pausing now and then to sip the coffee handed him by an attentive slave, and testifying his approval of the same by stroking his beard. In short, one could see at a glance that the Caliph was in an excellent humor.

Of all others, this was the hour when he might be most easily approached, as he was now quite indulgent and companionable; and therefore it was the custom of his Grand Vizier, Mansor, to visit him every day at this time.

As usual, he came to-day; but, as was unusual with him, his expression was quite serious.

The Caliph, removing the pipe from his mouth for a moment, said —

"Why do you wear so sober a face, Grand Vizier?"

The Vizier crossed his arms on his breast, bowed low before his master, and made answer—

"Sire, whether my face be sober or no, I know not. But beneath the castle walls stands a trader, who has such beautiful wares that I cannot help regretting that I have no spare money."

The Caliph, who had long wished for an opportunity to do his Vizier a favor, sent his black slave below to bring up the trader. The slave soon returned with the man, who was short and stout, of dark brown complexion, and clothed in rags. He carried a box containing all manner of wares: strings of pearls, rings, and richly-chased pistols, cups and combs. The Caliph and Grand Vizier looked them all over, and finally the Caliph selected a fine pair of pistols for Mansor and himself, as well as a comb for the Vizier's wife.

Now just as the merchant was about to close his box, the Caliph espied a small drawer therein, and desired to know if it contained still other valuables. By way of reply, the trader opened the drawer, disclosing a little box containing a blackish powder, and a paper covered with singular writing, that neither the Caliph nor Mansor was able to read.

"These two articles," explained the trader, " came into my possession through a merchant who found them on the street in Mecca. I do not know what they contain, but, for a small consideration, you are welcome to them, as I can make nothing of them."

The Caliph, who took pleasure in preserving old manuscripts in his library, even though he might not be able to read them, bought both the paper and the box, and dismissed the merchant. Then, curious to know what the manuscript contained, he inquired of the Vizier if he knew of any one who could decipher it.

"Most gracious master and benefactor," replied the Vizier, "near the great mosque lives a man called Selim the Learned, who understands all languages. Let him be summoned; perhaps he might know these secret characters."

The learned Selim was soon brought.

"Selim," began the Caliph, "it is said that you are very learned. Look for a moment at this writing, and see if you can make it out. If you can read it, you shall receive a new holiday cloak from me; if you cannot, you will get instead twelve lashes on the back and twenty-five on the soles of your feet, for being misnamed Selim the Learned."

Selim made an obeisance, saying, "Thy will be done, O Sire!"

He then examined the writing long and attentively, suddenly exclaiming, "If this be not Latin, Sire, then give me to the hangman!"

"Read what is written there, if it is Latin!" commanded the Caliph.

Selim thereupon began to translate as follows:

"*Man, whoever thou art, that findeth this, praise Allah for His goodness. He who takes a pinch of this powder, at the same time saying,* MUTABOR, *will be able to transform himself into any animal, and will also understand the language of animals. Whenever he wishes to re-assume the human form, he shall bow three times towards the East and pronounce the same word. But take care that thou dost not laugh while thou art transformed, or the magic word would vanish utterly from thy memory, and thou wouldst remain an animal.*"

When Selim the Learned had read this, the Caliph was pleased beyond measure. He made the scholar swear never to mention the secret to any one; presented him with a beautiful cloak, and then dismissed him. Then turning to his Vizier, he said—

"I call that a good investment, Mansor. I am impatient to become an animal. Come to me to-morrow morning early. We will then go together to the fields, take a little pinch of this magical snuff, and then listen to what is said in the air and the water, in the forest and field."

II.

No sooner had the Caliph Chasid dressed and breakfasted on the following morning, than the Grand Vizier arrived, as he had been commanded to do, to accompany him on his walk. The Caliph put the box containing the

magic powder in his sash, and after bidding his attendants remain in the castle, started off, attended only by
Mansor.

They first took their way through the extensive gardens of the Caliph, vainly searching for some living
thing, in order to make their experiment. The Vizier at
last proposed that they go farther on, to a pond, where
he had frequently seen many creatures, more especially
storks.

The Caliph consented to the proposal of Mansor, and
went with him towards the pond. Arriving there, they
saw a stork walking up and down, looking for frogs, and
occasionally striking out before him with his bill. At the
same time far up in the sky they discerned another stork
hovering over this spot.

"I will wager my beard, Most Worthy Master," said
the Vizier, "that these two storks will hold a charming
conversation together. What say you to our becoming
storks?"

"Well thought of!" answered the Caliph. "But first
let us carefully examine again the directions for resum-
ing our human form. All right! By bowing three times
towards the East and saying '*Mutabor*,' I shall be once
more Caliph, and you Grand Vizier. But, for heavens
sake! recollect! *No laughing, or we are lost!*"

While the Caliph spoke, he noticed that the stork
above their heads was gradually approaching the earth.
Quickly drawing the box from his girdle, he put a good
pinch to his nose, held out the box to the Vizier, who
also took a pinch, and both then cried out: "*Mutabor!*"

Their legs at once shrank up and became thin and
red; the beautiful yellow slippers of the Caliph and his
companion took on the shape of stork's feet; their arms
developed into wings; their necks were stretched until
they measured a yard in length; their beards vanished,
while white feathers covered their bodies.

"You have a beautiful bill, Mr. Grand Vizier," cried
the Caliph, after a long pause of astonishment. "By the

beard of the Prophet! I never saw any thing like it in my life."

"Thank you most humbly," replied the Vizier, bowing low; "but, if I dare venture the assertion, Your Highness presents a much handsomer appearance as a stork than as Caliph. But come; if agreeable to you, let us

keep watch on our companions over there, and ascertain whether we can really understand *Storkish.*"

In the meantime the other stork had alighted on the ground, cleaned its feet with its bill, smoothed its feathers nicely, and approached the first stork. The two newly-made storks now made haste to get near them, and, to their surprise, overheard the following conversation:

"Good morning, Mrs. Longlegs! So early in the meadow?"

"Thank you kindly, dear Clapperbill; I was just procuring a little breakfast for myself. How would a portion of lizard suit you, or a leg of a frog?"

"Much obliged; but, I have not the least appetite to-day. I come to the meadow for quite another purpose. I am to dance to-day before my father's guests, and therefore wish to practice a little in private."

So saying, the young stork stepped over the field in a series of wonderful evolutions. The Caliph and Mansor looked on in wonder. But when she struck an artistic attitude on one foot, and began to fan herself gracefully with her wings, the two could no longer contain themselves. An irrepressible fit of laughter burst forth from their bills, from which it took them a long time to recover. The Caliph was the first to compose himself.

"That was sport!" exclaimed he, "that money could not buy. It's too bad that the stupid creatures were frightened away by our laughter, or they would certainly have tried to sing."

Just here the Vizier remembered that laughing during the transformation was forbidden them. He communicated his anxiety to the Caliph.

"Zounds! By the Cities of the Prophet, that would be a bad joke if I were compelled to remain a stork! Try and think of that stupid word, Mansor! For the life of me, I can't recall it!"

"We must bow three times towards the East, calling: *Mu—Mu—Mu.*"

They turned towards the East, and bowed away so zealously that their bills nearly ploughed up the ground. But, O Horror! the magic word had escaped them; and no matter how often the Caliph bowed, or how earnestly his Vizier called out—*Mu—Mu*, their memory failed them; and the poor Chasid and his Vizier remained storks.

III.

Sadly the enchanted ones wandered through the fields, without the slightest idea of what course they had better pursue in their present plight. They could neither get rid of their feathers, nor could they return to the town with any hope of recognition; for who would believe a stork, were he to proclaim himself Caliph? or, even believing the story, would the citizens of Bagdad be willing to have a stork for their Caliph? So they stole about for several days, supporting themselves very poorly on fruits, which, on account of their long bills, they could eat only with great difficulty. For lizards and frogs they had no appetite, fearing lest such tit-bits might disagree with their stomachs. The only consolation left them in their wretchedness was the power of flight; and they

often flew to the roofs of Bagdad, that they might see what occurred there. For the first day or two, they noticed great excitement in the streets, followed by sadness. But about the fourth day after their enchantment, while they were resting on the roof of the Caliph's palace, they observed down in the street a brilliant procession. Trumpets and fifes sounded. A man in a gold-embroidered scarlet coat sat upon a richly caparisoned steed, surrounded by a gay retinue. Half Bagdad followed him, and all shouted:

"Hail Mizra! Ruler of Bagdad!"

The two storks perched on the palace roof, exchanged a glance, and Caliph Chasid said—

"Do you perceive now the meaning of my enchantment, Grand Vizier? This Mizra is the son of my deadly enemy, who, in an evil hour, swore to revenge himself on me. But still I will not give up all hope. Come with me, thou faithful companion of my misfortune, we will make a pilgrimage to the grave of the Prophet. Perhaps in that sacred place the spell will be removed"

They rose from the palace roof and flew in the direction of Medina. But so little practice had the two storks had in flying, that it fared hard with them.

"Oh, Sire!" groaned the Grand Vizier, after a few hours' flight, "with your permission I shall have to stop. You fly much too fast! And it is now evening, and we should do well to look out for a place on which to alight for the night."

Chasid harkened to the request of his follower, and, perceiving a ruin that promised to afford a shelter, they flew down to it. The place they had selected for the night bore the appearance of having once been a castle. Beautiful columns rose out of the ruins, while several rooms still in a fair state of preservation, testified to the former splendor of the building. Chasid and his companion strolled through the passages, seeking some dry sheltered spot, when suddenly the stork Mansor stopped.

"Sire," whispered he softly, "I wish it were not so unbecoming in a Grand Vizier, and even more in a stork, to fear ghosts! My courage is fast failing me, for near here there was a distinct sound of sighing and groaning!"

The Caliph also stopped, and very plainly heard a low sobbing that seemed to proceed from a human being, rather than from an animal. Full of curiosity, he was about to approach the place whence the sounds came, when the Vizier caught him by the wing with his bill, and begged him most earnestly not to plunge into new and unknown dangers. All in vain! for the Caliph, who even under a stork's wing, carried a stout heart, tore himself away with the loss of a few feathers, and hastened into a dark passage. He shortly came to a door, through which he plainly heard sighs intermingled with low groans. He pushed open the door with his bill, but remained standing on the threshold in surprise.

In the ruined room, lighted but dimly by a small lattice window, he saw a large owl sitting on the floor. Large tears fell from its great round eyes, while in passionate tones it poured forth its complaints from its curved beak. But when the owl saw the Caliph and his Vizier, who by this time had stolen up. it raised a loud cry of joy. Daintily brushing the tears from its eyes with the brown spotted wings, it exclaimed in pure human Arabic, to the wonder of the listeners:

"Welcome, storks! You are a good omen, as it was once prophecied that storks would be the bearers of good fortune to me."

As soon as the Caliph had sufficiently recovered from his astonishment, he made a bow with his long neck, brought his slender feet into a graceful position, and said—

"O owl of the night! from your words I believe I see in you a companion in misfortune. But, alas! Your hope that we can give you relief is doomed to disappointment. You will yourself appreciate our helplessness when you have heard our story."

The owl requested him to relate it; which the Caliph did, just as we have heard it.

IV.

When the Caliph had concluded his story, the owl thanked him, and said:

"Listen also to my tale, and learn that I am not less unfortunate than yourself. My father is king of India. I, his only and unhappy daughter, am named Lusa. That same sorcerer, Kaschnur, who transformed you, plunged me also into misery. One day he came to my

father and demanded me in marriage for his son Mizra.
But my father, who is a quick tempered man, had him
thrown down-stairs. The wretch found means, by as-
suming other forms, of approaching me; and one day,
as I was taking the air in my garden, he appeared, dressed
as a slave, and handed me a drink that changed me into
this horrible shape. He brought me here senseless from
fright, and shouted in my ears with a terrible voice:
'Here you shall remain, ugly, despised by every creature,
until death; or till some man voluntarily offers to marry
you in your present form! Thus do I revenge myself on
you and your proud father!' Since then many months
have passed. Lonely and sad, I live as a hermit within
these walls, abhorred by the world, despised even by
animals, shut out from all enjoyment of the beauties of
nature, as I am blind by day, and only at night, when
the moon sheds its pale light over these walls, does the
veil fall from my eyes."

The owl finished her story, and once more brushed
away with her wing the tears which the recital of her
sufferings had caused.

The Caliph was sunk in deep thought over the story
of the Princess.

"Unless I am greatly in error," said he, "there is a
hidden connection between our misfortunes; but where
shall I find the key to this riddle?"

"O, Sire," the owl replied, "I suspect that too, for
when I was a little child it was foretold me by a sooth-
sayer that a stork would sometime bring me great good
fortune. And I think I know a way by which we can
accomplish our own rescue."

In great surprise the Caliph asked her in what way
she meant.

"The sorcerer who has done this wrong to us both,"
she answered, "comes once a month to these ruins. Not
far from here there is a room in which he is accustomed
to hold a banquet with many of his fellows. Many times
have I heard them there. On these occasions they relate

to each other their shameful deeds. Perhaps then he will divulge the magic word you have forgotten."

"O, dearest Princess," cried the Caliph, "tell us, when does he come, and where is the banqueting hall?"

The owl remained silent for a moment, and then said: "Do not take it unkindly; but only on one condition can I inform you."

"Speak out! speak out!" exclaimed Chasid. "Whatever your condition it will be acceptable to me."

"Well then, I am also desirous of being set free; but this can only happen by one of you offering me his hand."

The storks were somewhat disconcerted at this proposal; and the Caliph beckoned his follower to leave the room with him.

"Grand Vizier," said the Caliph, closing the door behind them, "this is a pretty piece of business! But you, now, might take her."

' Indeed?" answered he, "and thus give my wife cause to scratch my eyes out, when I get home? Then, too, I am an old man; whereas you are young and unmarried, and therefore in a better position to offer your hand to a beautiful young princess."

"That's the very point," sighed the Caliph, as he sadly allowed his wings to droop to the ground. "It would be buying a cat in the bag; for what assurance have you that she is young and beautiful?"

They discussed the matter for a long time, until at last the Caliph, convinced that the Vizier would rather remain a stork than marry the Princess, concluded to fulfill the condition she had imposed on himself.

The owl was greatly rejoiced, and confessed that they could not have come at a better time, as it was probable that the sorcerers would assemble there that very night. The owl then left the room with the storks to show them to the banquet-room. For a long time they walked through a dark passage, when finally there streamed out bright rays of light through a broken wall. As they came up to the wall the owl cautioned the storks to re-

2

main perfectly quiet. The gap in which they stood overlooked a large room, adorned on all sides with marble
columns, and tastefully decorated; countless colored
lamps made the place light as day. In the centre of the
room stood a round table covered with various dainty
dishes, and upon the divan that encircled it, sat eight
men. In one of these men the storks recognized the
trader who had sold them the magic powder. The person who sat next to him called on him to relate his latest
deeds. The trader then told the story of the Caliph and
his Vizier.

V.

"What kind of a word did you give them?" asked the
other sorcerer.

"A very hard Latin word—*Mutabor.*"

When the storks from their place in the wall, heard
this, they were almost beside themselves with joy. They
ran so fast toward the outlet of the ruins that the owl
could hardly keep up with their long legs. Once clear
of the building, the Caliph said to the owl with much
feeling:

"Savior of my life and the life of my friend! As a lasting reward for what you have done, take me for your
husband."

Then he turned to the East. Three times the storks
bowed their long necks to the sun just rising above the
mountains, "*Mutabor!*" shouted they, and in a trice they
were men again. Then, in the joy of their newly-returned
life, master and follower were laughing and weeping by
turns in each other's arms.

But who could describe their astonishment when they
turned around and saw a beautiful lady, richly dressed,
standing before them? With a smile she gave the Caliph
her hand.

"Do you no longer recognize the owl?" she asked.

It really was the Princess. The Caliph was so enraptured by her beauty and grace, that he declared his transformation into a stork had been the best piece of fortune that had ever happened to him.

The three now set out together on their journey to Bagdad. The Caliph found in his clothes not only the box of magic powder, but his purse as well. He therefore bought in the next village whatever was necessary for their journey, and thus they soon reached the gates of Bagdad. There the arrival of the Caliph caused the greatest surprise. He had long since been given up for dead, and the joy of the people at getting back their beloved ruler knew no bounds. All the more was their wrath inflamed against the traitor Mizra. They rushed to the palace, and took the old sorcerer and his son prisoners.

The Caliph sent the old man to the ruins, and had him hanged in the very room that had been occupied by the Princess when an owl. But to the son, who understood nothing of the art of his father, he gave the choice of death or a pinch of the powder. As the prisoner chose the latter, the Grand Vizier offered him the box. A generous pinch, followed by the magic word of the Caliph, and he became a stork. The Caliph secured him in an iron cage, which was placed in the garden.

Long and happily Caliph Chasid lived with his wife, the Princess. His pleasantest hours were always those of the afternoon, when the Grand Vizier visited him. Then they often spoke of their adventures as storks, and whenever the Caliph felt unusually merry, he began to imitate the Grand Vizier as he appeared when a stork. He stalked up and down the room, set up a great clapping, waved his arms as though they were wings, and showed how the Vizier had turned to the East and called, "*Mu— Mu—Mu—*." All this was great sport for the Caliph's wife and children. But sometimes, when the Caliph clapped too long and cried, "*Mu—Mu—Mu—*" too often, the Vizier was wont to silence him with the threat that if he did not stop he would tell the Princess what their conversation had been before the door of her room in the ruin.

As Selim Baruch finished his story, the merchants testified their approval thereof most heartily.

"Of a truth, the afternoon has passed without our knowing it," said one of them, lifting the curtain of the tent. "The evening wind blows fresh; we could put behind us a good stretch of road."

As his companions were of the same opinion, the tents were folded, and the caravan started on its way in the same order in which it had entered camp.

They journeyed nearly all night, as the days were hot and sultry, while the night was cool and starlit. They came at last to a convenient camping place, pitched their tents and lay down to rest. But the merchants did not neglect to provide for the stranger as bountifully as if he had been their most honored guest. One gave him a cushion, another blankets, a third gave him slaves; in short, he was as well provided for as though he had been at home.

The heated hours of the day were already upon them when they arose from their slumbers, and they therefore unanimously decided to remain where they were until evening.

When night approached, the movement of the caravan was resumed, and its progress was continued until the following noon without impediment. After they had halted and refreshed themselves, Selim Baruch said to Muley, the youngest of the merchants —

"Although you are the youngest of us all, you are always cheerful, and could certainly give us a merry tale. Serve it up, so that we may refresh ourselves after the heat of the day."

"I should be glad to relate something that would amuse you," answered Muley. "Still, modesty in all things is becoming to youth; therefore, my older traveling companions should take precedence. Zaleukos is always so serious and silent, ought he not to tell us what it is that clouds his life? Perhaps we should be able to lighten his sorrow, if such he experiences; for we would willingly treat him as a brother, even though he is not of our religion."

The person thus addressed was a Greek merchant — a man in middle age, fine looking and of vigorous frame, but very grave. Although he was an unbeliever (that is, not a Musselman), he was much beloved by his fellow-travelers, as his whole conduct had won their esteem and confidence. He had but one hand, and some of his companions supposed that this loss was the cause of his grief.

Zaleukos replied to the confidential inquiries of Muley: "I am much honored by the interest you take in me, but have no grief—at least none that you, with even the best intentions, could dispel. Still, as Muley seems to lay so much stress on my sadness, I will tell you something that will perhaps account for my appearing sadder than other people. As you see, I have lost my left hand. It was not missing at my birth, but I was deprived of it in the darkest hours of my life. Whether my punishment was just — whether, under the circumstances, my features could be other than sad—you may judge for yourselves when you have heard the story of the Amputated Hand."

THE AMPUTATED HAND.

I WAS born in Constantinople. My father was an interpreter at the Sublime Porte, carrying on at the same time quite a lucrative trade in ottar of roses and silk goods. He gave me a good education, devoting a part of his own time to my instruction, and also employing one of our priests to superintend my studies. At first he designed me to be the successor of his business, but as I developed greater talents than even he had expected, he changed his mind, and, by the advice of his friends, concluded to make a physician of me; inasmuch as a doctor, whose acquirements were greater than those of the quacks on the market-place, was sure of making his way in Constantinople. Many Franks came to our house, and one of them persuaded my father to allow me to go to the city of Paris, in his country, where the best medical education might be had gratuitously. He proposed to take me with him on his return journey, and the trip should cost me nothing. My father, who had traveled widely in his youth, assented to the arrangement, and the Frenchman told me I should have three months in which to get ready.

I was beside myself with joy at the prospect of seeing foreign countries, and waited for the day of our departure with great impatience. At last the Frenchman finished his business, and prepared for the journey. On the evening before we started, my father led me into his bed-chamber. There I saw fine apparel and weapons lying on the table. But that which attracted my attention most was a large pile of gold, larger than I had ever before seen. My father embraced me, saying—

"See, my son, I have provided these clothes for your journey. These weapons are also yours; they are the same that your grandfather buckled on me when I went out into the world. I know that you can wield them; but never use them except in self-defense, and then strike hard. My fortune is not large; look, I have divided it into three parts: one is yours, another is for my own support, but the third is a sacred trust, to be well guarded, and meant to serve you in the hour of need."

Thus spake my good old father, while tears stood in his eyes, perhaps from a presentiment that he would never see me again.

Every thing went well on the journey. We soon arrived in the land of the Franks, and six days afterwards we entered the great city of Paris. My friend rented a room for me there, and advised me as to the best disposition to make of my money, which amounted in all to two thousand thalers.

I lived for three years in this city, and learned what a qualified physician should know; but I should be guilty of untruth were I to say that I lived there contentedly, for the customs of this people did not please me. I had but few good friends there, but these few were noble young men. In all this time I had heard nothing from my father. The desire to see my home finally prevailed over all other considerations. I therefore seized a favorable opportunity to return. An embassy from the Franks was bound to the Sublime Porte. I engaged as surgeon in the retinue of the ambassadors, and arrived safely once more in Stamboul.

I found my father's house closed. The neighbors were astonished to see me, and told me that my father had been dead for two months. The priest who had instructed me in my youth, brought me the key, and alone

and bereft I entered the desolate house.   I found every
thing as my father had left it, with the single exception
of the gold that he had promised to leave me—that was
missing.   I asked the priest about it.   He made a low
bow, and replied:

"Your father died as a holy man, leaving his gold to
the church."

This was incomprehensible to me, yet what should I
do?   I had no witnesses against the priest, and must
console myself with the reflection that he had not also
regarded the house and goods of my father as a legacy
to the church.   This was the first misfortune that happened to me, but from this time forth, stroke followed
stroke.   My reputation as a physician did not spread,
because I could not stoop to advertise myself on the
market-place; and, above all, I missed my father, whose
recommendation would have secured me admittance to
the wealthiest and most influential families, which now
never gave a thought to the poor Zaleukos.   Then, too,
my father's goods found no sale, as the old customers
disappeared after his death, and to gain new ones would
require time.

Once, as I was hopelessly thinking over my situation,
it occurred to me that I had often seen countrymen of
mine wandering through the land of the Franks, and dis-
playing their wares in the squares of the cities.   I remembered that their goods found a ready sale, because
they came from a strange country, and that the profits on
such merchandise were very large.   My resolution was
taken at once.   I sold the homestead, gave a part of the
sale money to a trustworthy friend to keep for me, and
with the remainder bought such goods as were not common among the Franks; shawls, silk stuffs, ointments,
oils, etc.   I then took passage on a ship, and so began
my second journey to the land of the Franks.

It seemed as though fortune smiled on me again the
moment we left the Dardanelles behind.   Our voyage
was short and fortunate.   I wandered through the cities

and towns of the Franks, and every-where found ready purchasers for my wares. My friend in Stamboul kept forwarding me consignments of fresh goods, and day by day my financial condition improved. When I thought I had made money enough to venture on some larger undertaking, I went to Italy with my goods. I have omitted speaking on one thing that brought me in quite a little sum of money; this was my knowledge of medicine. When I entered a town, I scattered notices announcing the arrival of a Greek physician, whose skill had restored many to health; and my balsams and medicines brought me in many a sequin.

At last I reached the city of Florence. It was my intention to remain some time in this place, partly because the city pleased me, and partly for the reason that I wished to recover from the fatigue of my wanderings. I rented a shop in the Santa Croce quarter, and not far from it, in an inn, I found a suite of beautiful rooms that overlooked a terrace. I then distributed notices that advertised me as a merchant and physician. I had no sooner opened my shop than a stream of customers poured in, and although my prices were rather high, I sold more than others, because I was polite and affable with my customers.

I had passed four days pleasantly in Florence, when one evening, after closing my shop, as I was counting over the profits of the day, I came across a note, in a little box, that I could not remember having put there. I opened the note, and found that it contained a request that I would come to the Ponte Vecchio that night punctually at twelve o'clock. I studied for a long time over the matter; but, as I did not know a soul in Florence, I concluded that somebody wished to lead me secretly to a sick person, as had happened more than once before. I therefore resolved to go; but, by way of precaution, I took along the sword that my father had given me.

Shortly before midnight I started, and soon came to

c

the Ponte Vecchio. I found the bridge deserted, and
determined to wait until the person who had invited me
there should appear. The night was cold; the moon
shone bright, and I looked down at the waves of the
Arno gleaming in the moonlight. The church clocks
struck twelve. I raised my head, and before me stood
a tall man, covered with a red mantle, a corner of which
he held before his face. I was somewhat startled at first
by his sudden appearance, but collecting myself immediately, said to him:

"If you are the person who ordered me here, tell me
what it is you desire?"

The man in the red mantle turned about and said
slowly: "Follow me!"

I felt somewhat uneasy about accompanying this
stranger, and replied: "Not so, dear sir, until you first
tell me where I am to follow you; and you might also
show me your face, so that I may assure myself that you
mean me no harm."

The stranger, however, assumed to be indifferent, and
said, "If you won't go, Zaleukos, then don't!"

This aroused my anger. "Do you think," exclaimed
I, "that a man like me will allow himself to be made
sport of by every fool? and that I should wait here in
this cold night for nothing?"

In three leaps I reached him, seized him by the cloak,
and shouted still louder, at the same time laying my
other hand on my sword; but the stranger had already
disappeared around the next corner, leaving the cloak in
my hand.

By and by my rage subsided; I still had the cloak,
and this should furnish the key to this singular adventure. I put it on and started to go home. But before I
had gone a hundred steps from the bridge, somebody
brushed by me, and whispered to me in French: "Take
care, Count; it can't be done to-night!" But before I
could look around, this person was far away, and I saw
only a shadow flitting by the houses. I saw at once that

these whispered words were meant for the owner of the cloak, and did not in any way concern me; but they shed no light on the mystery.

The next morning I considered what would better be done in the matter. My first thought was to have the mantle cried in the streets, as though I had found it, but in that case the owner could have sent for it by some third party, and I should be no wiser for my pains. While I was thinking of this, I examined the mantle closely. It was of heavy reddish-purple Genoese velvet, with a border of Astrachan fur, and richly embroidered with gold. The splendid appearance of the cloak led me to think of a plan that I resolved to put in execution. I took the cloak to my store, and offered it for sale; but placed such a high price on it that I was sure it would find no purchaser. My purpose in this was to look everybody who asked about the furred cloak directly in the eye. I thought that as I had had a momentary glimpse of the figure of the unknown man after the loss of his cloak, I would know it among a thousand. There were many admirers of the cloak, whose extraordinary beauty attracted all eyes; but none of them resembled the stranger, and not one of them would pay the exorbitant price of two hundred sequins. It struck me as strange that when I asked one and another whether such cloaks were common in Florence, they all answered, "no," and assured me that they had never before seen such a rich and elegant piece of work.

As evening drew near, a young man, who had often been in my shop, and who had already bid high for the cloak, came in, and threw down a purse of sequins, exclaiming:

"Before God. Zaleukos, I must have your cloak, even if it beggars me."

He at once began to count out his gold pieces. I was in quite a dilemma. I had only hung up the mantle in order that it might perhaps catch the eye of its owner; and along came a young fool to pay the monstrous price, but what could I do? I finally consented to the bargain, as from one point of view I should be well compensated for my night's adventure.   The youth put on the mantle and left, but turned on the threshold and detached a paper that was fastened to the mantle, which he threw to me, saying: "Here, Zaleukos, is something that evidently does not go with the cloak."

I took the paper unconcernedly, and found the following words were written on it: "Bring the cloak to the Ponte Vecchio to-night, at the appointed time, and you will receive four hundred sequins."

I was thunderstruck.   I had forfeited this chance, and had not even attained my purpose.   But not stopping to consider the matter, I gathered up the two hundred sequins, and rushed out after the man who had bought the cloak.   "Take back your money my good friend," said I, "and leave me the mantle, as it is impossible for me to part with it."

At first the young man looked on this as a joke; but when he saw that I was really in earnest, he angrily refused to comply with my demand, treated me as a fool, and thus we speedily came to blows.   I was so fortunate as to snatch the cloak away from him in the scuffle, and was hastening away with it, when the young man summoned the police, and we were taken to court.   The judge was surprised at the accusation against me, and awarded the cloak to my opponent.   But I offered the young man twenty, fifty, eighty, yes, one hundred sequins, over and above his two hundred, if he would leave me in possession of the mantle.   My gold accomplished what my entreaties could not.   He took my sequins, while I carried away the mantle in triumph, contenting myself with the thought that even if all Florence considered me insane, I knew, better than they, that I should clear something by this transaction.

Impatiently I awaited the night.   At the same hour as on the previous night, I went to the Ponte Vecchio with the mantle on my arm.   At the last stroke of the clock, a form approached out of the darkness. It was undoubtedly the man I had met the night before.

"Have you the mantle?" I was asked.

"Yes," replied I; "but it cost me a hundred sequins cash."

"I know it," was the reply, "look here, there are four hundred."

He walked with me up to the broad balustrade of the bridge, and counted out the gold pieces. They glistened brightly in the moonlight; their gleam rejoiced my heart. Oh, I dreamed not that it was the last joy it would ever experience. I put the money in my pocket, and attempted to get a good look at the stranger; but he wore a mask, through which dark eyes darted a formidable look on me.

"I thank you, sir, for your kindness," said I. "What now do you require from me? But I say to you beforehand that it must not be any thing wrong."

"Your anxiety is needless," replied he, as he placed the mantle on his shoulders. "I need your services as a doctor; still, not for a living patient, but for a dead one."

"How can that be?" cried I, in astonishment.

"I came with my sister from a distant country," began the stranger, beckoning me at the same time to follow him. "I lived with her here at the house of a friend. My sister had been ill, and yesterday she died suddenly. Her relatives will bury her to-morrow. But in accordance with an old custom in our family, all of its members must be buried in the tomb of their ancestors. Many who died in foreign lands were embalmed and brought home. I will permit our relatives here to keep my sister's body, but I must at least take to my father the head of his daughter, that he may see her once more."

This custom of cutting off the heads of beloved relatives seemed horrible to me; still I thought best not to offer any objections, lest the stranger should feel insulted. I therefore told him that I was acquainted with the

method of embalming the dead, and requested him to
conduct me to the deceased. Still I could not refrain
from inquiring why all this was to be conducted so
secretly and at night? He answered that his relatives,
holding his views on this subject to be wicked, would prevent him from carrying them out by day; but when the
head was once removed, they could say little more on the
subject. Of course he might have brought me the head
himself but a natural feeling held him back from removing it.

In the meantime we had reached a large and magnificent house, which my companion pointed out to me as
the end of our night's pilgrimage. We passed by the
principal gate, entering by a smaller one, which the
stranger closed carefully after him, and ascended a spiral
staircase in the darkness. It led into a dimly lighted
corridor, from which he gained a room which was lighted
by a lamp suspended from the ceiling.

In this room was a bed, on which the body lay. The
stranger turned his head away, apparently making an attempt to hide his tears. He pointed to the bed; ordered
me to do my work well and quickly, and walked out of
the door.

I took out my instruments, which as a physician I always carried with me, and approached the bed. Only
the head of the dead girl was visible, but this was so
beautiful that I was seized with the deepest pity. The
dark hair hung down in long braids; the face was pale;
the eyes were closed.

I first made a slight incision in the skin, as is the
practice with surgeons when they are about to remove a
limb. Then I selected my sharpest knife, and with one
stroke cut through the windpipe. But what a tragedy!
The girl opened her eyes, closing them again instantly,
and with a deep sigh, now, for the first time, breathed
out her life, while at the same time a warm stream of
blood gushed from the wound. I was sure that I had
taken the life of this poor creature; for that she was now

dead was beyond question, as there could be no recovery from this wound.

I stood some moments almost stupefied at what had taken place. Had the man in the red mantle betrayed

me, or had his sister been lying in a trance? The latter conjecture seemed the most plausible. But I dared not say this to the brother of the girl; therefore I resolved to take the head completely off. But one more groan came from the dying girl, a spasm shook her form, and all was

over. Overcome with horror, I rushed out of the room.
But the lamp in the corridor had gone out, and there was
no trace of my companion. In the darkness, I was compelled to feel my way along the wall to reach the stair-
way. I finally found it, and descended, slipping and
stumbling. Nor was there any one below. I found the
door unlocked, and breathed freer when I once more
stood upon the street. Urged on by terror, I ran to my
rooms, and buried myself in the cushions of my
couch.

But sleep fled from me, and the approach of morning
warned me to compose myself. It seemed altogether
likely to me that the man who had betrayed me into
doing this atrocious deed would not inform on me. I resolved to go on as usual with my business, and if possible to assume a cheerful manner. But a new circumstance, that I now noticed for the first time, increased
my terror. My cap and girdle, as well as my instruments, were missing, and I was uncertain whether I had
left them in the chamber of the murdered girl, or had lost
them in my flight. Unfortunately the first supposition
seemed the more probable, and thus the murder would
be traced to me.

I opened my shop at the usual time. My neighbor,
who was a talkative man, came in to see me as usual in
the morning.

"What do you say to the horrible tragedy that happened last night?" was his greeting. I acted as if I
knew nothing about it. "What, is it possible that you
don't know what the whole city is talking about? Not
know that the most beautiful flower of Florence, Bianca,
the Governor's daughter, was murdered during the night?
I saw her yesterday, looking so happy as she rode
through the streets with her lover; and to-day was to
have been her wedding day."

Every word was a stab in my heart. And how often
did I suffer these pangs, as one by one my customers repeated the story, each making it more horrible than the

other! And yet none of them could make it as terrible as it had been when presented to my own eyes.

About noon an officer from the court stepped into my shop, and requested me to send the people away.

"Signor Zaleukos," said he, producing the articles I had missed, "are these things yours?"

I hesitated for a moment whether I should deny all knowledge of them; but as I saw through the half open door my landlord and several acquaintances who could have borne witness against me, I determined not to make the matter worse by a lie, and acknowledged the ownership of the articles. The officer bade me follow him, and led me to a large building, which I soon recognized as the prison. There he showed me to a room, telling me that I should occupy it for the present.

My situation seemed desperate when I came to think it over in the solitude of the prison. The thought that I had committed murder, even though it was done accidentally, kept returning to my mind. Neither could I hide from myself the fact that the glitter of the gold had captivated my senses, or I should never have rushed so blindly into this affair.

Two hours after my arrest I was led out of my chamber. Passing down several steps, we entered a large hall. Twelve men, most of them of advanced age, sat at a long table, covered with a black cloth. On the side of the hall were ranged rows of benches, filled with the aristocracy of Florence. High up, in the galleries the spectators were crowded close together. When I was brought before the black-covered table, a man of dark and sad aspect arose. It was the Governor. He told those assembled that he, being the father of the murdered girl, could not preside over this case, and that he would vaoate his seat, for the present, in favor of the oldest senator. The oldest senator was a man of at least ninety years. He was bent with age, and his temples were fringed with thin white hairs; but his eyes were still brilliant, and his voice was clear and strong.

2*

He began by asking me if I confessed to the murder. I besought him to give me his attention, and related fearlessly and in distinct tones what I had done. I noticed that as I proceeded, the Governor first turned pale and then red; and when I had finished, he sprang up in a rage. "What, wretch!" he exclaimed to me, "it is your intention, then, to impute this crime, that you committed in a spirit of avarice, to another?"

The presiding senator reproved him for this outburst, and reminded him that he had of his own accord renounced his right to direct the trial; nor did it appear, he said, that I contemplated robbery, as, by his own admission, nothing was stolen from his daughter. The senator declared to the Governor that he must give an account of his daughter's past life, as this was the only means of judging whether I had spoken the truth or not. At the same time he would close the court for that day, in order, as he said, to get some further information from the papers of the deceased, which the Governor should turn over to him. I was led back to my prison, where I passed a miserable day, occupied with the eager wish that some connection might be established between the man in the red mantle and the deceased.

Full of expectation, I entered the hall of justice on the following day. There were several letters on the table. The aged senator asked me whether they were in my hand-writing. I looked at them, and found that they must have been written by the same hand that wrote me the two notes I had received. I expressed this belief to the senators, but they paid no attention to my opinion, and answered that I both could and did write those notes myself, as the signature at the end of the letters was certainly a Z, the initial letter of my name. And then the letters contained threats against the deceased, and warnings against the wedding which was about to take place.

The Governor seemed to have made some strange disclosures about me, as I was on this day treated more sternly and suspiciously. To justify myself, I called for all the papers that were to be found in my room. But I was told that search had already been made there, and nothing found. When the court broke up, my hope had entirely vanished; and when I was led back to the hall on the third day, the verdict was communicated to me. I had been convicted of willful murder, and sentenced to death. To this, then, I had come at last! Deprived of every thing that was still dear to me on earth, far from my home, I should die innocent of crime, and, in the bloom of my youth, under an ax!

I was sitting in my lonely prison on the evening of the day that had decided my fate, with my hopes all dissipated, and my thoughts earnestly turned on death, when my prison door opened, and a man entered, who regarded me long and silently. "And thus I find you once more, Zaleukos?" said he. I had not recognized him by the dull gleam of my lamp, but the tone of his voice awoke old memories in me. It was Valetty, one of the few friends I had made during my studies in Paris. He said that happening to come to Florence, where his father, who was a man of prominence, lived, he heard of my story; he had come to see me, to learn from my own lips how I had come to commit so terrible a crime. I told him the whole story. He seemed very much astonished, and implored me to tell him, my only friend, the whole truth, and not die with a lie on my lips. I swore to him by every thing that was sacred that I had spoken the truth, and that the only burden on my conscience was that, dazed by the glitter of the gold, I had not perceived the improbabilities in the stranger's story. "Then you did not know Bianca?" asked he. I assured him that I had never seen her before. Valetty then told me that a deep secret hung over the deed, that the Governor had passed sentence on me very hastily, and there was a rumor among the people that I had known Bianca for a long time, and had murdered her out of revenge for her approaching marriage with another. I remarked to

him that all this might apply to the man in the red
mantle, but that I was unable to prove his participation
in the deed. Valetty embraced me, weeping, and promised to make every effort to save my life. I had but
little hope, yet I knew that Valetty was a wise man and
experienced in the laws, and that he would do his best
to save me.

For two long days I remained in uncertainty. At
last Valetty appeared. "I bring you consolation, even
though it be painful," said he. "You will live and be
set at liberty; but with the loss of a hand."

Joyfully I thanked my friend for my life. He told
me that the Governor was inexorably opposed to opening the case again, but that finally, in order not to appear
unjust, he agreed that if a similar case could be found in
any books of Florentine history, then my punishment
should be regulated by the punishment there recorded.
Valetty and his father had thereupon looked through the
old books by day and night, and finally found a case the
exact counterpart of mine. The punishment there
awarded was stated thus: "His left hand shall be amputated, his goods confiscated, and he himself banished
forever." This was now to be my punishment; and I
had to prepare myself for the painful ordeal that awaited
me. But I will not dwell on that terrible hour when I
stood on the public square, laid my hand on the block,
and felt my own blood stream over me.

Valetty took me to his own house until I had recovered; then he generously provided me with money for
my journey; as all that I had acquired in my years of
labor was forfeited to the State. I traveled from Florence to Sicily, and there embarked on the first ship for
Constantinople. My hopes were turned upon the money
I had given into the keeping of my friend; I also asked
permission to live with him, but he astounded me with
the question, why I did not occupy my own house? He
informed me that a strange man had bought a house in my
name in the Greek quarter, and had told the neighbors

that I would soon be there to take possession of it. I immediately went there with my friend, and was warmly welcomed by all my old acquaintances. An old merchant gave me a letter, left by the man who had bought the house for me.

The letter was as follows: "Zaleukos, two hands will be always ready to provide so tirelessly for you that you will not feel the loss of one. The house that you see, and all it contains, is yours; and every year you will be given enough to place you in the ranks of your wealthiest countrymen. May you forgive him who is more unfortunate than yourself."

I suspected who had written this; and the merchant replied to my question that he had taken the man to be a Frank, and that he wore a red mantle. I knew enough to own to myself that the stranger was not entirely destitute of noble sentiments. I found my new house fitted up in the very best manner, and there was also a shop stocked with wares finer than I had ever owned before.

Ten years have passed since then; yet, more from habit than necessity, I continue to make these commercial journeys. I have never since visited that country where I met with my misfortune. Every year I receive a thousand gold pieces. But though it rejoices me to know that the unfortunate stranger has some noble traits of character, it is impossible for him to cure the sorrow of my soul, which is perpetually haunted by the terrible vision of the murdered Bianca.

While the Greek merchant had told his story, the others had listened to him with the deepest interest. Selim Baruch, particularly, had shown much emotion. having sighed deeply several times, while Muley was sure that at one time he had seen tears in his eyes. The merchants commented for some time on the story.

"And do you not hate the stranger who so basely endangered your life and caused the loss of so important a member of your body?" asked Selim Baruch.

"There was a time at first," answered the Greek, "when my heart accused him before God that he had brought this sorrow on me and poisoned my life. But I found consolation in the religion of my fathers, which commands me to love my enemies. And then he must be more unhappy than I."

"You are a noble man!" exclaimed Selim Baruch, as he pressed the Greek's hand warmly.

The leader of the guard here interrupted the conversation. He entered the tent with an anxious air, and reported that it would not do for them to retire to their couches, as this was the place where the caravans were usually attacked; and, besides, his sentinels believed they saw several horsemen in the distance.

The merchants were greatly disturbed at this news; but Selim Baruch, the stranger, expressed surprise at their consternation, and thought that they were so strongly guarded that they need not fear a troop of Arab robbers.

"True, Master!" answered the leader of the escort; "if it were only such fellows, one could lie down to sleep without anxiety. But for sometime past the terrible Orbasan has appeared occasionally; and therefore it behooves one to be on his guard."

Selim desired to know who this Orbasan might be, and one of the merchants answered him: "There are all sorts of reports current among the people about this wonderful man. Some believe him to be a supernatural being, because he has often overcome five or six men in a fight. Others hold that he is a brave Frank, whom misfortune has driven into these parts. But from all accounts this much is certain: that he is an infamous robber and thief!"

"But still you will hardly be able to maintain that," retorted Lezah, another of the merchants. "Even though a robber, he is a magnanimous man, and has shown himself such to my brother, as I could relate to you. He has made orderly men of his whole band, and while he roams over the desert, no other band dare show itself. Neither is he a common robber, but simply levies a tax on the caravans, and whoever pays this willingly may travel on without further molestation, for Orbasan is the Ruler of the Desert."

Thus the merchants discoursed in the tent; but the guard, who was stationed around the camp, began to be uneasy. A considerable troop of armed horsemen was seen at a distance of half an hour's ride, and seemed to be making directly for the camp. One of the guard therefore went into the tent to announce that they would probably be attacked. The merchants conferred with one another as to what was to be done: whether they had better ride out and meet the attack, or await it in camp. The two eldest merchants were in favor of the latter course; but the fiery Muley and Zaleukos chose the first, and called on Selim to follow their example. But Selim quietly drew a small blue cloth, covered with red stars, from his girdle, tied it to a spear, and ordered one of the slaves to fasten it to the top of the tent, saying he would pledge his life that when the horsemen saw this signal they would draw off quietly. Muley placed no faith in the result, but the slave fixed the lance on top of the tent. In the meantime all those in camp had seized their weapons, and looked for the horsemen in intense expectancy. But they had apparently caught sight of the signal on the tent, as they suddenly changed their course, and moved off from the camp in an opposite direction.

The merchants gazed in wonder, now at the vanishing horsemen, and then on Selim. But he stood before the tent, looking out unconcernedly over the plain, as if nothing unusual had happened. At length Muley broke the silence.

"Who are you, O mighty stranger?" cried he. "You that tame the wild hordes of the desert by a signal."

"You rate my power much higher than it is," answered Selim Baruch. "I provided myself with this

token when I fled from captivity. What it signifies, I do
not know myself; only this much I do know: that whoever travels with this sign stands under powerful protection."

The merchants thanked Selim and called him their
deliverer; and really the number of the horsemen was
so great that the caravan could not have resisted them
very long.

With lighter hearts the merchants laid down to rest;
and when the sun began to set, and the evening breeze
blew over the plains of sand, they broke camp, and
resumed their journey.

The next day they camped within a day's march of
the end of the desert. When the travelers had gathered
once more in the large tent, Lezah the merchant began
to speak:

"I told you yesterday that the dreaded Orbasan was
a magnanimous man; permit me to prove it to you
to-day, by the recital of my brother's fate. My father
was Cadi at Acara. He had three children, of whom I
was the eldest. My brother and sister were considerably
younger. When I was twenty years old, my father's
brother sent for me. He made me heir to his property,
with the condition that I should remain with him while
he lived. But he reached a good old age, so that I
could not return home until two years ago, having
learned nothing in the meantime of the dark cloud that
had overshadowed our family, and how graciously Allah
had dispersed it."

THE RESCUE OF FATIMA.

Y brother Mustapha and my sister Fatima were of nearly the same age. He was at the most, but two years older. They were devotedly attached to one another, and together strove, by e ery means in their power, to lighten the burden of our sick father's years.

On Fatima's sixteenth birthday, my brother arranged a celebration in her honor. He invited all her companions; served them with choice viands in the garden; and towards evening invited them to a ride on the sea, in a barge which he had hired, and decorated especially for the occasion. Fatima and her companions joyfully accepted the invitation, as the evening was fine, and the city viewed from the sea, especially by night, presented a magnificent appearance.

So highly did the young girls enjoy their ride, that they kept urging my brother to take them still further out to sea. Mustapha consented very unwillingly, as some days before a corsair had been seen standing off the coast. Not far from the city a point of land extended out into the sea. The young girls now expressed a desire to go there, that they might see the sun set in the sea. As they rounded the cape, they saw, at a little distance, a barge filled with armed men. With many misgivings, my brother ordered the oarsmen to turn the boat around and pull for shore. And in truth his fears did not seem to be groundless, for the other barge gave chase to them,

D

and, having more rowers, soon overtook them — keeping in a line between my brother's barge and the shore. When the young girls perceived their danger, they jumped up with cries and lamentations. It was in vain that Mustapha tried to quiet them; in vain did he urge them to be quiet, as, by their running about, the boat was in danger of upsetting. His entreaties were not listened to; and when finally the other boat came near, they all rushed to the further side of Mustapha's boat and capsized it.

But in the meantime the movements of the strange boat had been watched from land, and as for some time past fears had been entertained of corsairs, several barges pushed out from shore to render assistance to my brother. They arrived just in time to pick up the drowning ones. In the excitement, the hostile boat escaped; and in the two barges on which the rescued had been placed, there was some uncertainty as to whether all had been saved. These two boats were brought side by side, and alas! it was found that my sister and one of her companions were missing. At the same moment a man whom no one knew was discovered on one of the barges. Mustapha's threats extorted from him the admission that he belonged to the hostile ship that lay at anchor two miles to the eastward, and that his companions, in their hasty flight, had left him while he was in the very act of assisting the young girls out of the water. He further said that he had seen two of them drawn into the boat to which he belonged.

The anguish of my aged father was intense. Mustapha, too, was nearly wild with grief — not alone because his beloved sister was lost, and he must blame himself as the author of her misfortune, but the companion of Fatima's sad fate was his betrothed, though he had never dared to mention that circumstance to our father, as the young lady's parents were poor and low-born.

But my father was a stern man. As soon as he was able to control his grief, he sent for Mustapha, and said to him: "Your folly has robbed me of the comfort of my old age, and the light of my eyes. Go! I banish you forever from my sight; I curse you and all your descendants; and only when you bring Fatima back to me, shall your father's curse be lifted."

My brother had not expected this. He had already formed the resolution of going in search of his sister and her friend, and had come to his father intending to ask his blessing on the undertaking; and now he was sent out into the world with the weight of his father's curse on his head. But if before sorrow had bent him to the ground, this blow, so undeservedly given, steeled his soul.

He went to the imprisoned pirate, to ask him where his ship was bound, and learned that she was employed in the slave trade, and usually made Balsora her market.

When he returned home to prepare for his journey, his father's wrath seemed to have cooled somewhat, as he sent him a purse of gold for his support on the journey. Mustapha then took leave of the parents of Zoraide — his secretly betrothed bride, and started on his way to Balsora.

As there was no ship from our small town bound directly for Balsora, my brother made the journey by land; and in order that he might not arrive too long after the pirates had reached there, he was forced to make very long day's journeys. Still, as he had a fine horse, and no luggage, he counted on reaching Balsora at the close of the sixth day. But on the evening of the fourth day, as he was riding along quite alone, he was suddenly attacked by three robbers. Observing that they were powerful men and well armed, and believing that their purpose was to take his money and horse, rather than his life, he called out that he would surrender. Thereupon they dismounted from their horses, and bound his feet together under his horse's belly. One of the men then seized the bridle of Mustapha's steed, and, with my brother in their midst, they galloped off in great haste without having once spoken a word. Mustapha resigned himself to a gloomy despondency. His father's curse seemed in process of fulfillment; and how could he hope to rescue his sister and Zoraide, when, stripped of all he possessed, he could employ only a miserable life towards securing their freedom?

Mustapha and his silent escort had ridden on for about an hour, when they turned into a side valley, which was shut in by high trees. A soft, dark-green sod, and a brook rushing swiftly through the middle of the valley, invited them to rest. Scattered over the green were from fifteen to twenty tents. Camels and fine horses were tied to the tent stakes, while from one of the tents sounded the pleasing melody of a guitar, accompanied by two fine male voices.

To my brother it seemed that people who had displayed such good taste in the selection of their camping ground could entertain no sinister designs on him, and he, therefore, cheerfully obeyed the command of his guides to dismount as soon as they had unloosed his bonds. He was led into a tent much larger than the others, the interior of which was fitted up neatly, even elegantly. Gold embroidered cushions, woven carpets and gold plated censors would have indicated elsewhere the wealth and respectability of their owner; but here they were plainly the fruits of robbery. On one of the cushions sat a little old man of repulsive appearance. His skin was tanned and shiny, and a disagreeable expression of Turkish slyness lurked about his eyes and mouth. Although this man attempted to appear dignified, it did not take Mustapha long to decide that this tent had not been furnished so richly for him, while the conversation of his guards seemed to confirm his observation.

"Where is the Strong One?" they inquired of the little old man.

"On the chase," answered he. "But he bade me fill his place while he was gone."

"He didn't display much sense, then," replied one of

the robbers, "as it ought to be decided at once whether this dog shall die or be held for ransom, and the Strong One could decide that much better than you."

The old man arose with an assumption of dignity, and reached out as if to grasp his opponent's ear, or to revenge himself by a blow; but when he saw that his effort was fruitless, he began to curse and swear. Nor did the others remain long in his debt, but replied in kind, until the tent resounded with their quarrel.

All at once the door of the tent was opened, and a tall, stately man, young and handsome as a Persian prince, entered. His clothes and weapons were plain and simple, with the exception of a richly jeweled dagger and a gleaming sword; but his steady eye and whole appearance commanded attention, without inspiring distrust.

"Who is it that dares to make such a disturbance in my tent?" demanded he of the frightened participants.

For a little time there was deep silence; until finally, one of the men who had brought Mustapha in told him how the quarrel had originated The face of the Strong One, as they called him, flushed with anger at this recital.

"When did I ever put you in my place, Hassan?" cried he, in a fearful voice, to the little old man, who, shrinking with fear, stole towards the door, looking smaller than ever. The Strong One lifted his foot, and Hassan went flying through the doorway with some remarkable leaps.

When Hassan had disappeared, the three men led Mustapha up to the master of the tent, who was now reclining on the cushions, saying: "We have brought you the man whom you ordered us to capture." The Strong One looked for some time at the prisoner, and then said: "Pasha of Sulieika, your own conscience will tell you why your are the prisoner of Orbasan."

When my brother heard this, he threw himself down before Orbasan, and answered · "Oh, Master, you have made a mistake. I am only a poor unfortunate man, and not the Pasha whom you seek."

All in the tent were surprised at these words. But the master of the tent replied —

"It will not help you much to deny your identity, as I will produce people who know you well." He then commanded Zuleima to be brought. An old woman was led in, who, in response to the question whether she did not recognize in my brother the Pasha of Sulieika, said —

"Certainly! I swear by the graves of the prophets that he is the Pasha and no other."

"Do you see, poor fool, how your stratagem is frustrated?" sneered Orbasan. "You are so miserable a creature that I will not soil my dagger with your blood; but when to-morrow's sun rises, I will tie you to my horse's tail and chase through the forests with you until the sun sets behind the hills of Sulieika."

At this announcement my brother's courage entirely deserted him. "This is the result of my cruel father's curse that is driving me to an ignominious death!" exclaimed he, in tears. "And thou, too, sweet sister, and thou, Zoraide, art lost!"

"Your dissimulation will avail you nothing," said one of the robbers, who was engaged in tying Mustapha's hands behind his back. "Get out of the tent quickly, for the Strong One is biting his lips and glancing at his dagger. If you would live another night, come quickly!"

As the robbers were leading my brother out of the tent, they encountered three others, who were pushing in a prisoner before them. "We have brought you the Pasha as you commanded us," said they, and led the prisoner up to the cushions where Orbasan reclined. While the prisoner was being led forward, my brother had an opportunity to observe him closely, and he was forced to acknowledge the striking resemblance which this man bore to him, only the stranger's complexion was darker and he wore a black beard.

Orbasan seemed much astonished over the appearance

of the second prisoner. "Which of you, then, is the right one?" asked he, looking from one to the other.

"If you mean the Pasha of Sulieika," answered the prisoner, in a proud tone, "I am he."

Orbasan gazed at him some time with a stern, hard expression, and then silently beckoned the men to lead him away. When they had done so, Orbasan went up to my brother, cut his bonds with his dagger, and motioned to him to sit down with him on the cushions. "I am sorry, young stranger," said he, "that I mistook you for that monster. It was, indeed, a singular dispensation of fate which led you into the hands of my comrades at the same hour that was destined to see the fall of that traitor." My brother begged of him but one favor: that he might be allowed to continue on his journey at once, as the least delay would prove fatal to his purpose. Orbasan inquired what the nature of the affair was that required such haste, and when Mustapha had told him every thing, Orbasan persuaded him to remain in his tent over night, as he and his horse were in need of rest, and promised that in the morning he would show him a way by which he could reach Balsora in a day and a half.

My brother remained, was hospitably entertained, and slept soundly until morning in the tent of the robber chief. When he awakened he found himself all alone, but before the curtain of the tent he heard several voices, one of which belonged to Orbasan and another to Hassan. He listened, and heard, to his horror, that the little old man was urging upon Orbasan the necessity of killing him, lest he should betray them when he had regained his liberty. Mustapha felt sure that Hassan hated him, because he had been the cause of the little fellow's being handled so roughly the night before. Orbasan remained silent for some moments, and then replied: "No, he is my guest, and the laws of hospitality are sacred with me; neither does he look like an informer."

Thus saying, Orbasan flung aside the curtain and

entered. "Peace be with you, Mustapha," said he. "Let us take our morning draught, and then prepare yourself to start." He handed my brother a glass of sherbet, and when they had drunk, they saddled their horses, and with a lighter heart than he had entered the camp, Mustapha swung himself into his seat.

They had soon left the tents far behind, and followed a broad path that led into the forest. Orbasan told my brother that the Pasha who had been captured had promised that he would permit them to remain undisturbed in his territory; yet but a few weeks after he took one of their bravest men prisoner, and hanged him with the most horrible torture. Orbasan had had spies on his track for a long time, and now he must die. Mustapha did not venture to oppose his purpose, as he was thankful to get away with a whole skin himself.

At the end of the forest Orbasan stopped his horse, described the way to my brother, offered him his hand at parting, and said: "Mustapha, you became the guest of the robber Orbasan under singular circumstances. I will not require you to promise that you will not betray what you have seen and heard. You were unjustly forced to suffer the fear of death, and I am, therefore, in your debt. Take this dagger as a keepsake, and if you are ever in need of help, send it to me, and I will hasten to your assistance. This purse you may be able to use on your journey."

My brother thanked him for his generosity, and took the dagger, but refused the purse. Orbasan pressed his hand once more, letting the purse fall to the ground, and sprang with the speed of the wind into the forest. When Mustapha saw that Orbasan did not intend to return for the purse, he dismounted and picked it up, starting at the generosity of his host, as he found it contained a large sum of gold. He thanked Allah for his rescue, recommended the generous robber to His mercy, and continued on his way to Balsora with a lighter heart.

Lezah, the story-teller, paused, and looked inquiringly at the merchant who had spoken so bitterly of Orbasan. The latter said —

"Well, if all that be so, I will cheerfully reverse my judgment of Orbasan, for he really treated your brother handsomely."

"He behaved like a true Musselman," exclaimed Muley. "But I hope your story was not ended there, for we are all curious to hear more; how things went with your brother, and whether he rescued your sister Fatima and the beautiful Zoraide."

"If I do not weary you, I will willingly continue," replied Lezah; "for this story of my brother is certainly adventurous and wonderful."

With this, he continued his story.

At noon on the seventh day of his departure from home, Mustapha entered the gate of Balsora. As soon as he had reached a caravansary, he made inquiries as to when the slave auction, held there every year, opened. He received in reply the dreadful news that he had arrived two days too late. They deplored his delay, and told him that he had missed a fine sight, for on the last day of the auction two female slaves had been put up, of such extraordinary beauty as to attract the attention of all bidders. There was sharp competition for their possession, and the bidding ran up so high as to frighten off everybody but their present owner. Mustapha made more particular inquiries, until he had satisfied himself beyond a doubt that these slaves were the unfortunate objects of his search. He learned further that the name of the man who had bought them was Thiuli-Kos; that he lived a good forty-hours' journey from Balsora, and was a rich and elderly man of rank, who had formerly been senior Pasha of the Shah, but had now retired from official life to live upon his means.

At first thought, Mustapha was about to mount his

horse and hasten after Thiuli-Kos, who had only a day
the start of him; but, after reflecting that, alone and unattended, he could hardly approach so powerful and rich
a man, and still less hope to rob him of his possessions,
he tried to devise some other plan, and soon hit upon one
that appeared feasible. The singular mistake of con-
founding him with the Pasha of Sulieika, which had been
so nearly fatal to him, suggested the idea of visiting the
house of Thiuli-Kos, under this name, and then attempting the rescue of the unfortunate maidens. Accordingly
he hired horses and servants — for which purpose Orbasan's money proved very useful — provided fine clothes
for himself and servants, and set out for Thiuli's castle.

In five days he reached the vicinity of the castle,
which was situated in a beautiful plain, enclosed within
high walls, above which but little could be seen of the
buildings. Arriving there, Mustapha dyed his hair and
beard black, and painted his face with the juice of a plant,
that gave him quite as brown a complexion as the real
Pasha had possessed. Thereupon he sent one of his servants to the castle to request a night's lodging, in the
name of the Pasha of Sulieika. The servant soon returned, and with him came four finely costumed slaves,
who took hold of the bridle of Mustapha's horse, and led
him into the court of the castle. There they assisted him
to dismount, when four others conducted him up the
broad marble steps to the presence of Thiuli. The latter
proved to be a jovial old fellow, and he received my
brother with due honor, and set before him the best that
his cook could prepare.

After the table was cleared, Mustapha turned the conversation to the new slaves, and Thiuli boasted of their
beauty, while complaining of their sadness; this, however, he believed would soon disappear. My brother was
well pleased with his reception, and betook himself to
rest, feeling very hopeful. He had slept perhaps an hour,
when he was awakened by the gleam of a lamp that dazzled his eyes. As he raised himself in bed, he believed

that he must still be dreaming, for before him stood that little dark-skinned man whom he had seen in Orbasan's tent. He held a lamp in his hand, and his broad mouth was distorted by a horrible grimace. Mustapha pinched his own arm and pulled his nose, in order to convince himself that he was awake; but the apparition remained as before.

"What will you at my bed-side?" cried Mustapha, as soon as he had recovered from his astonishment.

"Don't trouble yourself, Master," replied Hassan, "I have found out your purpose in coming here; nor was your worthy face forgotten by me. But really, if I had not helped to hang the Pasha with my own hands, I might perhaps have been deceived. Now I have come to put a question."

"First of all, tell me how you came here," returned Mustapha, furious at being betrayed.

"I will tell you," replied Hassan, "I could not get along with Orbasan any longer; therefore I ran away. But you, Mustapha, was the cause of our quarrel, and therefore you must give me your sister to wed, and I will assist you in your flight. If you do not agree to this, I will go to my new master and tell him something about the new Pasha."

Mustapha was beside himself with rage and terror. Now, just as he believed himself about to attain his object, why must this wretch come and thwart his designs? There was only one way left in which he could carry out his plan: he must kill the ugly monster. With one spring he leaped from the bed and tried to seize the ugly wretch; but he, doubtless having expected such an attack, let the lamp fall and escaped in the darkness, shrieking murderously for help.

He was now compelled to give up the young girls, and turn his attention to his own safety. He went to the window to see whether he could jump out, and found it was quite a distance to the ground, while opposite stood a high wall. Suddenly he heard voices approaching his

room. As they reached his door, he grasped his clothes
and dagger in desperation, and swung himself out of the
window. The fall was a hard one, but he felt that no
bones were broken, and sprang up to run to the wall,
which he climbed, to the astonishment of the pursuers,
and was soon at liberty. He ran until he reached a
small wood, where he flung himself down exhausted.
Here he considered what was to be done.

His servants and horses he had been forced to leave,
but the money which he carried in his girdle was safe,
and his ingenuity shortly discovered another mode of
rescue. He went on through the forest until he came to
a village, where for a little money he bought a horse
that quickly carried him to a city. Once there he inquired for a physician, and an old and experienced man
was recommended to him. By the aid of some gold
pieces, he induced this physician to furnish him with a
medicine that would produce a death-like sleep, that
might, however, be instantly dispelled by some other
remedy. When he had procured these medicines, he
bought a false beard, a black gown, and all manner of
little boxes and alembics, so that he properly represented
a traveling physician — loaded his traps on an ass and
journeyed back to the castle of Thiuli-Kos. He was
certain this time of not being known, as the beard made
such a complete change in his appearance that he felt
doubtful of his own identity.

On arriving at Thiuli's, he announced himself as the
physician Chakamankabudibaba. The result was as he
had foreseen: the high-sounding name recommended
him so highly to the weak old Pasha that he was at once
invited to dinner. After an hour's conversation, the old
man resolved to submit all his female slaves to the treatment of the wise physician. Mustapha could now hardly
conceal his joy at the prospect of seeing his beloved
sister again, and followed Thiuli with a beating heart, as
he led the way to the seraglio. They came to a room
beautifully decorated but unoccupied.

"Chambaba, or whatever you call yourself, dear doctor," said Thiuli-Kos, " look for a moment at yonder hole in the wall ; each one of my slaves will put her arm through it in succession, and you can ascertain by the pulse who the sick are and who the well."

Mustapha's objections to this arrangement were of no

avail; he was not permitted to see the slaves; still Thiuli consented to inform him of each one's general state of health. Thiuli then drew out a long sheet of paper from his sash, and began to call the roll of his female slaves in a loud voice; and at each name a hand was thrust through the wall, and the physician felt the pulse. Six were called off, and pronounced in good health, when Thiuli called out the name "Fatima," as the seventh, and a small white hand slipped through the wall. Trembling with joy, Mustapha seized this hand and declared with an important air, that Fatima was seriously sick. Thiuli became very anxious, and ordered his wise Chakamankabudibaba to prepare at once some medicine for her. The physician went out of the room, and wrote on a small piece of paper:

"*Fatima! I will save you, if you have the strength of will to take a medicine that will deprive you of life for two days; still I possess a remedy that will restore you to life again. If you are willing to do this, speak these words: The medicine did not help me any,' and I shall take it as a sign of your assent.*"

Mustapha returned to the room where Thiuli was awaiting him. He brought with him a harmless drink, felt of Fatima's pulse once more, at the same time tucking the note under her bracelet, and passed the drink through the opening in the wall. Thiuli seemed to be very anxious about Fatima, and put off the examination of the rest until a more favorable opportunity. As he left the room with Mustapha, he said, in a sad tone: "Chidababa, tell me the exact truth; what is your opinion of Fatima's sickness?" Chakamankabudibaba replied with a deep sigh: "Oh Master! may the good Prophet send you consolation; she has a stealthy fever that may end her life." At this reply Thiuli's anger flamed up. "What's that you say, you cursed dog of a doctor! Do you mean to say that she, for whom I paid two thousand pieces of gold, will die on my hands like a cow? Know, then, that if you do not save her, I will take your head off!"

My brother at once saw that he had made a stupid mistake, so he hastened to assure Thiuli there was still hope for Fatima. While they were speaking together, a black slave came from the seraglio to say to the physician that *the drink did not help her any*. "Put forth all your art, Chakamdababelda, or whatever you call yourself, and I will pay you whatever you ask," exclaimed

Thiuli-Kos, wild with anxiety at the prospect of losing so much money. "I will give her a little decoction that will save her from danger," answered the physician. "Yes! by all means, give her the medicine," cried old Thiuli.

Mustapha, in high spirits, went to fetch the sleeping potion, and after handing it to the slave, with instructions as to the quantity to be taken, he returned to Thiuli, and told him that now he must go down to the sea and gather some healing herbs. He then hurried away to the sea, that was not far off, where he took off his various disguises and flung them into the water, where the waves tossed them about. He then concealed himself in the bushes until evening, when he stole quietly up to the burial vault of Thiuli's castle.

Hardly an hour after Mustapha had departed from the castle, word was brought Thiuli that his slave Fatima was dying. He at once sent down to the shore to have the physician brought back, but his messengers soon returned with the information that the poor doctor had fallen into the water and been drowned ; his black cloak was floating on the waves, and occasionally his magnificent black beard might be seen bobbing up and down in the water.

When Thiuli saw there was no hope of her recovery, he cursed himself and the whole world, tore out his beard, and butted his head against the wall. But all this availed nothing, for Fatima, under the care of the other women, soon ceased to breathe. When Thiuli heard of her death, he ordered a coffin to be hastily made, as he could not suffer a dead person to remain in the house, and had the body carried to the tomb. The bearers carried the coffin there, dropped it hastily, and fled, as they heard groans and sighs proceeding from the other coffins.

Mustapha, who had hidden behind the coffins and frightened away the bearers of Fatima's coffin, now came out from his hiding place, and lighted a lamp that he had provided for this purpose. Next he produced a phial containing the restorative, and raised the lid of Fatima's coffin. But what was his amazement when the rays of the lamp disclosed features entirely strange to him! It was neither my sister nor Zoraide, but quite another person, that lay in the coffin. It took him a long time to recover from this latest blow of fate, but finally pity overcame his vexation. He opened the phial, and poured some of the contents into the mouth of the sleeper. She breathed, opened her eyes, and seemed for a long time to be trying to make out her situation. At last she recalled all that had happened, and, stepping out of the coffin, flung herself at Mustapha's feet. "How can I thank you, gracious being?" cried she, "for freeing me from my terrible prison!" Mustapha interrupted her expressions of gratitude with the question how it happened that she and not his sister Fatima had been rescued. She looked at him in an astonished way before replying: "Now for the first time I understand what before was incomprehensible to me. You must know that I was called Fatima in the castle, and it was to me you gave the note and medicine." My brother requested her to give him news of his sister and Zoraide, and learned that they were both in the castle, but, in accordance with a custom of Thiuli's, had received other names, and were now called Mirza and Nurmahal.

When the freed slave, Fatima, saw that my brother was so cast down by this mistake, she consoled him with the assurance that she could point out another way by which both of the young girls might be rescued. Aroused by what she said, he begged her to tell him her plan, to which she replied —

"For some five months I have been Thiuli's slave; yet from the first I have planned to escape, but it was too much of a task for me to attempt alone. In the inner court of the castle you must have noticed a fountain that throws the water in a cascade from ten pipes. This fountain impressed me strongly, because I remembered a similar one in my father's house, the water of which was brought through a large aqueduct. In order to learn whether this fountain was built in the same way, I one day praised its beauty to Thiuli, and asked who had constructed it. 'I built it myself,' answered he; 'and what you see here is the least part of the work. as the water is brought from a brook, a thousand paces away, through an arched viaduct at least high enough for a man to walk in. And the construction of all this I directed myself.'

"Since hearing this, I have often wished for the strength of a man to pull out a stone in the side of the fountain, and thereby escape. I will now show you the aqueduct, through which you can obtain entrance to the castle at night, and set your sister free. But you ought to have at least two men with you, in order to overpower the slaves who watch the seraglio at night."

My brother Mustapha, although he had seen his plans twice frustrated, plucked up courage once more at these words, and hoped, with Allah's assistance, to carry out the scheme of the slave. He promised to see that she arrived safely at her home if she would assist him to enter the castle. But one point caused him some little perplexity: where should he obtain two or three men upon whom he could depend? Just then Orbasan's dagger occurred to him, and the promise he had received from the bandit that, in case of need, he would hasten to his assistance; and he therefore left the vault, in company with Fatima, to hunt up the robber.

In the same village which had witnessed his transformation into a physician, he bought a horse with what money remained to him, and procured a lodging for Fatima with a poor woman who lived in the suburb. He then hastened toward the hills where he had first met Orbasan, and arrived there in three days. He soon found their tents, and appeared unexpectedly to Orbasan, who greeted him with friendliness. He gave an account of his failures, at which the grave Orbasan could not

E   3*

refrain from laughing now and then, especially when he thought of the physician Chakamankabudibaba. But he was terribly enraged over the treachery of the ugly little monster, Hassan, and swore he would hang him up wherever he found him. He also promised that when my brother had refreshed himself after the fatigue of his journey, he would be ready to assist him.

Mustapha therefore spent the night in Orbasan's tent. With the early dawn they rode off, accompanied by three of Orbasan's bravest men well mounted and armed. They rode very fast and in two days' time reached the place where Mustapha had left Fatima. They took her with them, and journeyed on until they came to the small wood from whence Thiuli's castle could be seen, where they went into camp until night should come.

As soon as it was dark, guided by Fatima, they stole up to the brook where the aqueduct began, and soon discovered the entrance. There they left Fatima and a servant with the horses, and prepared to descend into the conduit; but before they went in, Fatima repeated once more her instructions to them—they would emerge from the fountain into the inner court, in the right and left corners of which were towers, and in the sixth door counting from the right tower, they would find Fatima and Zoraide, guarded by two black slaves. Well provided with weapons and crowbars, Mustapha, Orbasan, and two other men, descended into the aqueduct. They sank to their hips in the water, but none the less did they advance valiantly forward. In half an hour they came to the fountain, and at once began to use their crowbars. The wall was thick and solid but could not long withstand the united strength of the four men, and they had soon made an opening large enough to crawl through. Orbasan passed through first, and helped the others after him.

When they all stood in the court, they looked closely at the side of the castle facing them, to pick out the door that had been described. But they did not all agree on this point, for on counting from the right tower toward the left, they found one door that had been walled up, and they could not decide whether Fatima had passed this door by, or had counted it in with the others. But Orbasan did not hesitate long. "My good sword will open every door to me," exclaimed he, and went to one of the doors followed by his companions. They opened the door and discovered six black slaves lying on the floor asleep. They were about to withdraw quietly, as they saw they had missed the right door, when a man's form arose in the corner, and in a well-known voice, called for help. It was Hassan, the deserter from Orbasan's camp. But before the black guards could find out what had happened, Orbasan rushed at the little wretch, tore his girdle into two pieces, with one of which he bound his mouth, and with the other tied his hands behind his back; then he turned on the slaves, some of whom were already partially secured by Mustapha and his companions, and assisted to completely overpower them. At the point of the dagger, the slaves confessed that Nurmahal and Mirza were in the adjoining room. Mustapha rushed in, and found Fatima and Zoraide, who were already aroused by the noise. They quickly collected their clothing and ornaments, and followed Mustapha. The two robbers now begged permission of Orbasan to plunder whatever they found; but he forbade them, saying: "It shall never be said of Orbasan that he broke into a house at night to steal gold."

Mustapha and the young girls slid quickly into the aqueduct, Orbasan promising to follow immediately; but as soon as the others were out of sight, Orbasan and one of the robbers took Hassan out into the court, and tying a silk cord around his neck, hung him to the highest point of the fountain. After having inflicted this penalty on the wretch, they descended into the aqueduct and followed Mustapha.

With tears the two young girls thanked their noble

rescuer Orbasan, but he hurried them on in their flight,
as it was quite probable that Thiuli-Kos would pursue

them in all directions. With deep emotion, Mustapha
and the rescued ones parted from Orbasan on the following day. Of a truth, they will never forget him. Fatima, the freed slave, disguised herself and went to Balsora

to take passage for her home, and all reached there safely after a short and agreeable journey.

The joy of seeing them again almost killed my father; but the day after their arrival, he ordered an immense banquet, to which the whole town came. My brother had then to repeat his story before a large number of relatives and friends, and with one voice they praised him and the noble Orbasan.

When my brother had finished, my father rose and led Zoraide up to him. "Thus," said he in joyful tones, "do I lift the curse from thy head; take her as the reward, which thou hast won through thy tireless zeal; take my fatherly blessing; and may our city never be wanting in men who, in brotherly love, in wisdom and zeal, resemble thee."

The caravan had reached the end of the desert, and the travelers joyfully greeted the green meadows and the thick foliage of the trees; a delightful view, of which they had been deprived for many days. In a beautiful valley was situated a caravansary, which they chose for a night's lodging; and although it offered poor accommodation and refreshment, yet the whole company were in better spirits and more confidential than ever, as the feeling that they had escaped all the dangers and discomforts which a journey through the desert brings, opened all hearts and disposed all minds to jests and sports. Muley, the active young merchant, danced a comic dance, accompanying himself with songs, until even the sad features of Zaleukos, the Greek, relaxed into a smile. But not satisfied with having entertained his fellow travelers with dances and games, he related, as soon as he had somewhat recovered from his violent exercise, the story which he had promised them.

LITTLE MUCK.

I N Nicæa, my dearly-loved native city, lived a man who was called Little Muck. I can recall him distinctly, although I was quite young at the time, chiefly because of a severe chastisement I received from my father on his account. This Little Muck was already an old man when I knew him, and yet he was not more than four feet in height. His figure presented a singular appearance, as his body, small and child-like, seemed but a slender support for a head much larger than the heads of ordinary people. He lived all alone in a large house, and cooked his own meals, and had it not been for the smoke that rose from his kitchen chimney at midday, the townspeople would have remained in doubt as to whether he still lived; for he went out but once a month. He was, however, occasionally seen walking on the house-top, and to one looking up from the street there was presented the singular sight of a head moving to and fro. My companions and myself were rather bad boys, who took delight in teasing and making sport of everybody; so it was always a great holiday for us whenever Little Muck went out. We gathered before his house on the appointed day, and waited; and when now the door opened, and the large head, wrapped in a still larger turban, peeped out, followed by the rest of his little body, done up in a threadbare cloak, baggy breeches, and a wide sash, from which hung·a dagger so long that it could not be told whether Muck stuck on the dagger or the dagger on Muck—when he

thus made his appearance, the air echoed with our shouts;
we threw up our caps, and danced around him like mad.
Little Muck, however, returned our salute with a grave

nod of the head, and shuffled slowly down the street in
such great, wide slippers as I had never seen before.
We boys ran behind him, shouting: "Little Muck! Little Muck!" We also had a jolly little verse that we
now and then sang in his honor, which ran as follows:

Little Muck, little Muck,
Living in a house so fair,
Once a month you take the air,
You, brave little dwarf, 't is said,
Have a mountain for a head;
Turn around just once and look;
Run and catch us, little Muck!

Thus had we often entertained ourselves, and, to my
shame be it confessed, I behaved the worst—often catching him by the cloak, and once I trod on the heel of his
slipper so that he fell down. This struck me as a very
funny thing, but the laugh stuck in my throat as I saw
him go to my father's house. He went right in and
remained there for some time. I hid myself near the
front door, and saw Little Muck come out again, accompanied by my father, who held his hand and parted from
him on the door-step with many bows. Not feeling very
easy in my mind, I remained for a long time in my hiding
place; but I was at last driven out by hunger, which I
feared worse than a whipping, and, spiritless and with
bowed head, I went home to my father. "I hear that
you have been insulting the good Little Muck," said he,
in a grave tone. "I will tell you the story of Little
Muck, and you will certainly not want to laugh at him
again; but before I begin, and after I am through, you
will receive *'the customary.'* " Now "the customary" consisted of twenty-five blows, which he was accustomed to
lay on without making any mistake in the count. He
took for this purpose the long stem of a cherry pipe, un-
screwing the amber mouth-piece, and belaboring me
harder than ever before. When the five-and-twenty
strokes were completed, he commanded me to pay attention, and told me the story of Little Muck.

The father of Little Muck—whose proper name was
Mukrah—was a poor but respectable man, living here in
Nicæa. He lived nearly as solitary a life as his son now
does. This son he could not endure, as he was ashamed
of his dwarfish shape, and he therefore allowed him to
grow up in ignorance. Little Muck, though in his six-

teenth year, was only a child; and his father continually scolded him, because he who should have long since " put away childish things," still remained so stupid and silly.

However, the old gentleman got a bad fall one day, from the effects of which he shortly died, and left Little Muck poor and ignorant. The unfeeling relatives, to whom the deceased had owed more than he could pay, drove the poor little fellow out of the house, and advised him to go out into the world and seek his fortune. Little Muck replied that he was ready for the journey, but begged that he might be allowed to have his father's clothes; and these were given him. His father had been a tall, stout man, so that the clothes did not fit the little son very well; but Muck knew just what to do in this emergency: he cut off every thing that was too long, and then put the clothes on. He seemed, however, to have forgotten that he should have cut away from the width as well; hence his singular appearance just as he may be seen to-day—dressed in the large turban, the broad sash, the baggy trousers, the blue cloak, all heirlooms from his father, which he has ever since worn. The long Damascus poniard, that had also belonged to his father, he stuck proudly in his sash, and, supported by a little cane, wandered out of the city gate.

He tramped along merrily the whole day; for had he not been sent out to seek his fortune? If he came across a broken bit of pottery glistening in the sun, he straightway put it into his pocket, in the full belief that it would prove to be the most brilliant diamond. When he saw in the distance the dome of a mosque all ablaze with the sun's rays, or a lake gleaming like a mirror, he made all haste to reach it, believing he had arrived in an enchanted land. But alas, the illusions vanished as he neared them, while weariness and an empty stomach forcibly reminded him that he was still in the land of mortals. Thus hungry and sorrowful, and despairing of ever finding his fortune, he wandered on for two long days, with the fruits of the field for his only nourishment, and the hard earth for his couch.

On the morning of the third day he discovered, from a hill, a large city. The crescent shone brightly on its battlements, while gay banners waving from the roofs seemed to beckon him on. In great surprise, he stopped to look at the city and its surroundings. "Yes, there shall Little Muck find his fortune," said he to himself; and summoning all his strength, he started on towards the city. But, although the town seemed near by, it was nearly noon when he reached it, as his little legs almost refused to carry out his will, and he was forced to sit down in the shade of a palm tree to rest. At last he reached the gate. There he arranged his cloak with great care, gave a new fold to his turban, stretched out his sash to twice its usual width, stuck the long poniard in a little straighter, and wiping the dust from his shoes, grasped his stick more firmly and marched bravely in.

He had wandered through several streets, but not a door opened to him ; nor did any one call out — as he had fancied would be done — :

> Little Muck ! Come in and eat,
> And rest your weary little feet.

Once more he looked up very longingly at a large, fine house before him, when suddenly a window was opened, and an old woman looked down, calling out in a sing-song tone :

> O come, O come !
> The porridge is done,
> The table is spread,
> May you all be well-fed ;
> O good neighbors, come,
> The porridge is done !

The door of the house opened, and Muck saw many dogs and cats enter. He remained for some time in doubt whether he should accept the invitation, but at last he mustered up courage and walked in. Before him went two little kittens, and he concluded to follow them, as they might know the way to the kitchen better than he did.

As Muck ascended the stairs, he met the same old woman who had looked out from the window. She looked at him crossly, and asked him what he wanted. "Why, you invited everybody in to partake of your porridge," answered Little Muck; "and as I was very hungry, I came in too." The old woman laughed and said: "Where in the world do you come from, you odd little fellow? The whole city knows that I cook for nobody but my dear cats, and now and then I invite company for them out of the neighborhood, as you see." Little Muck told the old woman how hardly it had fared with him since his father's death, and begged that she would permit him to eat with her cats to-day. The woman, who was pleased with the simple-hearted manner in which the dwarf told his story, allowed him to be her guest, and provided food and drink for him bountifully.

When he had eaten his fill, and felt much stronger, the old woman looked at him for some time before saying: "Little Muck, remain in my service; you will have little to do, and will be well provided for." Little Muck, who had found the cats' soup very nice, consented, and became the servant of Ahavzi. His duties were light, but quite peculiar. Ahavzi had, for instance, six cats, and every morning Little Muck had to comb their fur and rub in costly ointments; when the old woman went out he had also to look after the cats; when they were to be fed, he had to set the dishes before them; and at night it was his duty to lay them on silken cushions and cover them with velvet blankets. There were also a few small dogs in the house, which he had to wait upon; still, these received but little attention as compared with the cats, which Ahavzi considered as her own children. As for the rest, Muck led as lonely a life as he had suffered in his father's house; for, with the exception of the old woman, he saw only dogs and cats the livelong day.

For a little while, however, all went well with him. He always had enough to eat and but little to do, and the old woman found no fault with him. But after a while the cats became unruly; when the old woman had gone out, they would fly around the room as if possessed, throwing things about, and breaking many a fine dish that stood in their way. But whenever they heard the old woman coming up the stairs, they crouched down on their cushions, and wagged their tails, as if nothing had occurred. Ahavzi got very angry when she found her rooms in such disorder, and laid it all to Muck's charge; and though he might protest his innocence as much as he pleased, she believed her cats, which looked so harmless, more than she did her servant.

Little Muck felt very sad that he had failed to find his fortune, and secretly resolved to leave the service of Ahavzi. But, as he had discovered on his first journey how poorly one lives without money, he resolved to help himself to the wages which his mistress had often promised but never given him. There was one room in Ahavzi's house that was always kept locked, and whose interior Muck had never seen. But he had often heard the old woman bustling about in there, and as often he would have given his life to know what she had hidden there. When he came to think about the money for his journey, it occurred to him that the treasures of Ahavzi might be concealed in that room. But the door was always locked, and therefore he was unable to get at the treasures.

One morning, when the old woman had gone out, one of the dogs—to whom Ahavzi accorded little more than a step-mother's care, but whose favor Muck had acquired by a series of kindly services—seized Muck by his baggy trousers, and acted as if he wished the dwarf to follow him. Muck, always ready for a game with the dog, followed him, and behold, he was escorted to the bed-room of Ahavzi, and up to a small door that he had never noticed before The door was soon opened, and the dog

went in followed by Muck, who was greatly rejoiced to
find that he was in the very room that he had so long
sought to enter. He searched every-where for money,
but found none. Only old clothes and strangely shaped
dishes were to be seen. One of these dishes attracted
his attention. It was crystal and in it were cut beautiful figures. He picked it up and turned it about to
examine all its sides. But, horrors! he had not noticed
that it had a lid which was insecurely fastened. The
cover fell off, and was broken into a thousand pieces!

For a long time Little Muck stood there, motionless
from terror. Now was his fate decided. Now he must flee,
or the old woman would surely strike him dead. His
journey was decided on at once; and as he took one
more look around to see if there were nothing among the
effects of Ahavzi that he could make use of on his march,
his eye was caught by a pair of large slippers. They
were certainly not beautiful; but those he had on would
not stand another journey, and he was also attracted by
this pair on account of their size, for when he once had
these on his feet everybody, he hoped, would see that
he had " put away childish things." He therefore quickly
kicked off his own shoes and stepped into the large slippers. A walking stick ornamented with a finely cut
lion's head, seemed to him to be standing too idly in the
corner; so he took that along also, and hastened to his
own bed-room, where he threw on his cloak, placed his
father's turban on his head, stuck the poniard in his
sash, and left the house and city as speedily as his feet
would carry him.

Once free of the town, he ran on, from fear of the old
woman, until he was ready to drop with exhaustion.
Never before had he run so fast; indeed it seemed to him
that some unseen force was hurrying him on so that he
could not stop. Finally he observed that his power
must have connection with the slippers, as these kept
sliding along, and carried him with them. He attempted
all kinds of experiments to come to a stand-still, but was

unsuccessful; when as a last resort, he shouted at himself, as one calls to horses: "Whoa! whoa! stop! whoa!" Thereupon the slippers halted, and Muck threw himself down on the ground utterly exhausted.

The slippers pleased him very much. He had, after all, acquired something by his service, that would help him along in the world, on his way to find his fortune. In spite of his joy, he fell asleep from exhaustion—as the small body of little Muck had so heavy a head to carry that it could not endure much fatigue. The little dog, that had helped him to Ahavzi's slippers, appeared to him in a dream, and said to him: "Dear Muck, you don't quite understand how to use those slippers; you must know that by turning around three times on the heel of your slipper, you can fly to any point you choose; and with this walking-stick you can discover treasures, as wherever gold is buried it will strike three times on the earth, and if silver, twice!" Such was the dream of Little Muck.

When he waked up, he recalled the wonderful dream, and resolved to test its truth. He put on the slippers, raised one foot and attempted to turn on his heel. But any one who will try the feat of turning three times in succession on the heel of such a large slipper, will not wonder that Little Muck did not at first succeed, especially if one takes into account his heavy head, that was constantly causing him to lose his balance. The poor little fellow got several hard falls on his nose, but he would not be frightened off from repeating his efforts, and at last he succeeded.

He whirled around like a wheel on his heel; wished himself in the next large city, and the slippers steered him up into the air, rushed him with the speed of the wind through the clouds, and before Little Muck could think how it had all happened, he found himself in a market-place, where many stalls had been put up, and a countless number of people were busily running to and fro. He mixed somewhat with the people but considered it wiser to take himself to a quieter street, as on the market-place every now-and-then somebody stepped on his slippers, so as to nearly throw him down, and then again, one and another, in hurrying by, would get a stab from his projecting poniard, so that he was continually in trouble.

Little Muck now began to think seriously of what he should do to earn some money. To be sure, he had a stick that would point out hidden treasures, but where might he hope to find a place where gold or silver was buried? He might have exhibited himself for money; but for that he was too proud. Finally his speed of foot occurred to him. Perhaps, thought he, my slippers may procure me a livelihood; and he resolved to hire himself out as a runner. Concluding that the king, who lived in this city, would pay the best wages, he inquired for the palace. At the door of the palace stood a guard, who asked him what business he had there? On answering that he was seeking service, he was referred to the head steward. To him he preferred his request, and begged him to give him a place among the king's messengers. The steward measured him with a glance from head to foot, and said: "How will you, with your little feet, scarcely a hand's breadth in length, become a royal messenger? Get away with you! I am not here to crack jokes with every fool." Little Muck assured him that he meant every word he had said, and that he would run a race with the fastest, on a wager. The steward took all this as a bit of pleasantry, and in that spirit ordered him to hold himself ready for a race that evening. He then took him into the kitchen, and saw that he was given food and drink, and afterwards, betook himself to the king, and told him about the little fellow, and his offer to run a race.

The king was a merry gentleman, and well pleased with the steward for affording him an opportunity of having some sport with Muck, and ordered him to make such preparations for a race on the meadow, back of the castle, that his whole court could view the scene in comfort; and commanded him once more to pay every attention to the wants of the dwarf. The king told the princes and princesses of the entertainment that would be furnished in the evening, and they, in turn, informed their servants, so that when evening set in, all was expectancy, and every body who had feet to carry them, went streaming out to the meadow, where staging had been erected in order that they might see the vainglorious Muck run a race.

When the king with his sons and daughters had taken their seats on the platform, Little Muck entered the meadow, and saluted the lords and ladies with an extremely elegant bow; universal acclamation greeted the appearance of the little fellow. Surely such a figure had never been seen there before. The small body and the big head, the cloak and baggy breeches, the long dagger stuck through the broad sash, the little feet enclosed in such huge slippers—it was impossible to look at such a droll figure and refrain from shouts of laughter. But Little Muck did not permit himself to be disturbed by the merriment his appearance caused. He stood, leaning proudly on his cane, awaiting his opponent. The steward, in accordance with Muck's wish, had selected the king's fastest runner, who now stepped up and placed himself beside the dwarf, and both awaited the signal to start. Thereupon, Princess Amarza waved her veil, as had been agreed on, and, like two arrows shot at the same mark, the two runners flew over the meadow.

Muck's opponent took the lead at the start, but the dwarf chased after him in his slipper-chariot and soon overtook him, passed him, and reached the goal long before the other came up, panting for breath. Wonder and astonishment for some moments held the spectators still; but when the king clapped his hands, the crowd cheered and shouted: "Long live Little Muck, the victor in the race!"

Meanwhile, Little Muck had been brought up before

the king. He prostrated himself and said: "Most High and Mighty King, I have given you here only a small test of my art. Will you now permit my appointment as one of your runners?" But the king replied: "No; you shall be my body-messenger, dear Muck, and be retained about my person. Your wages will be one hundred gold pieces a year, and you shall eat at the head servants' table."

So Little Muck came to believe that at last he had found the fortune he had so long been looking for, and in his heart he was cheerful and content. He also rejoiced in the special favor of the king, who employed him on his quickest and most secret messages, which the dwarf executed with accuracy and the most inconceivable speed.

But the other servants of the king did not feel very cordial towards him, because they found themselves superseded in the favor of their master by a dwarf, who knew nothing except how to run fast. They laid many plots to ruin him, but all these came to naught, because of the implicit confidence that the king placed in his chief body-messenger — for to this position had Little Muck been advanced.

Muck, who was quite sensible of this feeling against him, never once thought of revenge, such was his goodness of heart, but tried to hit upon some plan by which he might become useful to his enemies, and win their love. He thought of his little stick, which he had neglected since he had found his fortune, and he reflected that if he were to find treasures, his companions would be more favorably disposed towards him. He had often heard that the father of the present king had buried a great deal of treasure, when his country had been overrun by the enemy: and it was also said that the old king had died without being able to reveal the secret to his son. From this time forward Muck always carried his stick with him, in the hope of sometime passing over the place where the old king had hidden his money.

One evening he went, by chance, into an outlying part

F

of the palace gardens, which he seldom visited; when suddenly he felt the stick twitch in his hand, and it bent three times to the ground. Well did he know what this betokened. He therefore drew out his poniard, made some marks on the neighboring trees, and stole back into the castle, where he provided himself with a spade, and waited until it was dark enough for his undertaking.

The digging made Little Muck much more trouble than he had anticipated. His arms were very weak, while his spade was large and heavy; and he had worked a full two hours before he had dug as many feet. Finally, he struck something hard, that sounded like iron. He now dug very fast, and soon brought to light a large iron lid. This caused him to get down in the hole to find out what the lid might cover, and he discovered, as he had expected, a large pot filled with gold pieces. But he had not sufficient strength to raise the pot, therefore he put into his pockets, his cloak, and his sash, as much as he wished to carry, covered up the remainder carefully, and took his load on his back. But if he had not had his slippers on, he would never have been able to move from the spot, so great was the weight of the gold. However, he reached his room unnoticed, and secured the gold under the cushions of his couch.

When Little Muck found himself in possession of such wealth, he believed that a new leaf would be turned, and he should win many friends and followers among his enemies: from which reasoning one may readily perceive that the good Little Muck could not have received a very good bringing up, or he would never have dreamed of securing true friends through the medium of money. Alas, that he did not then step into his slippers, and scamper off with his cloak full of gold!

The gold, which Little Muck from this time forth distributed so generously, awakened the envy of the other court servants. The chief cook, Ahuli, said: ' He is a counterfeiter!" The steward, Achmet, declared: "He coaxes it out of the king!" But Archaz, the treasurer, and Muck's bitterest enemy, who occasionally dipped into the king's cash box himself, exclaimed decidedly: "He has stolen it!"

In order to make sure of their case, they all acted in concert; and the head cup-bearer placed himself in the way of the king, one day, looking very sad and cast-down. So remarkably sad was his countenance, that the king inquired the cause of his sorrow. "Alas!" replied he, "I am sad because I have lost the favor of my master." "What fancy is that, friend Korchuz? Since when have I kept the sun of my favor from lighting on you?" asked the king. The head cup-bearer replied that the king had loaded the confidential body-messenger with gold, but had given nothing to his poor, faithful servants.

The king was very much surprised at this news, and listened to an account of the liberal gifts of Little Muck, while the conspirators easily created the suspicion in the royal mind that Muck had by some means stolen the gold from the treasury. This turn of affairs was very welcome to the treasurer, who, without it, would not have cared to render an account of the cash in his keeping. The king, therefore, gave an order that a secret watch should be kept on every step of Little Muck, to catch him, if possible, in the act.

On the night following this unlucky day, as Little Muck took his spade and stole out into the garden, with the intention of replenishing the heap of gold in his chamber, which his liberality had so wasted, he was followed at a distance by a guard, led by Ahuli, the cook, and Archaz, the treasurer, who fell upon him at the very moment when he was removing the gold from the pot, bound him, and took him straight before the king. The king, who felt cross enough at having his slumber disturbed, received his confidential chief body-messenger very ungraciously, and at once began an examination of the case. The pot had been dug from the earth, and, together with the spade and the cloak full of gold, was placed at the king's feet. The treasurer stated that, with his watchman, he had surprised Muck in the very act of burying this pot full of gold in the ground.

The king asked the accused if this were true, and where he had got the gold. Little Muck, conscious of his innocence, replied that he had discovered it in the garden, and that he was attempting to dig it up, and not to bury it. All present laughed loudly at his defense, but the king, extremely enraged at what he believed to be the cool effrontery of the dwarf, cried: "What, wretch! Do you persist in lying so shamelessly to your king, after stealing from him? Treasurer Archaz, I call upon you to say whether you recognize this as the amount of money that is missing from my treasury?" The treasurer answered that, for his part, he was sure that this much, and still more, had been missing from the royal treasury for some time, and he would take his oath that this was part of the stolen money. The king thereupon commanded that Little Muck should be put in chains, and thrown into the tower; and handed the money over to his treasurer to put back into the treasury.

Rejoiced at the fortunate outcome of the affair, the treasurer withdrew, and counted over the gold pieces at home; but this wicked man never once noticed, that in the bottom of the pot lay a scrap of paper, on which was written: "The enemy has over-run my country, and therefore I bury here a part of my treasure; whoever finds it will receive the curse of a king if he does not at once deliver it to my son.—*King Sadi.*"

Little Muck, in his prison, was a prey to the most melancholy reflections. He knew that the penalty for robbery of royal property was death; and yet he hesitated to reveal to the king the magical powers of his stick, because he rightly feared that it, and his slippers, would then be taken away from him. But neither could his slippers give him any aid in his present condition, for he was chained so closely to the wall that, try as he might, he could not turn on his heel. But when notice of death was served on him the following day, he thought better of the matter, concluding it was wiser to live without the stick, than to die with it. He, therefore, sent to the king, begging to make a private communication, and disclosed the secret to him. The king would not credit his confession; but Little Muck promised a test of the stick's power, if the king would grant him his life. The king gave him his word on it, and, unseen by Muck, had some gold buried in the garden, and then ordered Muck to find it. After a few moments hunt, Muck's stick struck three times on the ground. This assured the king that his treasurer had deceived him, and he therefore sent him — as is customary in the Levant — a silken cord, with which to strangle himself. But to Little Muck he said: "It is true that I promised to spare your life, but as I believe that you possess more than one secret in connection with this stick, you will be imprisoned for life, unless you confess what connection there is between this stick and your fast running."

Little Muck, whose experience for a single night in the tower had given him no desire for a longer imprisonment, acknowledged that his whole art lay in the slippers; still he did not inform the king about the three turns on the heel. The king tried on the slippers himself, in order to test them, and run about the garden like a madman, making many attempts to stop, but he did not know how to bring the slippers to a stand-still, and Little Muck, who could not forego this bit of revenge, let him run around till he fell senseless.

When the king recovered consciousness, he was fearfully enraged at Little Muck, who had run him out of breath. "I have pledged my word to give you life and liberty, but if you are within my territory in twelve hours, I will have you imprisoned!" As for the stick and slippers, he had them locked up in his treasury.

Poor as at first, Little Muck wandered out into the country, cursing the folly that had led him to think he could play an important part at court. The country

from which he was driven was fortunately not a large one,
so that in the course of eight hours he had reached the
boundary line; although walking, after having been accustomed to his beloved slippers, was no pleasant task to
him.

As soon as he had crossed the border, he turned off
from the highways in order to reach the most desolate
part of the wilderness, where he might live alone by himself, as he was at enmity with all mankind. In the dense
forest he came across a place that seemed well suited to
his purpose. A clear brook, overgrown by large, shady
fig trees, and with banks of soft velvety turf, looked very
inviting. Here he threw himself down, with the firm resolve not to eat again, but to calmly await death. While
indulging in gloomy reveries, he fell asleep; but when he
waked up, and began to experience the pangs of hunger,
he reflected that starvation was rather an unpleasant
thing, and therefore looked about him to see whether
any thing was to be had to eat.

Delicious ripe figs hung on the tree under which he
had slept. He climbed up to pick some, and found them
just to his taste; and afterwards he went down to the
brook to slake his thirst. But how great was his horror,
when the brook reflected back his head, adorned with two
prodigious ears, and a long, thick nose! In great perplexity, he seized the ears in his hands, and truly they
were more than half a yard long.

"I deserve an ass's ears!" cried he, "for like an ass
I have trodden my fortune under foot." He strolled about
under the trees, and when he once more felt hungry, he
again had recourse to the figs, as they were the only eat-
able things to be found on the trees. After eating his
second meal of figs, while thinking whether he might not
find a place for his ears under his large turban, so that
he would not appear too comical, he became sensible of
the fact that his enormous ears had disappeared. He
rushed down to the brook, and found it actually true; his
ears had resumed their former shape; his long, unshape-

ly nose had vanished. He now saw how all this had come about; the fruit of the first tree had presented him with the long nose and ears, while that of the second had healed him. Joyfully he perceived that his good luck had once more suggested to him the means of getting satisfaction. He picked from each tree as much as he could carry, and went back to the country he had so lately left.

In the first town he came to, he disguised himself with

other clothes, and went on to the city where the king lived. It was just at the season when ripe fruits were not very plentiful, and Little Muck placed himself under the palace gate, knowing from experience that the chief cook was in the habit of purchasing delicacies here for the king's table. Muck had not sat there long before he saw the cook coming through the court, and examining the viands of the marketmen who were ranged about the gate. Finally his glance fell on Muck's basket. "Ah! a rare morsel," exclaimed he, " that will please His Majesty mightily ; what will you take for the whole basket? " Little Muck named a moderate price, and the bargain was quickly made. The cook turned the basket over to a slave and went on. Little Muck scampered off quickly, as he was afraid that when the figs had done their work on the heads of the court people, he might be hunted up and punished as the seller.

The king was in excellent spirits at table, and praised the cook repeatedly for his successes, and for the solicitude with which he always sought out the rarest dainties for him; but the cook, knowing well what delicacy he was holding back, smirked in a satisfied way, dropping now and then mysterious phrases, such as: "Don't crow till you are out of the woods;" or "All's well that ends well," so that the princesses were very curious to know what it was he was about to produce. But when the beautiful, inviting figs were placed on the table, an exclamation broke from the lips of all present "How ripe; how appetizing!" cried the king. "Cook, you are a clever fellow, and deserve our especial favor!" Thus speaking, the king, who was accustomed to be rather economical with such delicacies, distributed the figs around his table with his own hand; each prince and princess received two, the court ladies and viziers one, while he placed the rest before himself, and began to devour them with great delight.

"But, mercy on us, father! what makes you look so strange?" exclaimed Princess Amarza, soon after. Everybody looked at the king in astonishment. Monstrous ears were attached to his head, and a long nose hung down over his chin. Then, too, they began to look at one another, with horror and astonishment. All were more or less decorated with this singular head-gear.

Fancy the horror experienced by the court! All the physicians in the city were sent for, and came in great numbers, prescribed pills and mixtures; but without effect on the ears and noses. An operation was performed on one of the princes, but the ears grew right out again.

Muck heard the whole story in his hiding-place, and saw that now his opportunity had come. With the money received from the sale of his figs, he bought a costume suitable for a professional man, while a long beard of goat's hair completed his disguise. With a small bag of figs, he entered the king's palace, and offered his services as a foreign physician. At first, his representations were scouted; but when Little Muck restored the ears and nose of one of the princes to

their natural size, by giving him a fig to eat, all were anxious to be cured by this strange physician. But the king took him by the hand, without speaking, and conducted him into his own apartment, where he opened a door that led into his treasury, and beckoned Muck to follow him. "Here is my treasure," said the king; "choose for yourself, and let it be what it will, it shall be preserved for you, if you will free me of this disgraceful evil."

This was sweet music in Little Muck's ears. No sooner had he entered than he espied his slippers on the floor, and near them, his stick. He walked up and down the room, as if wondering at the riches of the

4*

king; but on coming to his slippers he slid into them, seized his stick, and tore off his false beard, revealing to the astonished king the well-known features of his exiled Muck. "Faithless King!" said he; "you, who reward fidelity with ingratitude, may keep as a well-merited punishment the deformity that you bear. I leave you those ears, that you may think daily on Little Muck." Thus speaking, the dwarf turned quickly on his heel, wished himself far away, and before the king could call for help, Little Muck had flown away.

Since then, Little Muck has lived here in comfort, but without society, as he disdains mankind. Through experience he has become a wiser man, who, notwithstanding his external appearance may be unusual, is more worthy of your admiration than your sport.

Such was the story my father told me. I assured him that I repented of my rude behavior towards the good little man, and my father administered the other half of the punishment he had designed for me. I related to my playmates the wonderful events of the dwarf's life, and we became so much attached to him that not one of us ever abused him again. On the contrary, we honored him as long as he lived, and always bowed as low to him as before the Cadi or Mufti.

The travellers decided to rest for a day at this caravansary, in order to strengthen themselves and their beasts for the journey still before them. The gaiety of the day before continued, and they amused themselves with all kinds of games. After dinner, they called on the fourth merchant, Ali Sizah, to perform his duty, as the others had done, by giving them a story. He replied that his own life had been so barren of incidents, that he could not interest them with any personal anecdote, but, instead, he would relate to them the legend of "The False Prince."

THE FALSE PRINCE.

HERE was once a respectable jour-
neyman-tailor, named Labakan, who
had learned his trade of a clever
master in Alexandria. It could not
be said that Labakan was unhandy
with the needle; on the contrary, he
was able to do very fine work. Neither
would one be justified in calling him
lazy; but still every thing was not just
as it should be with the workman, as
he often sewed away by the hour at such a rate that the
needle became red-hot in his hands, and the thread
fairly smoked, and would then show a better piece of
work than any one else. But, at another time — and,
sad to relate, this occurred more frequently — he would
sit plunged in deep thought, looking before him with a
fixed gaze, and with something so peculiar in his expression and conduct that his master and the other journeymen were wont to say at such times: "Labakan is
putting on airs again."

But on Fridays, when other people were returning
from prayers to their work, Labakan came out of the
mosque in a beautiful costume, which he had taken
great pains to prepare for himself. He walked slowly
and with proud steps through the squares and streets of
the city, and whenever he was greeted by any of his
comrades with, "Peace be with you," or, "How are
you, friend Labakan?" he condescendingly waved his
hand in reply, or gave his superior a princely nod. If
his master said to him, "Ah, Labakan, what a prince was

lost in you!" he, much flattered, would respond, "Have you, too, remarked that?" or, "That has been my opinion for a long time."

After this manner had the journeyman conducted himself for a long time; but his master indulged his folly, as otherwise he was a good fellow and a clever workman. But one day, Selim, the brother of the sultan, who was then traveling through Alexandria,

sent a court costume to the master, to have certain changes made in it; and the master gave it to Labakan to make the alterations, as he did the best work. At night, after the master and his journeymen had gone out to refresh themselves after their day's work, an irresistible desire impelled Labakan to go back into the shop where the costume of the sultan's brother hung. He stood before it, lost in admiration over the splendor of the embroidery and the various shades of velvet and silk. He could not refrain from trying it on; and behold, it fitted him as perfectly as though it had been made for him. "Am I not as good a prince as anybody?" said he to himself, while striding up and down the room. "Has not the master said that I was born to be a prince?" With the clothes, the journeyman seemed to have adopted some quite royal sentiments; he could not banish from his mind the fancy that he was the unacknowledged son of a king; and as such, he resolved to travel about the world, leaving a place where the people had been so foolish as not to recognize his true rank under the cover of his present low position. The splendid costume seemed to him sent by a good fairy. He therefore took care not to slight so welcome a present, pocketed what little ready money he possessed, and, favored by the darkness of the night, strolled out of Alexandria's gate.

Wherever he appeared, the new prince created quite a sensation; as the splendor of his dress and his grave and majestic air were hardly in keeping with his mode of traveling. When he was questioned on this subject, he was accustomed to reply, in a mysterious way, that there were some very good reasons for his traveling afoot. But when he noticed that he was making himself ridiculous by his foot wanderings, he invested a small sum in an old horse, which was very well adapted to his wants, as, by its lack of speed and spirit, he was never forced into the embarrassing position of showing his skill as a rider—a thing quite out of his line.

One day, as he walked Murva (such was the name he had given his horse) along the road, he was overtaken by a horseman who requested permission to travel with him, as the road would seem much shorter if he could enjoy Labakan's company. The horseman was a merry young man, of pleasing appearance and conversation. He began talking with Labakan, asking where he had come from and where he was going; and it soon appeared that he, too, like the journeyman-tailor, was traveling about the world without any definite plan. He said that his name was Omar; that he was the nephew of Elsi

Bey, the unfortunate Pasha of Cairo, and was traveling in order to execute a charge that his uncle had confided to him on his death-bed. Labakan was not so communicative about his own affairs, but gave Omar to understand that he was of high descent, and was traveling for pleasure.

The two young gentlemen were well pleased with each other, and continued their journey together. On the second day of their acquaintance, Labakan inquired of his companion Omar about the trust he had to execute, and learned to his astonishment that Elsi Bey, Pasha of Cairo, had brought up Omar from his earliest childhood, and the boy had never known his parents. Now, when Elsi Bey was attacked by his enemies, and after three unfortunate battles, was forced to fly from the field, mortally wounded, he disclosed to his pupil that he was not his nephew, but the son of a mighty ruler, who, frightened by the prophecies of his astrologist, had had the young prince removed from the palace, with the oath not to see him again until the prince should have reached his twenty-second birthday. Elsi Bey did not give him the name of his father, but had most particularly charged him that he must be present at the famous pillar El Serujah, a four days' journey east of Alexandria, on the fourth day of the coming month of Ramadan, on which day he would be twenty-two years old. Arriving there, he should hold out a dagger to the men who would be standing on the column, with the words: "Here am I whom you seek;" and if they answered, "Praised be the Prophet, who preserved you," he should follow them, and they would lead him to his father.

The journeyman-tailor, Labakan, was astonished at this communication. He looked on Prince Omar, from this time forth, with envious eyes; exasperated that fate should have selected his companion, who already passed for the nephew of a powerful pasha, to shower on him the still higher dignity of a prince's son, while he, Labakan, endowed with all the qualities of a prince, was degraded by a low birth and a common occupation. He made comparisons between himself and the prince, and was forced to confess that the prince was a youth of prepossessing appearance, with fine sparkling eyes, aquiline nose, a gentle and obliging manner—in short, all the external marks of a gentleman. But numerous as were the good traits he noticed in his companion, still, he whispered to himself, a Labakan would be far more welcome to a princely father than the real prince.

These reflections occupied Labakan's mind the whole day; and they were present in his sleep, at their next lodging-place. And when he woke, and his eye fell on the sleeping Omar at his side—sleeping so quietly, and dreaming, perhaps, of his happy fortune—the idea came into Labakan's brain to obtain, through stratagem or force, that which unwilling fate had denied him. The dagger, the token by which the home-returning prince was to be recognized, stuck in the sash of the sleeper. He drew it forth lightly, to plunge it into the sleeping breast of its owner. But the pacific soul of the tailor shrunk at the thought of murder. He contented himself with taking possession of the dagger, ordered Omar's fast horse to be saddled, and before the prince had awaked, his faithless companion had gained a start of several miles.

It was the first day of the sacred month of Ramadan when Labakan robbed the prince; and he had, therefore, four days in which to reach the pillar of El Serujah, the location of which he well knew. Although the distance could be easily covered in two days, yet Labakan fearing to be overtaken by the true prince, made all haste.

At the close of the second day, Labakan saw the column before him. It stood upon a small hill, in a broad plain, and could be observed at a distance of eight miles. Labakan's heart beat wildly at the sight. Although he had had time enough, in the last two days, to think over the part he was about to play, still his accusing conscience made him uneasy; but the thought that he had been born to be a prince hardened him once more, so that he went forward.

The region about the column El Serujah was uninhabited and desolate, and the new prince would have found himself in sad straights for sustenance, had he not made provision for a journey of several days. He went into camp, with his horse, under some palm trees, and awaited there his fate.

Near the middle of the following day, he saw a large procession of horses and camels coming over the plain, to the column of El Serujah. The train stopped at the foot of the hill on which the column stood; splendid tents were pitched, and the whole had the appearance of a rich pasha's or sheik's caravan. Labakan suspected that the many people whom he saw were there on the Prince Omar's account, and he would willingly have shown them their future ruler then and there; but he controlled his desire to step forth as a prince, as the following morning would certainly see his dearest hopes realized.

The morning sun woke the overjoyed tailor to the most important moment of his life—the moment that should see him lifted from an ignoble position to the side of a royal father. To be sure, the unlawfulness of the steps he was taking, occurred to him, as he saddled his horse to ride to the column; to be sure, he thought of the anguish Prince Omar would suffer, betrayed in his fair hopes; but the die was cast, and he could not undo what had already been done, and his vanity whispered to him that he looked stately enough to be presented to the most powerful king as a son. Encouraged by such thoughts, he swung himself into his saddle, mustered all his courage to stand the ordeal of a gallop, and in less than fifteen minutes he reached the foot of the hill. He dismounted from his horse and tied it to a bush, and then drew out Prince Omar's dagger and ascended the hill.

At the foot of the column stood six men around an aged man of kingly appearance. A splendid kaftan of cloth of gold, with a white cashmere shawl wound about it, and a white turban ornamented with sparkling jewels, denoted him to be a man of wealth and rank.

Labakan went up to him, made a low obeisance, and offered him the dagger, saying: "Here am I whom you seek."

"Praised be the Prophet, who preserved you!" replied

the old man with tears of joy. "Embrace your old father, my beloved son Omar!" The good tailor was much moved by these solemn words, and with a mixture of joy and shame sank into the arms of the aged prince.

But only for an instant was he permitted to enjoy undisturbed the delight of his new surroundings; for as he arose from the embrace of the elderly prince, he saw a horseman hastening across the plain towards the hill. The rider and his horse presented a singular appearance.

The horse, either from stubbornness or exhaustion, could hardly be urged forward, but moved with a stumbling gait that could be called neither a walk nor a trot, while his rider was using both hands and feet to force him to a faster pace. Only too soon Labakan recognized his horse, Murva, and the genuine Prince Omar; but the wicked Father of Lies once more took possession of him, and he determined that, whatever the result might be, he would maintain his pretended rights with a bold face.

The rider's gestures had been seen while he was still at a distance; but now, in spite of the feeble trot of his horse, he had arrived at the foot of the hill, thrown himself from his horse, and rushed up the hill.

"Stay, there!" cried he, "Stop, whoever you may be, and do not let yourselves be misled by the shameful impostor! My name is Omar, and no mortal may dare to assume my name!"

Deep astonishment was expressed in the faces of the bystanders, at the turn affairs had taken, and the old prince was especially perplexed, as he looked inquiringly from one to the other. But Labakan said, with forced composure: "Most gracious Sire and Father, do not allow this person to mislead you. He is, to my certain knowledge, a crazy tailor from Alexandria, called Labakan, and more deserving of our pity than our anger."

These words brought the prince to the verge of madness. Foaming with rage he attempted to spring on Labakan, but the bystanders interposed, and held him fast, while the old prince said: "Of a truth, my dear son, the poor fellow is mad; let him be bound and placed on one of our dromedaries; perhaps we may be able to render the unfortunate youth some assistance."

The anger of the prince was past. He threw himself, weeping, at the feet of his father: "My heart tells me that you are my father; by the memory of my mother, I charge you to listen to me!"

"Eh, God preserve us!" answered the old man. "He

is beginning to talk strangely again; how does the fellow come by such stupid notions!"

Thereupon he took Labakan's arm, and was conducted down the hill by him. They both mounted beautiful, richly-caparisoned horses, and rode at the head of the caravan, over the plain. The hands of the prince were bound, and he was tied fast on one of the dromedaries, while two horsemen rode on each side, and kept a careful watch on all his movements.

The elderly prince was Saaud, Sultan of Wechabiten. He had lived for years without children, until finally a son, whom he had so ardently desired, was born to him. But the astrologer of whom he inquired the destiny of the boy, gave the opinion that "until his twenty-second year the child would be in danger of being supplanted by an enemy," therefore to be on the safe side, the sultan had given the prince to his tried and true friend, Elsi Bey, to be brought up, and for twenty-two painful years had waited for his home-coming.

All this the sultan told his pretended son, and expressed himself as well pleased with his figure and demeanor.

On arriving in the sultan's country they were everywhere received by the inhabitants with acclamations, as the report of the prince's arrival had spread like wildfire to all the cities and villages. Arches covered with flowers and boughs were constructed in all the streets through which they passed, brilliant carpets of all colors adorned the houses, and the people praised God and His Prophets for sending them so beautiful a prince. All this filled the heart of the tailor with delight; but all the more unhappy did the real Omar feel, who, still bound, followed the caravan in silent despair. In the universal joy nobody troubled themselves about him who should have been the recipient of their welcome. Thousands upon thousands shouted the name of Omar, but he who rightly bore this name was noticed not at all. At the most, one and another would ask who it was that was bound so securely; and the reply of his escort, that it was a crazy tailor, echoed horribly in his ears.

The caravan at last reached the capital of the sultan, where a still more brilliant reception was awaiting them. The sultana, an elderly, venerable lady, awaited them with the entire court, in the splendid hall of the palace. The floor of this salon was covered with an immense carpet, the walls were tastefully adorned with a light-blue cloth, hung from great silver hooks with golden tassels and cords.

It was already night when the caravan arrived; therefore numerous round colored lamps were lighted in the salon, making it light as day. But the most lights were placed at the farther end of the salon, where the sultana sat upon a throne. The throne stood upon a dais, and was inlaid with pure gold, and set with large amethysts. Four of the most distinguished emirs held a canopy over the sultana's head, while the Sheik of Medina fanned her with a fan of peacock's feathers.

Under these surroundings, the sultana awaited her husband and her son. She had not seen her son since his birth, but the longed-for son had appeared in her dreams, so that she felt sure of knowing him amongst a thousand. Now the noise of the approaching caravan was heard, trumpets and drums mingled with the cheers of the crowd; the hoofs of the horses beat in the court of the palace; nearer and nearer sounded the steps of the expected ones; the doors of the salon flew open, and through the rows of prostrate servants, the sultan hastened to the throne of the sultana, leading his son by the hand.

"Here," said he, "I bring you the one for whom you have so long yearned."

But the sultana interrupted him with: "That is not my son! Those are not the features that the Prophet showed me in my dreams!"

Just as the sultan was about to upbraid her for her unbelief, the door of the salon opened, and Prince Omar rushed in, followed by his guards, from whom he had escaped by the exercise of all his strength. He threw himself breathless before the throne with the words:

"Here will I die! Let me be killed, inhuman father, for I can no longer endure this disgrace."

Everyone was amazed at this speech; they crowded about the unfortunate youth, and the guards, from whom he had escaped, were about to lay hold of him and bind him again, when the sultana, who had looked on all this in speechless surprise, sprang up from the throne.

"Stay, there!" cried she; "this and no other is the real prince; this is he whom my eyes have never beheld, and yet my heart has known!"

The guard had involuntarily released Omar, but the sultan, burning with anger, called to them to bind the crazy fellow. "It is my business to decide here," said he, in a commanding tone, "and here one does not judge by the dreams of old women, but by certain reliable signs. This youth (pointing to Labakan) is my son, for he brought me the dagger, the true token of my friend Elsi."

"He stole the dagger!" exclaimed Omar. "He abused my unsuspecting confidence with treachery!" But the sultan, accustomed to have his own way in every thing, would not listen to the voice of his son, and had the unhappy Omar forcibly dragged from the room. Then, accompanied by Labakan, he went to his own room, very angry with the sultana, with whom he had lived in peace for twenty-five years.

The sultana was very unhappy over these events. She was perfectly well satisfied that an impostor had taken possession of the sultan's heart, as the unfortunate youth who had been dragged away, had often appeared in her dreams as her son.

When she had in a measure quieted her sorrow, she tried to hit upon some method of convincing the sultan of his error. This was no easy task, as he who had usurped their son's place, had brought the token of recognition, the dagger, and had also, as she discovered, learned so much about Omar's early life from the prince himself, that he played his *rôle* without betraying himself.

She summoned the men who had accompanied the sultan to the pillar of El Serujah, in order to learn all the particulars, and then held a consultation with her most trustworthy slave-women. They chose and then rejected this and that expedient. At last Melechsalah, a wise old woman, said: "If I have heard rightly, honored mistress, the one who brought the dagger, called him whom you recognize as your son, Labakan, a crazy tailor."

"Yes, that is true," answered the sultana; "but what can you make out of that?"

"Suppose," continued the slave, "that this impostor had fastened his own name on your son? And if this supposition is correct, there is a fine way of catching the impostor, that I will tell to you as a secret."

The sultana bent her head, and the slave whispered in her ear some expedient that seemed to please the sultana, as she prepared to go at once to the sultan.

The sultana was a prudent woman, who knew the weak sides of the sultan and how to make use of them. She therefore appeared willing to submit to his judgment, and to recognize the son he had chosen; asking in return but one condition. The sultan, who was sorry for the anger he had shown his wife, granted her request, and she said: "I should dearly like to receive from both of these claimants a test of their cleverness. Another person might very likely have them ride, fight, or throw spears; but these are things that everybody can do, and I will give them something that will require ingenuity to accomplish. Each one shall make a kaftan, and a pair of trousers, and then we shall see who will make the finest."

The sultan laughed, and said: "Well, you have devised something extremely wise! The idea that my son

should compete with your crazy tailor at coat-making?
No, it won't do."

The sultana, however, insisted that he was bound by
the promise he had made her in advance; and the sultan, who was a man of his word, finally consented, although he swore that let the crazy tailor make his coat
ever so fine, he would never admit him to be his son.

The sultan went in person to his son, and requested
him to humor the caprice of his mother, who very much
wished for a kaftan made by his hands. Labakan was
greatly pleased. If that is all that is wanted, thought
he to himself, then madame the sultana will soon have
cause to be proud of me.

Two rooms were prepared, one for the prince, the
other for the tailor, where they were to try their skill;
and they were liberally provided with silk cloth, scissors,
needles and thread.

The sultan was very curious to see what sort of a
thing his son would bring to light for a kaftan; while the
sultana was very nervous lest her stratagem should fail.
Two days had been given to them in which to accomplish their task. On the morning of the third day, the
sultan sent for his wife, and when she had come, he sent
into the two rooms for the two kaftans and their makers.

Labakan entered triumphantly, and spread his kaftan
before the astonished eyes of the sultan. "Look here,
father!" said he, "see, honored mother, whether this is
not a master-piece of a kaftan? I would be willing to
lay a wager with the cleverest court tailor that he could
not produce such an one as that."

The sultana smiled, and turned to Omar: "And what
have you produced, my son?" Impatiently he threw
down the silk, cloth and scissors on the floor. "I was
brought up to break horses, and to the use of a sword,
and my spear will hit the mark at sixty paces; but the
science of the needle is strange to me, and would have
been an unworthy study for a pupil of Elsi Bey, the
ruler of Cairo!"

"O thou true son of my heart!" exclaimed the sultana. "Now, I can embrace thee, and call thee son! Pardon me, my Husband and Lord," continued she, turning to the sultan, "that I have plotted this stratagem against you. Do you not now see which is the prince, and which the tailor? Truly, the kaftan that your son has made is superb, and I should like to ask him of what master he learned his trade"

The sultan sat in deep thought, glancing suspiciously now at his wife and now at Labakan, who vainly tried to control his blushes and his discomfiture at having so stupidly betrayed himself.

"Even this proof will not suffice," said the sultan. "But praised be Allah, I know of a means of finding out whether I have been deceived or not."

He ordered his fastest horse to be led out, swung himself into the saddle, and rode into a forest near by, where lived, according to an old legend, a kind fairy named Adolzaide, who had often stood by the kings of his race with her counsel in the hour of need.

In the middle of the forest was an open place surrounded by tall cedars. There lived—so the story ran—the fairy, and it was seldom that a mortal ventured there, as a certain aversion to the spot had for ages descended from father to son.

Arriving there, the sultan dismounted, tied his horse to a tree, placed himself in the centre of the opening, and called out in a loud voice: "If it be true that you have given my ancestors good advice in the hour of need, then do not spurn the prayer of their grandson, and give me advice on a point for which human understanding is too frail."

He had hardly spoken the last word, when one of the cedars opened, and a veiled lady, in long white garments, stepped forth. "I know why you come to me, Sultan Saaud. Your purpose is just; therefore, you shall have my assistance. Take these two little boxes. Let each of the young men who claim to be your son choose

between these. I know that the true prince will not fail
to pick out the right one." Thus spake the fairy, at the
same time handing him two little ivory boxes richly set
with gold and pearls. On the lid, which the sultan
vainly tried to open, were inscriptions in diamond letters.

The sultan tried to think as he rode home what these
little boxes might contain; but all his efforts to open
them failed. Nor did the inscriptions throw any light on
the matter, for one read—*Honor and Fame ;* the other—
Fortune and Riches. The sultan thought to himself that
he would have great difficulty in making a choice between
these two things, that were alike desirable, alike alluring.

On arriving at his palace, he sent for the sultana, and
told her of the verdict of the fairy. A strange hope
assured the sultana that he to whom her heart drew her
would choose the box that should make plain his royal
descent.

Two tables were placed before the throne or the sultan, upon which the king placed the boxes with his own
hand. He then ascended the throne, and beckoned one
of his slaves to open the doors of the salon. A brilliant
assembly of pashas and emirs of the realm, whom the
sultan had summoned, streamed through the opened
doors. They took their places on splendid cushions that
were ranged lengthwise along the wall.

When they were all seated, the sultan beckoned a
second time, and Labakan was brought forward. With a
proud step he walked up the hall, prostrated himself
before the throne, and said: "What are the commands
of my Lord and Father?"

The sultan rose from his throne, and said : "My son,
doubts have been raised as to the justness of your claim
to this name; one of those little boxes contains the proof
of your real parentage. Choose; I do not doubt that you
will select the right one."

Labakan arose and stepped up to the tables, hesitated
for some time as to which he should choose, but finally
said : "Honored Father! What can be higher than the

fortune to be your son? what nobler than the riches of thy grace? I choose the box with the inscription — *Fortune and Riches*."

"We shall presently know whether you have chosen the right one; in the meantime sit down on the cushion by the side of the Pasha of Medina," said the sultan, and motioned to a slave.

Omar was brought forward. His look was gloomy, his air sad, and his appearance created universal interest among those present. He prostrated himself before the throne, and inquired after the commands of the sultan. The sultan signified to him that he was to choose one of the little boxes. Omar arose and approached the tables.

He read attentively both inscriptions, and then said: "The last few days have taught me how fickle is fortune, how unstable are riches; but they have also learned me that an indestructible gift dwells in the breast of Honor, and that the shining star of Fame does not vanish with fortune. And though I should renounce a crown, the die is cast: *Honor and Fame*, I choose you!"

He placed his hand on the box he had chosen; but the sultan ordered him to wait a moment, and beckoned Labakan to come forward, and lay his hand on his box also. Then the sultan had a basin of water, of the holy fountain of Zemzem in Mecca, brought, washed his hands for prayer, turned his face to the East, prostrated himself and prayed: "God of my fathers! Thou who for centuries hast preserved our race pure and uncontaminated, do not permit that an unworthy one should bring to shame the name of the Abasside; be near my true son with Thy protection, in this hour of trial!"

The sultan arose, and once more ascended his throne. Universal expectancy held those present in breathless attention; one could have heard a mouse run over the floor, so still were they all. Those farthest away stretched their necks to look over the heads of those in front, that they might see the little boxes. Then the sultan spoke:

"Open the boxes!" and although no force could have opened them before, they now flew open of themselves.

In the box chosen by Omar lay, on a velvet cushion, a small golden crown, and a sceptre; in Labakan's box—a large needle and a little package of thread! The sultan ordered them to bring their boxes to him. He took the minature crown in his hand, and wonderful was it to see how, as he took it, it began to grow larger and larger until it had attained the size of a genuine crown. He placed the crown on the head of Omar, who knelt before him, kissed him on the forehead, and bade him sit at his right hand. Then turning to Labakan, he said: "There is an old proverb that the shoemaker should stick to his last. It looks as if you should stick to the needle. To be sure, you do not deserve my pardon; but some one has interceded for you, to whom I can refuse nothing to-day; therefore I spare you your miserable life. But, to give you some good advice—you had better make haste to get out of my kingdom."

Ashamed, ruined as were all his pretensions, the poor journeyman-tailor could not reply. He threw himself at the feet of the prince, in tears. "Can you forgive me, Prince?" said he.

"Loyalty to a friend, magnanimity to a foe, is the boast of the Abasside," replied the prince, as he raised him up. "Go in peace!"

"Oh, my true son!" cried the aged sultan, with deep emotion, and sank on the breast of Omar. The emirs and pashas, and all the nobility of the kingdom, rose from their seats, and cried: "Hail to the new son of the king!" and amidst the universal joy, Labakan stole out of the room with the little box under his arm.

He went below to the stables of the sultan, saddled his horse, Murva, and rode out of the gate of the city towards Alexandria. His life as a prince appeared to him as a dream, and the splendid little box, set with pearls and diamonds, was the only thing left to remind him that he had not dreamed.

When he at length reached Alexandria, he rode up to the house of his old master, dismounted, tied his horse near the door, and entered the workshop. The master, not knowing him at first, made an obeisance, and asked him what might be his pleasure. But on taking a closer look, and recognizing Labakan, he called to his journeymen and apprentices, and they all rushed angrily at the

poor Labakan, who was not expecting such a reception, kicked and beat him with their irons and yard-sticks, pricked him with needles, and nipped him with sharp shears, until, utterly exhausted, he sank down on a heap of old clothes.

While he lay there, the master gave him a lecture on the clothes he had stolen. In vain did Labakan assure him that he had come back in order to make restitution; all in vain did he offer him three-fold indemnity; the master and his men fell upon him again, beat him black

and blue, and threw him out of the door. Torn and
bruised, Labakan crawled on his horse and rode to a caravansary. Then he laid his tired and aching head on a
pillow, and reflected on the sorrows of earth, on unappre-
ciated merit, and on the vanity and fickleness of riches.
He fell asleep with the resolution to forswear all great-
ness, and become a respectable citizen.

The succeeding day found him still steadfast in his
purpose, as the heavy hands of the master and his men
seemed to have beaten all his grand notions out of him.
He sold his little box to a jeweler for a high price, bought
a house with the proceeds, and fitted up a workshop for
his trade. When he had every thing arranged, and had
also hung out a sign before his window with the inscription, "*Labakan, Tailor*," he sat down, and with the needle
and thread he had found in the little box, began to mend his
coat that had been so badly torn by his old master. He
was called away from his work, and when he returned to
take it up again, what a singular sight met his eyes! The
needle was sewing busily away without any one to guide
it, making such fine, delicate stitches, as even Labakan
in his most artistic moments could not have equaled!

Surely even the commonest gift of a kind fairy is useful and of great value. Still another value was possessed
by this present, namely: the ball of the thread was
never exhausted, let the needle sew as fast as it would.

Labakan obtained many customers, and was soon the
most famous tailor in all that region. He would cut out
the clothes, and make the first stitch with the needle,
and the needle would then instantly go on with the work,
never pausing until the garment was done. Master
Labakan soon had the whole town for customers, as his
work was first-class, and his prices low; and only over
one thing did the people of Alexandria shake their
heads, namely: that he worked without journeymen, and
with locked doors.

Thus did the saying of the little box, promising *Fortune and Riches*, come to pass. Fortune and riches, even

though in moderate measure, attended the steps of the good tailor; and when he heard of the fame of the young sultan, Omar, that was on all lips; when he heard that this brave man was the pride and love of his people, and the terror of his enemies—then the false prince thought to himself: "It is after all better that I remained a tailor, for the quest of honor and fame is rather a dangerous business."

Thus lived Labakan, contented with his lot, respected by his fellow-citizens; and if the needle in the meanwhile has not lost its virtue, it still sews on with the endlesss thread of the kind fairy, Adolzaide.

At sunset the caravan started on, and soon reached Birket-el-Had, or Pilgrim's Fountain; from which it was only a three hours' journey to Cairo. The caravan was expected about this time, and therefore the merchants soon had the pleasure of seeing their friends coming from Cairo to meet them. They entered the city through the gate Bab-el-Falch, as it is considered a happy omen for those who come from Mecca to pass through this gate, as the Prophet went out of it.

On the market-place the three Turkish merchants took leave of the stranger Selim Baruch, and the Greek merchant Zaleukos, and went home with their friends. But Zaleukos showed the stranger a good caravansary, and invited him to take dinner with him. The stranger accepted the invitation, and promised to come as soon as he had made some changes in his dress.

The Greek made every preparation to entertain his guest, for whom he had acquired a strong liking on the journey; and when the dishes were all arranged in order, he sat down to await the coming of his guest.

At last he heard slow and heavy steps in the hall that led to his room. He arose to go and meet him and welcome him on the threshold; but no sooner had he opened the door, than he stepped back horrified, for that terrible man with the red mantle stepped towards him! He looked at him again; there was no illusion; the same tall, commanding figure, the mask through which the dark eyes shone, the red mantle with the gold embroidery, were only too closely associated with the most terrible hours of his life.

Conflicting emotions surged in Zaleukos's breast. He had long since become reconciled to this picture of memory, and had forgiven him who had injured him; yet the appearance of the man himself opened all his wounds afresh; all those painful hours when he had suffered almost the pangs of death,—the remorse that had poisoned his young life,—all this swept over his soul in the flight of a moment.

"What do you want, monster?" exclaimed the Greek, as the apparition stood motionless on the threshold. "Vanish quickly, before I curse you!"

"Zaleukos!" spoke a well-known voice, from beneath the mask, "Zaleukos! is it thus you receive your guest?" The speaker removed the mask, and threw the mantle back; it was Selim Baruch, the stranger.

But Zaleukos was not yet quieted. He shuddered at the stranger, for only too plainly had he recognized the unknown man of the Ponte Vecchio. But the old habit of hospitality prevailed; he silently beckoned to the stranger to take a seat at the table.

"I perceive your thoughts," said the stranger, after they were seated. "Your eyes look inquiringly at me. I could have remained silent, and never more appeared to your vision; but I owe you an explanation, and therefore I ventured to appear to you in my old form, knowing that I run the risk of your cursing me. But you once told me: *The religion of my fathers commands me to love him, and then he must be more unhappy than I.* Believe that, my friend, and listen to my vindication.

"I must begin far back, in order to make my story quite clear. I was born in Alexandria, of Christian parents. My father was the French consul there, and was the younger son of a famous old French family. From my tenth year up, I was under the care of my uncle, in France, and left my fatherland some years after the breaking out of the Revolution, with my uncle, who no longer felt safe in the land of his ancestors, in order to find a refuge with my parents across the sea. We landed in Alexandria, hopeful of finding in my parents' home that quiet and peace that no longer obtained in France. The outside storms of this excitable period had not, it is true, extended to this point, but from an unexpected quarter came the blow that crushed our family to the ground. My brother, a young man full of promise, and private secretary to my father, had but recently married the daughter of a Florentine nobleman who lived in my father's neighborhood. Two days before our arrival, my brother's bride disappeared; and neither our family, nor yet her father, could discover the slightest trace of her. We finally came to the conclusion that she had ventured too far away for a walk, and had fallen into the hands of brigands. This belief would have been a consolation to my brother, in comparison with the truth that was only too soon made known to us. The faithless woman had eloped with a young Neapolitan, whom she had been in the habit of meeting at her father's house. My brother, terribly excited by this act, used his utmost endeavors to bring the guilty one to account; but in vain. His attempts in this direction, which had aroused attention in Florence and Naples, only served to bring down misfortune on us all. The Florentine nobleman returned to his country under the pretext of assisting my brother, but with the real design of destroying us all. He put an end to all the investigations instituted by my brother in Florence, and used his influence so effectually that my father and brother fell under the suspicion of their government, were imprisoned in the most outrageous manner, and taken to France, where they were guillotined. My mother went crazy, and only after ten long months did death release her from her terrible condition. But she recovered her sanity a few days before her death. I was thus left all alone in the world, but only one thought occupied my soul, only one thought overshadowed my grief: it was the powerful flame of revenge that my mother kindled in my breast during the last hours of her life.

"As I have said, she recovered her senses towards the last. She called me to her side and spoke quietly of our fate and of her approaching death. Then she sent everybody out of the room, raised herself with a spirited air from her poor couch, and said that I could win her blessing if I would swear to carry out what she should confide to me. Influenced by the dying words of my mother, I bound myself with an oath to do her bidding. She broke out in imprecations against the Florentine and his daughter, and required me, under the penalty of incurring her curse, to revenge our unfortunate family on him. She died in my arms. The thought of revenge had long slumbered in my soul; now it was aroused to action. I collected the balance of my patrimony, and resolved to risk every thing on my revenge.

"I was soon in Florence, where I kept as quiet as possible. The difficulty of executing my plan was much increased by the situation in which I found my enemy. The old Florentine had become Governor, and had the power, should he have the least suspicion of my presence, to destroy me. An incident occurred just then that was of great assistance to me. One evening I saw a man passing along the street, in a familiar livery. His unsteady gait, sullen look, and manner of muttering *Santo sacramento* and *Maledetto diavolo*, assured me that it was Pietro, a servant of the Florentine's, whom I had known in Alexandria. I had no doubt that it was his master whom he was cursing, and I therefore determined to make use of his present frame of mind for my own benefit. He seemed very much surprised to see me in Florence, and complained to me that since his master had become Governor he could do nothing to suit him; so that my

H   5*

gold, together with his anger, brought him over to my side. The most difficult part of my plan had now been provided for. I had in my pay a man who could open the door of my enemy to me at any hour, and now my revenge seemed near its accomplishment. The life of the old Florentine seemed to me of too little account to offset the destruction of our family: he must lose the idol of his heart, his daughter Bianca. Was it not she who treated my brother so shamefully? Was it not she who was the chief cause of our misfortunes? The news that she was about to be married a second time was very welcome to my revengeful heart. This would but heighten the vengeance of my blow. It was settled in my mind that she *must* die. But I myself shrank from the deed, and I did not credit Pietro with nerve enough; so we looked about for a man who could accomplish the work. I did not dare approach any of the Florentines, as none of them would have dared to undertake such a thing against the Governor. It was then that the scheme I afterward carried out, occurred to Pietro, who at the same time pitched upon you, a stranger and physician, as being the most suitable person to do the deed. The rest of the story you know. The only danger to the success of my scheme lay in your sagacity and honesty; hence the affair with the mantle.

Pietro opened the side gate of the Governor's palace for us, and would have shown us out as secretly, had not he and I fled, horrified by the terrible sight we saw through a crack in the door. Pursued by terror and remorse, I ran some two hundred paces, and sank down on the steps of a church. There I collected my thoughts, and my first one was of you and your fate, should you be found in the house   I stole to the palace, but could find no trace of either you or Pietro. The side gate was open, so I could at least hope that you had taken advantage of the opportunity to flee. But when the day broke, fear of discovery and a sensation of remorse drove me from Florence. I hastened to Rome. But imagine my consternation when, in the course of a few days, this story reached Rome, with the additional report that the murderer, a Greek physician, had been captured! I returned to Florence with sad apprehensions, for, if my revenge had before seemed too strong, I cursed it now, as it would have been purchased too dearly with your life. I arrived in Florence on the day you lost your hand. I will be silent over what I felt as I saw you ascend the scaffold and suffer so heroically. But as your blood streamed out, I made the resolve to see that the rest of your life should be passed in comfort. What happened afterwards, you know. It only remains for me to tell why I made this journey across the desert with you. Like a heavy burden the thought pressed on me that you had not yet forgiven me; therefore I resolved to pass some days with you, and at last give you an account of the motives that had influenced my action."

The Greek had listened silently to his guest, and when he had finished, with a gentle expression he offered him his hand. "I knew well that you must be more unhappy than I, for that cruel deed, like a black cloud, will forever darken your life. As for myself, I forgive you from my heart. But permit me one more question: How did you happen to be in the desert in your present character? What did you do after buying me the house in Constantinople?"

"I went back to Alexandria. Hatred of all human kind raged in my breast, but especially hatred of those nations which are called civilized. Believe me, I was better pleased with my Moslems. I had been in Alexandria only a few months, when it was invaded by my countrymen. I saw in them only the executioners of my father and brother; therefore I gathered some young people of my acquaintance, who entertained similar views, and joined the brave Mameluke, who became the terror of the French army. When the campaign was ended, I could not bring myself to return to the arts of peace. With a few friends of similar tendencies, I lived an unsettled fugitive life, devoted to battle and the chase. I live contentedly with these people, who honor me as their prince; for if my Asiatics are not so civilized as your Europeans, yet envy and slander, selfishness and ambition are not their characteristics."

Zaleukos thanked the stranger for his communication, but he did not hide from him his opinion that it would be far better for one of his rank and culture, were he to live and work in Christian and European countries. He took the stranger's hand, and invited him to go with him, and to live and die with him.

Zaleukos's guest was deeply moved. "From this I know," said he, "that you have entirely forgiven me, that you even love me. Receive my heartfelt thanks."

He sprang up, and stood in all his majesty before the Greek, who shrank back at the warlike appearance, the dark glistening eyes, the deep mysterious voice of his guest. "Your proposal is good," continued he; "any other person might be persuaded; I can not accept it! My horse is saddled, my followers await me: farewell, Zaleukos!"

The friends whom destiny had so strangely united, embraced each other before parting.

"And what shall I call you? What is the name of my guest and friend who will live forever in my memory?" asked the Greek.

The stranger gave him a parting look, pressed his hand once more, and replied: "They call me the ruler of the desert: I am *the Robber Orbasan.*"

THE INN IN THE SPESSART.

ANY years ago, while yet the roads in the Spessart were in poor condition and but little traveled, two young journeymen were making their way through this wooded region. The one might have been about eighteen years old, and was by trade a compass-maker; the other was a goldsmith, and, judging from his appearance, could not have been more than sixteen, and was most likely making his first journey out into the world.

Evening was coming on, and the shadows of the giant pines and beeches darkened the narrow road on which the two were walking. The compass-maker stepped bravely forward, whistling a tune, playing occasionally with Munter, his dog, and not seeming to feel much concern that the night was near, while the next inn for journeymen was still far ahead of them. But Felix, the goldsmith, began to look about him anxiously. When the wind rustled through the trees, it sounded to him as if there were steps behind him; when the bushes on either side of the road were stirred, he was sure he caught glimpses of lurking faces.

The young goldsmith was, moreover, neither superstitious nor lacking in courage. In Wuerzburg, where he had learned his trade, he passed among his fellows for a fearless youth, whose heart was in the right spot; but on this day his courage was at a singularly low ebb. He had been told so many things about the Spessart. A large

band of robbers were reported as committing depre-
dations there; many travellers had been robbed within a
few weeks, and a horrible murder was spoken of as having
occurred here not long before. Therefore he felt no little
alarm, as they were but two in number and could not
successfully resist armed robbers. How often he regretted that he had not stopped over-night at the edge of the
forest, instead of agreeing to accompany the compass-
maker to the next station!

"And if I am killed to-night, and lose all I have with
me, you will be to blame, compass-maker, for you persuaded me to come into this terrible forest," said he.

"Don't be a coward," retorted the other. "A real
journeyman should never be afraid. And what is it you
are afraid of? Do you think that the lordly robbers of the
Spessart would do us the honor to attack and kill us?
Why should they give themselves that trouble? To gain
possession of the Sunday-coat in my knapsack, or the spare
pennies given us by the people on our route? One would
have to travel in a coach-and-four, dressed in gold and
silks, before the robbers would think it worth their while
to kill one."

"Stop! Didn't you hear somebody whistle in the
woods?" exclaimed Felix, nervously.

"That was the wind whistling through the trees.
Walk faster, and we shall soon be out of the wood."

"Yes, it's all well enough for you to talk that way
about not being killed," continued the goldsmith; "they
would simply ask you what you had, search you, and take
away your Sunday-coat and your change. But they
would kill me because I carry gold and jewelry with me."

"Why should they kill you on that account? If four
or five were to spring out of the bush there now with
loaded rifles pointed at us, and politely inquire, 'Gentlemen, what have you with you?' or 'If agreeable, we
will help you carry it,' or some such elegant mode of address, then you wouldn't make a fool of yourself, but
would open your knapsack and lay the yellow waist-coat,

the blue coat, two shirts, and all your necklaces, brace-
lets, combs, and whatever you had besides, politely on
the ground, and be thankful for the life they spared you."

"You think so, do you?" responded Felix warmly.
"You think I would give up the ornament I have here
for my godmother, the dear lady countess? Sooner
would I part with my life! Sooner would I be hacked
into small pieces. Did she not take a mother's interest
in me, and since my tenth year bind me out as apprentice?
Has she not paid for my clothes and every thing? And
now, when I am about to go to her, to carry her something of my own handiwork that she had ordered of the
master; now, that I am able to give her this ornament
as a sample of what I have learned; now you think I
would give that up, and my yellow waistcoat as well, that
she gave me? No, better death than to give to these base
men the ornament intended for my godmother!"

"Don't be a fool!" exclaimed the compass-maker.
"If they were to kill you, the countess would still lose
the ornament; so it would be much better for you to deliver it up and keep your life."

Felix did not answer. Night had settled down, and
by the uncertain gleam of the new moon he could not see
more than five feet before him. He became more and
more nervous, kept close by the side of his companion,
and was uncertain whether he ought to approve of the
arguments of his friend or not. Thus they continued on,
side by side for another hour, when they saw a light in
the distance. The young goldsmith was of opinion that
they should not prematurely rejoice, as the light might
come from a den of thieves; but the compass-maker informed him the robbers had their houses or caves under
ground, and that this must be the inn that a man had told
them of, as they entered the forest.

It was a long, low house, before which a wagon stood;
and adjoining the house was a stable from which came
the neighing of horses. The compass-maker beckoned
his comrade to a window whose shutters were open; and

by standing on their toes they were able to look into the
room. In a chair before the stove slept a man whose
clothes bespoke him a wagoner—very likely the owner of
the cart before the door. On the other side of the stove
sat a woman and a girl, spinning. Behind the table,
close to the wall, sat a man with a glass of wine before
him. His head was supported in his hands so that his
face could not be seen. But the compass-maker judged
from his clothes that he was a man of rank. While they
were peeping, a dog in the house began to bark; Munter,
the compass-maker's dog, barked a reply; and a servant-
girl appeared at the door and looked out at the strangers.

They were promised supper and a bed; so they entered, and laying their heavy bundles, sticks, and hats in
the corner, sat down at the table with the gentleman. He
looked up at their greeting, and they perceived him to be
a handsome young man, who returned their greeting
pleasantly.

"You are late on the road," said he; "were you not
afraid to travel through the Spessart on so dark a night?
For my part, I would have stabled my horse in this
tavern before I would have ridden an hour longer."

"You are quite right in that, sir," responded the compass-maker. "The hoof beats of a fine horse are music
in the ears of these highwaymen, and lure them from a
great distance; but when a couple of poor journeymen
like us steal through the woods—people to whom the
robbers would sooner think of making a present than of
taking any thing from them—then, they do not lift a
foot."

"That is very likely," chimed in the wagoner, who,
awakened by the arrival of the journeymen, had taken a
seat at the table. "They could not very well be
attracted by a poor man's purse, but there have been instances of robbers killing poor people, simply out of thirst
for blood, and of forcing others to join the band and serve
as robbers."

"Well, if such are the deeds of these people in the

forest, then this house will not afford us very good protection," observed the young goldsmith. "There are only four of us, or, counting the hostler, five; and if ten men were to attack us here, what could we do against them? And more than this," he added, in a low tone, "who can guarantee that the people of this inn are honest?"

"Nothing to fear there," returned the wagoner. "I have known this tavern for more than ten years, and have never seen any thing wrong about it. The master of the house is seldom at home; they say he carries on a wine trade; but his wife is a quiet woman who would not harm any one. No, you do them a wrong, sir."

"And yet," interposed the young gentleman, "I should not like to brush aside so lightly what he said. Don't you remember the reports about those people who suddenly disappeared in this forest and left no trace behind them? Several of them had previously announced their intention of passing the night at this inn; and as two or three weeks passed by without their being heard from, they were searched for, and inquiries made at this inn, when they were assured that the missing men had never been here. It looks suspicious, to say the least."

"God knows," cried the compass-maker, "we should do a much more sensible thing if we were to camp out under the next best tree we came to, than to remain within these four walls, where there is no chance of running away when they are once at the door, for the windows are grated."

All grew very thoughtful over these speeches. It did not seem so very improbable, after all, that these tavern people in the forest, be it under compulsion or of their free accord, were in league with the robbers. The night-time seemed particularly dangerous to them, for they had all heard many stories of travellers who had been attacked and murdered in their sleep; and even if their lives were not endangered, yet most of the guests of the inn were possessed of such moderate means that the robbery of even a part of their property would have been a very serious loss to them. They looked dolefully into their glasses. The young gentleman wished himself on the back of his horse, trotting through a safe open valley. The compass-maker wished for twelve of his sturdy comrades, armed with clubs, for a body-guard. Felix, the goldsmith, was more anxious for the safety of the ornament designed for his benefactress, than for his own life. But the wagoner, who had been blowing clouds of smoke before him, said softly : " Gentlemen, at least they shall not surprise us asleep. I, for my part, will remain awake the whole night, if one other will keep watch with me."

" I will "— " I too," cried the three others. "And I could not go to sleep," added the young gentleman.

" Well we had better contrive some means of keeping awake," said the wagoner. " I think while we number just four people, we might play cards, that would keep us awake and while away the time."

" I never play cards," said the young gentleman, "therefore you would have to count me out."

" Nor do I know any thing about cards," added Felix.

" What can we do, then, if we don't play cards," asked the compass-maker. " Sing ? That wouldn't do, for it would only attract the attention of the robbers. Give one another riddles to guess ? That would not last very long. How would it do if we were to tell stories ? Humorous or pathetic, true or imaginative, they would keep us awake and pass away the time as well as cards."

" I am agreed, if you will begin," said the young gentleman, smiling. " You gentlemen of trades visit all countries, and have something to tell ; for every town has its own legends and tales."

" Yes, certainly, one hears a great deal," replied the compass-maker. " But, on the other hand, gentlemen like you study diligently in books, where really wonderful things are written ; therefore, you would know how to tell a wiser and more entertaining story than a plain journeyman, such as one of us, could pretend to — for unless I am much mistaken you are a student, a scholar."

"A scholar, no," laughed the young gentleman; "but certainly a student, and am now on my way home for the vacation. But what one reads in books does not answer for the purpose of a story nearly as well as what one hears. Therefore begin, if the other gentlemen are inclined to listen."

"Still more than with cards," responded the wagoner, "am I pleased when I hear a good story told. I often keep my team down to a miserably slow pace, that I may listen to one who walks near by, and has a fine story to tell; and I have taken many a person into my wagon, in bad weather, with the understanding that he should tell me a story; and one of my comrades I love very dearly, for the reason that he knows stories that last for seven hours and even longer."

"That is also my case," added the young goldsmith. "I love stories as I do my life; and my master in Wuerzburg had to forbid me books lest I should neglect my work. So tell us something fine, compass-maker; I know that you could tell stories from now until day-break before your stock gave out."

The compass-maker complied by emptying his glass and beginning his story.

THE HIRSCH-GULDEN.

 N Upper-Suabia still stands the walls of a castle that was once the stateliest of the surrounding country, Hohen-Zollern. It rose from the summit of a round steep mountain, from whence one had a distant and unobstructed view of the country. Farther than this castle could be seen from the encircling horizon, was the brave race of the Zollerns feared; and their name was known and honored in all German countries.

There lived several hundred years ago, in this castle, a Zollern, who was by nature a singular man. One could not say that he oppressed his subjects, or that he lived at war with his neighbors; yet no one trusted him, on account of his sullen look, his knitted brow, and his moody, crusty manner. There were few people, outside of the castle servants, who had ever heard him speak properly like other people; for when he rode through the valley, if one met him, gave him the road, and said to him with uncovered head, "Good evening, Sir Count! It is a fine day," he would answer, "Stupid stuff," or, "I know it already." If, however, one had been inattentive to his wants or had neglected his charger, or if a peasant with his cart met him on a narrow road, so that the count could not pass him quickly enough, he broke out into a torrent of curses. Yet it was never said of him on these occasions that he had struck a peasant. But all through this region he was called "The Tempest of Zollern."

The Tempest of Zollern had a wife who was a complete

contrast to himself, and as mild and pleasant as a May morning. Often by her friendly words and her kind glance had she reconciled to her husband people whom he, by his rude speech, had deeply insulted. To the poor she did all the good in her power; nor could the

warmest days of Summer or the most terrible snow storms of Winter prevent her from descending the steep mountain to visit poor people or sick children. If the count met her on these errands, he would say in a surly manner, " Know already — stupid stuff," and proceed on his way.

Many ladies would have been discouraged or intimidated by such a crusty manner; one would have thought, "why should I concern myself with poor people when my husband calls it all stupid stuff?" another, through pride or sorrow, might have lost her love for so moody a husband; but not so with the Countess Hedwig of Zollern. She was constant in her affection, strove to smooth the lines on his brow with her beautiful white hand, and loved and honored him. And when after a long time Heaven bestowed upon them the gift of a son, she loved her husband none the less while conferring all the duties of a tender mother on her little boy.

Three years went by, and the Count of Zollern saw his son only on Sunday afternoons, when the child was handed to him by the nurse. He looked at him without

changing a feature of his face, growled something through his beard, and gave him back to the nurse. But when the boy was able to say "father," the count gave the nurse a gulden, but showed no pleasanter face to the boy.

On his third birthday, however, the count had his son put on the first pair of breeches and had him dressed splendidly in velvet and silk. Then he ordered his horse, and also another fine horse for his son, took the child up on his arm, and began to descend the spiral staircase. The countess was astonished as she saw this. She was not accustomed to inquire where he was going and when he would return; but this time anxiety for her child opened her lips.

"Are you going to ride out, Sir Count?" she asked.

He made no reply. "For what purpose do you take the child?" continued she, "Cuno will take a walk with me."

"Know already," replied the Tempest of Zollern; and kept on his way till he stood in the court-yard, where he took the boy by one of his little feet and lifted him into the saddle, bound him fast, and then swinging himself on his horse, trotted out of the castle gate with the bridle of his son's horse in his hand.

At first the little fellow regarded it as a great treat to ride down the mountain with his father. He clapped his hands, laughed, shook the mane of his horse to make him go faster, all of which pleased the count so much that he called out several times: "You will make a brave lad!"

But when they came to the foot of the mountain, and the count's horse began to trot, the boy lost his courage, and begged, at first very quietly, that his father would ride slower; but as the count spurred on his horse, and the strong wind nearly took poor Cuno's breath away, the boy began to cry, became more and more impatient, and finally howled at the top of his lungs.

"Know already! stupid stuff!" began his father. "The young one howls on his first ride; be still, or——"

But in the moment he was about to stop the boy's cries by a curse, his horse reared, and the bridle of his son's horse slipped from his hand. He gave his attention to quieting his horse, and when he had mastered it and looked around for his child, he saw the other horse running up the mountain without its little rider.

Stern and unfeeling as was the Count of Zollern, this sight struck him to the heart. He believed his son had been dashed to the ground and killed. He pulled his beard and groaned; but nowhere could he find a trace of the boy. He had just began to think that the frightened horse had thrown him into the ditch that ran along the road, full of water, when he heard a child's voice call his name, and as he quickly turned, there sat an old woman

I

under a tree, not far from the road, rocking the child on her knees.

"How do you come by that boy, old witch?" shouted the count angrily. "Bring him to me at once."

"Not so fast, not so fast, your Honor!" laughed the ugly old woman, "or you too might meet with an accident on your proud horse. How did I come by the boy, did you ask? Well, his horse ran by and he was hanging down by one little foot, with his hair touching the ground, when I caught him in my apron."

"Know already!" cried the Count of Zollern, ill-humoredly. "Bring him here now; I can not very well dismount, my horse is wild and might kick him."

"Give me a hirsch-gulden, then," pleaded the woman humbly.

"Stupid stuff!" cried the count, and flung some copper coins to her under the tree.

"Oh, no! Come, I could make good use of a hirsch-gulden," continued the old woman.

"What, a hirsch-gulden! You are not worth that much yourself!" said the count angrily. "Quick with that child, or I will set the dogs on you!"

"So, I am not worth a hirsch-gulden, eh?" replied the old woman with a mocking laugh. "Well, it shall be seen what part of your heritage is worth a hirsch-gulden; but there, keep your money!" So saying, she tossed the three copper coins to the count; and so well could the old woman throw, that all three of the coins fell into the purse that the count still held in his hand.

The count was struck dumb with astonishment at this exhibition of skill, but at last his surprise was changed into anger. He grasped his gun, cocked it, and took aim at the old woman. But she, unmoved, hugged and kissed the boy, holding him up before her so as to protect herself from the bullet "You are a good little fellow," said she. "Only remain so, and you will never want for any thing." Then she let him go, shook her finger threateningly at the count, and said: "Zollern, Zollern!

you owe me a hirsch-gulden!'' With that she moved off slowly into the forest, leaning on a staff of box-wood. Conrad, the attendant, dismounted from his horse trembling, lifted his little master into the saddle, vaulted up behind him, and followed the count up to the castle.

This was the first and last time that the Tempest of Zollern took his son out riding with him; for because the boy had cried when his horse broke into a trot, the count regarded him as a spiritless child out of whom nothing was to be made, and looked on him with displeasure; and when the boy, who loved his father dearly, came in a friendly, coaxing way to his knee, he would motion him to go away, exclaiming: "Know it already! Stupid stuff!"

The countess had patiently borne all the unpleasant caprices of her husband, but this unfatherly behavior towards an innocent child affected her deeply. She fell sick several times with terror, when the sullen count had punished the boy severely for some trivial offense, and died at last in her best years, and was mourned by her servants, by the people for miles around, but especially by her little son.

From this time forth the aversion of the count for his son steadily progressed. He turned the lad over to the nurse and the house-chaplain to bring up, and looked after him but little himself — especially as shortly after his wife's death he married a rich young lady, who in a twelvemonth presented him with twins.

Cuno's favorite walk was to the house of the old woman who had once saved his life. She told him many things about his dead mother, and how much the countess had done for her. The men and maid-servants often warned him that he should not visit the Frau Feldheimerin so often, because she was nothing more nor less than a witch; but the boy was not frightened by their tales, as the chaplain had taught him that there were no witches, and that the stories that certain women could bewitch one, and ride through the air on broomsticks to

the Brocken Mountains, were lies. To be sure, he had
seen many things about Frau Feldheimerin that he could
not understand; the trick with the three coins that
she had thrown so cleverly into his father's purse, he remembered distinctly. Then too she could prepare all
manner of salves and decoctions with which she healed
people and cattle; but it was not true, as was said of
her, that she had a weather-pan, which, whenever she

placed it over the fire, produced a terrible thunder-storm.
She taught the little count much that was useful to him—
various remedies for sick horses, a drink to cure hydro-
phobia, a bait for fishes, and many other things. The
Frau Feldheimerin was soon his only company, for his
nurse died, and his step-mother did not trouble herself
much about him.

With his half-brothers, Cuno had a more sorrowful life
than before. They had the good fortune to stick to their
horses on their first ride, and the Tempest of Zollern,
therefore, regarded them as apt and promising boys, and

took them out to ride every day, and taught them all
that he knew himself.

But they did not learn much that was good from him,
for he could neither read nor write, and he would not
have his two precious sons wasting their time over such
matters; but by the time they were ten years old they
could swear as terribly as their father, quarreled with
everybody, lived together as peacefully as would a dog
and cat, and only when they joined hands to do Cuno a
wrong were they at all friendly with each other.

Their mother did not grieve over this state of things,
as she considered it healthful and strengthening for the
boys to fight; but a servant told the count about their
quarrels one day, and although he answered, "Know it
already! stupid stuff!" yet he tried to hit upon some
plan for the future that would prevent his sons from killing each other, as he dreaded that threat of the Frau
Feldheimerin, whom he held to be a witch: "Well, it
shall be seen what part of your heritage is worth a hirsch-
gulden."

One day as he was hunting in the vicinity of his castle, his attention was attracted by two mountains, which
from their form seemed well adapted for castles; and he
at once resolved to build there. Upon one of these

mountains he built the Castle Schalksberg, naming it after the smaller of the twins, who, on account of his many naughty tricks, had long ago received the nickname of the little Schalk from his father. The castle he built on the other hill he thought at first of calling Hirschguldenberg, in order to propitiate the old witch, because she did not esteem his heritage worth a hirsch-gulden; but he finally concluded to give it the simple name of Hirschberg. Such are the names of the two mountains to-day; and he who travels through the Suabian Alps can have them pointed out to him.

The Tempest of Zollern had at first designed to make a will bequeathing Zollern to his eldest son, Schalksberg to the little Schalk, and Hirschberg to the other twin; but his wife did not rest until he had changed it. "The stupid Cuno —" such was the way she spoke of the poor boy, because he was not so wild and ungovernable as her sons —"the stupid Cuno is rich enough from what he inherited from his mother, without getting the beautiful castle of Zollern. And shall my sons get only a castle, to which nothing belongs but a forest?"

It was in vain that the count represented to her that one could not justly rob Cuno of his birthright; she wept and scolded, until the Tempest of Zollern who never gave way to any one, at last, for the sake of peace, surrendered to her, and willed Schalksberg to Schalk, Zollern to Wolf, the larger of the twins, and Hirschberg, with the village of Balinger, to Cuno. Soon afterwards he was taken severely ill. When the doctor told him he was going to die, he replied, "Know it already;" and when the chaplain begged him to prepare for the future life, he answered, "Stupid stuff," cursed and stormed, and died, as he had lived, a great sinner.

But before his body was laid to rest, the countess produced the will, and sneeringly told Cuno that he might show his learning by reading what was written therein—namely, that he no longer had any business at Zollern. With her sons she rejoiced over the fine estate and the two castles which they had taken away from him, the first-born.

Cuno submitted, without complaint, to the provisions of the will; but with tears, he took leave of the castle where he was born, where his mother lay buried, and where the good chaplain lived, while not far away was the home of his only woman friend, Frau Feldheimerin. The castle of Hirschberg was, it is true, a fine stately building; but still it was so lonely and desolate for him, that he felt very homesick.

The countess and the twin brothers, who were now eighteen years old, sat one evening on the balcony looking down the mountain-side, when they perceived a stately knight riding up the road, followed by several servants and two mules bearing a sedan chair. They speculated for some time as to who he might be, when at last the little Schalk cried out: "Why, that is no other than our brother from Hirschberg!"

"The stupid Cuno!" said the countess in surprise. "Why, he is about to do us the honor of inviting us to visit him, and has brought along that splendid sedan to carry me to Hirschberg. Such kindness and politeness I had not given my son, the stupid Cuno, the credit of possessing. One politeness deserves another; let us go down to the gate to receive him; look pleased to see him, and perhaps he will make us some presents at Hirschberg — you a horse, and you a harness; and I have long wished to own his mother's ornaments."

"I don't want any presents from the stupid Cuno," replied Wolf, "neither will I appear glad to see him; and for aught I care, he might follow our blessed father; then we should inherit Hirschberg and everything, and to you, madame, we would sell those ornaments at a low price."

"Indeed, you good-for-nothing!" exclaimed his mother angrily, "I should have to buy the ornaments, should I? Is that your gratitude for my procuring Zollern for you? Little Schalk, I can have the ornaments free, can I not?"

"No pay, no work, lady mother!" replied Schalk,

laughing. "And if it be true that the ornaments are worth as much as most castles are, we certainly should not be fools enough to hang them around your neck. As soon as Cuno shuts his eyes for good, we will ride over there, divide every thing, and I will sell my part of the ornaments. Then if you will give more than the Jew, you shall have them."

Thus speaking, they came to the castle gate, and the countess had great difficulty in concealing the rage she felt, as Count Cuno rode over the draw-bridge. When he saw his step-mother and brothers standing there, he stopped his horse, dismounted, and greeted them politely; for although they had done him much wrong, still he remembered that they were his brothers and that his father had loved this woman.

"Well, this is nice to have my son visit us," said the countess, in a sweet voice, and with a gracious smile. "How do you like Hirschberg? Can one feel at home there? And you have furnished yourself with a sedan. Why, how splendid it is! an empress would have no cause to be ashamed of it; a wife will not be long wanting, I'm thinking, to ride around the country in it."

"I have not thought about that yet, gracious mother," replied Cuno, "and will therefore take home other company for my entertainment; for this purpose I have brought along the sedan."

"Why, you are very kind and thoughtful," interrupted the countess, as she bowed and smiled.

"For he can not ride a horse very well now," continued Cuno, quietly. "Father Joseph, I mean, the chaplain. I will take him home with me, for he is my old teacher, and we made that arrangement when I left Zollern. I will also pick up the old Frau Feldheimerin at the foot of the mountain. Why, bless me, she's as old as the hills, and saved my life once when I rode out for the first time with my blessed father. I have plenty of room in Hirschberg, and she shall live and die there."

So saying, he passed through the court-yard to call the chaplain.

The youngster Wolf bit his lips angrily; the countess became livid with rage; while Schalk laughed aloud. "What will you give me for the horse that I received as a present from him?" said he. "Brother Wolf, will you trade off your harness for it? Is he going to take home the chaplain and the old witch? They will make a fine pair; in the forenoon he can learn Greek from the chaplain, and in the afternoon take lessons in witchcraft from

Frau Feldheimerin. Why, what kind of tricks is the stupid Cuno up to!"

"He is a low, vulgar fellow," cried the countess, "and you shouldn't laugh about it, little Schalk. It is a shame for the whole family, and we shall be the sport of the neighborhood when it is reported that the Count of Zollern has fetched the old witch home to live with him in a splendid sedan. He gets that from his mother, who was also familiar with the sick and with miserable servants. Alas, his father would turn in his coffin if he could know of it."

"Yes," added Schalk, "father would say in his grave: 'Know already! stupid stuff!'"

"As sure as you live! there he comes now with the old man, and is not ashamed to take him by the arm,"

6*

exclaimed the countess, in disgust. " Come, I don't
wish to meet him again."

They went off, and (uno conducted his old teacher to
the drawbridge, and assisted him into the sedan. They
stopped at the foot of the mountain, before the hut of
Frau Feldheimerin, and found her waiting with a bundle
full of glasses, dishes, and medicines.

But Cuno's action was not looked at in the light
prophesied by the countess. It was thought to be noble
and praiseworthy that he should try to cheer the last days
of the old Frau Feldheimerin, and that he should take
Father Joseph into his castle. The only ones who dis-
liked and slandered him were his brothers and his step-
mother. But only to their own hurt; for everybody took
an aversion to such unnatural brothers, and by way of
retaliation the story went that they lived in continual
strife with their mother and did all they could to harm
one another. Count Cuno made several attempts to
reconcile his brothers to himself, for it was unbearable to
him when they rode by his castle without stopping, or
when they met him in the field and forest and greeted
him as coldly as though he were a stranger. But his
attempts failed, and only increased their bitterness towards him.

One day a plan occurred to him by which he might
perhaps win their hearts, for he knew that they were
miserly and avaricious. There was a pond situated at
about an equal distance from the three castles, but lying in
Cuno's domain. This pond contained the finest pike and
carp to be found any where; and it was one of the chief
grievances of the twin-brothers, who were fond of fishing,
that their father had not included this pond in the land
he had given them. They were too proud to fish there
without their brother's knowledge, neither would they ask
permission of him. But Cuno knew that his brothers
had set their hearts on this pond, so he sent an invitation to them to meet him there on a certain day.

It was a beautiful Spring morning, as, nearly at the

same moment, the three brothers from the three castles
met.

"Why, look you!" said Schalk; "we are well met! I
rode away from Schalksberg just on the stroke of
seven."

"So did I,"—"and I," repeated the brothers from
Hirschberg and Zollern.

"Well, then, the pond must lie precisely in the middle," continued Schalk. "It is a beautiful sheet of
water."

"Yes, and for that reason did I choose this spot for
our meeting. I know that you are both fond of fishing,
and although I sometimes throw a line myself, yet there
are fish enough here for three castles, and on these banks
there is room enough for us three, even were we all to
meet here at the same time. Therefore, I propose from
this time forth that this pond shall be the common property of us three, and each one of you shall have the same
rights here that I do."

"Why, our brother is certainly graciously minded,"
said Schalk, in a jeering way. "He really gives us six
acres of water and a few hundred little fishes! And
what shall we have to give in return?"

"You shall have it free," said Cuno. "I should like
to see and speak with you at this pond now and then.
We are the sons of one father."

"No," exclaimed Schalk; "that would not do at all,
for there is nothing more silly than to fish in company;
one is always frightening off the other's fishes. We
might, however, decide on days for each one—say Monday and Thursday for you, Cuno, Tuesday and Friday for
Wolf, and Wednesday and Saturday for me. Such an arrangement would suit me."

"But I won't agree to that," cried the surly Wolf. "I
don't want any free gift, neither will I divide my rights
with any one. You were right, Cuno, in making your
offer, for in justice the pond belongs as much to one as to
the other: but let us throw the dice to decide who shall

have the entire ownership for the future, and if I am
more fortunate than you, then you will have to come to
me for permission to fish."

"I never throw," replied Cuno, sad at this display of
obduracy on the part of his brothers.

"Of course not," sneered Schalk. "Our brother is so
pious that he thinks it is a deadly sin to throw dice. But
I will make another proposal, to which the most religious
recluse could offer no objection : Let us get some bait
and hooks, and he who shall have caught the most fish
this morning when the bell of Zollern strikes twelve, will
be the owner of the pond."

"I am truly a fool," responded Cuno, "to strive for
that which is mine by right of inheritance ; but that you
may see that my offer of a division was made in earnest,
I will fetch my fishing tackle."

They rode home, each one to his own castle. The
twins sent their servants out in all haste, with orders to
turn over all the old stones near by, and to collect what
worms they found underneath them for bait. But Cuno
took his usual fishing tackle, together with the bait which
Frau Feldheimerin had once learned him to prepare, and
was the first to reach the pond again. On the arrival of
the twins he allowed them the first choice of position,
and then threw in his own line. Then it was as if the
fish seemed to recognize in him the owner of the pond.
Whole schools of carp and pike drew near and swarmed
about his line. The oldest and largest crowded the small
fry aside ; every moment he landed a fish, and each time
he cast his line twenty or thirty darted at the hook with
open mouths. Before two hours had passed, the ground
around him was covered with fish ; then he laid down his
line and went over to where his brothers sat, to see how
they were getting along. Schalk had one poor little carp
and two paltry shiners ; while Wolf had caught three
barbels and two little gudgeons, and both looked sadly
down into the water, for they had seen from their place
the vast number that Cuno had caught.

When Cuno approached his brother Wolf, the latter sprang up in a rage, tore off his line, broke his rod into small pieces and flung them into the pond. "I wish I had a thousand hooks to throw in there, instead of one, and that a fish was wriggling on every one of them," cried he; "but this could never have occurred in a natural way, it is sorcery and witchcraft, or how should you, stupid Cuno, catch more fish in one hour than I could take in a year?"

"Yes, that's so," echoed Schalk. "I remember now that he learned how to fish from that vile witch, Frau Feldheimerin; and we were fools to fish with him; he will be a wizard himself one of these days."

"You wicked fellows!" returned Cuno, sadly. "I have had time enough this morning to get an insight into your avarice, your shamelessness, and your insolence. Go now, and never return here; and believe it would be better for your souls if you were half as pious and good as she whom you have called a witch"

"No, she is not a genuine witch," sneered Schalk. "Such wives can prophesy; but Frau Feldheimerin is about as much of a prophetess as a goose is a swan. Didn't she tell our father that one would be able to buy a good part of his heritage for a hirsch-gulden? And yet at his death everything within sight of the towers of Zollern belonged to him. Frau Feldheimerin is nothing more than a silly old hag, and you the stupid Cuno."

Thus saying, Schalk ran off as fast as he could, for he feared the strong arm of his brother Cuno; and Wolf followed him, shouting back all the curses he had learned from his father.

Grieved to the soul, Cuno returned home; for he now saw plainly that his brothers would never be reconciled to him. And he took their bitter words so seriously to heart that he fell sick the next day, and only the consoling words of good Father Joseph, and the strengthening remedies of Frau Feldheimerin, rescued him from death.

But when his brothers heard that Cuno lay very sick,

they sat down to a jovial banquet, and over their cups made an agreement that the one who should be the first to hear of his death was to fire off a cannon, in order to notify the other of the event, and he who fired first might take the best cask of wine in Cuno's cellar. From this time forth Wolf stationed a watchman in the vicinity of Hirschberg, while Schalk bribed one of Cuno's servants with a large sum of money, to inform him, without delay, when Cuno was breathing his last.

But this servant was more faithful to his good and gentle master than to the wicked Count of Schalksberg. He inquired one evening of Frau Feldheimerin, very solicitously, after his master's health, and when she told him that the count was doing quite well, he related to her the project of the brothers of firing off guns when the Count Cuno should die. The old woman was infuriated, and quickly repeated this story to the count, who could hardly believe his brothers were so utterly heartless; so she advised him to put the matter to the proof by spreading a report of his death. The count summoned the servant to whom his brother had given a bribe, questioned him closely, and then ordered him to ride to Schalksberg and announce his approaching death.

As the servant was riding hastily down the hill, he was seen and stopped by the servant of Count Wolf, who asked him where he was riding to in such a hurry. "Alas!" was his reply, "my poor master will not outlive the night, they have all given him up."

"Indeed! Has his time come?" cried the spy, as he ran to his horse, sprang on his back, and rode so fast towards Zollern, that his horse sank down at the gate, and he was himself only able to call out: "Count Cuno is dying!" before he fell down senseless. Thereupon, the cannon of Hohen-Zollern thundered, and Count Wolf rejoiced with his mother, in anticipation of the cask of wine, over the castle and its belongings, the jewels, the pond, and the echo of his cannon.

But what he had taken for its echo, was the cannon

of Schalksberg, and Wolf said smilingly to his mother:
" It seems Schalk has had a spy there too, and therefore
he and I will have to divide the wine equally, as well as
the rest of the property " With this he mounted his
horse, fearing lest Schalk should arrive at Hirschberg
before he did, and perhaps take away some of the jewels
of the deceased. But the twins met at the fish-pond, and
each blushed before the other, so apparent was the desire
of both to be the first-comer at Hirschberg. They said
not a word about Cuno, as they continued on their way
together, but discussed in a brotherly manner how things
should be arranged in the future, and to which of them
Hirschberg should belong. But as they rode over the
draw-bridge into the court, they saw their brother, safe
and sound, looking out of the window; but anger and
scorn flashed from his features.

The brothers shrank back in terror, taking him at first
to be a ghost, and crossed themselves; but when they
saw that he was still in flesh and blood, Wolf exclaimed:
"Stupid stuff! I thought you were dead."

"Omittance is no quittance," said Schalk, darting up
at his half-brother a venomous look.

Cuno replied in a threatening voice : " From this hour,
all bonds of brotherhood between us are broken. I
heard the salute you fired; but know this, that I have
five field-pieces here in the court that were loaded to do
you honor. Take care to keep out of the range of my
cannon, or you shall have a sample of our shooting at
Hirschberg."

They did not wait to be spoken to a second time,
for they saw that their brother was fully in earnest; so
they gave their horses the spurs and raced down the
mountain, while their brother sent a parting shot after
them, that whistled above their heads, so that they both
made a low and polite bow together; but he only wished
to frighten and not to wound them.

"Why did you fire off your gun?" asked Schalk of

his brother Wolf, in an ill-humored tone. "I only shot because I heard your gun, you fool!"

"On the contrary," replied Wolf. "I'll leave it to mother if you were not the first to shoot; and you have brought this disgrace on us, you little badger."

Schalk returned all his brother's epithets with interest; and when they came to the pond, they hurled at one another some of the choicest curses that the "Tempest of Zollern" had bequeathed them, and parted in hate and anger.

Shortly after this occurrence, Cuno made his will, and Frau Feldheimerin said to Father Joseph: "I would wager something that he has not left much to the twins." But with all her curiosity, and much as she urged her favorite, he would not tell her what was written in the will; nor did she ever learn, for a year afterwards the good woman passed away in spite of her salves and potions. She died, not of any disease, but of her ninety-eighth year, which might well bring even the most healthy person to the grave. Count Cuno had her buried with as much ceremony as if she had been his own mother and not a poor old woman, and he grew more and more lonely in his castle, especially as Father Joseph soon followed Frau Feldheimerin.

Still he did not suffer this solitude very long; for in his twenty-eighth year the good Cuno died, and, as wicked people asserted, of poison administered by Schalk. Be that as it may, some hours after his death the thunder of cannon was heard once more from Zollern and Schalksberg.

"This time he will have to acknowledge the truth of the reports," said Schalk to his brother Wolf, as they met on the road to Hirschberg.

"Yes," answered Wolf; "but even if he should rise from the dead and abuse us from the window as before, I have a rifle with me that will make him polite and dumb."

As they rode up the castle hill, they were joined by a

horseman with his retinue, whom they did not know. They believed, however, that he must be a friend of their brother's who had come to attend the funeral. Therefore they demeaned themselves as mourners, were loud in their praises of the deceased, lamented his early death, and Schalk even managed to squeeze out a few crocodile tears. The stranger paid no attention to what they said, but rode silently by their side up to the castle. "Now, then, we will make ourselves comfortable; and, butler, bring some wine, the very best!" cried Wolf, as he dismounted. They went up the spiral staircase into the salon, where they were followed by the silent stranger; and just as the twins had sat down to the table, he took from his purse a silver coin, and throwing it down on the slate table, where it rolled about and settled down with a ring, said:

"Then and there you have your inheritance; it is a good piece of silver, a hirsch-gulden."

The two brothers looked at one another in astonishment, laughed, and asked him what he meant by this.

The stranger, by way of reply, produced a parchment, attached to which were many seals, in which Cuno had recorded all the instances of malevolence that his brothers had shown him in his life-time, and at the close decreed and made known that his entire estate, real and personal, with the exception of his mother's jewels, should, in the event of his death, become the property of Wuertemberg, in consideration of *a pitiful hirsch-gulden!* But with his mother's jewels, a poor-house should be built in the town of Balingen.

The brothers were astonished anew; but instead of laughing this time, they ground their teeth together, for they could not hope to dispute the claim of Wuertemberg. They had lost the beautiful castle, the forest and field, the town of Balingen, and even the fish-pond, and inherited nothing but a miserable hirsch-gulden. This, Wolf stuck into his purse with a defiant air, put on his

K   7

cap, passed the Wuertemberg officer without a word, sprang on his horse, and rode back to Zollern.

When, on the following morning, his mother reproached him with having trifled away the estate and jewels, he rode over to Schalksberg and said to his brother:

"Shall we gamble with our inheritance, or drink it up?"

"Let's drink it away," replied Schalk; "then we shall both have won. We will ride down to Balingen and let the people see our disdain, even if we have lost the village in a most outrageous manner."

"And at 'The Lamb' tavern they have as good red wine as any the emperor drinks," added Wolf.

So they rode down together to "The Lamb," and inquired the cost of a quart of this red wine, and drank the worth of the gulden. Then Wolf got up, took from his purse the silver coin with the leaping stag stamped on it, threw it down on the table, and said:

"There's your gulden, that will make it right."

But the landlord picked up the gulden, looked at it first on one side and then on the other, and said smilingly:

"Yes, if it was any thing but a hirsch-gulden; but last night the messenger came from Stuttgart, and early this morning it was proclaimed in the name of the Count of Wuertemberg, to whom this town now belongs, that these coins would be no longer current; so give me some other money."

The brothers looked at one another in dismay. "Pay up," said one. "Haven't you got any change?" replied the other; and, in short, they were obliged to remain in debt to "The Lamb" for a gulden.

They started back home without speaking to one another until they came to the cross-road, where the road to the right ran to Zollern and the one to the left to Schalksberg. Then Schalk said:

"How now? We have inherited less than nothing; and moreover, the wine was miserable."

"Yes, to be sure," replied his brother, "but what Frau Feldheimerin said, has come to pass: 'We shall see what part of your inheritance is worth a hirsch-gulden.' And now we were not able to pay for even a measure of wine with it."

"Know it already!" answered he of Schalksberg.

"Stupid stuff!" returned the Count of Zollern, as he rode off moodily, towards his castle.

"That is the Legend of the Hirsch-Gulden," concluded the compass-maker, "and said to be a true one. The landlord at Duerrwangen, which is situated near the three castles, related it to one of my best friends, who often acted as guide through the Suabian Alps, and always put up at Duerrwangen."

The guests applauded the compass-maker's story. "What curious things one hears in the world!" exclaimed the wagoner. "Really, I feel glad now that we did not spoil the time with cards; this is much better, and so interested was I in the story, that I can tell it to-morrow to my comrades without missing a single word of it."

"While you were telling your story, something came into my mind," said the student.

"Oh, tell it, tell it!" pleaded the compass-maker and Felix.

"Very well," replied he, "it makes no difference whether my turn comes now or later. Still, what I tell you must be considered in confidence, for the incidents are reported to have really occurred."

He changed his position to a more comfortable one, and was just about to begin his story, when the landlady put away her distaff and went up to her guests at the table. "It is time now, gentlemen, to go to bed," said she. "It has struck nine, and to-morrow will be another day."

"Well, go to bed then," said the student. "Set another bottle of wine on the table for us, and we won't keep you up any longer."

"By no means," returned she, fretfully; "so long as guests remain in the public-room, it is not possible for the landlady and servants to retire. And once for all, gentlemen, I must request you to go to your rooms; the time hangs heavy on me, and there shall be no carousing in my house after nine o'clock."

"What's the matter with you, landlady?" said the compass-maker in surprise. "What harm can it do you if we sit here even after you have gone to sleep? We are honest people, and won't run off with any thing, nor leave without paying. I won't be ordered around in this way in any tavern."

The woman's eyes flashed angrily. "Do you suppose I will change the rules of my house to suit every raga-muffin of a journeyman and every vagrant who pays me only twelve kreuzers? I tell you for the last time that I won't submit to this nuisance."

The compass-maker was about to make a retort, when the student gave him a significant look, winked at the others, and said: "Very well, if the landlady will have it so, then let us go up to our rooms. But we should like some candles to find our way."

"I cannot accommodate you in that," responded the landlady, sullenly; "the others can find their way in the dark, and this stump of a candle will suffice for your needs; it's all I have in the house."

The young gentleman got up and took the light without replying. The others followed him, the journeymen taking their bundles up with them to keep them near their side.

When they got up to the head of the stairs, the student cautioned them to step very lightly, opened his door, and beckoned them to come in. "There can now be no doubt," said he, "that she means to betray us. Did you not notice how anxious she was to have us go to bed, and the means she took to prevent our remaining awake and together? She probably thinks that we will go to bed now, and thus play into her hands."

"But do you think that escape is impossible?" asked Felix. "In the forest one might more reasonably hope for rescue than in this room."

"These windows are also grated," said the student, vainly trying to wrench out one of the iron bars. "There is but one way by which we can get out, if we wish to escape, and that is by way of the front door; but I do not believe that they would let us out."

"We might make the attempt," said the wagoner; "I will see whether I can get into the yard. If it is possible then I will return for you."

The others assented to this proposal, so the wagoner took off his shoes and stole on tiptoe to the stair-case, while his companions listened anxiously from their room. He had got half-way down, safely and unnoticed, when suddenly a bull-dog rose up before him, placed its paws on his shoulders, and displayed a gleaming set of teeth right before his face. He did not dare to step either forward or backward, for at the least movement the dog would have seized him by the throat. At the same time the dog began to growl and bark, until the landlady and hostler appeared with lights.

"Where were you going? What do you want?" cried the woman.

"I wanted to fetch something from my cart," answered the wagoner trembling in every limb; for as the door opened he had caught a glimpse of several dark suspicious faces of armed men in the room.

"You might have done that before you went up-stairs," replied the woman crossly. "Come here, Fassan! Jacob, lock the yard-gate and light the man out to his wagon."

The dog drew back his muzzle from the wagoner's face, removed his paws from the man's shoulders, and lay down once more across the stair-way. In the meantime the hostler had secured the yard-gate, and now lighted the wagoner to his cart. An escape was not to be thought of. But when he came to consider what he

should take from his wagon, he recollected that he had
a pound of wax candles that were to be delivered in the
next town. "That short piece of candle won't last more
than fifteen minutes longer," said he to himself, "and
yet we must have light!" He therefore took two wax
candles from the wagon, concealed them in his sleeve,
and also took his cloak as an excuse for his errand, telling the hostler that he needed it for a blanket.

Without further incident he got back to the room up-
stairs He told his companions about the big dog that
guarded the stair-case, of the glimpse he had caught of
the armed men, and of all the precautions that had been
taken to prevent their escape; and concluded with a
groan : "We shall not survive the night."

"I don't think that," said the student. "I cannot
believe that these people would be so foolish as to take
the lives of four men for the sake of the few little things
we have with us. But we had better not try to defend
ourselves. For my part I shall lose the most; my horse
is already in their hands, and it cost me fifty ducats only
four weeks ago; my purse and my clothes I will give up
willingly, for after all my life is dearer to me than all
these."

"You talk sensibly," responded the wagoner. "Such
things as you have can be easily replaced; but I am the
messenger from Aschaffenburg, and have all kinds of
goods in my wagon, and in the stable two fine horses, all
I possess in the world."

"I can hardly believe that they would harm you,"
said the goldsmith; "the robbery of a messenger would
cause an alarm to be given all through the country. But
then I agree with what the young gentleman said: sooner
would I give up every thing I possess, and bind myself
with an oath never to speak of this matter and never to
make complaint against them, than to attempt to defend
my little property against people who have rifles and
pistols."

During these words, the wagoner had taken out his

wax candles. He stuck them on the table and lighted them. "Here let us await, in the name of God, whatever may happen to us," said he; "let us sit down together again, and banish sleep with stories."

"We will do that," answered the student; "and as the turn came to me down-stairs, I will now begin."

THE MARBLE HEART.

FIRST PART.

WHOEVER travels through Suabia should not neglect to take a peep into the Black Forest; not on account of the trees, although one does not find every-where such a countless number of magnificent pines, but because of the inhabitants, between whom and their outlying neighbors there exists a marked difference. They are taller than ordinary people, broad-shouldered and strong-limbed. It seems as though the balmy fragrance exhaled by the pines had given them a freer respiration, a clearer eye, and a more resolute if somewhat ruder spirit than that possessed by the inhabitants of the valleys and plains. And not only in their bearing and size do they differ from other people, but in their customs and pursuits as well. In that part of the Black Forest included within the Grand Duchy of Baden, are to be seen the most strikingly dressed inhabitants of the whole forest. The men let nature have her own way with their beards; while their black jackets, close-fitting knee breeches, red stockings, and peaked hats bound with a broad sheaf, give them a picturesque, yet serious and commanding appearance. Here the people generally are occupied in the manufacture of glass ; they also make watches and sell them to half the world.

On the other side of the forest formerly dwelt a branch of this same race ; but their employment had given them other customs and manners. They felled and trimmed their pine trees, rafted the logs down the Nagold into the Neckar, and from the Upper-Neckar to the Rhine, and thence far down into Holland, and even at the sea coast these raftsmen of the Black Forest were known. They stopped on their way down the rivers at each city that lined the banks, and proudly awaited purchasers for their logs and boards, but kept their largest and longest logs to dispose of for a larger sum, to the Mynheers for ship-building purposes. These raftsmen were accustomed to a rough, wandering life. Their joy was experienced in floating down the streams on their rafts ; their sorrow in the long walk back on the banks. Thus from the nature of their occupation they required a costume entirely different from that worn by the glass-makers on the other side of the Black Forest. They wore jackets of dark linen, over which green suspenders of a hand-breadth's width crossed over their broad breasts ; black leather knee breeches, from the pockets of which projected brass foot-rules like badges of honor ; but their joy and pride lay in their boots, the largest perhaps that ever came into vogue in any part of the world, as they could be drawn up two spans of the hand above the knee, so that the raftsmen could wade around in a yard of water without wetting their feet.

Up to quite a recent period, the inhabitants of this forest believed in spirits of the wood. But it is somewhat singular that the spirits who, as the legend ran, dwelt in the Black Forest, took sides in these prevailing fashions. Thus, it was averred that the Little Glass-Man, a good little spirit, only three-and-a-half feet high, never appeared otherwise than in a peaked hat with a wide brim, as well as a jacket and knee breeches and red

stockings; whereas, Dutch - Michel, who haunted the
other part of the forest, was a giant-sized broad-shouldered fellow in the dress of a raftsman, and several people who had seen him, asserted that they would not care
to pay for the hides that would be used to make him a
pair of boots. "And so tall," said they, "that an ordinary
man would not reach to his neck."

With these spirits of the forest, a young man of this
region is reported to have had a strange experience, which
I will relate:

There lived in the Black Forest a widow by the name
of Frau Barbara Munkin; her husband had been a charcoal-burner, and after his death she brought up her son
to the same business. Young Peter Munk, a cunning
fellow of sixteen, was much pleased to sit all the
week round on his smoking piles of wood, just as he had
seen his father do; or, all black and sooty as he was, and
a scarecrow to the people, he would go down to the towns
to sell his charcoal. But a charcoal-burner has plenty of
time to think about himself and others; and when Peter
Munk sat on his half-burned piles of wood, the dark
trees about him and the deep stillness of the forest disposed him to tears and filled his heart with nameless
longings. Something troubled him, and he could not
well make out what it was. Finally he discovered what
it was that had so put him out of sorts; it was his occupation. "A lonely black charcoal-burner," reflected he.
"It is a miserable life. How respectable are the glass-
makers, the watchmakers, and even the musicians of a
Sunday evening! And when Peter Munk, cleanly-washed
and brushed, appears dressed in his father's best jacket
with silver buttons and with bran-new red stockings, and
when one walks behind me and thinks, Who is that
stylish-looking fellow? and inwardly praises my stockings and my stately walk—when he passes by me and
turns around to look, he is sure to say to himself: 'Oh,
it's only Charcoal Pete!'"

The raftsmen on the other side of the forest also

aroused his envy. When these giants came over among
the glass-makers, dressed in their elegant clothes, wearing at least fifty pounds of silver in buttons, buckles, and
chains, when they looked on at a dance, with legs spread
wide apart, swore in Dutch, and smoked pipes from
Cologne three feet long in the stem, just like any distinguished Mynheer — then was Peter convinced that such
a raftsman was the very picture of a lucky man. And
when these fortunate beings put their hands into their
pockets and drew out whole handfuls of thalers and shook
for half a-dozen at a throw—five guldens here, ten there
—then he would nearly lose his senses, and would steal
home to his hut in a very melancholy mood. On many
holiday nights he had seen one or another of these timber
merchants lose more at play than his poor father had ever
been able to earn in a year.

Distinguished above all others were three of these men,
and Peter was uncertain which one of them was most
wonderful. One was a large heavy man, with a red face,
who passed for the richest man of them all. He was
called Stout Ezekiel. He went down to Amsterdam
twice a year with timber, and always had the good fortune to sell it at so much higher a price than others could
sell theirs, that he could afford to ride back home in good
style, while the others had to return on foot. The second
man of the trio was the lankest and leanest person in the
whole forest, and was called Slim Schlurker. Peter envied
him for his audacity; he contradicted the most respectable people, occupied more room when the inn was crowded
than four of the stoutest, either by spreading his elbows
out on the table, or by stretching his legs out on the
bench, and yet no one dared to interfere with him, for he
had an enormous amount of money. But the third was
a handsome young man, who was the best dancer far and
wide, and had, therefore, received the title of King of the
Ball. He had been a poor boy, and had been a servant
to one of the lumber dealers, when he suddenly became
very rich. Some said that he had found a pot of gold

under an old pine tree, others asserted that he had fished up a packet of gold pieces near Bingen on the Rhine, with the pole with which the raftsmen sometimes speared for fish; and that the packet was part of the great Nibe-

lungen treasure that lies buried there. In short, he had suddenly become a rich man, and was looked upon by young and old with the respect due a prince. Charcoal Pete often thought of these three men, as he sat so lonely in the forest of pines. It is true that all three had a common failing that made them hated by the people; this was their inhuman avarice—their utter lack of sym-

pathy for the poor and unfortunate; for the inhabitants
of the Black Forest are a kind-hearted people. But you
know how it goes in the world; if they were hated on account of their avarice, they yet commanded deference by
virtue of their money; for who but they could throw
away thalers as if one had only to shake them down from
the pines?

"I won't stand this much longer" said Peter, deject-
edly. to himself one day; for the day before had been a
holiday, and all the people had been down to the inn.
"If I don't make a strike pretty soon, I shall make away
with myself. Oh, if I were only as rich and respectable
as the Stout Ezekiel, or so bold and mighty as the Slim
Schlurker, or as famous and as well able to throw thalers
to the fiddlers as the King of the Ball! Where can the
fellow get his money?" He thought over all the ways
by which one could make money, but none of them
suited him. Finally there occurred to him the traditions
of people who had become rich through the aid of
Dutch Michel and the Little Glass-Man. During his
father's life-time, other poor people often came to visit
them, and Peter had heard them talk by the hour of rich
people and of the way their riches were acquired. The
name of the Little Glass-Man was often mentioned in
these conversations, as one who had helped these rich
men to their wealth; and Peter could almost remember
the verse that had to be spoken at the Tannenbuehl in
the centre of the forest in order to summon him. It ran
thus:

> " Schatzhauser im grünen Tannenwald,
>   Bist schon viel' hundert Jahre alt,
>   Dir gehört all' Land wo Tannen stehn—"

But strain his memory as he would, he could not recall another line. He often debated within himself
whether he should not ask this or that old man what the
rest of the rhyme was, but was held back by a certain
dread of betraying his thoughts — and then, too, the tradition of the Glass-Man could not be very widely known,

and the rhyme must be known to but very few, for there were not many rich people in the forest; and, strangest of all, why had not his father and the other poor people tried their luck? He finally led his mother into speaking about the Little Glass-Man; but she only told him what he knew before, and knew only the first line of the rhyme, although she did add afterwards that the spirit only showed himself to people who were born on a Sunday between eleven and two o'clock. In that respect, she told him, he would fill the requirements, if he could only remember the verse; as he was born on a Sunday noon.

When Charcoal Pete heard this, he was almost beside himself with joy at the thought of undertaking this adventure. It appeared to him sufficient that he knew a part of the verse, and that he was born on a Sunday; so he thought that the Glass-Man would appear to him. Therefore, after he had sold his charcoal one day, he did not kindle any more fires, but put on his father's best jacket, his new red stockings and his Sunday hat, grasped his black-thorn cane, and bade good-bye to his mother, saying: "I must go to town on business; we shall soon have to draw lots again to see who shall serve in the army, and I will once more call the justice's attention to the fact that I am the only son of a widow."

His mother commended his resolution, and he started off for Tannenbuehl. The Tannenbuehl lies on the highest point of the Black Forest; and within a radius of a two-hours' walk, not a village nor even a hut was to be found, for the superstitious people held the Tannenbuehl to be an unsafe place. And tall and splendid as were the trees in this region, they were now but seldom disturbed by the woodman's ax; for often when the wood-choppers had ventured in there to work, the axes had flown from the helves and cut them in the foot, or the trees had fallen unexpectedly before they could get out of the way, and had killed and injured many. Then, too, these magnificent trees could only be sold for firewood, as the raftsmen would never take a single log from this locality into their rafts, for the tradition was current among them that both men and rafts would come to grief if they were to do so.   Therefore, it was that the trees of the Tannenbuehl had been left to grow so thick and tall that it was almost as dark as night there on the clearest day; and Peter Muck began to feel rather timid there, for he heard not a voice, not a step save his own, not even the ring of an ax, while even the birds appeared to shun these dark shadows.

Charcoal Pete at last reached the highest point of the Tannenbuehl, and stood before a pine of enormous girth, for which a ship-builder in Holland would have given many hundred guldens, delivered at his yard. "Here," thought he, "the Little Glass-Man would be most likely to live." So he took off his Sunday hat, made a low bow before the tree, cleared his throat, and said in a trembling voice: "I wish you a very good afternoon, Mr. Glass-Man." But there was no answer, and every thing about was as still as before.   "Perhaps I have to speak the verse first," thought he, and mumbled:

> "Schaßhauſer im grünen Tannenwald,
>   Biſt ſchon viel' hundert Jahre alt,
>   Dir gehört all' Land wo Tannen ſtehn—"

As he spoke these words, he saw, to his great terror, a very small, strange figure peep out from behind the great tree. To Peter it seemed to be the Little Glass-Man, just as he had heard him described: a black jacket, red stockings, a peaked hat with a broad brim, and a pale but fine and intelligent little face. But alas, as quickly as the Little Glass-Man had looked around the tree, so quickly had he disappeared again. "Mr. Glass-Man," cried Peter Munk after a long pause, "be so kind as not to make a fool of me. Mr. Glass-Man, if you think I didn't see you, you are very much mistaken. I saw you very plainly when you looked around the tree."   Still no answer; but occasionally Peter believed he heard a low, amused chuckle behind the tree.   Finally his impa-

tience conquered the fear that had held him back.
"Wait, you little fellow," cried he; "I will soon catch
you." With one leap he sprang behind the tree, but
there was no

" Schatzhauser im grünen Tannenwald,"

and only a small squirrel ran up the tree.

Peter Munk shook his head; he saw that he had the
method of conjuration all right up to a certain point, and
that perhaps only another line was needed to induce the
Little Glass-Man to appear. He thought over this and
that, but found nothing to the purpose. The squirrel
was to be seen on the lower branches of the tree, and
acted as if it were either trying to cheer him up or was
making sport of him. It smoothed down its fur, waved
its fine bushy tail, and looked at him with intelligent
eyes. But at last he was afraid to remain here alone
with this little creature; for now the squirrel would
appear to have a human head and a three-peaked hat,
and then again it would be just like other squirrels, with
the exception of red stockings and black shoes on its
hinder legs. In short, it was a merry creature; but
nevertheless Charcoal Pete stood in dread of it, believing
that there was some magic in all this.

Peter left the spot at a much faster pace than he had
approached it. The shadows of the pine wood seemed
to deepen, the trees to be taller, and such terror took
possession of him that he broke into a run, and experienced a sense of security only when he heard dogs barking in the distance, and saw between the trees the smoke
rising from a hut. But when he came nearer, and perceived the dress worn by the people in the hut, he found
that in his alarm he had taken the wrong direction, and
instead of arriving among the glass-makers, he had come
to the raftsmen. The people who dwelt in the hut were
wood-choppers; an old man, his son, who was the owner
of the house, and some grandchildren They gave Charcoal Pete a hospitable reception, without asking for his

name and residence; brought him cider to drink, and for supper a large blackcock, the most tempting dish in the Black Forest, was set on the table.

After supper the housewife and her daughters gathered, with their distaffs, around the light which the children fed with the finest resin; the grandfather, the guest, and the master of the house smoked and looked at the busy fingers of the women, while the boys were occupied in cutting out wooden forks and spoons. Out in the forest a storm was raging; one heard every now and then heavy peals of thunder, and often it sounded as though entire trees had been snapped off and crushed together. The fearless children wanted to go out into the forest to view this wild and beautiful scene; but their grandfather restrained them by a sharp word and look. " I would not advise any one to go outside the door," exclaimed he; " he would never come back again, for Dutch Michel is cutting a fresh link of logs to-night."

The children all stared at him. They might have heard the name of Dutch Michel mentioned before, but now they begged their grandfather that he would tell them all about him. And Peter Munk, who had heard Dutch Michel spoken of on the other side of the forest only in a vague way, joined in the children's request, and asked the old man who Dutch Michel was and where he was to be seen. " He is the master of this forest; and, judging from such an inquiry from a man of your age, you must live on the other side of the Tannenbuehl, or even farther away, not to have heard of him. I will tell you what I know about Dutch Michel, and the stories that are circulated regarding him:

"About a hundred years ago — at least so my ancestors said — there was not a more honorable race of people on the face of the earth than the inhabitants of the Black Forest. But now, since so much money has come into the country, the people are dishonest and wicked; the young fellows dance and sing on Sunday, and swear most terribly. But at the time of which I speak there

was a very different state of things; and even though
Dutch Michel is looking in at the window now, I say, just
as I have often said before, that he is to blame for all this
woful change. There lived a hundred years or more
ago, a rich timber merchant, who employed a large number of men. He traded far down the Rhine, and his business prospered, as he was a God-fearing man. One
evening a man came to his door, the like of whom he had
never seen before. His clothing did not differ from that
of the Black Forest workingmen, but he was a good head
taller than any of them, and it had not been believed
that such a giant existed any where. He asked for work,
and the timber merchant, seeing that he was strong and
so well adapted to carrying heavy loads, made a bargain
with him. Michel was a workman such as this man had
never had before. As a wood-chopper he was the equal
of any other three men; and he would carry one end of
a tree which required six men to carry the other end.

" But after cutting trees for six months, he went to his
employer and said : ' I have cut wood here long enough
now, and should like to see where my tree-trunks go to ;
so how would it do if you were to let me go down on the
rafts ? '   The timber merchant replied: ' I will not
stand in the way of your seeing a little of the world,
Michel. To be sure, I need strong men to fell the trees,
while on the raft more cleverness is required ; but it shall
be as you wish for this time.'

" The raft on which he was to go, consisted of eight
sections, the last of which was made up of the largest
timbers. But what do you think happened? On the
evening before they started, the tall Michel brought eight
more logs to the water, thicker and longer than any that
had ever been seen before, and each one he had carried
as lightly on his shoulder as if it were simply a raft pole,
so that all were amazed. Where he had cut them remains
a mystery to-day. The heart of the timber merchant
rejoiced as he saw them, and began to reckon up what
they might be worth; but Michel said: 'There, those

are for me to travel on. I shouldn't get very far on those other chips.' His master, by way of thanks, presented him with a pair of high boots; but Michel threw them aside, and produced a pair that my grandfather assured me weighed a hundred pounds and stood five feet high.

"The raft was started off, and if Michel had astonished the wood-choppers before, it was now the turn of the raftsmen to be surprised; for instead of the float going more slowly down the stream, as had been expected on account of these enormous logs, as soon as they touched the Neckar they flew down the river with the speed of an arrow. If they came to a curve in the Neckar, that had

usually given the raftsmen much trouble to keep the raft
in the middle of the stream and prevent it from ground-
ing on the gravel or sand, Michel would spring into the
water and push the raft to the right or the left, so that it
passed by without accident. But if they came to a
stand-still, he would run forward to the first section, have
all the other men throw down their poles, stick his own
enormous beam into the gravel, and with a single push
the float flew down the river at such a rate that the land
and trees and villages seemed to be running away from
them.

"Thus in half the time usually consumed, they
reached Cologne on the Rhine, where they had been accustomed to sell their float. But here Michel spoke up
once more : ' You seem to be merchants who understand
your own interests. Do you then think that the people
of Cologne use all this timber that comes from the Black
Forest? No, they buy it of you at half its cost, and sell
it to Holland merchants at an immense advance. Let us
sell the smaller logs here, and take the larger ones down
to Holland ; what we receive above the usual price will
be our own gain.'

"Thus spake the crafty Michel, and the others were
content to do as he advised — some because they had a
desire to see Holland, and others on account of the money
they would pocket. Only one of the men was honest,
and tried to dissuade his companions from exposing their
master's property to further risks, or to cheat him out of
the higher price they might receive ; but they would not
listen to him, and forgot his words. Dutch Michel, however, did not forget them. They continued on down the
Rhine, and Michel conducted the raft and soon brought
it to Rotterdam. There they were offered four times
the former price, and the enormous logs that Michel had
brought sold for a large sum. When these raftsmen
found themselves the possessors of so much money, they
could hardly contain themselves for joy. Michel made
the division, one part for the timber merchant and the

three others among the men. And now they frequented
the taverns with sailors and other low associates, gam-
bled and threw away their money; but the brave man
who had advised against their going to Holland was sold
to a slave-dealer by Dutch Michel, and was never again
heard of. From that time forth Holland was the paradise of the raftsmen of the Black Forest, and Dutch
Michel was their king. The timber merchants did not
learn of the swindle practiced on them for some time;
and money, oaths, bad manners, drunkenness and gambling were gradually imported from Holland unnoticed.

"When the story of these doings came out, Dutch
Michel was nowhere to be found. But he is not by any
means dead For a hundred years he has carried on his
ghostly deeds in the forest, and it is said that he has been
the means of enriching many; but at the cost of their
souls. How that may be, I will not say; but this much
is certain : that on these stormy nights he picks out the
finest trees in the Tannenbuehl, where none dare to chop,
and my father once saw him break off a tree four feet
thick as easily as if it had been a reed. He makes a
present of these trees to those who will turn from the
right and follow him; then at midnight they bring down
these logs to the river, and he goes with his followers
down to Holland. But if I were the King of Holland, I
would have him blown to pieces with grape-shot; for
every ship that has in it any of Dutch Michel's timber,
even if it be only a single stick, must go to the bottom.
This is the cause of all the shipwrecks we hear of; for
how else could a fine strong ship, as large as a church,
be destroyed on the water ? And whenever Dutch Michel
fells a pine in the Black Forest on a stormy night, one of
his timbers springs from a ship's side, the water rushes
in, and the ship is lost with all her crew. Such is the
legend of Dutch Michel; and it is sure that all that is
bad in the Black Forest may be ascribed to him. But
oh, he can make one rich!" added the old man mysteri-
ously; "yet I wouldn't have any thing to do with him—

I would not for any money stand in the shoes of the Stout Ezekiel or in those of the Slim Schlurker; and the King of the Ball is reported to belong to him also."

During the recital of the old man's story, the storm had ceased. The girls now timidly lighted their lamps and went off to bed; while the man gave Peter a bag of leaves for a pillow on the settee, and wished him good-night.

Never before did Charcoal Pete have such dreams as on this night. Now the sullen giant, Dutch Michel, would raise the window and hold out before him with his enormously long arm a purse full of gold pieces, which he chincked together; then he would see the good-natured Little Glass-Man riding about the room on a monstrous green bottle, and he could hear his merry laugh just as it sounded in the Tannenbuehl; then again there was hummed into his left ear:

> "In Holland there is gold;
> You can have it if you will
> For very little pay;
> Gold, Gold!"

then in his right ear he heard the song of the " Schaßhaufer im grünen Tannenwald," and a soft voice whispered: " Stupid Charcoal Pete! stupid Peter Munk can't think of any thing to rhyme with *stehen*, and yet was born on Sunday at twelve o'clock. Rhyme, stupid Peter, rhyme!"

He sighed and groaned in his sleep. He tried his best to think of a rhyme for that word; but as he had never made a rhyme in his life, all his efforts in his dream were fruitless. But on awaking with the early dawn, his dream recurred to his mind. He sat himself down behind the table with folded arms, and thought over the whispers he could still hear. "Rhyme, stupid Charcoal Pete, rhyme," said he to himself, meanwhile tapping his forehead with his finger; but the rhyme would not come forth at his bidding.

While he was sitting thus, looking sadly before him

with his mind intent on a rhyme for *stehen*, three fellows passed by the house, one of whom was singing:

> "Am Berge that ich stehen
> Und schaute in das Thal,
> Da hab' ich sie gesehen
> Zum allerletzten Mal."

That struck Peter's ear instantly, and springing up he rushed hastily out of the house, ran after the three men, and seized the singer roughly by the arm. "Stop, friend," cried he, "what was your rhyme for *stehen?* Be so kind as to recite what you sang."

"What's the trouble with you, young fellow?" retorted the singer. "I can sing what I please, so let go of my arm, or ——"

"No, you must tell me what you sang!" shouted Peter, taking a firmer grip on his arm. The two others did not hesitate long on seeing this but fell upon Peter with their hard fists and gave him such a beating that he was forced to let go his hold on the first man and sank exhausted to his knees. "You have got your share now," said they laughing, "and mind you, stupid fellow, never to jump upon people again on the highway."

"Oh, I will surely take care!" replied Charcoal Pete sighing; "but now that I have had the blows, be so good as to tell me plainly what it was that man sang."

They began to laugh again, and made sport of him; but the one who had sung the song repeated it to him, and laughing and singing they continued on their way.

"Also *gesehen*," said the beaten one, as he raised himself up with some difficulty; "*gesehen* rhymes with *stehen*. Now then, Little Glass-Man, we will speak a word together." He went back to the hut, took his hat and stick, and bade farewell to the inmates of the hut, and started on his way back to the Tannenbuehl.

He walked on slowly and thoughtfully, for he had a line to make up; finally as he came into the neighborhood of the Tannenbuehl, and the pines grew taller and thicker, he had completed the verse, and in his joy made a leap into the air. Just then appeared a man of giant size, who held in his hand a pole as long as a ship's mast. Peter's courage failed him as he saw this giant walking along very slowly near him; for, thought he, that is none other than Dutch Michel. But the giant remained silent, and Peter occasionally took a half-frightened look at him. He was fully a head taller than the largest man Peter had ever seen; his face was neither young nor old, and yet full of lines; he wore a linen jacket, and the enormous boots drawn over the leather breeches, Peter recognized from the legend he had heard the night before.

"Peter Munk, what are you doing in the Tannenbuehl?" inquired the King of the Wood, in a deep threatening voice.

"Good morning, neighbor," replied Peter, with an effort to hide his uneasiness: "I was going back home through the Tannenbuehl."

"Peter Munk," returned the giant, darting a piercing look at him, "your way does not lie through this grove."

"Well, no, not directly," said Peter; "but it is warm to-day, and I thought it would be cooler up here."

"Don't tell a lie, Charcoal Pete!" cried Dutch Michel, in a voice of thunder, "or I will beat you to the ground with my pole. Do you think I didn't hear you pleading with the Little Glass-Man?" continued he more gently. "Come, come, that was a foolish thing to do, and it is fortunate that you did not know that verse; he is a niggard, the little churl, and doesn't give much, and those to whom he does give don't enjoy life very much. Peter, you are a poor simpleton, and it grieves me to the soul to see such a lively, handsome fellow, who might do something in the world, burning charcoal. While others are throwing about great thalers or ducats, you can hardly raise a sixpence: 't is a miserable life."

"That's all true, and you are right; it is a miserable life."

"Well, I shouldn't mind giving you a lift," continued

the terrible Michel. " I have already helped many a brave fellow out of his misery, so you would not be the first. Speak up, now; how many hundred thalers do you want to start with ? "

With these words, he shook the gold pieces in his immense pocket, and they jingled as Peter had heard them last night in his dream. His heart beat wildly and painfully; he was warm and cold by turns, and Dutch Michel did not look as if he was in the habit of giving away money in compassion without receiving something in return. The mysterious words of the old man in the hut recurred to his mind, and driven by unaccountable anxiety and terror, he cried: " Best thanks, master; but I won't have any dealings with you, for I know you too well," and ran off at the top of his speed.

But Dutch Michel strode after him muttering in a hollow, threatening voice: " You will regret it, Peter; it is written on your forehead and can be read in your eye, you will not escape me. Don't run so fast; listen to just one word of reason. There is my boundary line now." But when Peter heard this, and saw not far ahead of him a small trench, he increased his speed in order to get beyond the line, so that Michel, too, had to run much faster and followed him with curses and threats. The young man made a desperate leap over the trench, as he saw Dutch Michel raise his pole to destroy him. He landed safely on the other side, and saw the pole shattered in the air as though it had struck an invisible wall, and a long splinter fell at Peter's feet. He picked it up triumphantly with the intention of hurling it back at Michel; but at that moment he felt it moving in his hand, and discovered, to his horror, that it was an enormous snake, which with darting tongue and glistening eyes reared its head to strike at him. He let go his hold, but the reptile had coiled itself tightly about his arm, and its fangs were already close to his face, when of a sudden a blackcock swooped down, seized the snake's head in its bill and flew up into the air with its prey, while Dutch Michel, who had seen all this from the boundary line, howled and stormed as the snake was carried off by its more powerful enemy.

Trembling and staggering, Peter continued on his way. The path became steeper, the region wilder, and soon he found himself at the base of the large pine tree. He made his obeisance as yesterday to the invisible Little Glass-Man, and then recited his verse:

> " Schatzhauser im grünen Tannenwald,
> Bist schon viel' hundert Jahre alt,
> Dein ist all' Land, wo Tannen stehn,
> Läßt Dich nur Sonntagskindern sehn."

" You haven't quite hit it, but seeing it's you, Charcoal Pete, we'll let it pass," said a low soft voice near him. He looked around him in surprise, and beneath a splendid pine sat a little old man, dressed in a black jacket and red stockings, with a large hat on his head. He had a delicate, pleasing face, and a beard as fine as a spider's web. He smoked from a pipe of blue glass; and on approaching nearer, Peter saw, to his astonishment, that the clothing, shoes, and hat of the little man were all made of colored glass, but it was as flexible as though still hot, for it bent like cloth with every movement of the little man.

" You have met that churl, Dutch Michel?" said the little man, coughing peculiarly after every word. " He meant to scare you badly; but I have taken away his magic pole and he will never recover it again."

" Yes, Mr. Schatzhauser," replied Peter, with a low bow. " I was in a pretty bad fix. Then you must have been the blackcock who killed the snake! My best thanks for your kindness. But I have come here to counsel with you. Things are in a bad way with me; a charcoal burner doesn't get ahead any, and as I am still young I thought that perhaps something better might be made out of me. When I look at others, I see how they have progressed in a short time — the stout Ezekiel for

8

instance, and the King of the Ball; they have money like hay."

"Peter," said the little man, gravely blowing the smoke from his pipe to a great distance, "do not talk to me in that way. How much would you be benefitted by being apparently happy for a few years, only to be still more unhappy afterwards? You must not despise your calling; your father and grandfather were honorable people, and followed the same pursuit. Peter Munk! I will not think that it is laziness that brings you to me."

Peter shrank back before the earnestness of the little man, and reddened. "Idleness, Herr Schatzhauser im Tannenwald, is, I well know, the beginning of all burdens; but you should not think poorly of me for desiring to better my condition. A charcoal burner is of very little account in the world, while the glass-makers and raftsmen and watchmakers are all respectable."

"Pride often comes before a fall," replied the master of the pine wood, in a more friendly manner. "You mortals are a strange race. Seldom is one of you contented with the lot to which he was born and brought up. And what would be the result of your becoming a glass-maker? You would then want to be a timber merchant; and if you were a timber merchant, the life of the ranger or the magistrate's dwelling would seem more attractive still. But it shall be as you wish, provided you promise to work hard. I am accustomed to grant every Sunday child who knows how to find me three wishes; the first two are free, the third I can set aside if it is a foolish one. So announce your wishes, Peter, but let them be something good and useful."

"Hurrah! You are an excellent Little Glass-Man, and you are rightly called Schatzhauser, for with you the treasures are always at home. Well, if I am at liberty to wish for what my heart longs, my first wish shall be that I could dance better than the King of the Ball, and that I had as much money in my pocket as the Stout Ezekiel."

"You fool!" exclaimed the little man scornfully;
What a pitiful wish is that, to dance well and have
money to gamble with! Are you not ashamed, stupid
Peter, to fool away your chance in such a fashion? Of
what use will your dancing be to you and your poor
mother? Of what use will money be to you, when, as
can be seen from your wish, it is destined for the tavern,
and like that of the miserable King of the Ball, will remain there? Then you would have nothing for the rest
of the week, and will suffer want as before. I will give
you another wish free; but look to it that you choose
more intelligently?"

Peter scratched his head, and said, after some hesita-
tion: "Well, I wish for the most beautiful and costly
glass-works in the whole Black Forest, together with suitable belongings for it, and money to keep it going."

"Nothing else?" inquired the little man in an appre-
hensive manner; "nothing else, Peter?"

"Well, you might add a horse and carriage to all
this."

"Oh, you stupid Charcoal Pete!" cried the little man,
and threw his glass pipe in a fit of anger at a large pine
tree, so that it broke into a hundred pieces. "Horses?
Wagons? Intellect, I tell you, intellect, a sound human
understanding and foresight, you should have wished for,
and not horses and wagons. Well, don't look so sad;
we will see that you don't come to much harm by it, for
your second wish was not such a bad one. Glass-works
will support both man and master; and if you had wished
for foresight and understanding with it, wagons and
horses would have followed as a matter of course."

"But, Herr Schatzhauser," returned Peter, "I have
one more wish left, and if you think that intellect is such
a desirable thing, why, I might wish for it now."

"Not so. You will get into many difficulties when you
will rejoice that you still have one wish left. And so you
had better now start on your way home. Here," said the
little man, drawing a purse from his pocket, "are two

thousand guldens, and it should be enough, so don't come back to me begging for more money, or I should have to hang you up to the highest pine tree. Three days ago old Winkfritz, who had the glass-works in the valley, died. Go there to-morrow early, and make a suitable bid for the business Conduct yourself well, be diligent, and I will visit you occasionally and assist you with word and deed, as you did not wish for understanding. But — and I say this to you in all seriousness — your first wish was a bad one. Take care, Peter, how you run to the tavern; no one ever received any good thereby."

While thus speaking, the little man had produced a second pipe of alabaster glass, filled it with crushed pine cones, and lighted it by holding a large burning-glass in the sun. When he had done this, he shook Peter's hand in a friendly manner, accompanied him a short distance on his way, giving him some valuable advice, meanwhile blowing out thicker and thicker volumes of smoke, and finally disappearing in a cloud of smoke, that, as if from genuine Dutch tobacco, curled slowly about the tops of the pine trees.

When Peter arrived at home, he found his mother in a state of great alarm about him, for the good woman could believe nothing else but that her son had been drawn as a soldier. He, however, was in a very happy mood, and told her how he had met a good friend in the forest, who had advanced him money to undertake a better business than that of charcoal burning. Although his mother had lived in this hut for thirty years, and was as much accustomed to the sight of sooty faces as every miller's wife is to the flour on her husband's face, yet she was vain enough when Peter held out the prospect of a more brilliant life, to despise her early condition, and said : "Yes, as mother of a man who owns the glass-works, I am somewhat better than neighbor Grete and Bete, and for the future I shall take a front seat in the church among respectable people."

Peter soon concluded a bargain with the heirs for the

glass-works. He retained the workmen whom he found there, and made glass by day and night. In the beginning he was much pleased with the business. He was accustomed to walk proudly about the works, with his hands in his pockets, looking into this and that, advising here and there, over which his workmen laughed not a little; but his great delight was to see the glass blown, and he often attempted this work himself, forming the most singular shapes out of the molten mass. But before long he tired of the business, and spent only an hour a day at the works; then only an hour in two days, and finally he went only once a week, so that his workmen did what they pleased.

All this resulted from his visits to the tavern. The Sunday after he had met the little man in the wood, he went to the tavern, and found the King of the Ball already leading the dance, while the Stout Ezekiel was sitting down to his glass and shaking dice for crown-thalers. Peter put his hand in his pocket to see if the Little Glass-Man had kept faith with him, and behold, his pockets were bulged out with silver and gold. His legs, too, began to twitch and move as though they were about to dance and leap; and when the first dance was over, he placed himself with his partner opposite, near the King of the Ball, and if this man sprang three feet high, Peter would fly up four, and if the other accomplished wonderfully intricate steps, Peter would throw out his legs in such a marvelous style that all present were beside themselves with delight and amazement. But as soon as it was known that Peter had bought a glass-factory, and as the dancers saw him tossing sixpences to the musicians every time he passed them in the dance, their astonishment knew no bounds. Some thought he must have found treasure in the forest; others, that he had inherited an estate; but all deferred to him and looked upon him as a great man, simply because he had money. On the same evening he lost twenty guldens at play; and still the coins chinked in his pocket as though there were still a hundred guldens there.

When Peter saw how important a person he had become, he could not contain himself for joy and pride He threw his money right and left, and divided it generously among the poor, remembering how sorely poverty pressed on him. The skill of the King of the Ball was brought to shame by the supernatural art of the new dancer, and Peter was dubbed Emperor of the Ball. The most adventurous gamblers of a Sunday did not risk as much as he; but neither did they lose as much. And yet the more he lost the more he won. This happened through the agency of the Little Glass-Man. He had wished always to have as much money in his pocket as the Stout Ezekiel had in his; and the latter was the very man to whom Peter lost his money. And when he lost twenty or thirty guldens at a throw, he had just as many more when Ezekiel pocketed them.

By degrees, however, he got deeper into gambling and drinking than the worst topers in the Black Forest, so that he was oftener called Gambler Pete than Emperor of the Ball, for he played now nearly every work-day as well. Hence it was that his business was soon ruined, and Peter's lack of understanding was to blame for it. He had as much glass made as the works could possibly produce; but he had not bought with the business the secret of how to dispose of the glass. He did not know what in the world to do with his stock, and finally sold it to peddlers at half the cost price, in order to pay the men's wages.

One evening he was returning home as usual from the tavern, and in spite of the wine he had drunk in order to make himself merry, he reflected with terror and anguish on the ruin of his glass-works business, when suddenly he felt conscious that some one was walking at his side. He turned around and, behold, it was the Little Glass-Man. At once Peter fell into a passion, and protested with high and boastful words that the little man was to blame for his misfortunes.

"What do I want now with a horse and wagon?" cried he "Of what use is the glass-foundry and all my glass? Even when I was a poor charcoal burner, I was far happier, and had no cares. Now I do not know how soon the magistrate will come and seize my property for debt!"

"Indeed?" replied the Little Glass-Man, "indeed? I should bear the blame for your misfortunes? Is this your gratitude for what I have done for you? Who advised you to wish so foolishly? You were bound to be a glass-manufacturer, and yet did not know where to sell your wares. Didn't I caution you to wish wisely? Judgment, Peter, and wisdom, you were lacking in."

"What do you mean by judgment and wisdom?" demanded Peter. "I am as wise a man as any body, Little Glass-Man, and will prove it to you." With these words he seized the Little Glass-Man violently by the neck, shouting: "Now I have you, Schatzhauser im grünen Tannenwald! and now I will make my third wish, which you must grant me. I want right here on the spot two hundred thousand thalers, and a house and —— oh dear!" shrieked he, as he wrung his hands, for the Little Glass-Man had transformed himself into a glowing glass that burned his hand like flaming fire. And nothing more was to be seen of the little man.

For many days Peter's blistered hand reminded him of his folly and ingratitude; but when his hand healed his conscience became deadened, and he said: "Even if my glass-works and every thing I have should be sold, I still have the Stout Ezekiel to fall back on. As long as he has money of a Sunday I shall not want for it."

True, Peter! But if he should have none? And this very thing happened one day. For one Sunday Peter came down to the tavern, and the people stretched their necks out of the window, one saying, "There comes Gambler Pete!" and another, "Yes, the Emperor of the

Ball, the rich glass-manufacturer!" while a third one
shook his head, saying,"Every-where his debts are spoken
of, and in the town it is said that the magistrate will not
be put off much longer from seizing his glass-works."
The rich Peter greeted the guests at the window politely
as he stepped out of his wagon, and called out: "Good
evening, landlord! has the Stout Ezekiel come yet?"
And a deep voice replied: "Come right in, Peter. We
have already set down to the cards, and have kept a
place for you." So Peter entered the public room, put
his hand into his pocket and found that the Stout Ezekiel
must be pretty well provided with money, for his own
pocket was crammed full.

He sat down at the table with the others, and played
and won, losing now and then; and so they played until
evening came on, and all the honest folk went home, and
then they continued to play by candle-light, until two
other players said: "Come, we've had enough, and must
go home to our wife and children." But Gambler Pete
challenged the Stout Ezekiel to remain. For some time
Ezekiel would not consent to do so, but finally he said:
"Very well, I will just count my money and then we
throw for five gulden stakes, for less than that would be
child's play." He took out his purse and counted out
one hundred guldens, so Gambler Pete knew how much
money he had without troubling himself to count. But
although Ezekiel had won all the afternoon, he now began to lose throw after throw, and swore fearfully over
his losses. If he threw threes, Peter would immediately
throw fives. At last he flung down his last five guldens
on the table, and said: "Once more, and even if I lose
these I won't quit, for you must lend me from your winnings Peter; one honest fellow should help another!"

"As much as you like, even if it was a hundred guldens," said the Emperor of the Ball, pleased with his
gains; and the Stout Ezekiel shook the dice and threw
fifteen. "Three fives!" cried he, "now we will see!"

M

But Pete threw eighteen, and a hoarse well-known voice behind him said: "There, that was the last!"

He turned about, and behind him stood the giant form of Dutch Michel. Horrified, he let the money he had just grasped fall from his hand. Ezekiel, however, did not see Michel, but requested a loan of ten guldens from Gambler Pete. Quite dazed, Peter put his hand in his pocket, but found no money there. He searched his other pocket but found none there; he turned his pockets inside out, but not a farthing rolled out. Now for the first time he remembered that his first wish had been to always have as much money in his pocket as the Stout Ezekiel had. It had all disappeared like smoke.

The landlord and Ezekiel looked on in surprise while he was searching for his money; they would not believe him when he declared that he had no more money, but finally, when they felt in his pockets themselves, they got very angry and denounced him as a base sorcerer who had wished all his winnings and his own money at home. Peter defended himself as well as he could, but appearances were against him. Ezekiel declared that he would tell this terrible tale to every body in the Black Forest, and the landlord promised Ezekiel that he would go to town early in the morning and enter a complaint against Peter Munk as a sorcerer, and he would live to see Peter burned, he added. Thereupon they fell upon Peter, tore off his jacket, and pitched him out of doors.

Not a star was to be seen in the sky as Peter stole sadly back towards his home; yet in spite of the darkness he could perceive a form that walked near him, and finally heard it say: "It's all up with you, Peter Munk! All your magnificence is at an end; and I could have told you how it would turn out when you would not listen to me but ran over to the Little Glass-Man. Now you can see what comes of despising my advice. But try me once; I have pity on your hard fate. Not one who has come to me has regretted it; and if you are not afraid of the road, you can speak to me any time to-morrow in the Tannenbuehl."

Peter knew well who it was that spoke to him, and he shuddered. He made no reply, but walked on to his house.

The story-teller was interrupted just here by a commotion before the inn. A wagon was heard to drive up; several voices called for a light; there was a loud rapping on the yard gate, and the barking of several dogs. The room occupied by the wagoner and the journeymen looked out on the street. The four men sprang up and rushed in there in order to see what had happened. As nearly as they could make out by the gleam of a lantern, a large traveling carriage stood before the inn, and a tall man was assisting two veiled ladies to alight from it, while a coachman in livery was taking out the horses and a servant was unstrapping the trunk. "God be merciful to them!" sighed the wagoner. "If they leave this inn with a whole skin I shall cease to feel uneasy about my cart."

"Keep still!" whispered the student. "I have a suspicion that it is not for us, but for these ladies that the ambush has been laid. Probably the people below had information of the journey these ladies were to take. If we could only contrive to warn them of their danger! Stop a moment. In the whole inn there is but one room that would be fit for a lady, and that one adjoins mine. They will be conducted there. Remain quietly in this room, and I will try to let their servants know the state of affairs."

The young man stole silently to his room and blew out the wax candles, leaving only the light that the landlady had given them. Then he listened at the door.

Presently the landlady came up the stairs with the ladies, and conducted them in a most obsequious manner to their room. She besought her guests to retire soon, as they must be exhausted by their ride, and then went

down-stairs again. Soon afterwards, the student heard
the heavy steps of a man ascending the stairs; he opened
the door cautiously a little ways, and peering through the
crack saw the tall man who had helped the ladies from
the wagon. He wore a hunter's costume, with a hunting
knife in his belt, and was most likely the equerry of the
ladies.

As soon as the student could make sure that this man
was alone, he opened his door quickly and beckoned the
man to come in. The equerry came up to him with a
surprised look, but before he could ask what was wanted,
the student whispered to him: "Sir, you have been led
into a den of thieves to-night."

The man shrank back, but the student drew him inside
of the room and related to him all the suspicious circumstances about the house.

The huntsman was much alarmed as he heard this,
and informed the young man that the ladies, a countess
and her maid, were at first anxious to travel right through
the night; but they were met a short distance from this
inn by a horseman who had hailed them and asked where
they were bound. When he learned that their intention
was to travel through the Spessart all night, he advised
them against doing so, as being very unsafe at the present time. "If you will take the advice of an honest
man," he had added, "you will give up that purpose;
there is an inn not far from here, and poor and incon-
venient as you may find it, it is better for you to pass the
night there than to expose yourself unnecessarily to
danger." The man who thus advised them appeared to
be honest and respectable, and the countess, fearing an
assault from robbers, had given orders to have the carriage stopped at this inn.

The huntsman considered it his duty to inform the
ladies of the danger that threatened them. He went
into their room, and shortly afterwards opened the door
connecting with the student's room. The countess, a
lady some forty years of age, came in to the student, pale

with terror, and had him repeat his suspicions to her. Then they consulted together as to what steps they had better take in this critical situation, finally deciding to summon the two servants, the wagoner and the journeymen, so that in case of an attack they might all make common cause.

The door that opened on the hall in the countess's room was locked and barricaded with tables and chairs. She, with her maid, sat down on the bed, and the two servants kept watch by her, while the huntsman, the student, the journeyman and the wagoner sat around the table in the student's room, and resolved to await their fate.

It was now about ten o'clock; every thing was quiet in the house, and still no signs were made of disturbing the guests, when the compass-maker said: "In order to remain awake it would be best for us to take up our former mode of passing the time. We were telling all kinds of stories; and if you, Mr. Huntsman, have no objections, we might continue." The huntsman not only had no objections, but to show his entire acquiescence he promised to relate something himself, and began at once with the following tale:

SAID'S ADVENTURES.

IN the time of Haroun-al-Raschid, the ruler of Bagdad, there lived in Balsora a man named Benezar. He was possessed of considerable means, and could live quietly and comfortably without resorting to trade. Nor did he change his life of ease when a son was born to him. "Why should I, at my time of life, dicker and trade?" said he to his neighbors, "just to leave Said a thousand more gold pieces if things went well, and if they went badly a thousand less? 'Where two have eaten, a third may feast,' says the proverb; and if he is only a good boy, Said shall want for nothing." Thus spake Benezar, and well did he keep his word, for his son was brought up neither to a trade nor yet to commerce. Still Benezar did not omit reading with him the books of wisdom, and as it was the father's belief that a young man needed, with scholarship and veneration for age, nothing more than a strong arm and courage, he had his son early educated in the use of weapons, and Said soon passed among boys of his own age, and even among those much older, for a valiant fencer, while in horsemanship and swimming he had no superior.

When he was eighteen years old, his father sent him to Mecca, to the grave of the Prophet, to say his prayers and go through his religious exercises on the spot, as required by custom and the commandment Before he departed, his father called him to his side and praised his conduct, gave him good advice, provided him with money, and then said:

"One word more, my son Said. I am a man above sharing in the superstitions of the rabble. I listen with pleasure to the stories of fairies and sorcerers as an agreeable way of passing the time; still I am far from believing, as so many ignorant people do, that these genii, or whatever they may be, exert an influence on the lives and affairs of mortals. But your mother, who has been dead these twelve years, believed as devoutly in them as in the Koran; yes, she even confided to me once, after I had pledged her not to reveal the fact to any one but her child, that she herself from her birth up had had association with a fairy. I laughed at her for entertaining such a notion; and yet I must confess, Said, that certain things happened at your birth that caused me great astonishment. It had rained and thundered the whole day, and the sky was so black that nothing could be seen without a light. But at four o'clock in the afternoon I was told that I was the father of a little boy. I hastened to your mother's room to see and to bless our first-born; but all her maids stood before the door, and in response to my questions, answered that no one would be allowed in the room at present, as Zemira (your mother) had ordered every body out of her chamber because she wished to be alone. I knocked on the door, but all in vain; it remained locked. While I waited somewhat indignantly, before the door, the sky cleared more quickly than I had ever seen it do before, — but the most wonderful thing about it was, that it was only over our loved city of Balsora that the clear blue sky appeared, for the black clouds rolled back, and lightning flashed on the outskirts of this circle. While I was contemplating this spectacle curiously, my wife's door flew open. I ordered the maids to wait outside, and entered the chamber alone to ask your mother why she had locked herself in. As I entered, such a stupefying odor of roses, pinks, and hyacinths greeted me that I almost lost my senses. Your mother held you up to me, at the same time pointing to a little silver whistle that was attached to your neck by a

golden chain as fine as silk. 'The good woman of whom
I once spoke to you has been here,' said your mother,
'and has given your boy this present.' 'And was it the
old witch also who swept away the clouds and left this
fragrance of roses and pinks behind her?' said I with an
incredulous laugh. 'But she might have left him something better than this whistle: say a purse full of
gold, a horse, or something of the kind.' Your mother
besought me not to jest, because the fairies, if angered,
would transform their blessings into maledictions. To
please her, and because she was sick, I said no more;
nor did we speak again of this strange occurrence until
six years afterwards, when, young as she was, she felt that
she was going to die. She gave me then the little whistle,
charging me to give it to you only when you had reached
your twentieth year, and before that hour not to let it go
out of my possession. She died. Here now is the
present," continued Benezar, producing from a little box
a small silver whistle, to which was attached a long gold
chain; "and I give it to you in your eighteenth, instead
of your twentieth year, because you are going away, and
I may be gathered to my fathers before you return home.
I do not see any sensible reason why you should remain
here another two years before setting out, as your anxious mother wished. You are a good and prudent young
man, can wield your weapons as bravely as a man of
four-and-twenty, and therefore I can as well pronounce
you of age to-day as if you were already twenty; and
now go in peace, and think, in fortune and misfortune —
from which last may heaven preserve you — on your
father."

Thus spake Benezar of Balsora, as he dismissed his
son. Said took leave of him with much emotion, hung
the chain about his neck, stuck the whistle in his sash,
swung himself on his horse, and rode to the place where
the caravan for Mecca assembled. In a short time
eighty camels and many hundred horsemen had gathered
there: the caravan started off, and Said rode out of the

gate of Balsora, his native city, that he was destined not to see again for a long time.

The novelty of such a journey, and the many strange objects that obtruded themselves upon his attention, at first diverted his mind; but as the travelers neared the desert and the country became more and more desolate, he began to reflect on many things, and among others, on the words with which his father had taken leave of him. He drew out his whistle, examined it closely, and put it to his mouth to see whether it would give a clear and fine tone; but, lo! it would not sound at all. He puffed out his cheeks, and blew with all his strength; but he could not produce a single note, and vexed at the useless present, he thrust the whistle back into his sash. But his thoughts shortly returned to the mysterious words of his mother. He had heard much about fairies, but he had never learned that this or that neighbor in Balsora had had any relations with a supernatural power; on the contrary, the legends of these spirits had always been located in distant times and places, and therefore he believed there were to-day no such apparitions, or that the fairies had ceased to visit mortals or to take any interest in their fate. But although he thought thus, he was constantly making the attempt to believe in mysterious and supernatural powers, and wondering what might have been their relations with his mother; and so he would sit on his horse like one in a dream nearly the whole day, taking no part in the conversation of the travellers, and deaf to their songs and laughter.

Said was a very handsome youth; his eye was clear and piercing, his mouth wore a pleasing expression, and, young as he was, he bore himself with a certain dignity that one seldom sees in so young a man, and his grace and soldierly appearance in the saddle commanded the attention of many of his fellow-travellers. An old man who rode by his side was much pleased with his manner, and sought by many questions to become more acquainted with him. Said, in whom reverence for old age had

been early inculcated, answered modestly, but wisely
and with circumspection, so that the old man's first im-
pressions of him were strengthened. But as the young
man's thoughts had been occupied the whole day with
but one subject, it followed that the conversation between the two soon turned upon the mysterious realm
of the fairies; and Said finally asked the old man bluntly
whether he believed in the existence of fairies, who took
mortals under their protection, or sought to injure them.

The old man shook his head thoughtfully, and stroked
his beard, before replying: "It can not be disputed that
there have been instances of the kind, although I have
never seen a dwarf of the spirits, a giant of the genii, a
sorcerer, or a fairy." He then began to relate so many
wonderful stories that Said's head was fairly in a whirl,
and he could believe nothing else than that everything
which had happened at his birth — the change in the
weather, the sweet odor of roses and hyacinths — were
the signs that he was under the special protection of a
kind and powerful fairy, and that the whistle was given
him for no less a purpose than to summon the fairy in
case of need. He dreamed all night of castles, winged
horses, genii and the like, and dwelt in a genuine fairy
realm.

But, sad to relate, he was doomed to experience on
the following day how perishable were all his dreams,
sleeping or waking. The caravan had made its way
along in easy stages for the greater part of the day, Said
keeping his place at the side of his elderly companion,
when a dark cloud was seen on the horizon. Some held
it to be a sand-storm, others thought it was clouds, and
still others were of opinion that it was another caravan. But Said's companion, who was an old traveller,
cried out in a loud voice that they should be on their
guard, for this was a horde of Arab robbers approaching.
The men seized their weapons, the women and the goods
were placed in the centre, and everything made ready
against an attack. The dark mass moved slowly over

the plain, resembling an immense flock of storks taking their flight to distant lands. By-and-by, they came on faster, and hardly was the caravan able to distinguish men and lances, when, with the speed of the wind, the robbers swarmed around them.

The men defended themselves bravely, but the robbers, who were over four hundred strong, surrounded them on all sides, killed many from a distance, and then made a charge with their lances. In this fearful moment, Said, who had fought among the foremost, was reminded of his whistle. He drew it forth hastily, put it to his lips, and blew; but let it drop again in disappointment, for it gave out not the slightest sound. Enraged over this cruel disillusion, he took aim at an Arab conspicuous by his splendid costume, and shot him through the breast. The man swayed in his saddle, and fell from his horse.

"Allah! what have you done, young man?" exclaimed the old man at his side. "Now we are all lost!" And thus it seemed, for no sooner did the robbers see this man fall, than they raised a terrible cry, and closed in on the caravan with such resistless force that the few who remained unwounded were soon scattered. In another moment, Said found himself surrounded by five or six of the enemy. He handled his lance so dexterously, however, that not one of them dared approach him very closely; at last one of them bent his bow, took aim, and was just about to let the arrow fly, when another of the robbers stopped him. The young man prepared for some new mode of attack; but before he saw their design, one of the Arabs had thrown a lasso over his head, and, try as he might to remove the rope, his efforts were unavailing — the noose was drawn tighter and tighter, and Said was a prisoner.

The caravan was finally captured, and the Arabs, who did not all belong to one tribe, divided the prisoners and the remaining booty between them, and left the scene of the encounter, part of them riding off to the South and

the remainder to the East. Near Said rode four armed
guards, who often glared at him angrily, uttering savage
oaths. From all this, Said concluded that it must have
been one of their leaders, very likely a prince, whom he
had slain. The prospect of slavery was to him much
worse than that of death; so he secretly thanked his stars
that he had drawn the vengeance of the whole horde on
himself, for he did not doubt that they would kill him
when they reached their camp. The guards watched his
every motion, and if he but turned his head, they
threatened him with their spears; but once, when the
horse of one of his guards stumbled, he turned his head
quickly, and was rejoiced at the sight of his fellow-traveller
whom he had believed was among the dead.

Finally, trees and tents were seen in the distance;
and as they drew nearer, they were met by a crowd of
women and children, who had exchanged but a few words
with the robbers, when they broke out into loud cries,
and all looked at Said, shook their fists, and uttered imprecations on his head. "That is he," shrieked they,
"who has killed the great Almansor, the bravest of men!
he shall die, and we will throw his flesh to the jackals of
the desert for prey." Then they rushed at Said so fero-
ciously, with sticks and whatever missiles they could lay
their hands on, that the robbers had to throw themselves
between the women and the object of their wrath. " Be
off, you scamps! away you women! " cried they, dispers-
ing the rabble with their lances; " he has killed the great
Almansor in battle, and he shall die; not by the hand of
a woman, but by the sword of the brave."

On coming to an open place surrounded by the tents,
they halted. The prisoners were bound together in pairs,
and the booty carried into the tents, while Said was bound
separately and led into a tent larger than the others,
where sat an elderly and finely dressed man, whose proud
bearing denoted him to be the chief of this tribe. The
men who had brought Said in approached the chief with
a sad air and with bowed heads. " The howling of the

women has informed me of what has happened," said their majestic leader, looking from one to the other of his men; "your manner confirms it — Almansor has fallen."

"Almansor has fallen," repeated the men, "but here, Selim, Ruler of the Desert, is his murderer, and we bring him here that you may decide as to the form of death that shall be inflicted on him. Shall we make a target of him for our arrows? shall we force him to run the gauntlet of our lances? or do you decree that he shall be hung or torn asunder by horses?"

"Who are you?" asked Selim, looking darkly at the prisoner, who, although doomed to death, stood before his captors with a courageous air.

Said replied to his question briefly and frankly.

"Did you kill my son by stealth? Did you pierce him from behind with an arrow or a lance?"

"No, Sire!" returned Said. "I killed him in an open fight, face to face, while he was attacking our caravan, because he had killed eight of my companions before my eyes."

"Does he speak the truth?" asked Selim of the men who had captured Said.

"Yes, Sire, he killed Almansor in a fair fight," replied one of the men.

"Then he has done no more and no less than we should have done in his place," returned Selim; "he fought his enemy, who would have robbed him of liberty and life, and killed him; therefore, loose his bonds at once!"

The men looked at him in astonishment, and obeyed his order in a slow and unwilling manner.

"And shall the murderer of your son, the brave Almansor, not die?" asked one of them, casting a look of hate at Said. "Would that we had disposed of him on the spot!"

"He shall not die!" exclaimed Selim. "I will take him into my own tent, as my fair share of the booty, and he shall be my servant."

Said could find no words in which to express his
thanks. The men left the tent grumbling; and when they
communicated Selim's decision to the women and children, who were waiting outside, they were greeted by terrible shrieks and lamentations, and threats were made
that they would avenge Almansor's death on his murderer themselves, because his own father would not take
vengeance.

The other captives were divided among the tribe.
Some were released, in order that they might obtain ransom for the rich merchants; others were sent out as
shepherds with the flocks; and many who had formerly
been waited upon by ten slaves, were doomed to perform
menial services in this camp. Not so with Said, however.
Was it his courageous and heroic manner, or the mysterious influence of a kind fairy, that attached Selim to him
so strongly? It would be hard to say; but Said lived in
the chief's tent more as a son than as servant. Soon,
however, the strange partiality of the old chief drew down
on Said the hatred of the other servants. He met every-
where only savage looks, and if he went alone through
the camp he heard on all sides curses and threats directed
against him, and more than once arrows had flown by
close to his breast — and that they did not hit him he
ascribed to the silver whistle that he wore constantly in
his bosom. He often complained to Selim of these
attempts on his life; but the chief's efforts to discover the
would-be assassin were in vain, for the whole tribe seemed
to be in league against the favored stranger. So Selim
said to him one day: "I had hoped that you might possibly replace the son who fell by your hand. It is not
your fault or mine that this could not be. All feel bitter
hatred toward you, and it is not in my power to protect
you for the future, for how would it benefit either you or
myself to bring the guilty ones to punishment after they
had stealthily killed you? Therefore, when the men return from their present expedition, I will say to them that

your father has sent me a ransom, and I will send you by some trusty men across the desert "

" But could I trust myself with any of these men ? " asked Said in amazement. " Would they not kill me on the way ? "

" The oath that they will take before me will protect you; it has never yet been broken," replied Selim calmly.

Some days after this the men returned to camp, and Selim kept his promise. He presented the young man with weapons, clothes and a horse, summoned all the available men, and chose five of their number to conduct Said across the desert, and bound them by a formidable oath not to kill him, and then took leave of Said with tears.

The five men rode moodily and silently through the desert with Said, who noticed how unwillingly they were fulfilling their commission; and it caused him not a little anxiety to find that two of them were present at the time he killed Almansor. When they were about an eight hours' journey from the camp, Said heard the men whispering among themselves, and remarked that their manner was more and more sullen. He tried to catch what they were saying, and made out that they were conversing in a language understood only by this tribe, and only employed by them in their secret or dangerous undertakings. Selim, whose intention it had been to keep the young man permanently with him in his tent, had devoted many hours to teaching the young man these secret words ; but what he now overheard was not of the most comforting nature.

" This is the spot," said one; " here we attacked the caravan, and here fell the bravest of men by the hand of a boy."

" The wind has covered the tracks of his horse," continued another, " but I have not forgotten them."

"And shall he who laid hands on him still live and be at liberty, and thus cast reproach on us ? When was it ever heard before that a father failed to revenge the death of his only son? But Selim grows old and childish."

"And if the father neglects it," said a fourth, "then it becomes the duty of the fallen man's friends to avenge him. We should cut the murderer down on this spot. Such has been our law and custom for ages."

" But we have bound ourselves by an oath to the chief not to kill this youth," said the fifth man, " and we cannot break our oath."

"It is true," responded the others; "we have sworn, and the murderer is free to pass from the hands of his enemies."

"Stop a moment!" cried one, the most sullen of them all. "Old Selim has a wise head, but is not so shrewd as he is generally credited with being. Did we swear to him that we would take this boy to this or that place? No; our oath simply bound us not to take his life, and we will leave him that; but the blistering sun and the sharp teeth of the jackals will soon accomplish our revenge for us. Here, on this spot, we can bind and leave him."

Thus spake the robber; but Said had now prepared himself for a last desperate chance, and before the final words were fairly spoken he suddenly wheeled his horse to one side, gave him a sharp blow, and flew like a bird across the plain. The five men paused for a moment in surprise; but they were skilled in pursuit, and spread themselves out, chasing him from the right and left, and as they were more experienced in riding on the desert, two of them had soon overtaken the youth, and when he swerved to one side he found two other men there, while the fifth was at his back. The oath they had taken prevented them from using their weapons against him, so they lassoed him once more, pulled him from his horse, beat him unmercifully, bound his hands and feet, and laid him down on the burning sands of the desert.

Said begged piteously for mercy; he promised them a large ransom, but with a laugh they mounted their horses and galloped off. He listened for some moments to the receding steps of their horses, and then gave himself up for lost. He thought of his father and of the old man's sorrow if his son should never more return; he thought on his own misery, doomed to die so young; for nothing was more certain than that he must suffer the torments of suffocation in the hot sands, or that he should be torn to pieces by jackals.

The sun rose ever higher, and its hot rays burnt into his forehead; with considerable difficulty he rolled over, but the change of position gave him but little relief. In

making this exertion, the whistle fell from his bosom. He moved about until he could seize it in his mouth, then he attempted to blow it; but even in this terrible hour of need it refused to respond to his will. In utter despair, he let his head fall back, and before long the sun had robbed him of his senses.

After many hours, Said was awakened by sounds close by him, and immediately after was conscious that his shoulder had been seized. He uttered a cry of terror, for he could believe nothing else than that a jackal had attacked him. Now he was grasped by the legs also, and became sensible that it was not the claws of a beast of

N   9

prey but the hands of a man who was trying to restore his senses, and who was speaking with two or three other men. " He lives," whispered they, " but he believes that we are his foes."

At last Said opened his eyes, and perceived above his own the face of a short, stout man, with small eyes and a long beard, who spoke kindly to him, helped him to get up, handed him food and drink, and while he was partaking of the refreshments told him that he was a merchant from Bagdad, named Kalum-Bek, and dealt in shawls and fine veils for ladies. He had made a business journey, and was now on his way home, and had seen Said lying half-dead in the sand. The splendor of the youth's costume, and the sparkling stone in his dagger had attracted his attention; he had done all in his power to revive him, and his efforts had finally succeeded. The youth thanked him for his life, for he saw clearly that without the interposition of this man he would have perished miserably ; and as he had neither the means of getting away, nor the desire to wander over the desert on foot and alone, he gratefully accepted the offer of a seat on one of the merchant's heavily-laden camels, and decided to go to Bagdad with the merchant, with the chance of finding there a company bound for Balsora, which he could join.

On the journey, the merchant related to his travelling companion a great many stories about the excellent Ruler of the Faithful, Haroun-al-Raschid. He told anecdotes showing the caliph's love of justice and his shrewdness, and how he was able to smooth out the knottiest questions of law in a simple and admirable way ; and among others he related the story of the ropemaker, and the story of the jar of olives,—tales that every child now knows, but which astonished Said.

"Our master, the Ruler of the Faithful," continued the merchant, "is a wonderful man. If you have an idea that he sleeps like the common people, you are very much mistaken. Two or three hours at day-break is all the sleep he takes. I am positive of that, for Messour, his head chamberlain, is my cousin; and although he is as silent as the grave concerning the secrets of his master, he will now and then let a hint drop, for kinship's sake, if he sees that one is nearly out of his senses with curiosity. Instead, then, of sleeping like other people, the caliph steals through the streets of Bagdad at night; and seldom does a week pass that he does not chance upon an adventure; for you must know — as is made clear by the story of the jar of olives, which is as true as the word of the Prophet,— that he does not make his rounds with the watch, or on horseback in full costume, his way lighted by a hundred torch-bearers, as he might very well do if he chose, but he goes about disguised sometimes as a merchant, sometimes as a mariner, at other times as a soldier, and again as a mufti, and looks around to see if every thing is right and in order. And therefore it happens that in no other town is one so polite towards every fool upon whom he stumbles on the street at night, as in Bagdad; for it would be as likely to turn out the caliph as a dirty Arab from the desert, and there is wood enough growing round to give every person in and around Bagdad the bastinado."

Thus spake the merchant; and Said, strong as was his desire to see his father once more, rejoiced at the prospect of seeing Bagdad and its famous ruler, Haroun-al-Raschid.

After a ten-days' journey, they arrived at their destination; and Said was astonished at the magnificence of this city, then at the height of its splendor. The merchant invited him to go with him to his house, and Said gladly accepted the invitation; as it now occurred to him for the first time, among the crowd of people, that with the exception of the air, the water of the Tigris, and a lodging on the steps of the mosque, nothing could be had without money.

The day after his arrival in Bagdad, as soon as he had dressed himself — thinking that he need not be ashamed to show himself on the streets of Bagdad in his splendid soldierly costume — the merchant entered his room, looked at the handsome youth with a knavish smile, stroked his beard and said: "That's all very fine, young man! but what shall be done with you? You are, it appears to me, a great dreamer, taking no thought for the morrow; or have you money enough with you to support such style as that?"

"Dear Kalum-Bek," replied the young man, greatly disconcerted, "I certainly have no money, but perhaps you will furnish me with the means to reach home; my father would surely repay you."

"Your father, fellow?" cried the merchant, with a loud laugh. "I think the sun must have scorched your brain. Do you think I would take your simple word for that yarn you spun me in the desert — that your father was a rich citizen of Balsora, you his only son? — and about the attack of the robbers, and your life with the tribe, and this, that, and the other? Even then I felt very angry at your frivolous lies and utter impudence. I know that all the rich people in Balsora are traders; I have had dealings with all of them, and should have heard of a Benezar, even if he had not been worth more than six thousand Tomans. It is, therefore, either a lie that you hail from Balsora, or else your father is a poor wretch, to whose runaway son I would not lend a copper. Then, too, the attack in the desert! Who ever heard, since the wise Caliph Haroun has made the trade routes across the desert safe, that robbers dared to plunder a caravan and lead the men off into captivity? And then, too, it would have been known; but on my entire journey, as well as here in Bagdad, where people gather from all parts of the world, there has not been a word said about it. That is the second lie, you shameless young fellow!"

Pale with anger, Said tried to interrupt the wicked little man, but the merchant talked still louder, and gesticulated wildly with his arms. "And the third lie, you audacious liar, is the story of your life in Selim's camp.

Selim's name is well known by every body who has ever
seen an Arab, but Selim has the reputation of being the
most cruel and relentless robber on the desert, and you
pretend to say that you killed his son and was not at
once hacked to pieces; yes, you even pushed your impudence so far as to state the impossible, — that Selim had
protected you against his own tribe, had taken you into
his own tent, and let you go without a ransom, instead
of hanging you up to the first good tree; he who has
often hanged travellers just to see what kind of faces they
would make when they were hung up. O you detestable
liar!"

"And I can only repeat," cried the youth, "that by
my soul and the beard of the Prophet, it was all true!"

"What! you swear by your soul?" shouted the merchant, "by your black, lying soul? Who would believe
that? And by the beard of the Prophet,— you that have
no beard? Who would put any trust in that?"

"I certainly have no witnesses," continued Said;
"but did you not find me bound and perishing?"

"That proves nothing to me," replied the merchant.
"You were yourself dressed like a robber, and it might
easily have happened that you attacked some one stronger
than yourself, who conquered and bound you."

"I should like to see any one, or even two," returned
Said, "who could floor and bind me, unless they came up
behind me and flung a noose over my head. Staying in
your bazar as you do, you cannot have any notion of
what a single man is able to do when he has been brought
up to arms. But you saved my life, and my thanks are
due you. What would you have me do? If you do not
support me I must beg; and I should not care to ask a
favor of any one of my station. I will go to see the
caliph."

"Indeed!" sneered the merchant," you will ask assistance of no one but our most gracious master? I should
call that genteel begging! But look you, my fine young
gentleman! access to the caliph can be had only through

my cousin Messour, and a word from me would acquaint him with your capacity for lying. But I will take pity on your youth, Said. You shall have a chance to better yourself, and something may be made out of you yet. I will take you into my shop at the bazar; you can serve me there for a year; and when that time is past, if you don't choose to remain with me any longer, I will pay you your wages and let you go where you will, to Aleppo or Medina, to Stamboul or Balsora, or, for aught I care, to the Infidels. I will give you till noon to decide; if you agree to my proposal, well and good; if you do not, I will make out an estimate of the expense you put me to on the journey, and for your seat on the camel, pay myself by taking your clothes and all you possess, and then throw you into the street; then you can beg where you like, of the caliph or the mufti, at the mosque or in the bazar."

With these words the wicked man left the unfortunate youth. Said looked after him with loathing. He rebelled against the wickedness of this man, who had designedly taken him to his house so that he might have him in his power. He looked about to see if he could escape, but found the windows grated and the door locked. Finally, after his spirit had long revolted at the idea, he decided to accept the merchant's proposal for the present. He saw clearly that nothing better remained for him to do; for even if he were to run away, he could not reach Balsora without money. But he made up his mind to seek the caliph's protection as soon as possible.

On the following day, Kalum-Bek led his new servant to his shop in the bazar. He showed Said the shawls, veils, and other wares in which he dealt, and instructed the youth in his strange duties. These required that Said, stripped of his soldierly costume and clad like a merchant's servant, should stand in the doorway of the shop, with a shawl in one hand and a splendid veil in the other, and cry out his wares to the passers-by, name the price, and invite the people to buy. And now, too it became evident to Said why Kalum-Bek had selected him for this business. The merchant was a short, ugly-looking man, and when he himself stood at the door and cried his wares, many of the neighbors, as well as the passers-by, would make fun of his appearance, or the boys would tease him, while the women called him a scarecrow; but everybody was pleased with the appearance of young Said, who attracted customers by his graceful deportment and by his clever and tasteful way of exhibiting his shawls and veils.

When Kalum-Bek saw that customers thronged to his shop since Said had taken his stand at the door, he became more friendly with the young man, gave him better things to eat than before, and was careful to keep him finely dressed. But Said was little touched by this display of mildness in his master; and the whole day long, and even in his dreams, tried to hit upon some means of returning to his native city.

One day when the sales had been very large, and all the errand boys who delivered parcels at the houses were out on their rounds, a woman entered and made several purchases. She then wanted some one to carry her packages home. "I can send them all up to you in half an hour," said Kalum-Bek; "you will either have to wait that long or else take some outside porter."

"Do you pretend to be a merchant and advise your customers to employ strange porters?" exclaimed the woman. "Might not such a fellow run off with my parcels in the crowd? And then whom should I look to? No, you are bound by the practice of the bazar to send my bundles home for me, and I insist on your doing it!"

"But wait for just half an hour, worthy lady!" exclaimed the merchant excitedly. "All my errand boys have been sent out."

"It's a poor shop that don't have errand boys constantly at hand," interrupted the angry woman. "But there stands one of your good-for-nothings now! Come, young fellow, take my parcel and follow after me."

"Stop! Stop!" cried Kalum-Bek. "He is my sign-board, my crier, my magnet! He cannot stir from the threshold!"

"What's that!" exclaimed the old lady, thrusting her bundle under Said's arm without further parley. "It is a poor merchant that depends on such a useless clown for a sign, and those are miserable wares that cannot speak for themselves. Go, go, fellow; you shall earn a fee to-day."

"Go then, in the name of Ariman and all evil spirits!" muttered Kalum-Bek to his magnet, "and see that you come right back; the old hag might give me a bad name all over the bazar if I refuse to comply with her demands."

Said followed the woman, who hastened through the square and down the streets at a much quicker pace than one would have believed a woman of her age capable of. At last she stopped before a splendid house, and knocked; the folding doors flew open, and she ascended a marble stair-case, beckoning Said to follow. They came shortly to a high and wide salon, more magnificent than any Said had ever seen before. The old woman sank down exhausted on a cushion, motioned the young man to lay down his bundle, handed him a small silver coin, and bade him go.

He had just reached the door, when a clear, musical voice called: "Said!" Surprised that any one there should know him, he looked around and saw, in place of the old woman, an elegant lady sitting on the cushion, surrounded by numerous slaves and maids. Said, mute with astonishment, crossed his arms and made a low obeisance

"Said, my dear boy," said the lady, "much as I deplore the misfortune that is the cause of your presence in Bagdad, yet this was the only place decided on by destiny where you might be released from the fate that would surely follow you if you left the homestead before your twentieth year. Said, have you still your whistle?"

"Indeed I have," cried he joyfully, drawing out the golden chain, "and you perhaps are the kind fairy who gave me this token at my birth?"

"I was the friend of your mother, and will be your friend also as long as you remain good. Alas! would that your father — unthinking man — had followed my counsel! You would then have been spared many sorrows."

"Well, it had to come to pass!" replied Said. "But, most gracious fairy, harness a strong northeast wind to your carriage of clouds, and take me up with you, and drive me in a few minutes to my father in Balsora; I will wait there patiently until the six months are passed that close my nineteenth year."

The fairy smiled. "You have a very proper mode of addressing us," answered she; "but, poor Said! it is not possible. I cannot do anything wonderful for you at present, because you left your homestead. Nor can I even free you from the power of the wretch, Kalum-Bek. He is under the protection of your worst enemy."

"Then I have not only a kind female friend but a female enemy as well?" said Said. "I believe I have often experienced her influence. But at least you might assist me with your counsel. Had I not better go to the caliph and seek his protection? He is a wise man, and would protect me from Kalum-Bek."

"Yes, Haroun is a wise man," replied the fairy; "but, sad to say, he is also only a mortal. He trusts his head chamberlain, Messour, as much as he does himself; and he is right in that, for he has tried Messour and found him true. But Messour trusts his friend Kalum-Bek as he does himself; and in that he is wrong, for Kalum is a bad man, even if he is a relative of Messour's. Kalum has a cunning head, and as soon as he had returned from his trip he made up a very pretty fable about you, which he confided to his cousin the chamberlain, who in turn told it to the caliph, so that you would not be very well received were you to go to the palace. But there are other ways and means of approaching him, and it is written on the stars that you shall experience his mercy."

"That is really too bad," said Said, mournfully. "I must then serve for a long time yet as the servant of that scoundrel Kalum-Bek. But there is one favor, honored fairy, that is in your power to grant me. I have been educated to the use of arms, and my greatest delight is a tournament where there are some sharp contests with the lance, bow and blunt swords. Well, every week just such a tournament takes place in this city between the young men. But only people of the finest costume, and besides that only *free* men will be allowed to enter the lists, and clerks in the bazar are particularly excluded. Now if you could arrange that I could have a horse, clothes and weapons every week, and that my face would not be easily recognizable ——"

"That is a wish befitting a noble young man," interrupted the fairy. "Your mother's father was the bravest man in Syria, and you seem to have inherited his spirit. Take notice of this house; you shall find here every week a horse, and two mounted attendants, weapons and clothes, and a lotion for your face that will completely disguise you. And now, Said, farewell! Be patient, wise and virtuous. In six months your whistle will sound, and Zulima's ear will be listening for its tone."

The youth separated from his strange protectress with expressions of gratitude and esteem. He fixed the house and street clearly in his mind, and then went back to the bazar, which he reached just in the nick of time to save his master from a terrible beating. A great crowd was gathered before the shop, boys danced about the merchant and jeered at him, while their elders laughed. He stood just before the shop, trembling with suppressed rage, and sadly harassed — in one hand a shawl, in the other a veil. This singular scene was caused by a circumstance that had occurred during Said's absence. Kalum had taken the place of his handsome clerk at the door, but no one cared to buy of the ugly old man. Just

then two men came to the bazar wishing to buy presents
for their wives. They had gone up and down the bazar
several times, looking in here and there, and Kalum-
Bek, who had observed their actions for some time,
thought he saw his chance, so he called out: "Here,
gentlemen, here! What are you looking for? Beautiful
veils, beautiful wares?"

"Good sir," replied one of them, "your wares may do
very well, but our wives are peculiar, and it has become

the fashion in this city to buy veils only of the handsome
clerk, Said. We have been looking for him this half-
hour, but cannot find him; now if you can tell us where
we will meet him, we will buy from you some other time."

"Allah il Allah!" cried Kalum-Bek with a smirk.
"The Prophet has led you to the right door. You wish
to buy veils of the handsome Said? Good, just step inside;
this is his place."

One of the men laughed at Kalum's short and ugly
figure, and his assertion that he was the handsome clerk;

but the other, believing that Kalum was trying to make
sport of him, did not remain long in his debt, but paid
the merchant back in his own coin. Kalum-Bek was
beside himself; he called his neighbors to witness that
his was the only shop in the bazar that went by the name
of "the shop of the handsome clerk;" but the neighbors,
who envied him the run of custom he had enjoyed for
some time, pretended not to know anything about the
matter, and the two men then made an attack upon the
old liar, as they called him. Kalum defended himself
more with shrieks and curses than by the use of his fists,
and thus attracted a large crowd before his shop. Half
the city knew him to be a mean, avaricious old miser,
nor did the bystanders grudge him the cuffs he received;
and one of his assailants had just plucked the old man
by the beard, when his arm was seized, and with a sudden jerk he was thrown to the ground with such violence
that his turban fell off and his slippers flew to some distance.

The crowd, which very likely would have been rejoiced
to see Kalum-Bek well punished, grumbled loudly. The
fallen man's companion looked around to see who it was
that had ventured to throw his friend down; but when
he saw a tall, strong youth, with flashing eyes and courageous mien, standing before him, he did not think it
best to attack him, especially as Kalum regarding his
rescue as a miracle, pointed to the young man and
cried: "Now then! what would you have more? There he
stands beyond a doubt, gentlemen; that is Said, the
handsome clerk." The people standing about laughed,
while the prostrate man got up shamefacedly, and limped
off with his companion without buying either shawl or
veil.

"O you star of all clerks, you crown of the bazar!"
cried Kalum, leading his clerk into the shop; "really,
that is what I call being on hand at the right time, and
the right kind of interference too. Why, the fellow was
laid out as flat on the ground as if he had never stood on

his legs, and I — I should have had no use for a barber again to comb and oil my beard, if you had arrived two minutes later! How can I reward you ?"

It had been only a momentary sensation of pity which had governed Said's hand and heart; but now that that feeling had passed, he regreted that he had saved this wicked man from a good chastisement. A dozen hairs from his beard, thought Said, would have kept him humble for twelve days. And now the young man thought best to make use of the favorable disposition of the merchant, and therefore asked to be given one evening in each week for a walk or for any other purpose he pleased. Kalum consented, knowing full well that his clerk was too sensible to run off without money or clothes.

On the following Wednesday, the day on which the young men of the best families assembled in the public square in the city to go through their martial exercises, Said asked Kalum if he would let him have this evening for his own use; and on receiving the merchant's permission, he went to the fairy's house, knocked, and the door was immediately opened The servants seemed to have prepared everything before his arrival; for without questioning him as to his desire, they led him upstairs to a beautiful room, and there handed him the lotion that was to disguise his features. He moistened his face with it, and then glanced into a metallic mirror; he hardly recognized himself, for he was now sunburnt, wore a hadsome black beard, and looked to be at least ten years older than he really was.

He was now conducted into a second room, where he found a complete and splendid costume, of which the Caliph of Bagdad need not have been ashamed, on the day when he reviewed his army in all his magnificence. Together with a turban of the finest texture, with a clasp of diamonds and a long heron's plume, Said found a coat of mail made of silver rings, so finely worked that it conformed to every movement of his body, and yet was so firm that neither lance nor sword could find a way through

it. A Damascus blade in a richly ornamented sheath,
and with a handle whose stones seemed to Said to be of
priceless value, completed his warlike appearance. As
he came to the door, armed at all points, one of the servants handed him a silk cloth and told him that the mistress of the house sent it to him, and that when he wiped
his face with it, the beard and the complexion would disappear.

In the court-yard stood three beautiful horses; Said
mounted the finest, and his attendants the other two, and
rode off with a light heart to the square where the contest was to be held. The splendor of his costume and
the brightness of his weapons drew all eyes upon him,
and a general buzz of astonishment followed his entrance
into the ring. It was a brilliant assemblage of the
bravest and noblest youths of Bagdad, where even the
brothers of the caliph were seen flying about on their
horses and swinging their lances. On Said's approach,
as no one seemed to know him, the son of the grand
vizier, with some of his friends, rode up to him, greeted
him politely, and invited him to take part in their contests, at the same time inquiring his name and whence
he came. Said represented to them that his name was
Almansor, and he hailed from Cairo; that he had set out
upon a journey, but having heard so much said about the
skill and bravery of the young noblemen of Bagdad, he
could not refrain from delaying his journey in order to
get acquainted with them. The young men were highly
pleased with the bearing and courageous appearance of
Said-Almansor; handed him a lance, and had him
select his opponent,— as the whole company were divided
into two parties, in order that they might assault one
another both singly and in groups.

But the attention which had been attracted by Said
was now concentrated upon the unusual skill and dex-
terity which he displayed in combat. His horse was
swifter than a bird, while his sword whizzed about in still
more rapid circles. He threw the lance at its mark as

easily and with as much accuracy as if it had been an
arrow shot from a bow.   He conquered the bravest of
the opposing force, and at the end of the tournament

was so universally recognized as the victor, that one of
the caliph's brothers and the son of the grand vizier,
who had both fought on Said's side, requested the pleasure of breaking a lance with him. Ali, the caliph's
brother, was soon conquered by Said ; but the grand

vizier's son withstood him so bravely that after a long contest they thought it best to postpone the decision until the next meeting.

The day after the tournament, nothing was spoken of in Bagdad but the handsome, rich, and brave stranger. All who had seen him, even those over whom he had triumphed, were charmed by his well-bred manners. He even heard his own praises sounded in the shop of Kalum-Bek, and it was only deplored that no one knew where he lived.

The next week, Said found at the house of the fairy a still finer costume and still more costly weapons. Half Bagdad had rushed to the square, while even the caliph looked on from a balcony; he, too, admired Almansor, and at the conclusion of the tournament he hung a large gold medal, attached to a gold chain, about the youth's neck, as a mark of his favor.

It could not very well be otherwise than that this second and still more brilliant triumph of Said's should excite the envy of the young men of Bagdad. "Shall a stranger," said they to one another, "come here to Bagdad, and carry off all the laurels? He will now boast in other places that among the flower of Bagdad's youth there was not one who was a match for him." They therefore resolved, at the next tournament, to fall upon him, as if by chance, five or six at a time.

These tokens of discontent did not escape Said's sharp eye. He noticed how the young men congregated at the street corners, whispered to one another, and pointed angrily at him. He suspected that none of them felt very friendly toward him, with the exception of the caliph's brother and the grand vizier's son, and even they rather annoyed him by their questions as to where they might call on him, how he occupied his time, what he found of interest in Bagdad, etc., etc. It was a singular coincidence that one of these young men, who surveyed Said-Almansor with the bitterest looks, was no other than the man whom Said had thrown down when the assault was made on Kalum-Bek a few weeks before, just as the man was about to tear out the unfortunate merchant's beard. This man looked at Said very attentively and spitefully. Said had conquered him several times in the tournament; but this would not account for such hostile looks, and Said began to fear lest his figure or his voice had betrayed him to this man as the clerk of Kalum-Bek — a discovery that would expose him to the sneers and anger of the people.

The project which Said's foes attempted to carry out at the next tournament failed, not only by reason of Said's caution and bravery, but by the assistance he received from the caliph's brother and the grand vizier's son. When these two young men saw that Said was surrounded by five or six who sought to disarm or unseat him, they dashed up, chased away the conspirators, and threatened the men who had acted so treacherously with dismissal from the course.

For more than four months, Said had excited the astonishment of Bagdad by his prowess, when one evening, on returning home from the tournament, he heard some voices which seemed familiar to him. Before him walked four men at a slow pace, apparently discussing some subject together. As Said approached nearer, he discovered that they were talking in the dialect which the men in Selim's tribe had used in the desert, and suspected that they were planning some robbery. His first thought was to draw back from these men; but when he reflected that he might be the means of preventing some great wrong, he stole up still nearer to listen to what they were saying.

"The gate keeper expressly said it was the street to the right of the bazar," said one of the men; "he will certainly pass through it to-night, in company with the grand vizier."

"Good!" added another. "I am not afraid of the grand vizier; he is old, and not much of a hero; but the caliph wields a good sword, and I wouldn't trust

o   9*

him; there would be ten or twelve of the body-guard stealing after him."

".Not a soul!" responded a third. "Whenever he has been seen and recognized at night, he was always unattended except by the vizier or the head chamberlain. He will be ours to-night; but no harm must be done him."

"I think," said the first speaker, "that the best plan would be to throw a noose over his head; we may not kill him, for it would be but a small ransom that they would pay for his body, and, more than that, we shouldn't be sure of receiving it."

"An hour before midnight, then!" exclaimed they, and separated, one going this way, another that.

Said was not a little horrified at this scheme. He resolved to hasten at once to the caliph's palace and warn him of the threatened danger. But after running through several streets, he remembered the caution that the fairy had given him — that the caliph had received a bad report about him. He reflected that his warning might be laughed at, or regarded as an attempt on his part to ingratiate himself with the Caliph of Bagdad; and so he concluded that it would be best to depend on his good sword, and rescue the caliph from the hands of the robbers himself.

So he did not return to Kalum-Bek's house, but sat down on the steps of a mosque and waited there until night had set in. Then he went through the bazar and into the street mentioned by the robbers, and hid himself behind a projection of one of the houses. He might have stood there an hour, when he heard two men coming slowly down the street. At first he thought it must be the caliph and his grand vizier; but one of the men clapped his hands, and immediately two other men hurried very noiselessly up the street from the bazar. They whispered together for a while, and then separated; three hiding not far from Said, while the fourth paced up and down the street. The night was very dark, but still, so that Said had to depend almost entirely upon his acute sense of hearing.

Another half-hour had passed, when footsteps were heard coming from the bazar. The robber must have heard them too, for he stole by Said towards the bazar. The steps came nearer, and Said was just able to make out some dark figures, when the robber clapped his hands, and, in the same moment, the three men waiting in ambush rushed out. The persons attacked must have been armed, for Said heard the ring of clashing swords. At once he drew his own Damascus blade, and sprang upon the robber's with the cry: "Down with the enemies of the great Haroun!" He struck one of them to the ground with the first blow, and turned upon two others, who were just in the act of disarming a man over whom they had thrown a rope. Said lifted the rope blindly in order to cut it, but in the effort to use his sword he struck one of the robber's arms such a blow, as to cut off his hand, and the robber fell to his knees with cries of pain. The fourth robber, who had been fighting with another man, now came towards Said, who was still engaged with the third, but the man who had been lassoed no sooner found himself free than he drew his dagger, and, from one side, plunged it into the breast of the advancing robber. When the remaining robber saw this, he threw away his sword and fled.

Said did not remain long in doubt as to whom he had saved, for the taller of the two men said: "The one thing is as strange as the other; this attack upon my life or liberty, as the incomprehensible assistance and rescue. How did you know who I was? Did you know of the scheme of these robbers?"

"Ruler of the Faithful," answered Said, "for I do not doubt that you are he, I walked down the street El Malek this evening behind some men, whose strange and mysterious dialect I had once learned. They spoke of taking you prisoner and of killing your vizier. As it was too late to warn you, I resolved to go to the place where they would lie in ambush for you, and give you my assistance."

"Thank you," said Haroun; "but it is not best to remain long in this place; take this ring, and come in the morning to my palace; we will then talk over this affair, and see how I can best reward you. Come, vizier, it is best not to stop here; they might come back again."

Thus saying, he placed a ring on Said's finger, and attempted to lead off the grand vizier, but the latter, begging him to wait a moment, turned and held out to the astonished Said a heavy purse: "Young man," said he, "my master, the caliph, can do anything for you that he feels inclined to do, even to making you my successor; but I myself can do but little, and that little had better be done to-day, rather than to-morrow. Therefore, take this purse. That does not, however, cancel my debt of gratitude; so whenever you have a wish, come in confidence to me."

Overpowered with his good fortune, Said hurried home. But here he was not so well received. Kalum-Bek was at first angry at his long absence, and then anxious, for the merchant thought he might easily lose the handsome sign of his shop. Kalum therefore received him with abusive words, and raved like a madman. But Said — who had taken a look into his purse and found it filled with gold pieces, and reflected that he could now travel home, even without the caliph's favor, which was certainly not worth less than the gratitude of his vizier — declared roundly that he would not remain in his service another hour. At first Kalum was very much frightened by this declaration; but shortly he laughed sneeringly and said:

"You loafer and vagabond! You miserable creature! Where would you run to, if I were to give up supporting you? Where would you get a dinner or a lodging?"

"You need not trouble yourself about that, Mr. Kalum-Bek," answered Said audaciously. "Farewell; you will never see me again!"

With these words, Said left the house. while Kalum-

Bek looked after him speechless with astonishment. The following morning, however, after thinking over the matter well, he sent out his errand boys, and had the runaway sought for every-where. For a long time their search was a vain one; but finally one of the boys came back and reported that he had seen Said come out of a mosque and go into a caravansary. He was, however, much changed, wore a beautiful costume, a dagger sword, and splendid turban.

When Kalum-Bek heard this, he shouted with an oath: "He has stolen from me, and bought clothes with the money. Oh, I am a ruined man!" Then he ran to the chief of police, and as he was known to be a relative of Messour, the head chamberlain, he had no difficulty in having two policemen sent out to arrest Said. Said sat before a caravansary, conversing quietly with a merchant whom he had found there, about a journey to Balsora, his native city, when suddenly he was seized by some men, and his hands tied behind his back before he could offer any resistance. He asked them whose authority they were acting under, and they replied that they were obeying the orders of the chief of police, on complaint of his rightful master, Kalum-Bek. The ugly little merchant then came up, abused and jeered at Said, felt in the young man's pocket, and to the astonishment of the bystanders, and with a shout of triumph, drew out a large purse filled with gold.

"Look! He has robbed me of all that, the wicked fellow!" cried he, and the people looked with abhorrence at the prisoner, saying: "What! so young, so handsome, and yet so wicked! To the court, to the court, that he may get the bastinado!" Thus they dragged him away, while a large procession of people of all ranks followed in their wake, shouting: "See, that is the handsome clerk of the bazar; he stole from his master and ran away; he took two hundred gold pieces!"

The chief of police received the prisoner with a dark look. Said tried to speak, but the official told him to be

still, and listened only to the little merchant. He held
up the purse, and asked Kalum whether this gold had
been stolen from him. Kalum-Bek swore that it had;
but his perjury, while it gained him the gold, did not help
to restore to him his clerk, who was worth a thousand
gold pieces to him, for the judge said : "In accordance
with a law that my all-powerful master, the caliph, has
recently made, every theft of over a hundred gold pieces
that transpires in the bazar, is punished with banishment
for life to a desert island. This thief comes at just the
right time; he makes the twentieth of his class, and so
completes the lot; to-morrow they will be put on a vessel
and taken out to sea."

Said was in despair. He besought the officers to listen
to him, to let him speak only one word with the caliph;
but he found no mercy. Kalum-Bek, who now repented
of his oath, also pleaded for him, but the judge said:
"You have your gold back, and should be contented; go
home and keep quiet, or I will fine you ten gold pieces
for every contradiction." Kalum quieted down; the
judge made a sign, and the unfortunate Said was led
away.

He was taken to a dark and damp dungeon, where
nineteen poor wretches, scattered about on straw, received him as their companion in misfortune, with wild
laughter and curses on the judge and caliph. Terrible as
was the fate before him, fearful as was the thought of
being banished to a desert island, he still found consolation in the thought that the morrow would take him out
of this horrible prison. But he was very greatly in error
in supposing that his situation would be bettered on the
ship. The twenty men were thrown into the hold, where
they could not stand upright, and there they fought among
themselves for the best places.

The anchor was weighed, and Said wept bitter tears
as the ship that was to bear him far away from his fatherland began to move They received bread and fruits,
and a drink of sweetened water, but once a day : and it

was so dark in the ship's hold, that lights always had to be brought down when the prisoners were to be fed. Every two or three days one of their number was found dead, so unwholesome was the air in this floating prison, and Said's life was preserved only by his youth and his splendid health.

They had been on the sea for fourteen days, when one day the waves roared more violently than ever, and there was much running to and fro on the deck. Said suspected that a storm was at hand, and he welcomed the prospect of one, hoping that then he might be released by death.

The ship began to pitch about, and finally struck on a ledge with a terrible crash. Cries and groans were heard on the deck, intermingled with the roar of the storm. At last all was still again; but at the same time one of the prisoners discovered that the water was pouring into the ship. They pounded on the hatch-door, but could get no answer; and as the water poured in more and more rapidly, they united their strength and managed to break the hatch open.

They ascended the steps, but found not a soul on board. The whole crew had taken to the boats. Most of the prisoners were in despair, for the storm increased in fury, the ship cracked and settled down on the ledge. For some hours they sat on the deck and partook of their last repast from the provisions they found in the ship, then the storm began to rage again, the ship was torn from the ledge on which it had been held, and broken up.

Said had climbed the mast, and held fast to it when the ship went to pieces. The waves tossed him about, but he kept his head up by paddling with his feet. Thus he floated about, in ever-increasing danger, for half an hour, when the chain with whistle attached once again fell out of his bosom, and once more he tried to make it sound. With one hand he held fast to the mast, and with the other put the whistle to his lips, blew, and a clear musical tone was the result. Instantly the storm

ceased, and the waves became as smooth as if oil had
been poured on them. He had hardly looked about him,
with an easier breath, to see whether he could discern
land, when the mast beneath him began to expand in a
very singular manner, and to move as well; and, not a
little to his terror, he perceived that he was no longer
riding on a wooden mast, but upon the back of an enormous dolphin. But after a few moments his courage returned; and as he saw that the dolphin swam along on
his course quietly and easily, although swiftly, he ascribed
his wonderful rescue to the silver whistle and to the kind
fairy, and shouted his most earnest thanks into the air.

His wonderful horse carried him through the waves
with the speed of an arrow; and before night he saw land,
and also a broad river, into which the dolphin turned. Up
stream it went more slowly, and, that he might not starve,
Said, who remembered from old stories of enchantment
how one should work a charm, took out the whistle again,
blew it loudly and heartily, and wished that he had a good
meal. The dolphin stopped instantly, and out of the
water rose a table, as little wet as if it had stood in the
sun for eight days, and richly furnished with the finest
dishes. Said attacked the food like a famished person,
for his rations during his imprisonment were scant and of
miserable quality; and when he had eaten to his fill, he
expressed his thanks; the table sank down again, while

he jogged the dolphin in the side, and the fish at once responded by continuing on its course up stream.

The sun was setting when Said perceived in the dim distance a large city, whose minarets seemed to bear a resemblance to those of Bagdad. This discovery was not a pleasant one; but his confidence in the kind fairy was so great that he felt sure she would not permit him to fall again into the clutches of the unscrupulous Kalum-Bek. To one side, about three miles distant from the city, and close to the river, he noticed a magnificent country house, and, to his astonishment, the fish seemed to be making directly towards this house.

Upon the roof of the house stood a group of handsomely dressed men, and on the bank of the river Said saw a large crowd of servants, who were looking at him in wonder. The dolphin stopped at some marble steps that led up to the house, and hardly had Said put foot on the steps when the dolphin disappeared. A number of servants now ran down the steps, and requested him in the name of their master to come up to the house, at the same time offering him a suit of dry clothes. Said dressed himself quickly, and followed the servants to the roof, where he found three men, of whom the tallest and handsomest came forward to meet him in a pleasant manner.

"Who are you, wonderful stranger," said he, "you who tame the fishes of the sea, and guide them to the right and left, as the best horseman governs his steed? Are you a sorcerer, or a being like us?"

"Sir," replied Said, "things have gone very badly with me for the last few weeks; but if it will please you to hear me, I will relate my story."

Then he told the three men all of his adventures, from the moment of leaving his father's house up to his wonderful rescue from the sea. He was often interrupted by their expressions of astonishment; and when he had ended, the master of the house, who had received him in so kind a manner, said: "I trust your words, Said; but

10

you tell us that you won a medal in the tournament, and
that the caliph gave you a ring; can you show them to
us?"

"I have preserved them both upon my heart," said the
youth, "and would sooner have parted with my life than
with these precious gifts, for I esteem it my most valiant
and meritorious deed that I freed the caliph from the
hands of his would-be murderers." So saying, he drew
from his bosom the medal and ring, and handed them to
the men.

"By the beard of the Prophet! It is he! It is *my*
ring!" cried the tall, handsome man. "Grand vizier,
let us embrace him, for here stands our savior." To
Said it was like a dream. The two men embraced him,
and Said, prostrating himself, said:

"Pardon me, Ruler of the Faithful, that I have spoken
so freely before you, for you can be no other than Haroun-
al-Raschid, the great Caliph of Bagdad."

"I am he, and your friend," replied Haroun; "and
from this hour forth, all your sad misfortunes are at an
end. Follow me to Bagdad, remain in my dominion, and
become one of my most trustworthy officers; for you
have shown you were not indifferent to Haroun's fate,
though I should not like to put all of my faithful servants
to such a severe test."

Said thanked the caliph, and promised to remain with
him, — first requesting permission to make a visit to his
father, who must be suffering much anxiety on his account;
and the caliph thought this just and commendable.
They then mounted horses, and were soon in Bagdad.
The caliph showed Said a long suite of splendidly decorated rooms that he should have, and, more than that,
promised to build a house for his own use.

At the first information of this event, the old brothers-
in-arms of Said's — the grand vizier's son and the caliph's brother — hastened to the palace and embraced
Said as the deliverer of their noble caliph, and begged
him to become their friend. But they were speechless

with astonishment when Said, drawing forth the prize medal, said: "I have been your friend for a long time." They had only seen him with his false beard and dark skin; and when he had related how and why he had disguised himself — when he had the blunt weapons brought to prove his story, fought with them, and thus gave them the best proof that he was the brave Almansor — then did they embrace him with joyful exclamations, considering themselves fortunate in having such a friend.

The following day, as Said was sitting with the caliph and grand vizier, Messour, the chamberlain, came in and said: "Ruler of the Faithful, if there is no objection, I would like to ask a favor of you."

"I will hear it first," answered Haroun.

"My dear first-cousin, Kalum-Bek, a prominent merchant of the bazar, stands without," said Messour. "He has had a singular transaction with a man from Balsora, whose son once worked for Kalum-Bek, but who afterward stole from him and then ran away, no one knows whither. Now the father of this youth comes and demands his son of Kalum, who hasn't him. Kalum therefore begs that you will do him the favor of deciding between him and this man, by the exercise of your profound wisdom."

"I will judge in the matter," replied the caliph. "In half an hour your cousin and his opponent may enter the hall of justice."

When Messour had expressed his gratitude and gone out, Haroun said: "That must be your father, Said; and now that I am so fortunate as to know your story, I shall judge with the wisdom of Salomo. Conceal yourself, Said, behind the curtain of my throne; and you, grand vizier, send at once for that wicked police justice. I shall want his testimony in this case."

Both did as the caliph ordered. Said's heart beat fast as he saw his father, pale and stricken with grief, enter the hall of justice with tottering steps; while Kalum-Bek's smile of assurance, as he whispered to his

cousin, made Said so furious that he had difficulty in
refraining from rushing at him from his place of conceal-
ment, as his greatest sufferings and sorrows had been
caused by this cruel man.

There were many people in the hall, all of whom
were anxious to hear the caliph speak. As soon as the
Ruler of Bagdad had ascended the throne, the grand
vizier commanded silence, and asked who appeared as
complainant before his master.

Kalum-Bek approached with an impudent air, and
said: " A few days ago I was standing before the door of
my shop in the bazar, when a crier, with a purse in his
hand, and with this man walking near him, went among
the booths, shouting: 'A purse of gold to him who can
give any information about Said of Balsora.' This Said
had been in my service, and therefore I cried: ' This
way, friend! I can win that purse.' This man, who is
now so hostile to me, came up in a friendly way and
asked me what information I possessed. I answered:
' You must be Benezar, Said's father? and when he
affirmed that he was, I told him how I had found the
young fellow in the desert, rescued him and restored him
to health, and brought him back with me to Bagdad. In
the joy of his heart he gave me the purse. But when
now this unreasonable man heard, as I went on to tell
him, how his son had worked for me, had been guilty of
very wicked acts, had stolen from me and then run away,
he would not believe it, and quarrelled with me for several days, demanding his son and his money back; and
I can not return them both, for the gold is mine as
compensation for the news I furnished him, and I can not
produce his ungrateful son."

It was now Benezar's turn to speak. He described
his son, how noble and good he was, and the impossi-
bility of his ever having become so degraded as to steal.
He requested the caliph to make the most thorough examination of the case.

"I hope," said Haroun, "that you reported the theft, Kalum-Bek, as was your duty?"

"Why, certainly!" exclaimed that worthy, smiling. "I took him before the police justice."

"Let the police justice be brought!" ordered the caliph.

To every body's astonishment, this official appeared as suddenly as if brought by magic. The caliph asked whether he remembered that Kalum-Bek had come before him with a young man, and the official replied that he did.

"Did you listen to the young man; did he confess to the theft?" asked Haroun.

"No, he was actually so obstinate that he would not confess to any one but yourself," replied the justice.

"But I don't remember to have seen him," said the caliph.

"But why should you? If I were to listen to them, I should have a whole pack of such vagabonds to send you every day."

"You know that my ear is open for every one," replied Haroun; "but perhaps the proofs of the theft were so clear that it was not necessary to bring the young man into my presence. You had witnesses, I suppose, Kalum, that the money found on this young man belonged to you?"

"Witnesses?" repeated Kalum, turning pale; "no, I did not have any witnesses, for you know, Ruler of the Faithful, that one gold piece looks just like another. Where, then, should I get witnesses to testify that these one hundred gold pieces are the same that were missing from my cash-box."

"How, then, can you tell that that particular money belonged to you?" asked the caliph.

"By the purse," replied Kalum.

"Have you the purse here?" continued the caliph.

"Here it is," said the merchant, drawing out a purse which he handed to the vizier to give to the caliph.

But the vizier cried with feigned surprise: "By the beard of the Prophet! Do you claim the purse, you dog? Why it is my own purse, and I gave it filled with a hundred gold pieces, to a brave young man who rescued me from a great danger."

"Can you swear to that?" asked the caliph.

"As surely as that I shall some time be in paradise," answered the vizier, "for my daughter made the purse with her own hands."

"Why, look you then, police Justice!" cried Haroun, "you were falsely advised. Why did you believe that the purse belonged to this merchant?"

"He swore to it," replied the justice, humbly.

"Then you swore falsely?" thundered the caliph, as the merchant, pale and trembling, stood before him.

"Allah, Allah!" cried Kalum. "I certainly don't want to dispute the grand vizier's word; he is a truthful man, but alas! the purse does belong to me and that rascal of a Said stole it. I would give a thousand tomans if he was in this room now."

"What did you do with this Said?" asked the caliph. "Speak up! where shall we have to send for him, that he may come and make confession before me?"

"I banished him to a desert island," said the police justice.

"O Said! my son, my son!" cried the unhappy father.

"Indeed, then he acknowledged the crime, did he?" inquired Haroun.

The police justice turned pale. He rolled his eyes about restlessly, and finally said: "If I remember rightly — yes."

"You are not certain about it, then?" continued the caliph in a terrible voice; "then we will ask the young man himself. Step forth, Said, and you Kalum-Bek, to begin with, will count out one thousand gold pieces, as Said is now in the room."

Kalum and the police justice thought it was a ghost that stood before them. They prostrated themselves and cried: "Mercy! Mercy!" Benezar, half-fainting with joy, fell into the arms of his long-lost son. But, with great severity of manner, the caliph said: "Police Justice, here stands Said; did he confess?"

"No," whined the justice; "I listened only to Kalum's testimony, because he was a respectable man."

"Did I place you as a judge over all that you might listen only to the people of rank?" demanded Haroun-al-Raschid, with noble scorn. "I will banish you for ten years to a desert island in the middle of the sea; there you can reflect on justice. And you, miserable wretch, who bring the dying back to life, not in order to rescue them, but to make them your slaves — you will pay down, as I said before, the thousand tomahs that you promised if Said were only present to be called as witness."

Kalum congratulated himself at having got out of a very bad scrape so easily, and was just going to thank the kind caliph, when Haroun continued: "For the perjury you committed about the hundred gold pieces, you will receive a hundred lashes on the soles of your feet. Further than this Said will have the choice of taking your shop and its contents and you as a porter, or of contenting himself with ten gold pieces for every day's work he did for you."

"Let the wretch go, Caliph!" cried the youth; "I would not take anything that ever belonged to him."

"No," replied Haroun, "I prefer that you should be compensated. I will choose for you the ten gold pieces a day, and you can reckon up how many days you were in his claws. Away with this wretch!"

The two offenders were led away, and the caliph conducted Benezar and Said to another apartment, where he related to Benezar his rescue by Said, interrupted by the shrieks of Kalum-Bek, upon the soles of whose feet a hundred gold pieces of full weight were being counted out.

The caliph invited Benezar to come to Bagdad and

live with him and Said. Benezar consented, and made
only one more journey home in order to fetch his large
possessions. Said lived in the palace which the grateful
caliph built for him, like a prince. The caliph's brother
and grand vizier's son were his constant companions;
and it soon became a proverb in Bagdad: "I would that
I were as good and as fortunate as Said, the son of
Benezar."

"I could keep awake for two or three nights without experiencing the least sensation of sleepiness, with such
entertainment," said the compass-maker, when the
huntsman had concluded. "And I have often proved
the truth of what I say. I was once apprentice to a
bell-founder. The master was a rich man and no miser,
and therefore our wonder was all the more aroused on a
certain occasion, when we had a big job on hand, by a
display of parsimony on his part. A bell was being cast
for a new church, and we apprentices had to sit up all
night and keep the fire up. We did not doubt that the
master would tap a cask of the best wine for us. But
we were mistaken. He began to talk about his travels,
and to tell all manner of stories of his life; then the
head apprentice's turn came, and so on through the whole
row of us, and none of us got sleepy, so intent were we
all in listening. Before we knew it, day was at hand.
Then we perceived the master's stratagem of keeping us
awake by telling stories; for when the bell was done he
did not spare his wine, but brought out what he had
wisely saved on those nights."

"He was a sensible man," said the student. "There
is no remedy for sleepiness like conversation. And I
should not have cared to sit alone to-night, for about
eleven o'clock I should have succumbed to sleep."

"The peasantry have found that out also," said the
the huntsman. "In the long Winter evenings the women
and girls do not remain alone at home to spin, lest they
should fall asleep in the middle of their task; but a

large number of them meet together, in a well-lighted room, and tell stories over their work."

"Yes," added the wagoner, "and their stories are often of a kind to make one shudder, for they talk about ghosts that walk the earth, goblins that create a hubbub in their rooms at night, and spirits that torment men and cattle."

"They don't entertain themselves very well then, I fear," said the student. "For my part, I confess that there is nothing so displeasing to me as ghost stories."

"I don't agree with you at all," cried the compass-maker. "I find a story that causes one to shudder very entertaining. It is just like a rain-storm when one is sheltered under the roof. He hears the drops *tick-tack*, *tick-tack*, on the tiles, and then run off in streams, while he lies warm and dry in bed. So when one listens to ghost stories in a lighted room, with plenty of company, he feels safe and at ease."

"But how is it afterwards?" asked the student. "When one has listened who shares in this silly belief in ghosts, will he not tremble when he is alone again and in the dark? Will he not recall all the horrible things he has heard? I can even now work myself into quite a rage over these ghost stories, when I think of my child-hood. I was a cheerful, lively boy, but perhaps some-what noisier than was agreeable to my nurse, who could not think of any other means to quiet me than of giving me a fright. She told me all sorts of horrible stories about witches and evil spirits who haunted the house. I was too young then to know that all these stories were untrue. I was not afraid of the largest hound, could throw every one of my companions; but whenever I was alone in the dark, I would shut my eyes in terror. I would not go outside the door alone after dark without a light; and how often did my father punish me when he noticed my conduct! But for a long time I could not free my mind from this childish fear, for which my fool-ish nurse was wholly to blame."

"Yes, it is a great mistake," observed the huntsman, "to fill a child's head with such absurdities. I can answer you that I have known brave, daring men, huntsmen, who did not fear to encounter several of their foes at once — who, when they were searching for game at night, or on the lookout for poachers, would, all of a sudden, lose their courage, taking a tree for a ghost, a bush for a witch, and a pair of fire-flies for the eyes of a monster that was lurking for them in the dark."

"And it is not only for children," said the student, "that I hold entertainment of that kind to be in the highest degree hurtful and foolish, but for every body; for what intelligent person could amuse himself with the doings and sayings of things that exist only in the brain of a fool? There is where the ghost walks, and nowhere else. But these stories do the most harm among the country people. Their faith in absurdities of this kind is firm and unwavering, and this belief is nourished in the inns and spinning rooms, where they huddle close together and in a timid tone relate the most horrible stories they can call to mind."

"Yes," responded the wagoner; "many a misfortune has occurred through these stories, and, indeed, my own sister lost her life thereby."

"How was that? Through these ghost stories, did you say?" exclaimed the men, in surprise.

"Yes, certainly, by such stories," continued the wagoner. "In the village where our father lived it was the custom for the wives and maidens to get together with their spinning on a Winter's evening. The young men would also be there and tell many stories. So it happened that one evening when they were speaking about ghosts, the young men told about an old store-keeper who died ten years before, but found no rest in his grave. Every night he would throw up the earth, rise from his grave, steal slowly along to his store, coughing as was his wont in life, and there weigh out sugar and coffee, mumbling meanwhile:

Twelve ounces, twelve ounces, at dark midnight,
Equal sixteen, in broad daylight.

Many claimed that they had seen him, and the maids
and wives got quite frightened. But my sister, a girl of
sixteen, wishing to show that she was less foolish than
the others, said: 'I don't believe a word of that; he who
is once dead never comes back!' She said this, unfortunately, without a conviction of its truth, for she had
been frightened many times herself. Thereupon one of
the young people said: 'If you believe that, then you
would have no reason to be afraid of him; his grave is
only two paces from that of Kate's, who recently died.
If you dare, go to the church-yard, pick a flower from
Kate's grave, and bring it to us; then we will begin to
believe that you are not afraid of the store-keeper's
ghost. My sister was ashamed of being laughed at by
the others, therefore she said: 'Oh, that's easy enough;
what kind of a flower do you want?' 'The only white
rose in the village blooms there; so bring us a bunch of
those,' answered one of her friends. She got up and
went out, and all the men praised her spirit; but the
women shook their heads and said: 'If it only ends
well!' My sister passed on to the cemetery; the moon
shone brightly, but she began to tremble as the clock
struck twelve while she was opening the church-yard
gate. She clambered over many mounds which she knew,
and her heart beat faster and faster the nearer she came
to Kate's white rose bush and the ghostly store-keeper's
grave. At last she reached it, and kneeled down, trembling with fear, to pluck some roses. Just then she
thought she heard a noise close by; she turned around,
and saw the earth flying out of a grave two steps away
from her, and a form straightened itself up slowly in the
grave. It was that of an old, pale-faced man, with a
white night-cap on his head. My sister was greatly
frightened; she turned to look once more to make sure
that she had seen aright; but when the man in the grave

began to say, in a nasal tone: 'Good evening, Miss!
where do you come from so late?' she was seized with a
deathly terror, and collecting all her strength, she sprang
over the graves, ran to the house she had just left, and
breathlessly related what she had seen; then she became
so weak that she had to be carried home. Of what use
was it that we found out the next day that it was the
grave-digger who was making a grave there, and who had
spoken to my poor sister? Before she could comprehend this she had fallen into a high fever, of which she
died three days afterwards. She had gathered the roses
for her own burial wreath."

A tear dropped from the wagoner's eye as he concluded, while the others regarded him with sympathy.

" So the poor child died in this implicit faith," said the
young goldsmith. " I recollect a legend in that connection, which I should like to tell you, and that unfortunately is connected with such a tragedy."

THE CAVE OF STEENFOLL.

A SCOTTISH LEGEND.

IN one of Scotland's rocky islands, there dwelt many years ago, two fishermen, who lived in complete harmony. Both were unmarried; neither of them had any relatives living; and their common labor, although differently directed, sufficed to support them both. They were of about the same age, but in person and disposition they resembled each other as little as do an eagle and a sea-calf.

Kaspar Strumpf was a short, stout man, with a broad, fat, full-moon face, and good-natured, laughing eyes, to which sorrow and care appeared to be strangers. He was not only fat, but sleepy and lazy as well; and therefore the house work, cooking and baking, and repairing of nets for the capture of fish for their own table and for the market, devolved on him, as well as a large part of the cultivation of the small field attached to their cabin. Quite the opposite was his companion — tall and lank, with Roman nose and keen eyes; he was known as the most industrious and luckiest fisherman, the most daring cliff-climber after birds and down, the hardest field worker, on the whole island. Besides all this, he was considered the keenest trader on the Kirkwall market; but as his wares were good, and his transactions above reproach, every one dealt willingly with him. Thus William Falcon and Kaspar Strumpf — with whom the former, avaricious as he was, freely divided his hardly-earned gains — not only made a good living, but were in a fair way of acquiring a certain degree of wealth. But a competence would not satisfy Falcon's covetous soul; he wanted to be rich, extremely rich, and as he had already found out that riches accumulate but slowly in the usual course of industry, he at last settled into the conviction that he should have to attain his riches through some extraordinary stroke of fortune. When this idea had once taken possession of his mind, there was no room left for any thing else, and he began to talk this shadowy windfall over with Kaspar Strumpf, as though it had already come to pass. Kaspar, who received everything that Falcon said as scripture, repeated all this to his neighbors; and so the report was spread abroad that William Falcon had either sold his soul to the evil one, or had at least received an offer for it from the prince of the infernal regions.

At first, these reports caused much amusement to Falcon; but gradually he began to entertain the notion that a spirit might sometime reveal a treasure to him, and he no longer contradicted his acquaintances when they twitted him on the subject. He continued his usual occupations, but with far less zeal than before, and often consumed a great part of the time, that he had formerly passed in fishing or other useful avocations, in idle search for some kind of an adventure by which he should suddenly become rich. To still further complete this unfortunate tendency of his mind, it happened that as he was standing one day on the lonely sea-shore, looking out on the restless sea as if he were expecting his good fortune would come from thence, a large wave rolled a yellow ball to his feet amongst a mass of moss and loosened stone — a ball of gold!

Falcon stood as if bewitched. His hopes, then, had not been unsubstantial dreams; the sea had given him gold, beautiful shining gold, the fragment probably of a heavy bar of gold which the sea had rolled on its bottom into the size and shape of a musket ball. And now it was clear to his mind that somewhere on this coast there must have been a treasure ship wrecked, and that he had been selected as the chosen one to raise this buried treasure from the sea. From this time forth, this search for treasure became the passion of his life. He strove to conceal the golden nugget even from his friend, so that others might not discover his purpose. He neglected everything else, and spent his days and nights on this coast, not casting his net for fishes, but throwing out a scoop, that he had specially prepared for the purpose, for gold.

But he found poverty instead of wealth; for he earned nothing now himself, and Kaspar's sleepy efforts would not support them both. In the search for the larger mass of gold, not only the nugget was used up, but the entire property of the two men as well. But as Strumpf had formerly received the largest part of his living by Falcon's efforts, taking it all as a matter of course, so now he looked on the profitless undertaking of his friend silently and without a murmur; and it was just this meek forbearance on the part of his friend that spurred Falcon on to continue his restless search for wealth. But what made him still more active in his search was, that as often as he laid down to rest and closed his eyes in sleep, a word was sounded in his ear that he seemed to have heard very plainly, and that always appeared to be the same word, and yet he could never recall it. To be sure, he did not see what connection this circumstance, singular as it was, might have with his present purpose; but upon a spirit like William Falcon's everything made an impression, and even this mysterious whisper helped to strengthen his belief that great good luck was in store for him, which he expected to find only in a heap of gold.

One day he was surprised by a storm on the shore in the same place where he had found the nugget, and he was forced to take refuge from its fury in a cave near by. This cave, which the inhabitants called the cave of

Steenfoll, consists of a long underground passage opening
on the sea, with two entrances, and permitting a free passage of the waves that were continually foaming through
them with a loud roar.   This cave could be entered only
from one place — through a fissure from above, that was
but seldom approached except by venturesome boys, as
in addition to the natural dangers of the spot, the cavern
was reported to be haunted.   Falcon let himself down
through this opening with some difficulty, for about twelve
feet, and took a seat on a projecting piece of rock beneath an overhanging ledge, where, with the roaring
waves beneath his feet and the raging storm above his
head, he fell into his usual train of thought about the
wrecked ship and what kind of a ship it might have been ;
for in spite of all his inquiries, he could not obtain any
information of a vessel having been wrecked on this spot,
even from the oldest inhabitants.   How long he sat thus
he did not know himself ; but when he finally awoke from
his reveries, he found that the storm was over, and he
was about to clamber up again, when a voice from out of
the depths pronounced the word "*Car-milhan*" very distinctly. He climbed up to the top again, and looked down
into the abyss once more in great terror.   "Great
Heavens ! " exclaimed he "that is the word that dis-
turbs my sleep ! What does it mean ? "   "*Carmilhan !* "
was the sighing response that came once more from the
cave ; and he fled to his hut like a frightened deer.

Falcon was no coward ; his fright was more from surprise than fear ; and, more than this, the greed for
gold was too powerful in him to allow of his being
easily driven from his dangerous path. Once, as he
was fishing with his scoop for treasure by moonlight, opposite the cave of Steenfoll, his scoop caught
on something. He pulled with all his strength, but the
mass was immovable. In the meantime the wind had
risen, dark clouds overcast the sky, the boat rocked and
threatened to turn over ; but Falcon did not lose his
presence of mind ; he pulled and pulled at his scoop

until the resistance ceased, and as he felt no weight he concluded that his rope had broken. But just as the clouds were about to obscure the moon's light, a round, black mass appeared on the surface of the water, and the word that haunted him, "*Carmilhan*," was spoken. He made a quick effort to seize the object; but as soon as he stretched out his arm it disappeared in the darkness, and the coming storm forced him to seek protection under the rocks near by. Here, overcome by exhaustion, he fell asleep, only to be tormented in dreams by an unbridled imagination, and to suffer anew the pangs experienced in his waking hours, caused by his restless search for wealth.

When Falcon waked, the first rays of the rising sun fell upon the bosom of the sea, as smooth now as a mirror. He was just about to set out on his accustomed work, when he saw something coming towards him from the distance. He soon recognized it as a boat. Within it sat a human figure; but what aroused his greatest astonishment was that the vessel came on without the aid of sail or oar, and its prow pointed for land without the person sitting in the boat paying any attention to the rudder, if there were one. The boat came nearer, and finally stopped near William's boat. Its occupant proved to be a little dried-up old man, dressed in yellow linen, and wearing a red peaked night-cap. His eyes were closed, and he sat as motionless as a mummy. After vainly shouting at him and jarring the boat, Falcon was in the act of making a line fast to the boat to tow it off, when the little man opened his eyes, and began to bestir himself in such a manner as to fill even the bold fisherman's mind with dread.

"Where am I?" asked he in Dutch, after a deep sigh. Falcon who had learned something of that language from the Dutch herring-fishermen, told him the name of the island, and inquired who he was and what errand brought him here.

"I have come to look for the *Carmilhan*."

10*

"The *Carmilhan*? for Heaven's sake, what is that?" cried the curious fisherman.

"I won't give an answer to questions addressed to me in such a manner," replied the little man.

"Well then," shouted Falcon, "what is the *Carmilhan*?"

"The *Carmilhan* is nothing now; but once it was a beautiful ship, carrying more gold than ever a vessel carried before"

"Where was it wrecked, and when?"

"It was a hundred years ago; where, I do not know exactly. I come to search for the spot and recover the lost gold; if you will help me we will divide what we find."

"With my whole heart; only tell me what I must do."

"What you will have to do requires courage. You must go just before midnight to the wildest and loneliest region on the island, leading a cow, which you must slaughter there, and get some one to wrap you up in the cow's fresh hide. Your companion must then lay you down and leave you alone, and before it strikes one o'clock you will know where the treasures of the *Carmilhan* lies."

"It was in just such a way that old Engrol was destroyed, body and soul!" cried Falcon, with horror. "You are the evil one himself," continued he as he rowed quickly away. "Go back to hell! I won't have anything to do with you."

The little man gnashed his teeth, and cursed him; but Falcon, who had seized both oars, was soon out of hearing, and on turning round a rocky promontory was out of sight as well.

But the discovery that the evil one was taking advantage of his avarice by seeking to ensnare him with gold, did not open the eyes of the blinded fisherman, but on the contrary he determined to make use of the information the little man had given him, without putting himself in the power of the evil one. So while he continued

to fish for gold on the desolate coast, he neglected the
prosperity offered by large schools of fish off other parts
of the coast as well as all other expedients to which he
had once turned his attention, and sank with his companion into deeper poverty from day to day, until the
common necessaries of life began to fail them.   But
although this ruin might be wholly ascribed to Falcon's
obstinacy and cupidity, and the maintenance of both had
fallen on Kaspar Strumpf alone, yet the latter r.ever once
reproached his companion, but on the other hand continued to display the same subjection to him, and the
same confidence in his superior understanding, as at the
time when every one of his undertakings was successful.
This circumstance increased Falcon's sorrows not a little,
but drove him into a still keener search for gold, hoping
thereby soon to be able to indemnify his companion for so
great forbearance.   The word *Carmilhan* still haunted
him in his sleep.   In short, need, disappointed hopes,
and avarice, drove him finally into a species of insanity,
so that he really resolved to do that which the little man
had advised — although knowing that, as the legend ran,
he thereby gave himself up to the powers of darkness.

Kaspar's objections were all in vain.   Falcon became
the more determined, the more Kaspar besought him to
give up his desperate purpose; and finally the good,
weak-minded fellow consented to accompany him and
assist him in carrying out his plan.   The hearts of both
men were saddened, as they tied a rope to the horns of
a beautiful cow that they had owned since she was a
calf, and that was now their last piece of property; they
had often refused to sell her before, because they could
not bear the thought of letting her go into strange hands.
But the evil spirit that now controlled Falcon's actions
triumphed over his better nature; nor did Kaspar know
how to restrain him in anything.

It was now September, and the long nights of the
Scottish Winter had already begun.   The night clouds
were driven along before the raw night wind, and were

banked up in masses like icebergs. Deep shadows filled
the ravines between the mountains and the peat-bogs, and
the troubled channels of the streams appeared black and
fearful. Falcon led the way and Strumpf followed, shud-
dering at his own boldness. Tears filled Kaspar's eyes as
often as he looked at the poor creature that was going so
unconsciously and trustfully to its death, to be dealt it by
the hand that had always fed and caressed it.

With much difficulty they entered a narrow marshy
valley, which was here and there strewn with rocks, with
patches of moss and heathers, and was shut in by a chain
of wild mountains whose outlines were lost in a gray mist,
and whose steep sides had seldom been ascended by a
human foot. They approached a large rock in the centre of
the valley over the shaking bog, from which a frightened
eagle flew screaming into the sky. The poor cow lowed,
as if aware of the terrors of the place and the fate that
awaited her. Kaspar turned aside to wipe away the fast
falling tears. He looked down to the rocky opening
through which they had come, from which point could be
heard the breakers on the distant coast, and then up to
the mountain peaks, upon which a coal-black cloud had
settled, from which might be heard from time to time dull
mutterings of thunder. As he looked toward Falcon he
found that his friend had made the cow fast to the rock,
and now stood with uplifted ax in the very act of dealing
her death blow.

This was too much for Kaspar. Wringing his hands,
he fell upon his knees. "For God's sake, William Falcon!" shouted he in despairing tones, "save yourself!
Spare the cow! Save yourself and me! Save your soul!
Save your life! And if you will persist in tempting God,
wait at least until to-morrow and sacrifice some other
animal than our own cow!"

"Kaspar, are you crazy?" shrieked Falcon, like a madman, while he still held the ax swinging in the air.
"Shall I spare the cow and starve?"

"You shall not starve," answered Kaspar, resolutely.

"As long as I have hands you shall not suffer hunger. I will work for you day and night, so that you do not endanger the peace of your soul, and let the poor creature live for my sake!"

"Then take the ax and split my head!" shouted Falcon, in desperation. "I won't move from this spot until I have what I desire. Can you raise the treasures of the *Carmilhan* for me? Can your hands earn more than the merest necessaries of life? But you can put an end to my misery. Come, and let me be the victim!"

"William, kill the cow, kill me! It does not matter to me, I was only anxious about the salvation of your soul. Alas! this was the altar of the Picts, and the sacrifice that you would bring belongs to the darkness."

"I don't know anything about that," cried Falcon, laughing wildly, like one who is resolved not to listen to anything that might swerve him from his purpose. "Kaspar, you are crazy and make me crazy, too. But there," continued he, throwing away the ax and picking up his knife from the stone as if about to stab himself; "there, I will kill myself instead of the cow!"

Kaspar was at his side in a twinkling, tore the murderous weapon from his hand, seized the ax, poised it high in the air, and brought it down with such a force on the poor cow's head, that she fell dead at her master's feet.

A flash of lightning, accompanied by a peal of thunder, followed this rash act, and Falcon stared at his friend in astonishment. But Strumpf was disturbed neither by the thunder-clap nor by the fixed stare of his companion; and without speaking a word, fell to work at removing the hide. When Falcon had recovered from his amazement, he assisted his companion at this task, but with as evident aversion as he had before manifested eagerness to see the sacrifice completed. During their work the thunder-storm had gathered, the thunder reverberated among the mountains, and fearful flashes played about the rock; while the wind roared through the lower val-

leys and along the coast. And when at last the two fishermen had stripped the hide off, they found that they
were wet through to the skin. They spread the hide out
on the ground, and Kaspar wrapped and tied Falcon up
in it. Then, for the first time, when all this was done,
poor Kaspar broke the long silence by saying in a trembling voice, as he looked down at his deluded friend:
" Can I do anything more for you, William? "

" Nothing more," replied the other; "farewell!"

" Farewell," responded Kaspar. " God be with you,
and pardon you, as I do."

These were the last words Falcon heard from him, for
Kaspar disappeared in the darkness; and immediately
thereafter the most terrible thunder-storm occurred that
William had ever experienced. It began with a flash,
that revealed to Falcon's sight not only the mountains
and rocks in his immediate vicinity, but also the valley
below, with the foaming sea and the rocky islets in the
bay, between which he thought he had a vision of a large
foreign ship, dismasted; though the sight was instantly
lost again in the inky darkness. The thunder-claps were
deafening. A mass of splintered rock rolled down the
mountain-side and threatened to crush him. The rain
poured down in such torrents that the narrow, marshy
valley was flooded with a stream that soon reached to
Falcon's shoulders; fortunately Kaspar had laid him with
the upper part of his body on a slight elevation, else he
would surely have drowned The water rose still higher,
and the more Falcon exerted himself to get out of his
dangerous situation, the tighter did the hide seem to
wrap itself about his limbs. All in vain did he call for
Kaspar. Kaspar was far away. He did not dare to call
on God in his distress, and a shudder ran through his
frame whenever he thought of appealing for assistance to
the powers into whose clutches he was conscious of
having delivered himself.

Already the water crept into his ears; now it touched
the edge of his lips. " Oh, God! I am lost! ' screamed

he, as he felt the water sweep over his face; but in the
same instant the sound of a waterfall close by came
dimly to his ears, and his face was immediately uncovered. The flood had forced a passage through the stone;
and as the rain slackened and the sky grew lighter, so
did his despair abate, and a ray of hope returned to his
mind. But although he felt as exhausted as if just
emerged from a death-struggle, and ardently wished to be
released from his imprisonment, still the purpose of his
desperate efforts was not yet accomplished, and with the
vanishing of immediate deadly peril, the demon of greed
returned to his breast. But, convinced that he must remain in his present situation in order to attain his end,
he kept very quiet, and finally, overcome by cold and
exhaustion, fell into a sound sleep.

He might have slept two hours, when a cold wind
blowing over his face, and a roaring, as of oncoming
waves, aroused him from his happy state of oblivion.
The sky was darkened anew. A flash, like that which
had ushered in the first storm, lighted up once more the
surrounding region, and he fancied he had another vision
of the strange ship, that was now poised for an instant
on the crest of an enormous wave close to the Steenfoll
cliffs, and then appeared to shoot suddenly into the
rocky chasm. He continued to stare after the phantom,
as the sea was now illuminated by unceasing flashes of
lightning, when suddenly a water-spout rose from the
valley, near where he lay, and dashed him so violently
against a rock as to deprive him of his senses. When he
recovered consciousness, the weather had cleared, the
sky was bright, but the lightning still continued.

He lay close at the base of the mountains that shut
in this valley, feeling so badly bruised that he had
no desire to stir. He heard the quieter beating of the
surf, mingled with a solemn melody like that of a psalm.
These tones were at first so faint that he thought they
must be an illusion; but they occurred again and again,
each time clearer and nearer, and at last he thought he

could distinguish the melody of a psalm which he had
heard on board a Dutch fishing-smack the Summer before. Finally he could also make out voices, and he
seemed to be able to distinguish the words of the song.
The voices were now in the valley, and he pushed himself, with difficulty, to a stone, upon which he raised his
head, and perceived a procession of human figures, evidently the singers he had heard, and who were coming
directly towards him. Care and grief were expressed on
the faces of these people; and water was dripping from
their clothes. Now they were close to him, and their
song ceased. At their head were several musicians;
then followed some seamen, and after these came a tall
and strong man in a costume richly decorated with gold,
apparently belonging to a past age. A sword hung at his
side, and he carried in his hand a stout Spanish cane
with a gold head. At his left side walked a negro boy,
who, from time to time, handed his master a long-stemmed
pipe, from which the latter would take several grave
puffs and then walk on. He stopped bolt upright before
Falcon, while other men, less splendidly dressed, ranged
themselves on either side of him. They all had pipes in
their hands, not, however, as costly as that of their
leader. Behind them came still other persons, among
them being several women, some of whom had children
in their arms or at their apron-strings, and all in costly
foreign costumes. A crowd of Dutch sailors brought up
the rear of the procession, each one having a quid of
tobacco in his mouth, and holding between his teeth a
little cutty-pipe, which he smoked in gloomy silence.

The fisherman shuddered as he looked at this singular
assembly; but his expectation that something would
come of it all kept his courage up. For some time the
strange people stood around him thus, and the smoke
from their pipes floated over them like a cloud, through
which peeped the stars. The men closed in on Falcon
in an ever-narrowing circle; the smoking became more

and more vehement, and the clouds that arose from pipe and mouth increased in density.

Falcon was a bold, daring man; he had prepared himself beforehand for extraordinary occurrences; but when he saw this innumerable crowd pressing in on him as if to crush him by their numbers, his courage failed him, great drops of sweat stood out on his forehead, and he thought he would perish in a spasm of fright. But one may imagine his horror when, as he chanced to turn his eyes, he saw, sitting motionless and erect, close by his head, the little old man in the yellow linen suit, looking just as he had the first time except that now, as if making fun of the whole assembly, he, too, had a pipe in his mouth. In the mortal fright that now took possession of him, Falcon cried out to the leader of this assembly:

"In the name of whomsoever you serve, who are you? and what do you want with me?"

The tall man drew three whiffs, even more gravely than before; then gave the pipe to his servant and answered very coldly:

"I am Alfred Frank van Swelder, commander of the ship *Carmilhan*, of Amsterdam, which, on the voyage home from Batavia, went to the bottom with man and mouse on this rocky coast. These are my officers, those my passengers, and beyond, my brave crew who were all drowned with me. Why have you summoned us from our dwellings deep in the sea? Why do you disturb our rest?"

"I wish to know where the treasure of the *Carmilhan* lies."

"On the bottom of the sea."

"Where?"

"In the cave of Steenfoll."

"How can I recover it?"

"A goose dives into the abyss for a herring; is not the treasure of the *Carmilhan* of as much value?"

"How much of it shall I recover?"

"More than you will ever spend."

Q   11

The little man in yellow grinned horribly at this reply, while all the others laughed aloud.

"Are you through?" inquired the commander, further.

"I am. Farewell!"

"Farewell, until we meet again!" replied the Dutch-
man, and turned to go; the musicians took the lead
again, and the whole procession marched away in the
same order in which it had come, and with the same
solemn song, which grew ever fainter and fainter in the
distance, until finally it was lost in the roar of the
breakers.

Falcon now exerted his utmost strength to get out of
the hide, and he at last succeeded in freeing one arm,
with which he was able to loosen the rope that was
wound round him, and soon had stepped out of the hide.
Without stopping to look about him, he hastened down to
his hut, and found poor Kaspar Strumpf lying on the
ground in an insensible condition   With some difficulty
he restored him to consciousness, and the good fellow
shed tears of joy on once more beholding the friend of
his youth, whom he had given up for lost. But this
happy consolation vanished quickly, when he learned
what a desperate undertaking Falcon now had in mind.

"I would rather cast myself into hell than to look any
longer at these bare walls and reflect on our misery.
Follow me, or stay here; I am going at any rate."

With these words, Falcon seized a torch, a tinder-box,
and a rope, and hastened away. Kaspar ran after him as
fast as he could, and found his friend standing on the ledge
of the rock upon which he had once sought safety from
the storm, and ready to let himself down into the raging
abyss. When Kaspar found that his entreaties had no
effect on the crazed man, he prepared to descend after
him; but Falcon ordered him to remain where he was
and hold on to the rope. With an amount of exertion
that could only have been supplied by the blindest of
passions, greed, Falcon clambered down into the cave,
and at last came to a projecting piece of rock, just below

which the black waves, crested with foam, rushed along
with a dreadful roar. He looked about him eagerly,

and finally saw something glistening in the water directly
beneath where he stood. He laid down his torch, plunged

in, and seized a heavy object which he managed to bring
back with him. It was an iron box filled with gold
pieces. He shouted up to his companion what he had
found; but he would not pay the least attention to Kaspar's entreaties to content himself with what he had.
Falcon believed that this was only the first fruit of his
long endeavors. He plunged into the waves once
more—a peal of laughter arose from the sea, and William
Falcon was never seen again.

Kaspar went back to the hut, but as a changed man.
The strange shocks which his weak head and sensitive
heart had experienced, wrecked his mind. He wandered
about, day and night, staring before him in an imbecile
way, pitied and yet avoided by all his former acquaintances. One stormy night a fisherman claimed to have recognized William Falcon on the shore among the crew of
the *Carmilhan,* and on that same night Kaspar Strumpf
disappeared. He was sought for every-where, but no
trace of him was ever found; but the legend runs that
he has often been seen, together with Falcon, among the
crew of the spectre ship, which since his loss appears at
stated times at the cave of Steenfoll.

"It is long past midnight," said the student, when the
young goldsmith had concluded his story; "there cannot
well be any further danger, and I, for my part, am so
sleepy that I would advise that we all lay down and go to
sleep with a sense of perfect security."

"I should not feel safe before two o'clock in the morning," said the huntsman; "the proverb says, from eleven
till two is the thief's hour."

"I am of the same opinion," observed the compass-
maker; "for if they mean us any harm, there is certainly
no time so well adapted to their purpose as the small
hours. Therefore, I think it would be well if the student
were to continue his story, which he did not finish."

"I will not refuse your request," responded the student, " although our neighbor, the huhtsman, did not hear the beginning of it."

" I will try to imagine it, only go on," replied the huntsman.

" Well then," — the student had just begun, when they were interrupted by the barking of a dog. All held their breaths and listened. At the same instant one of the servants rushed in from the countess's room, and announced that from ten to twelve armed men were approaching the inn.

The huntsman seized his rifle, the student his pistol, the journeymen their canes, while the wagoner drew a large knife from his pocket. Thus they stood staring at one another helplessly.

" Let us station ourselves at the head of the stairs ! " cried the student. " Two or three of these villains shall meet their death before we are overpowered. So saying he gave the compass-maker his other pistol, with the understanding that they should fire one after the other. They took their places on the stairs — the student and the huntsman first, and near them the courageous compass-maker, who kept his pistol pointed down the centre of the stair-way. The goldsmith and the wagoner stood behind them, ready to do their best if it should come to a hand-to-hand fight.

They had stood thus but a few moments, when the house-door opened, and they heard several voices whispering.

Now they heard the steps of many men nearing the stair-way. The steps came up the stairs, and when about half way up three men were made out, who were evidently not prepared for the reception that awaited them. As they turned round the pillar that supported the flooring above, the huntsman called out: " Halt! One step further, and you are dead men. Cock your guns, friends, and take good aim ! "

The robbers shrank back; returned hastily to their companions below, and conferred with them. After a

while one of them came back and said: " Gentlemen, it
would be folly in you to sacrifice your lives for nothing,
for there are enough of us to completely destroy you; but
return to your rooms and not one of you shall be harmed
in the least, nor will we take a farthing from you."

" What is your purpose, then ? " demanded the student.
" Do you think we will trust such villains as you ? No
indeed ! If you have any business with us, come on, in
God's name ; but the first one who ventures up here I
will brand on the forehead so that he will never suffer
from headache again ! "

" Surrender the lady to us then," answered the robber.
"She shall not suffer harm ; we will merely conduct her to
a safe place, where she can remain in comfort, while her
servants return to the count and inform him that he can
ransom her for twenty thousand guldens ! "

" Shall we listen to such propositions ? " exclaimed the
huntsman, furious with rage as he cocked his gun. " I
will count three, and if you are not off before I say three,
I will pull the trigger ! One, two —"

" Hold ! " shouted the robber in a tone of command.
" Is it customary to shoot at an unarmed man, who is
holding a friendly parley with you ? Foolish fellow, you
might shoot me dead, and after all not perform a very
heroic deed ; but here stand twenty of my comrades who
would avenge me. How would it benefit your lady countess if you lay dead or stunned on the floor ? Believe
me, if she will go with us without offering resistance she
shall be treated with every consideration, but if you don't
put down your gun before I have counted three, it shall
fare hard with her. Put down your gun ! — One, two,
three ! "

" These dogs are not to be trifled with," whispered
the huntsman to his companion, as he obeyed the robber's command. " Really I am not afraid of my own life,
but if I were to shoot down one of them, it might be so
much the worse for my lady. I will consult with the
countess." Then turning to the robber he continued:

"Give us a truce of half an hour in order to prepare the countess. It would kill her if she were to be informed of this suddenly."

"Granted," replied the robber, at the same time stationing a guard of six men on the stair-case.

Bewildered and irresolute, the unfortunate travellers followed the huntsman to the countess's chamber, which was close to the stairs, and so loudly had the men spoken that the lady had not missed a word of what had been said. She was pale, and trembled violently, but nevertheless was firmly resolved to accept her fate.

"Why should I jeopardize the lives of so many brave men?" said she. "Why demand of you, to whom I am a stranger, an idle defence? No; I see no other chance of rescue than to follow these wretches."

All were impressed by the lady's spirit and misfortune. The huntsman wept, and swore that he could not survive this disgrace. The student reviled himself and his stature of six feet. "If I were only half a head shorter and had no beard," said he, "I should know how to act; I would dress myself in the lady countess's clothes, and these wretches should find out only too late what a blunder they had made"

Felix also had been deeply moved by the lady's misfortune. Her whole presence came so familiarly and affectingly before him, that it seemed to him as if the mother whom he had lost in his youth was now in this terrible situation. He would cheerfully have given his life for hers. And, as the student spoke, his words awakened an idea in his mind; he forgot all anxiety and every consideration but that of the rescue of this lady.

"If that is all," said he, stepping forward timidly, and coloring as he spoke, "if only a short stature, a beardless chin, and a courageous heart are needed to rescue this lady, then perhaps I am not unfit for that purpose. Put on my coat, gracious lady, hide your beautiful hair beneath my hat, take my bundle on your back and go your way as Felix, the goldsmith."

All were astonished at the youth's spirit, while the huntsman fell on his neck in an ecstasy of joy. "Goldsmith" cried he, "you will do that? You will slip into my gracious lady's clothes and thus save her? The good God has prompted you to do it. But you shall not go alone; I will share your captivity, will remain at your side as your best friend, and while I live they shall not harm you."

"I too will go with you, as true as I live!" exclaimed the student.

Much persuasion was required before the countess would consent to this scheme. She could not bear the thought that a stranger should sacrifice himself for her; she could not help thinking that if the robbers should afterward discover the deception practiced on them, they would take a terrible revenge on the unfortunate youth. But finally she was over-persuaded, partly by the entreaties of the young man, and partly by the reflection that if she was saved she would make every exertion to rescue her savior. The huntsman and the other travellers accompanied Felix into the student's room, where he quickly threw on some of the countess's clothes. To still further disguise him, the huntsman secured some locks of the maid's false hair to the goldsmith's head, and tied on the lady's hat. All declared that he would never be known; while the compass-maker roundly asserted that if he had met him on the street he should take off his hat without the slightest suspicion that he was bowing to his courageous comrade.

The countess in the meanwhile, with the help of her maid, had dressed herself in the clothes she found in the goldsmith's knapsack. With the hat drawn down over the forehead, the staff in her hand, and the knapsack on her back, she was completely disguised; and the travellers would have laughed not a little at any other time, over this comical masquerade. The new travelling journeyman thanked Felix with tears, and promised the speediest assistance.

"I have only one request to make," answered Felix. "In the knapsack you have on your back there is a small box; preserve this with the utmost care, for if it should be lost, I should never be happy again. I must carry it to my godmother and ——"

"Godfried, the huntsman, knows where my castle is," interrupted the lady. "Every thing shall be given back to you just as it was; for I hope you will come yourself, noble young man, to receive the thanks of my husband and myself."

Before Felix could reply, the harsh voices of the robbers were heard calling from the stairs that the time was up, and that everything was ready for the countess's journey. The huntsman went down to them, and declared that he could not leave the countess, and would rather go with them, wherever they might lead, than to return to his master without his mistress. The student also insisted that he should be allowed to accompany the lady. The robbers discussed the matter for some time, and finally consented to the arrangement, provided that the huntsman should at once surrender his weapons. Then they gave orders that the other travellers should remain perfectly quiet while the countess was being taken away.

Felix pulled down the veil that was spread over his hat, sat down in a corner with one hand supporting his head, and, with the manner of one in deep grief, awaited the robbers. The travellers had withdrawn to the other room, but left the door ajar so that they could see all that occurred. The huntsman sat down with an appearance of sadness, but keeping a sharp eye on the corner of the room that the countess had occupied. After they had sat thus for a few moments, the door opened, and a handsome stately man of about thirty-six years of age entered the room. He wore a kind of military uniform, an order on his breast, a long sabre at his side, and in his hand he carried a hat decorated with beautiful feathers.

Two of his men guarded the door immediately after his entrance.

He approached Felix with a low bow; he seemed to be somewhat embarrassed in the presence of a lady of rank, as he made several attempts before he was able to speak connectedly.

"Gracious lady," said he, "cases happen now and then in which one must have patience; such an one is yours. Do not think that I shall for even a moment lose sight of the respect due to so superior a lady. You shall have every comfort, and will have nothing to complain of except perhaps the fright you have suffered this evening." He paused here, as if awaiting an answer; but as Felix made no reply, he continued: "Do not look upon me as a common thief. I am an unfortunate man, whom adverse circumstances have forced into this life. We are desirous of leaving this region forever, but need money for that purpose. It would have been an easy matter for us to fall upon merchants and stages, but thereby we should have brought lasting misfortune on many people. Your husband, the count, inherited half a million thalers not six weeks ago. We ask for twenty thousand guldens of this superabundance; certainly a just and moderate demand. You will, therefore, have the goodness to write a note to the count at once, informing him that we are holding you for a ransom, that he must send the money as quickly as possible, and that unless he does so—you understand me, we should be compelled to treat you with much less consideration. The ransom will not be accepted unless brought by a single man, under a pledge of the strictest secrecy."

This scene was viewed with the most anxious interest by all the guests of the inn, but most anxiously of all by the countess. She trembled every moment lest the young man should betray himself. She was firmly resolved to ransom him for a large sum, but just as strong was her resolve not to take a single step with these robbers for any earthly consideration. She had found a knife in the goldsmith's coat pocket. She held it open in her hand, prepared to kill herself rather than suffer such a fate. Not less anxious was Felix himself. To be sure, he was consoled and strengthed by the reflection that it was a manly and praiseworthy act to come to the assistance of a helpless lady as he was doing, but he feared lest he should betray himself by each movement or by his voice. His alarm increased when the robber spoke of his writing a letter. How should he write it? By what title should he address the count? In what style should he write the letter, without betraying himself? But his anxiety rose to the highest pitch, when the robber chief laid paper and pen before him, and requested him to lift his veil and write the letter.

Felix did not know how becoming this disguise was to him, or he would not have entertained the least fear of discovery. For, as he finally felt forced to raise his veil, the robber chief, surprised by the beauty of the lady and her somewhat manly and spirited features, regarded her with still greater respect. This fact did not escape the young goldsmith's attention; and satisfied that at least for a moment there was no danger of discovery, he took up the pen and wrote to his pretended husband, after a form that he had once read in an old book:

"My Lord and Husband:—I, unhappy woman, have been seized, on my journey, in the dead of night, by people whom I cannot credit with good intentions. They will keep me a prisoner until you, Sir Count, have paid down the sum of twenty thousand guldens for me. This is provided you do not inform the authorities of this matter, or seek their assistance; and that you send the money by a single messenger to the forest inn in the Spessart. Otherwise I am threatened with a long and severe imprisonment. Begging for the speediest deliverance,

I am your unhappy
Wife."

He handed this remarkable letter to the robber chief, who read it through and signified his approbation.

"It rests with you now to decide," said he, "whether you will be accompanied by the huntsman or your maid. I shall send one of them to your husband with this letter."

"The huntsman, and that gentleman there, will accompany me," answered Felix.

"Very well," returned the robber, going to the door and summoning the countess's maid "Just give this woman her instructions."

The maid appeared, shivering and shaking. Felix too turned pale when he reflected that here he was in danger once more of betraying himself. Still the unexpected courage that had carried him safely through the former ordeal, returned. "I have no further commands for you," said he, "except that you desire the count to take me from this unfortunate situation as quickly as possible."

"And," added the robber, "that you recommend the count most earnestly and explicitly to keep silent about all this, and not to undertake any action against us, before his wife is in his hands. Our spies would give us timely warning of any such demonstrations on his part, and I would not then be answerable for the consequences."

The trembling maid promised to obey these instructions. She was further ordered to pack what dresses and linen the lady countess might need in a small bundle, as they could not hamper themselves with much luggage; and when this had been done, the robber chief, with a low bow, requested the lady to follow him. Felix stood up, the huntsman and the student followed, and, preceded by the robber, all three descended the stairs.

Before the inn stood a large number of horses. One of them was pointed out to the huntsman; another, a beautiful pony provided with a side-saddle, stood ready for the countess; while a third was given to the student. The leader lifted the young goldsmith to the saddle, fixed him firmly in his seat, and then mounted a horse himself. He rode to the right of the lady, while another of the robbers rode at her left side. The student and huntsman were similarly guarded. As soon as the band of robbers were mounted, the leader gave a loud and clear whistle as a signal to start, and shortly the whole troop had disappeared in the forest.

The company gathered in the chamber of the inn, gradually recovered from their terror after the departure of the robbers. As is generally the case after some great misfortune or sudden danger has passed by, they would have been very cheerful had not their thoughts been occupied with their three companions, who had been led away before their very eyes. They all broke out in praise of the young goldsmith, and the countess wept when she reflected how deeply she was indebted to one upon whom she had no claim, whom she had never even known. It was a consolation for them all to know that the heroic huntsman and the brave student had accompanied him, and could comfort him in his hours of despondency. They even entertained a hope that the experienced forester would discover a means of escape for himself and companions. They consulted together as to what they had better do. The countess resolved that, as she was bound by no oath to the robbers, she would at once return to her husband, and make every exertion to discover their hiding-place, and set their prisoners free. The wagoner promised to go to Aschaffenburg and summon the officials to organize a pursuit of the robbers, while the compass-maker was to continue his journey.

The travellers were not disturbed any more that night; silence reigned in the forest inn, that had an hour before been the theatre of terrible scenes. But in the morning, when the servants of the countess went below to prepare for her departure, they came running back, and reported that they had found the landlady and her hostler bound on the floor, and begging for assistance.

The travellers gazed at one another in astonishment.

"What?" cried the compass-maker. "Then these people must have been innocent. We have done them wrong, for they can have no association with the robbers."

"I will allow myself to be hanged in their place," returned the wagoner, "if we were not right after all. This is only a sham, designed to prevent their conviction. Don't you remember the suspicious appearance of this inn? Don't you remember how, when I started to go down-stairs, the trained dog would not let me pass? how the landlady and the hostler appeared instantly, and asked in a surly way what I was after? Still, all this was well for us, or at least for the lady countess. If things had worn a less suspicious air in the public room, if the landlady had not aroused our distrust, we should not have remained together, nor have kept awake. The robbers could have attacked us in our sleep, or at least would have guarded our doors, so that the substitution of the brave young goldsmith for the countess would not have been possible."

They all agreed with the wagoner, and determined to lodge a complaint against the landlady and her servant, before the magistrate. Still, in order to be on the safe side, they concluded not to manifest the least token of suspicion just yet. The servants and the wagoner went down-stairs, loosened the bonds of the robbers' accomplices, and conducted themselves as sympathetically and sorrowfully as possible. In order to conciliate her guests still more, the landlady charged each one but a very small amount, and extended them a hearty invitation to call again.

The wagoner paid his reckoning, took leave of his companions in misfortune, and started on his road. After him the two jouneymen went off. Light as the goldsmith's bundle had been made, it still seemed heavy to the delicate lady. But still heavier was her heart, when the traitorous landlady stretched out her hand to take leave of her at the door. "Why," cried she, "what kind of a spark are you, to be going out into the world so young? You must be a spoiled fellow, whom the master chased out of his shop. But that's none of my business; do me the honor to stop here on your return journey. Good luck to you!"

The countess was so nervous, and trembled so, that she did not dare reply, least she should be betrayed by her voice. The compass-maker, noticing her confusion, took his companion by the arm, bade good-bye to the landlady, and sang a jovial song as they struck out into the forest.

"Now I am really in safety," cried the countess, when they had put a hundred paces between them and the inn. "To the last moment I feared that the landlady would recognize me, and have her servant lock me up. Oh, how can I thank you for all you have done? Come to my castle; you must at least return to meet your travelling companions again."

The compass-maker consented, and while they were thus speaking, the countess's carriage came rolling up behind them; the door was quickly opened, the lady sprang inside, waved a farewell to the young journeyman, and was driven rapidly away.

About this time, the robbers and their prisoners reached the camping place of the band. They had ridden over a rough forest road at a fast trot, exchanging not a word with their prisoners, and conversing among themselves in low tones only when they changed their course. They finally came to a halt just above a deep ravine. The robbers dismounted, and their leader assisted the goldsmith from his horse, apologizing for the fast and wearisome ride he had forced him to take, and inquiring whether the gracious lady felt very much fatigued.

Felix answered him in as gentle a tone as he could assume, that he was in need of rest; and the robber offered his arm to escort him into the ravine. The descent was a very steep one, and the footpath was narrow and precipitous. At last they were safely down. Felix saw before him by the faint light of the opening day, a small narrow valley not more than a hundred paces in circumference, that lay deep in a basin formed by the precipitous rocks. Some six or eight small, board and log huts were built in this ravine. A few untidy women peeped out curiously from these hovels, and a pack of twelve large dogs and their countless puppies surrounded the new-comers, howling and barking. The chief led the countess to the best one of these huts, and told her that this was exclusively for her own use; and granted Felix's request that the huntsman and the student might be permitted to remain with him.

The hut was furnished with deer-skins and mats, which served at once for a carpet and for seats. Some jugs and dishes, made out of wood, a rusty old fowling-piece, and in the further corner a couch made of a couple of boards and a few woollen blankets, which could hardly be dignified by the name of a bed, were the only appointments of the place.

Left alone together for the first time in this miserable hut, the three prisoners had time to think over their strange situation. Felix, who did not for a moment repent of his noble action, but who was still nervous as to what would become of him in case of a discovery, gave utterance to loud complaints; but the huntsman quickly checked him, and whispered:

"For God's sake, be quiet, dear boy; don't you know that they will be listening to us?"

"Each word uttered in such a tone as that would create suspicion in their minds," added the student.

Nothing remained to poor Felix but to weep silently. "Believe me, Mr. Huntsman," said he, "I do not weep for fear of these robbers, or because of this miserable hut; no, it is quite another kind of sorrow that oppresses me. How easily might the countess forget what I said to her so hastily, and then I should be considered a thief and thus made miserable forever.

"But what is it, then, that causes you so much anxiety?" inquired the huntsman, wondering at the demeanor of the young man, who, up to this time, had borne himself so courageously.

" Listen, and you will do me justice," answered Felix. " My father was a clever goldsmith of Nuremberg, and my mother, previous to her marriage, had served as maid to a lady of rank, and when she married my father she was finely fitted out by the countess whom she had served. The countess remained a good friend to my parents, and after my birth she stood as my godmother and made me many presents. And when my parents died of a pestilence, and I, left alone in the world, was about to be sent to the poorhouse, this lady godmother heard of my misfortune and placed me in a boarding-school. When I was of the proper age, she wrote to know if I would like to learn my father's trade. I jumped at the chance, and she apprenticed me to a master of the art in Wuerzburg. I took readily to the work, and had soon made such progress that I was given a certificate, and could set out as a travelling journeyman. I wrote this to my lady godmother, and she answered at once that she would give me the money for my outfit. With the letter she sent some splendid stones, and requested me to give them a beautiful setting, and bring the ornament to her myself as a proof of my skill, and receive my travelling money at the same time. I have never seen my lady godmother, and you may imagine with what pleasure I undertook her commands. I worked day and night on the ornament, and turned out such a beautiful and delicate piece of work that even the master was astonished at my skill. When it was completed, I packed my knapsack carefully, took leave of my master, and started out on the journey to my lady godmother's castle. Then," continued he, breaking into tears, "these villainous robbers happened along and destroyed all my hopes. For if your lady countess loses the ornament, or forgets what I told her and throws away my old knapsack, how shall I ever face my lady godmother? How should I prove my story? How could I replace the stones? And my travelling

R   11*

money would also be lost, and I should appear as an ungrateful fellow who had foolishly surrendered his charge. And, finally, would any one believe me if I were to relate this wonderful adventure?"

"Be of good cheer!" replied the huntsman. "I do not believe that your ornament can be lost while in the keeping of the countess; and even if such a thing should occur, she would be sure to make the loss good to her deliverer, and would herself bear witness to these mischances. We will leave you now for some hours, for we really need sleep, and after the excitement of this night you ought to take some rest. Afterwards in conversing with one another let us forget our misfortune for the time being, or, better still, let us think about our escape."

They went away Felix remained alone, and made an attempt to follow the huntsman's advice. When, after some hours, the student and huntsman returned, they found their young friend in a much better mood. The huntsman told the goldsmith that the chief of the band had assured him that the lady should have every attention; and that in a few moments one of the women whom they had seen about the huts would serve the lady countess with coffee, and offer her services as attendant. They resolved, in order not to be disturbed, to refuse this favor; and when the ugly old gypsy woman came, set the breakfast before them, and inquired in an obsequious manner whether she could be of any further service, Felix motioned to her to leave, and as she still lingered, the huntsman drove her out of the door. The student then narrated all that they had learned about the camp.

"The hut in which you live, beautiful lady countess," began he, "seems originally to have been designed for the leader of the band. It is not so roomy, but it is much finer than the others. Beside this, there are six others, in which the women and children live, for there are seldom more than six robbers at home. One stands guard not far from this hut; another below him, on the way to the path that leads out of the ravine; and a third stands as sentinel above, at the entrance to the ravine. Every second hour they are relieved by the three others. More than this, each guard has two large dogs near him, and they are all so wide-awake that one can not set foot outside the hut without being barked at. I have no hope that we can steal out of this place."

"Don't make me sad; I feel more cheerful after my nap," returned Felix. "Don't give up all hope, and if you fear discovery, let us rather talk about something else, and not be troubled about the future. Herr Student, you began a story in the inn; continue it now, for we have time to amuse ourselves."

"I can scarcely remember what it was," answered the young man.

"You were relating the legend of 'The Marble Heart,' and had reached the point where the landlord and the other gambler had put Charcoal Pete out of doors."

"All right; it comes back to me now," replied he. "Well, if you wish to hear more of it, I will continue."

THE MARBLE HEART.

SECOND PART.

WHEN Peter went to his glass-works on Monday morning, he found not only his workmen there, but also other people who do not make very pleasant visitors—the sheriff and three bailiffs. The sheriff bade Peter good morning, asked how he had slept, and then took out a long register, on which were inscribed the names of Peter's creditors. "Can you pay or not?" demanded the sheriff in a severe tone. "And be quick about the matter too, for I have not much time to spare, and the prison is a three hours ride from here." Peter, in great despondency, confessed that he was unable to pay the claims, and left it to the sheriff to appraise his house, glass-works, stable, and horses and carriage.

While the officials were conducting their examination, it occurred to Peter that the Tannenbuehl was not far away, and as the little man had not helped him, he would try the big man. He ran to the Tannenbuehl as fast as though the officers had been at his heels; and it seemed to him, as he rushed by the spot where he had first spoken to the Little Glass-Man, that an invisible hand seized him —but he tore himself out of its grasp, and ran on till he came to the boundary line, which he remembered well; and hardly had he shouted: "Dutch Michel! Dutch Michel!" when the giant raftsman, with his immense pole, stood before him.

"Have you come at last?" said the giant, laughing.

"Do they want to strip you for the benefit of your creditors? Well, be quiet; your whole trouble comes, as I told you it would, from the Little Glass-Man—the hypocrite. When one gives, one should give generously, and not like this miser. But come," continued he, turning towards the forest, "follow me to my house, and we will see whether we can make a trade."

"Make a trade?" reflected Peter. "What can he want from me? How can I make a bargain with him? Does he want me to do him some service, or what is it he's after?"

They walked over a steep forest path, and suddenly came upon a dark and deep ravine. Dutch Michel sprang down the rocks as if they were an easy marble stair-case; but Peter came near fainting with fright, when Dutch Michel on reaching the bottom, made himself as tall as a church steeple, and stretched out an arm as long as a weaver's beam, with a hand as broad as the table in the tavern, and shouted in a voice that echoed like a deep funeral bell: "Set down on my hand and hold fast to the fingers, and you will not fall." Peter tremblingly obeyed him, taking a seat on the giant's hand, and holding on to his thumb.

They went down and down for a great distance, but still, to Peter's astonishment it did not grow darker; on the contrary, it seemed to be lighter in the ravine, so that for some time his eyes could not endure the light. The farther they descended, the smaller did Dutch Michel make himself, and he now, in his former stature, stood before a house neither better nor worse than those owned by wealthy peasants in the Black Forest. The room into which Peter was conducted did not differ from the rooms of other houses, except that an indescribable air of loneliness pervaded it. The wooden clock, the enormous Dutch tile stove, the utensils on the shelves, were the same as those in use every-where. Michel showed him to a seat behind the large table and then went out, returning soon with a pitcher of wine and glasses. He poured out the wine, and they talked at random, until Dutch Michel began to tell about the pleasures of the world, of strange lands, and of beautiful cities and rivers, so that Peter at last became possessed of a strong desire to travel also, and told the giant so openly.

"However desirous you might be of undertaking anything, a couple of quick beats of your silly heart would make you tremble; and as for injured reputation, for misfortune, why should a sensible fellow trouble himself with such matters? Did you feel the insult in your head when recently you were called a cheat and swindler? Did your stomach pain you when the sheriff came to turn you out of house and home? Tell me, where were you conscious of pain?"

"In my heart," answered Peter, laying his hand on his breast; for it seemed to him as though his heart was swinging to and fro unsteadily.

"You have—don't take it amiss — you have thrown away many hundred guldens on idle beggars and other low fellows; how did that benefit you? They blessed you, and wished you a long life; do you therefore expect to live the longer? For the half of that wasted money you could have employed physicians in your illness. Blessings? — Yes, it's a fine blessing to have your property seized and yourself put out of doors! And what was it that induced you to put your hand in your pocket whenever a beggar held out his tattered hat?—your heart, once more your heart; and neither your eyes nor your tongue, your arms nor your legs, but your heart. You took it—as the saying is—too much to heart."

"But how can one train himself so that it would not be so any more? I am exerting myself now to control my heart, and still it beats and torments me."

"Yes, no doubt you find that the case," replied the giant, with a laugh. "You, poor fellow, can not manage it at all; but give me the little beating thing, and then you will see how much better off you will be."

"Give you my heart?" shrieked Peter in terror. "I should certainly die on the spot! No, never!"

"Yes, if one of your learned surgeons was to perform the operation of removing the heart from your body, you would certainly die; but with me it would be quite another thing. Still, come this way, and satisfy yourself." So saying, he got up, opened a chamber door, and took Peter inside. The young man's heart contracted spasmodically as he stepped over the sill, but he paid no attention to it, for the sight that met his eyes was strange and surprising. On a row of shelves stood glasses filled with a transparent fluid, and in each of these glasses was a human heart; the glasses were also labeled with names, written on paper slips, and Peter read them with great curiosity. Here was the heart of the magistrate at F., of the Stout Ezekiel, of the King of the Ball, of the head gamekeeper; there were the hearts of six corn factors, of eight recruiting officers, of three scriveners — in short, it was a collection of the most respectable hearts within a circumference of sixty miles.

"Look!" said Dutch Michel. "All these have thrown away the cares and sorrows of life. Not one of these hearts beats anxiously any longer, and their former possessors are glad to be well rid of their troublesome guests."

"But what do they carry in the breast in place of them?" asked Peter, whose head began to swim at what he had seen.

"This," answered the giant, handing him, from a drawer, a *stone heart*.

"What!" exclaimed Peter, as a chill crept over him. "A heart of marble? But look you, Dutch Michel, that must be very cold in the breast."

"Certainly; but it is an agreeable coolness. Why should a heart be warm? In winter the warmth of it is of no account; good cherry rum you would find a better protection against the cold than a warm heart, and in summer, when you are sweltering in the heat, you can not imagine how such a heart will cool you. And, as I said before, there will be no further anxiety or terror, neither any more silly pity, nor any sorrow, with such a heart in your breast."

"And is that all you are able to give me?" asked Peter discontentedly. "I hope for money, and you offer me a stone!"

"Well, I think a hundred thousand guldens will do you to start with. If you handle that well, you can soon become a millionaire."

"One hundred thousand!" shouted the poor charcoal burner joyfully. "There, don't beat so violently in my breast, we will soon be through with one another. All right, Michel; give me the stone and the money, and you may take the restless thing out of its cage."

"I thought you would show yourself to be a sensible fellow," said Dutch Michel smiling. "Come, let us drink once more together, and then I will count out the money."

So they sat down to the wine again, and drank until Peter fell into a deep sleep. He was finally awakened by the ringing notes of a bugle horn, and behold, he sat in a beautiful carriage, driving over a broad highway, and as he turned to look out of the carriage, he saw the Black Forest lying far behind him in the blue distance. At first he could hardly realize that it was he himself who sat in the carriage; for even his clothes were not the same that he had worn yesterday. But he remembered every thing that had occurred so clearly, that he said: "I am Charcoal Pete, that is certain, and nobody else."

He was surprised that he felt no sensation of sorrow, now that for the first time he was leaving behind him his home and the woods where he had lived so long. He could neither sigh nor shed a tear, as he thought of his mother whom he was leaving in want and sorrow; for all this was a matter of indifference to him now. "Tears and sighs," thought he, "homesickness and melancholy, come from the heart, and—thanks to Dutch Michel—mine is cold and stony."

He laid his hand on his breast, and it was perfectly quiet there. "If he has kept his word as well with the hundred thousand guldens as he has about the heart, I shall be happy," said he, and at once began a search in his carriage; he found all manner of clothes, as fine as he could wish them, but no money. At last he came upon a pocket which contained many thousand thalers in gold, and drafts on bankers in all the large cities. "Now it's all just as I wanted it," thought he; and settling himself comfortably in a corner of the carriage, he journeyed out into the wide world.

He traveled for two years about the world, looking out from his carriage to the right and left at the buildings he passed by; and when he entered a city he looked out only for the sign of the tavern. After dinner he would be driven about the town, and have the sights pointed out to him. But neither picture, house, music, dancing, nor any thing else, rejoiced him. His heart of stone could not feel an interest in any thing, and his eyes and ears were dulled to all that was beautiful. No pleasures remained to him but those of eating, drinking and sleeping. Now and then, it is true, he recalled the fact, that he had been happier when he was poor and worked for his own support. Then every beautiful view in the valley, the sound of music and song, had rejoiced him; then he had been satisfied with the simple fare that his mother had prepared and brought out to his fires. When he thus thought of the past, it seemed very singular to him that he could not laugh at all now, while then every little jest had amused him. When others laughed, he simply affected to do the same as a mere matter of politeness; but his heart did not join in the merriment. He felt then that although he was destitute of emotion, yet he was far from being contented. It was not homesickness or melancholy, but dullness, weariness, and a joyless life, that finally drove him back to his native place.

12

As he passed by Strasbourg and saw the dark forest
in the distance, as he once more saw the strong forms
and honest, faithful faces of the inhabitants of the Black
Forest, as his ear caught the strong, deep, well-remem-
bered tones of his countrymen's voices, he put his hand
quickly to his heart, for his blood danced through his
veins, and he thought he should both weep and rejoice;
but — how could he be so foolish? — he had only a heart
of stone, and stones are without feeling, and neither
laugh nor weep.

His first visit was to Dutch Michel, who received him
with much show of friendliness. "Michel," said Peter,
"I have travelled and have seen every thing, but experienced only weariness. Upon the whole, the stone I
carry in my breast saves me from many things; I never
get angry, am never sad, but at the same time I am
never happy, and it seems to me as if I only half lived.
Can not you make the stone heart a little more sensitive?
or, give me back rather my old heart. I was accustomed
to it for twenty-five years, and even if it did sometimes
lead me into a foolish act, still it was a contented and
happy heart."

The Spirit of the Forest laughed scornfully. "When
you are once dead, Peter Munk," replied he, "your heart
shall not be missing; then you shall have back your soft,
sensitive heart, and then you will have an opportunity to
feel whatever comes, joy or sorrow. But in this world it
can never be yours again. Still, Peter, although you
have travelled, it won't do you any good to live in the
way you have been doing. Settle down somewhere here
in the forest, build a house, marry, double your wealth;
you were only in want of some employment. Because
you were idle, you experienced weariness; and now you
would charge it all to this innocent heart."

Peter saw that Michel was right, so far as idleness
was concerned, and resolved to devote his energies to acquiring more and more riches. Michel presented him

with another hundred thousand guldens, and the two parted on the best of terms.

The news soon spread throughout the Black Forest that Charcoal Pete, or Gambler Pete, was back again, and richer than before. Things went on as they had done. When he had been reduced to beggary, he was kicked out of the tavern door; and when now, on one Sunday afternoon he drove up to the tavern, his old associates shook his hand, praised his horse, inquired about his journey; and when he began to play with the Stout Ezekiel again for silver thalers, he stood higher than ever in the esteem of the hangers-on. Instead of the glass business, he now went into the timber trade; but this was only for sake of appearance, as his chief business was that of a corn factor and money lender. Fully half of the inhabitants of the Black Forest gradually fell into his debt, as he only lent money at ten per cent interest, or sold corn to the poor, who could not pay cash for it, at three times what it was worth. He stood in intimate relations with the sheriff, and if one did not pay Mr. Peter Munk on the day his note fell due, the sheriff would ride over to the debtor's place, seize his house and land, sell it without delay, and drive father, mother and child into the forest. At first this course of action caused Peter some little trouble, for the people who had been driven out of their homes blockaded his gates,— the men pleading for time, the women attempting to soften his heart of stone, and the children crying for a piece of bread. But when he had provided himself with a couple of savage mastiffs, this charivari, as he called it, very soon ceased. He whistled to the dogs, and set them on the pack of beggars, who would scatter with screams in all directions. But the most trouble was given him by an old woman, who was none other than Peter's mother. She had been plunged into misery and want, since her house and lot had been sold, and her son, on his return, rich as he was, would not look after her wants. Therefore she occasionally appeared at his door, weak and old, leaning on a staff. She dared not enter the house, for he had once chased her out of the door; but it pained her to live on the charity of other people, when her own son was so well able to provide for her old age. But the cold heart was never disturbed by the sight of the pale, well-known features, by her pleading looks or by the withered, out-stretched hand, or the tottering form. And when on a

Saturday she knocked at his door, he would take out a sixpence, grumbling meanwhile, roll it up in a piece of paper, and send it out to her by a servant. He could hear her trembling voice as she returned thanks and wished that all happiness might be his; he heard her steal away from the door coughing, but gave her no further thought, except to reproach himself with having thrown away a good sixpence.

Finally Peter began to think about getting married. He knew that there was not a father in the whole Black Forest who would not have been glad to give him his daughter; but he meant to be particular in his choice, for he wished that in this matter, too, his luck and his judgment should be recognized. Therefore he rode all through the forest, searching here and there, but not one of the beautiful Black Forest maidens seemed beautiful enough for him. Finally, after he had looked through all the ball rooms in a vain search for his ideal beauty, he one day heard that the daughter of a certain wood-chopper was the most beautiful and virtuous of all the Black Forest maidens. She lived a very quiet life, kept her father's house in the neatest order, and never showed herself at a ball, not even on holidays. When Peter heard of this Black Forest beauty, he resolved to obtain her, and rode to the hut to which he was directed. The father of the beautiful Lisbeth received the gentleman in much surprise, but was still more astonished to hear that this was the wealthy Mr. Peter Munk, and that the gentleman wished to become his son-in-law. Believing that now all his cares and his poverty were at an end, the old man did not hesitate very long, but consented to the match without stopping to consult his daughter's inclinations, and the good child was so dutiful that she made no objections, and soon became Mrs. Peter Munk.

But things did not go as well with the poor girl as she had dreamed. She thought she had a perfect knowledge of how to manage a house; but she could not do any thing that seemed to please her husband. She had sympathy with poor people, and, as her husband was so rich, she thought it would be no sin to give a farthing to a poor beggar woman or to hand an old man a cup of tea. But when Peter saw her do this one day, he said, in a harsh voice and with angry looks: "Why do you waste my means on idlers and vagabonds? Did you bring anything into the house, that you can throw money away like a princess? If I catch you at this again, you shall feel my hand!"

The beautiful Lisbeth wept in her chamber over the cruel disposition of her husband, and often did she feel that she would rather be back in her father's hut than to live with the rich but miserly and hard-hearted Peter. Alas, had she known that her husband had a marble heart, and could neither love her nor any one else, she would not have wondered so much at his actions. But whenever she sat at the door, and a beggar came up, took off his hat and began to speak, she now cast her eyes down that she might not see the poor fellow, and clasped her hands tighter lest she should involuntarily feel in her pocket for money. So it happened that the beautiful Lisbeth came to be badly spoken of throughout the entire Forest, and it was asserted that she was even more miserly than Peter himself.

But one day while Lisbeth was sitting before the house, spinning, and humming a song — for she felt in unusually good spirits, as the weather was fine and Peter had ridden off — a little old man came up the road, carrying a large, heavy sack. Lisbeth had heard him panting while he was still at some distance, and she looked at him sympathetically, thinking that so old and weak a man ought not to carry so heavy a burden.

In the meantime the man had staggered and panted up, and when he was opposite Lisbeth, he almost fell down under the sack. "Alas, take pity on me, madame, and hand me a glass of water," said the little man; "I can not go another step, and I fear I shall faint."

"But at your age you ought not to carry such a heavy load," said Lisbeth.

"Yes, if I was not forced by poverty to serve as a messenger," answered he. "Alas, a rich lady like you does not know how poverty pinches, and how refreshing a drink of water would be on such a hot day."

On hearing this Lisbeth rushed into the house, took a pitcher from the shelf and filled it with water; but when she returned with it, and had come within a few feet of the man, she saw how miserable he appeared as he sat on the sack, and, remembering that her husband was not at home, she set the pitcher of water to one side, got a goblet and filled it with wine, laid a slice of rye bread on top of it, and brought it out to the old man. "There; a sip of wine, at your age, will do you more good than water," said she. "But don't drink it so hastily, and eat your bread with it."

The little man looked at her in astonishment, while tears gathered in his eyes. He drank the wine and then said: "I have grown old, but I have seen few people who were so merciful, and who knew how to make gifts as handsomely and heartily as you do, Frau Lisbeth. And for this your life on earth shall be a happy one; such a heart will not remain without a reward."

"No, and she shall have her reward on the spot!" shouted a terrible voice; and as they turned, there stood Peter with an angry face.

"So you were pouring out my best wine for beggars, and giving my own goblet·to the lips of a vagrant? There, take your reward!"

Lisbeth threw herself at his feet and begged his forgiveness; but the heart of stone felt no pity; he turned the whip he held in his hand, and struck such a blow with the butt of it on her beautiful forehead, that she sank lifeless into the arms of the old man. When Peter saw this, he seemed to regret it on the instant, he bent down to see if there was still life in her, but the little man said to him in a well-known voice: "Don't trouble yourself, Charcoal Peter! It was the sweetest and loveliest flower in the Black Forest; but you have destroyed it, and it will never bloom again."

The blood left Peter's cheeks, as he said: "It is you then, Herr Schatzhauser? Well, what is done, is done, and must have come to pass. I hope, however, that you won't charge me with being her murderer before the magistrate."

"Wretch!" exclaimed the Little Glass-Man, "how would it console me to bring your mortal frame to the gallows? It is not earthly judges whom you have to fear, but other and severer ones, for you have sold your soul to the evil one."

"And if I have sold my heart," shrieked Peter, "you and your miserable treasures are to blame for it! You, malicious spirit, have led me to perdition, driven me to seek help of another, and you are answerable for it all."

But hardly had Peter said this, when the Little Glass-Man swelled and grew, and became both tall and broad, while his eyes were as large as soup plates, and his mouth was like a heated oven from which flames darted forth. Peter threw himself on his knees, and his marble heart did not prevent his limbs from trembling like an aspen tree. The Spirit of the Forest seized him by the neck with the talons of a hawk, and whirled him about as a whirlwind sweeps up the dead leaves, and then threw him to the ground with such force that all his ribs cracked. "Earth-worm!" cried he, in a voice like a roll of thunder, "I could dash you to pieces if I chose, for you have insulted the Master of the Forest. But for this dead woman's sake, who has given me food and drink, you shall have an eight days' reprieve. If you don't mend your ways by that time, I will come and grind your limbs to powder, and you shall die in all your sins!"

Night had come on, when some men who were passing saw the rich Peter Munk lying on the ground. They turned him over, and searched for signs of life; but for some time their efforts to restore him were in vain. Finally one of them went into the house and brought out some water, with which they sprinkled his face. Thereupon Peter drew a long breath, groaned, and opened his eyes, looked about him, and inquired after Lisbeth; but none of them had seen her. He thanked the men for the assistance they had rendered him, slipped into his house and searched every-where; but Lisbeth was nowhere to be found, and what he had taken for a horrible dream was the bitter truth.

While he was sitting there quite alone, some strange thoughts came into his mind; he was not afraid of anything, for his heart was cold; but when he thought of his wife's death, the thought of his own death came to him and he reflected how heavily he should be weighted on leaving the world — burdened with the tears of the poor, with thousands of their curses, with the agony of the poor wretches on whom he had set his dogs, with the silent despair of his mother, with the blood of the good and beautiful Lisbeth; and if he could not give an account to the old man, her father, if he should come and ask, "Where is my daughter?" how should he respond to the question of Another, to whom all forests, all seas, all mountains, and the lives of all mortals, belong?

His sleep was disturbed by dreams, and every few moments he was awakened by a sweet voice calling to him: "Peter, get a warmer heart!" And when he woke he quickly closed his eyes again; for the voice that gave him this warning was the voice of Lisbeth, his wife.

The following day he went to the tavern to drown his reflections in drink, and there he met the Stout Ezekiel. He sat down by him; they talked about this and that, of the fine weather, of the war, of the taxes, and finally came to talk about death, and how this and that one had died suddenly. Peter asked Ezekiel what he thought about death and a future life. Ezekiel replied that the body was buried, but that the soul either rose to heaven or descended to hell.

"But do they bury one's heart also?" asked Peter, all attention.

"Why, certainly, that is also buried."

"But how would it be if one did not have his heart any longer?" continued Peter.

Ezekiel looked at him sharply as he spoke those words. "What do you mean by that? Do you imagine that I haven't a heart?"

s

"Oh, you have heart enough, and as firm as a rock," replied Peter.

Ezekiel stared at him in astonishment, looked about him to see if any one had overheard Peter, and then said :

"Where do you get this knowledge? Or perhaps yours does not beat any more?"

"It does not beat any more, at least not here in my breast!" answered Peter Munk. "But tell me — now that you know what I mean — how will it be with *our* hearts!"

"Why should that trouble you, comrade?" asked Ezekiel laughing. "We have a pleasant course to run on earth, and that's enough. It is certainly one of the best things about our cold hearts, that we experience no fear in the face of such thoughts."

"Very true; but still one will think on these subjects, and although I do not know what fear is, yet I can remember how much I feared hell when I was a small and innocent boy."

"Well, it certainly won't go very easy with us," said Ezekiel. "I once questioned a school-master on that point, and he told me that after death the hearts were weighed, to find out how heavily they had sinned. The light ones then ascended, the heavy ones sank down; and I think that our stones will have a pretty good weight."

"Alas, yes," replied Peter; "and I often feel uncomfortable, that my heart is so unsympathetic and indifferent, when I think on such subjects."

On the next night, Peter heard the well-known voice whisper in his ear, five or six times: "Peter, get a warmer heart!" He experienced no remorse at having killed his wife, but when he told the domestics that she had gone off on a journey, the thought had instantly occurred to him: "Where has she probably journeyed to?"

For six days he had lived on in this manner, haunted by these reflections, and every night he heard this voice, which brought back to his recollection the terrible threat of the Little Glass-Man; but on the seventh morning he sprang up from his couch crying: "Now, then, I will see whether I can procure a warmer heart, for this emotionless stone in my breast makes my life weary and desolate." He quickly drew on his Sunday attire, mounted his horse, and rode to the Tannenbuehl.

In the Tannenbuehl the trees stood too closely together to permit of his riding further, so he tied his horse to a tree, and with hasty steps went up to the highest point of the hill and when he reached the largest pine he spoke the verse that had once caused him so much trouble to learn:

> "Keeper of green woods of pine,
> All its lands are only thine;
> Thou art many centuries old;
> Sunday-born children thee behold."

Thereupon the Little Glass-Man appeared, but not with a pleasant greeting as before; his expression was sad and stern. He wore a coat of black glass, and a long piece of crape fluttered down from his hat. Peter well knew for whom the Spirit of the Wood sorrowed.

"What do you want of me, Peter Munk?" asked the Little Glass-Man in a hollow voice.

"I have still one wish left, Herr Schatzhauser," answered Peter, with downcast eyes.

"Can hearts of stone have any wishes?" said the Glass-Man. "You have every thing needful for your wicked course of life, and it is doubtful whether I should grant your wish."

"But you promised me three wishes; and I have one left yet."

"Still, I have the right to refuse it if it should prove a foolish one," continued the Glass-Man. "But proceed, I will hear what it is you want."

"I want you to take this lifeless stone out of my breast, and give me in its place my living heart," said Peter.

"Did I make that bargain with you? Am I Dutch

Michel, who gives riches and cold hearts? You must look to him for your heart."

"Alas, he will nevermore give it back to me," replied Peter.

"Wicked as you are, I pity you," said the Little Glass-Man after a pause. "But as your wish is not a foolish one, I can not refuse you my assistance at least. So listen. You can not recover your heart by force, but possibly you may do so by stratagem; and this may not prove such a hard matter after all, for Michel, although he thinks himself uncommonly wise, is really a very stupid fellow. So go directly to him, and do just as I shall tell you."

The Little Glass-Man then instructed Peter in what he was to do, and gave him a small cross of clear crystal. "He can not harm you while you live, and he will let you go free if you hold this up before him and pray at the same time. And if you should get back your heart, then return to this place, where I shall be awaiting you."

Peter Munk took the cross, impressed on his memory all the words he was to say, and went to Dutch Michel's ravine. He called him three times by name, and immediately the giant stood before him.

"Have you killed your wife?" asked the giant, with a fiendish laugh. "I should have done it in your place, for she was giving away your wealth to the beggars. But you had better leave the country for a while, for an alarm will be given if she is not found. You will need money, and have probably come after it."

"You have guessed rightly," said Peter, "and make it a large amount this time, for America is far away."

Michel preceded Peter into the hut, where he opened a chest in which was piled a large amount of money, and took out whole rolls of gold. While he was counting them out on the table, Peter said: "You are a frivolous fellow, Michel, to cheat me into thinking that I had a stone in the breast and that you had my heart!"

"And is that not so?" asked Michel, surprised. "Can

you feel your heart? Is it not as cold as ice? Can you experience fear or sorrow, or can any thing cause you remorse?"

"You have only made my heart stand still, but I have it just the same as ever in my breast, and Ezekiel, too, says that you have lied to us. You are not the man who can tear a heart from another's breast without his knowing it, and without endangering his life; you would have to be a sorcerer to do that."

"But I assure you," cried Michel indignantly, "that you and Ezekiel, and all the rich people who have had dealings with me, have hearts as cold as your own, and I have their true hearts here in my chamber."

"Why, how the lies slip over your tongue!" laughed Peter. "You may tell that to some body else. Do you suppose that I haven't seen dozens of just such imitations on my travels? The hearts in your chamber are fashioned from wax! You are a rich fellow, I admit, but no sorcerer."

The giant, in a rage, flung open the chamber door. "Come in here, and read all these labels; and look! that glass there holds Peter Munk's heart. Do you see how it beats? Can one imitate that too in wax?"

"Nevertheless, it is made of wax;" exclaimed Peter. "A real heart doesn't beat in that way; and besides, I still have my own in my breast. No indeed, you are not a sorcerer!"

"But I will prove it to you!" cried the giant, angrily. "You shall feel it yourself, and acknowledge that it is your heart." He took it out, tore Peter's jacket open, and took a stone from the young man's breast and held it up to him. Then taking up the beating heart, he breathed on it, and placed it carefully in its place, and at once Peter felt it beating in his breast, and he could once more rejoice thereat.

"How is it with you now?" asked Michel smiling.

"Verily, you were right," answered Peter, meanwhile

drawing the little crystal cross from his pocket. "I would not have believed that one could do such a thing!"

"Is it not so? And I can practice magic, as you see; but come, I will put the stone back again now."

"Gently, Herr Michel!" cried Peter, taking a step backward, and holding up the cross between them. "One catches mice with cheese, and this time you are trapped." And forthwith, Peter began to pray, speaking whatever words came readily to his mind.

Thereupon, Michel became smaller and smaller, sank down to the floor, writhed and twisted about like a worm, and gasped and groaned, while all the hearts began to beat and knock against their glass cages, until it sounded like the workshop of a clock-maker. Peter was very much frightened, and ran out of the house, and, driven on by terror, scaled the cliffs; for he heard Michel get up from the floor, stamp and rage, and shout after him the most terrible curses. On arriving at the top of the ravine, Peter ran towards the Tannenbuehl. A terrible thunderstorm came up; lightning flashed to the right and left, and shattered many trees, but he reached the Little Glass-Man's territory unharmed.

His heart beat joyfully, because of the very pleasure it seemed to take in beating. But soon he looked back at his past life with horror, as at the thunder storm that had shattered the trees behind him He thought of Lisbeth, his good and beautiful wife, whom he had murdered in his avarice. He looked upon himself as an outcast from mankind, and wept violently as he came to the Glass-Man's hill.

Herr Schatzhauser sat under the pine tree, smoking a small pipe, but looking more cheerful than before.

"Why do you weep, Charcoal Pete?" asked he. "Did you not get your heart? Does the cold one still lie in your breast?"

"Alas, Master!" sighed Peter, "when I had the cold stone heart, I never wept. My eyes were as dry as the earth in July; but now the old heart is nearly broken in thinking of what I have done. I drove my debtors into misery and want, set my dogs on the poor and sick, and — you yourself saw how my whip fell on her beautiful forehead!"

"Peter, you were a great sinner!" said the Little Glass-Man. "Money and idleness ruined you, until your heart, turned to stone, knew neither joy nor sorrow, remorse nor pity. But repentance brings pardon, and if I were only sure that you were very sorry for your past life, I might do something for you."

"I do not want any thing more," replied Peter, with drooping head. "It is all over with me. I shall never know happiness again. What can I do, now that I am alone in the world? My mother will never pardon my behavior toward her; and perhaps I, monster that I am, have already brought her to the grave. And Lisbeth, my wife! No; rather kill me, Herr Schatzhauser, and make an end of my miserable life at once."

"Very well," replied the little man, "if you will have it so; my ax is close by." He took his pipe quietly from his mouth, knocked out the ashes, and stuck it in his pocket. Then he rose slowly and went behind the tree. Peter sat weeping on the grass, caring nothing for his life, and waiting patiently for the death-blow. After some time he heard light steps behind him, and thought: "Now he is coming."

"Look round once more, Peter Munk!" shouted the little man. Peter wiped the tears from his eyes and looked about him, and saw—his mother, and Lisbeth, his wife, who both looked at him pleasantly. He sprang up joyfully saying:

"Then you are not dead, Lisbeth? And you too, mother, have you forgiven me?"

"They will forgive you," said the Little Glass-Man, "because you feel true repentance, and every thing shall be forgotten. Return home now to your father's hut, and be a charcoal burner as before, and if you are honest and just you will honor your trade, and your neighbors will love and esteem you more highly than if you had ten tons of gold." Thus spake the Little Glass-Man, and bade them farewell.

The three praised and blessed him, and then started home. The splendid house of the rich Peter Munk had vanished. The lightning had struck and consumed it, together with all its treasures. But it was not far to his mother's hut; thence they took their way, untroubled by the loss of Peter's palace.

But how astonished were they on coming to the hut to find that it had been changed into a large house, like those occupied by the well-to-do peasants, and every thing inside was simple, was good and substantial.

"The good Little Glass-Man has done this!" exclaimed Peter.

"How beautiful!" cried Lisbeth; "and here I shall feel much more at home than in the great house with so many servants."

From this time forth, Peter Munk was a brave and industrious man. He was contented with what he had, carried on his trade cheerfully, and so it came to pass that through his own efforts he became well-to-do and was well thought of throughout the Black Forest. He never quarreled again with his wife, honored his mother, and gave to the poor who passed his door. When, in due course of time, a beautiful boy was born to him, Peter went to the Tannenbuehl and spoke his verse. But the Little Glass-Man did not respond. "Herr Schatzhauser," cried Peter, "hear me this time; I only want to ask you to stand as godfather to my little boy!" But there was no reply; only a puff of wind blew through the pines and threw some cones down into the grass. "I will take these with me as a memento, since you will not show yourself," said Peter. He put the cones in his pocket, and went home; but when he took off his Sunday jacket and gave it to his mother to put away, four large rolls of coin fell from the pockets, and when they were opened they proved to be good, new Baden thalers, with not a counterfeit among them. And this was the godfather's gift from the little man in the Tannenbuehl to the little Peter.

Thus they lived on, quietly and contentedly ; and often afterwards, when the gray hairs began to show on Peter's head, he would say : " It is better to be contented with a little than to have gold and estates with a *marble heart.*"

Some five days had now passed, and Felix, the huntsman and the student were still the prisoners of the robbers. They were well treated by the chief and his men, but still they longed for their freedom, for each day that passed added to their fear of discovery. On the evening of the fifth day, the huntsman declared to his companions in misfortune that he was fully resolved to escape that night or die in the attempt. He incited his companions to the same resolve, and showed them how they should set about the attempt. "The guard who is posted nearest to us, I will look after," said he. "It is a case of necessity, and necessity knows no law ;—he must die !"

"Die !" repeated Felix in horror; "you would kill him ? "

" I am firmly resolved to do it, when it comes to the question of saving two human lives. You must know that I overheard the robbers whispering, in an anxious manner, that the woods were being scoured for them; and the old women, in their anger, let out the wicked designs of the band; they cursed about us, and it is an understood thing that if the robbers are attacked we shall die without mercy."

"God in Heaven !" exclaimed the young man, hiding his face in his hands.

"Still, they have not put the knives to our throats as yet," continued the huntsman, " therefore, let us get the start of them. When it gets dark I will steal up to the nearest guard ; he will challenge me; I shall whisper to him that the countess has been suddenly taken very sick,

12*

and while he is off his guard I will stab him. Then I will return for you, and the second guard will not escape us any more easily; and between us three the third sentinel will not stand much of a show."

The huntsman, as he spoke, looked so terrible that Felix was actually in fear of him. He was about to beg of him to give up these bloody designs, when the door of the hut opened softly, and a man's form stole in quickly. It was the robber chief. He closed the door carefully behind him, and motioned to the prisoners to keep quiet. He then sat down near Felix, and said:

"Lady countess, your situation is a desperate one. Your husband has not kept faith with us; not only has he failed to send the ransom, but he has also aroused the government against us, and the militia are scouring the forest in all directions to capture me and my men. I have threatened your husband with your death, if an attempt was made to seize us; still either your life must be of very little account to him, or else he does not think we are in earnest. Your life is in our hands, and is forfeited under our laws. Have you any thing to say on the subject?"

The prisoners looked down in great perplexity; they knew not what to answer, for Felix felt sure that a confession of his disguise would only increase their danger.

"It is impossible for me," continued the robber, "to place a lady, for whom I have the utmost esteem, in danger. Therefore I will make a proposition for your rescue; it is the only way out that is left you; *I will fly with you.*"

Surprised, astonished beyond measure, they all looked at him while he continued: "The majority of my comrades have decided to go to Italy, and join a band of brigands there; but for my part it would not suit me to serve under another, and therefore I shall make no common cause with them. If, now, you will give me your word, lady countess, to speak a good word for me, to use your influence, with your powerful connections, for my protection, then I will set you free before it is too late."

Felix was at a loss what to say. His honest heart was opposed to willfully exposing a man, who was offering to save his life, to a danger from which he might not afterwards be able to protect him. As he still remained silent, the robber continued: "At the present time, soldiers are wanted every-where; I will be satisfied with the most common position. I know that you have great influence, but I will not ask for any thing further than your promise to do something for me in this case."

"Well, then," replied Felix, with eyes cast down, "I promise you to do what I can, whatever is in my power, to be of use to you. There is some consolation for me in the fact that of your own free will you are anxious to give up this life of a brigand."

The robber chief kissed his hand with much emotion, and added, in a whisper, that the countess must be ready to go two hours after night had set in; and then left the hut with as much caution as he had entered it. The prisoners breathed freer, when he had gone.

"Verily," exclaimed the huntsman, "God has softened his heart. How wonderful our means of escape! Did I ever dream that any thing like this could happen in the world, and that I should fall in with such an adventure?"

"Wonderful, certainly!" said Felix; "but have I done right in deceiving this man? What will my protection amount to? Shall I not be luring him to the gallows, if I do not confess to him who I am?"

"Why, how is it possible you can have such scruples, dear boy?" exclaimed the student; "and after you have played your part to such perfection, too! No, you needn't feel anxious on that score at all; that is nothing but a lawful subterfuge. Did he not attempt the outrage of kidnapping a noble lady? No, you have not done wrong; moreover I believe he will win favor with the authorities, when he, the head of the band, voluntarily surrenders himself."

This last reflection comforted the young goldsmith. In joyful anticipations alternating with uneasy apprehen-

sions over the success of the plan of escape, they passed
the succeeding hours It was already dark when the
chief returned, laid down a bundle of clothes, and said:

"Lady countess, in order to facilitate our flight, it is
necessary for you to put on this suit of men's clothes.
Get all ready. In an hour we shall begin our march."
With these words, he left the prisoners; and the huntsman had great difficulty in refraining from laughter.
"This will be the second disguise," cried he, "and I am
sure that this will be better suited to you than the first
one was!"

They opened the bundle and found a handsome hunting costume, with all its belongings, which fitted Felix well.
After he had put it on, the huntsman was about to throw
the countess's clothes into a corner of the hut; but Felix
would not consent to leave them there; he made a small
bundle of them, and hinted that he meant to ask the
countess to present them to him, and that he would preserve them all his life as a memento of these eventful
days.

Finally the robber chief came. He was fully armed,
and brought the huntsman the rifle that had been taken
away from him, and a powder-horn as well. He also
gave the student a musket, and handed Felix a hunting
knife, with the request that he would carry it and use it
in case of necessity. It was fortunate for the three men
that it was so dark, for the eager air with which Felix
received this weapon might have betrayed his sex to the
robber. As they stole carefully out of the hut, the huntsman noticed that the post near their hut was not guarded,
so that it was possible for them to slip away from the
huts unnoticed; yet the leader did not take the path that
led up out of the ravine, but brought them all to a cliff
that was so nearly perpendicular as to seem quite impas-
sible. Arriving there, their guide showed them a rope-
ladder secured to the rocks above. He swung his rifle
on his back, and climbed up a little way, telling the

countess to follow him, and offering his hand to assist her. The huntsman was the last to climb up. Arriving

at the top of the cliff, they soon struck a foot-path, and walked away at a fast pace.

"This foot-path," said their guide, "leads to the Aschaffenburg road. We will go to that place, as I have received information that your husband, the count, is stopping there now."

They walked on in silence, the robber chief keeping the lead, and the others following close at his heels. After a three hours' walk, they stopped. The robber recommended Felix to sit down and rest. He then brought out some bread, and a flask of old wine, and offered this refreshment to the weary ones. " I believe that within an hour we shall strike some of the outposts established by the militia all around the forest. In that case I beg you to bespeak good treatment for me of the commanding officer."

Felix assented, although he expected but little good to result from his interference. They rested for half an hour, and then continued their walk. They had gone on for about an hour, and had nearly reached the highway; the day was just breaking, and the shadows of night were disappearing from the forest, when their steps were suddenly arrested by a loud "Halt!" Five soldiers surrounded them, and told them that they must be taken before the commanding officer, and give an account of their presence in the forest. When they had gone fifty paces further, under the escort of the soldiers, they saw weapons gleaming in the thicket to the right and left of them; a whole army seemed to have taken possession of the forest.

The mayor sat, with several other officers, under an oak tree. When the prisoners were brought before him, and just as he was about to question them as to whence they came and whither they were bound, one of the men sprang up exclaiming: "Good Heaven! what do I see? that is surely Godfried, our forester!"

"You are right, Mr. Magistrate!" answered the huntsman, in a joyful voice. " "It is I, and I have had a wonderful rescue from the hands of those wretches."

The officers were astonished to see him; and the huntsman asked the mayor and the magistrate to step aside with him, when he related to them, in a few words, how they had escaped, and who the fourth man that accompanied them was.

Rejoiced at this news, the mayor at once made preparations to have this important prisoner conveyed to another point ; and then he led the young goldsmith to his comrades, and introduced him as the heroic youth that had, by his courage and presence of mind, saved the countess; and they all took Felix by the hand, praised him, and could not hear enough from him and the huntsman about their adventures.

In the meantime it had become broad daylight The mayor decided to accompany the rescued ones to the town. He went with them to the nearest village, where a wagon stood, and invited Felix to take a seat with him in the wagon ; while the student, the huntsman, the magistrate, and many other people, rode before and after them ; and thus they entered the city in triumph. Reports of the attack on the forest inn, and of the sacrifice of the young goldsmith, had spread over the country like wildfire ; and just as rapidly did the news of their rescue now pass from mouth to mouth. It was, therefore, not to be wondered at, that they found the streets of the city crowded with people who were eager to catch a glimpse of the young hero. Everybody pressed forward, as the wagon rolled slowly through the streets. "There he is ! " shouted the crowd. "Do you see him there in the wagon beside the officer ! Long live the brave young goldsmith ! " And the cheers of a thousand voices rent the air.

Felix was deeply moved by the hearty welcome of the crowd. But a still more affecting reception awaited him at the court-house. A middle-aged man met him on the steps, and embraced him with tears in his eyes. "How can I reward you, my son ? " cried he. "You have saved me my wife, and my children their mother; for the shock of such an imprisonment her gentle frame could not have survived."

Strongly as Felix insisted that he would not accept of any reward for what he had done, the more did the count seem resolved that he should. At last the unfortunate fate of the robber chief occurred to the youth's mind, and he related to the count how this man had rescued him, thinking that he was the countess, and that therefore the robber was really entitled to the count's gratitude. The count, moved not so much by the action of the robber chief as by this fresh display of unselfishness on Felix's part, promised to do his best to save the robber from the punishment due his crimes.

On the same day, the count took the young goldsmith, accompanied by the stout-hearted huntsman, to his palace, where the countess, still anxious for the fate of the young man, was waiting for news from the forest. Who could describe her joy when her husband entered her room, holding her deliverer by the hand? She was never through questioning and thanking him; she brought her children and showed to them the noble-hearted youth to whom their mother owed so much, and the little ones seized his hands, and the child-like way in which they spoke their thanks and their assurances that, next to their father and mother, they loved him better than any one else in the whole world, were to him a most blessed recompense for many sorrows, and for the sleepless nights he had passed in the robbers' camp.

After the first moments of rejoicing were over, the countess beckoned to a servant, who presently brought the clothes and the knapsack that Felix had turned over to the countess in the forest inn. "Here is every thing," said she, with a kindly smile, "that you gave me on that terrible night; they enveloped me with a glamour that blinded my pursuers. They are once more at your service; still I will make you an offer for these clothes, that I may have some mementoes of you. And I ask you to take in exchange the sum which the robbers demanded for my ransom."

Felix was confounded by the munificence of this present; his nobler self revolted against accepting a reward for what he had done voluntarily. "Gracious

countess," said he, deeply moved, "I can not consent
to this. The clothes shall be yours as you wished; but
the money of which you spoke I can not take. Still, as
I know that you are desirous of rewarding me in some
way, instead of any other reward, let me continue to be
blessed with your best wishes, and should I ever happen
to be in need of assistance, you may be sure that I will
call on you." In vain did the countess and her husband
seek to change the young man's resolution; and the servant was about to carry the clothes and knapsack out
again, when Felix remembered the ornament, which the
occurrence of these happy scenes had put out of his
mind.

"Wait," cried he; "there is one thing in my knapsack, gracious lady, that you must permit me to take;
every thing else shall be wholly and entirely yours."

"Just as you please," said she; "although I should
like to keep every thing just as it is, to remember you
by; so please take only what you can not do without.
Yet, if I may be permitted to ask, what is it that lies so
near to your heart that you don't wish to give it to me?"

While she was speaking, the young man had opened
the knapsack, and now produced a small red morocco
case. "Every thing that belongs to me, you are welcome to," replied he, smiling; "but this belongs to my
dear lady godmother. I did the work on it myself, and
must carry it to her with my own hands. It is a piece
of jewelry, gracious lady," continued he as he opened
the case and held it out to her, "an ornament that I
myself prepared"

She took the case, but hardly had she looked at the
ornament when she started back in surprise.

"Did you say that these stones were intended for
your godmother?" exclaimed she.

"Yes, to be sure," answered Felix; "my lady godmother sent me the stones, I set them, and am now on
the way to deliver them to her myself."

The countess looked at him with deep emotion; the

tears started from her eyes. "Then you are Felix Perner of Nuremberg?" said she.

"Yes; but by what means did you find out my name so quickly?" asked the youth, in great perplexity.

"O wonderful dispensation of heaven!" exclaimed she, turning to her astonished husband. "This is Felix, our little godson, the son of our maid, Sabine! Felix! I am the one whom you were on your way to see; and you saved your godmother from the robbers without knowing it."

"What? Are you then the Countess Sandau, who did so much for me and my mother? And is this the Castle Maienburg, to which I was bound! How grateful I am to the kind fate that brought us together so strangely; thus I have been able to prove indeed, even if in small measure, my great thankfulness to you."

"You did more for me than I shall ever be able to do for you; still while I live I shall try to show you how deeply indebted to you we all feel. My husband shall be to you a father, my children shall be as sisters, while I will be your true mother; and this ornament, that led you to me in the hour of my greatest need, shall be my most precious souvenir, for it will always remind me of you and of your noble spirit."

Thus spake the countess; and well did she keep her word. She gave the fortunate Felix abundant support on his wanderings, and when he returned as a clever master of his art she bought a house for him in Nuremberg and fitted it up completely. Not the least striking among the appointments of his parlor were finely painted pictures, representing the scenes in the inn, and Felix's life among the robbers.

There Felix lived as a clever goldsmith. The fame of his work, together with the wonderful story of his heroism, brought him customers from all parts of the realm. Many strangers, on coming to the beautiful city of Nuremberg, found their way to the shop of the famous Master Felix, in order to have a look at him, also to order an ornament made by him. But his most welcome visitors were the forester, the compass-maker, the student, and the wagoner. Whenever the latter travelled from Wuerzburg to Fuerth, he stopped to speak with Felix. The huntsman brought him presents from the countess nearly every year; while the compass-maker, after wandering about in all lands, settled down with Felix

One day they were visited by the student. He had grown to be an important man in the country, but was not ashamed to drop in now and then and take supper with Felix and the compass-maker. They lived over again all the scenes in the forest inn, and the former student related that he had seen the robber chief in Italy; he had improved very much for the better, and served as a brave soldier under the King of Naples.

Felix was rejoiced to hear this. Without this man, it is true, he might never have been placed in so dangerous a situation as in those days of his captivity; but neither could he have escaped from the robber band without his aid. And thus it was that the brave master goldsmith had only peaceful and agreeable recollections of the *Inn in the Spessart.*

PART III.

TALES OF THE PALACE

TALES OF THE PALACE.

THE SHEIK'S PALACE AND HIS SLAVES.

ALI BANU, Sheik of Alessandria, was a singular man. When he passed down the street of a morning, with a superb cashmere turban wound about his head, and clad in a festival habit, and sash worth not less than fifty camels, walking with slow and solemn steps, his forehead so contracted that his eyebrows met, his eyes cast down, and at every fifth step stroking his long black beard with a thoughtful air — when he thus took his way to the mosque, to give readings from the Koran to the Faithful, as required by his office; then the people on the street paused, looked after him, and said to one another: " He is really a handsome, stately man." " And rich, — a rich gentleman," another added; " extremely wealthy; has he not a palace on the harbor of Stamboul? Has he not estates and lands, and many thousand head of cattle, and a great number of slaves?" " Yes " spoke up a third; " and the Tartar who was recently sent here from Stamboul, with a message for the sheik from the sultan (may the Prophet preserve him), told me that our sheik was thought highly of by the minister of foreign affairs, by the lord high admiral, by all the ministers, in fact; yes, even by the sultan." " Yes," exclaimed a fourth, " fortune attends his steps. He is a wealthy distinguished gentleman; but — but — you know

what I mean!" Yes, certainly," interrupted the others;
"it is true he has his burden to carry, and I wouldn't care
to change places with him. He is rich, and a man of
rank, but, but—"

Ali Banu had a splendid house on the finest square
in Alessandria. In front of the house was a broad terrace, surrounded by a marble wall, and shaded by palm
trees. Here the sheik often sat of an evening smoking
his nargileh. At a respectable distance, twelve richly
costumed slaves awaited his orders; one carried his betel,
another held his parasol, a third had vessels of solid gold
filled with rare sherbet, a fourth carried a fan of peacock's
feathers to drive away the flies from his master's person,
others were singers and carried lutes and wind instruments to entertain him with music when he so desired,
while the best educated of them all carried scrolls from
which to read to their master.

But they waited in vain for him to signify his pleasure.
He desired neither music nor song; he did not wish to
hear passages or poems from the wise poets of the past; he
would not taste of the sherbet, nor chew of the betel; and
even the slave with the fan had his labor for his pains,
as the master was indifferent to the flies that buzzed about
him.

The passers-by often stopped and wondered over the
splendor of the house, at the richly dressed slaves, and
the signs of comfort that prevailed every-where; but
when their eyes fell on the sheik, sitting so grave and
melancholy under the palms, with his gaze never once
wandering from the little blue clouds of his nargileh, they
shook their heads and said: "Truly, this rich man is a
poor man. He, who has so much, is poorer than one
who has nothing; for the Prophet has not given him the
sense to enjoy it." Thus spake the people; they laughed
at him and passed on.

One evening, as the sheik again sat under the palms
before his door, in all his pomp, some young men standing in the street looked at him and laughed.

"Truly," said one, "Sheik Ali Banu is a foolish man; had I his wealth, I should make a different use of it. Every day I would live sumptuously and in joy; my friends should dine with me in the large *salons* of the house, and song and laughter should fill these sad halls."

"Yes," rejoined another, "all that might be very fine; but many friends would make short work of a fortune, even were it as large as that of the sultan (whom the Prophet preserve); but if I sat there under the palms, fronting this beautiful square, my slaves should sing and play, my dancers should come and dance and leap and furnish all sorts of entertainment. Then, too, I should take pleasure in smoking the nargileh, should be served with the costly sherbet, and enjoy myself in all this like a king of Bagdad."

"The sheik," said a third young man, who was a writer, "should be a wise and learned man; and really his lectures on the Koran show him to be a man of extensive reading. But is his life ordered as is beseeming in a man of sense? There stands a slave, with an armful of scrolls; I would give my best suit of clothes just to read one of them, for they are certainly rare treasures. But he! Why, he sits and smokes, and leaves books — books — alone! If I were Sheik Ali Banu, the fellow should read to me until he was entirely out of breath, or until night came on; and even then he should read to me till I had fallen asleep."

"Ha! you will grant that my plan for enjoying life is the best," laughed a fourth. "Eating and drinking, dancing and singing, hearing the tales and poems of miserable authors! No, I would have it all another way. He has the finest of horses and camels, and abundance of money. In his place, I would travel — travel to the ends of the earth, to the Muscovites, to the Franks; no distance should prevent my seeing the wonders of the world. That's what I would do, if I were that man yonder."

"Youth is a beautiful season, and the age at which

one is joyful," said an old man, of insignificant appearance, who stood near them, and had overheard their conversation. "But permit me to say that youth is also foolish, and talks thoughtlessly now and then without knowing what it says."

"What were you saying, old man?" asked the young men in surprise. "Did you mean us? How does it concern you, if we find fault with the sheik's mode of life?"

"If one is better informed than another, he should correct the other's errors; so says the Prophet," rejoined the old man. "The sheik, it is true, is blessed with plenty, and has every thing that the heart could desire; yet he has reason to be sad and melancholy. Did you suppose he was always thus? No; fifteen years ago he was cheerful and active as the gazelle, lived merrily, and enjoyed life. At that time he had a son, the joy of his life, handsome and talented, and those who saw and heard him talk envied the sheik his idol, for he was not more than ten years old, and yet there were few youths of eighteen as well educated."

"And he died? The poor sheik!" cried the young writer.

"It would be a consolation to the sheik to know that he had gone to the mansions of the Prophet, where he would be better off than here in Alessandria; but that which the sheik had to suffer is far worse. It was at the time when the Franks, like hungry wolves, invaded our land, and waged war against us. They took Alessandria, and from here they went on further and attacked the Mamelukes. The sheik was a wise man, and understood how to get along with the enemy. But whether it was because they had designs on his treasure, or because he had taken the Faithful into his house, I do not know for a certainty; but they came one day to him and accused him of having secretly supplied the Mamelukes with provisions, horses and weapons. It was of no use that he proved his innocence, for the Franks are a rough, hard-hearted people, when it is a question of extorting money.

They took his young son, Kairam, as a hostage to their camp. The sheik offered a large sum of money for his return, but they held on to the boy for a still higher bid. In the meantime they received an order from their pasha, or whatever his title might be, to embark on their vessels. Not a soul in Alessandria knew a thing about it, and all at once they were seen standing out to sea, having, it is believed, taken little Kairam with them, as nothing has ever been heard of him since."

"Oh, the poor man! how terribly Allah has chastened him!" the young men exclaimed in concert, looking with pity at the sheik, who, with such magnificent surroundings, sat sad and lonely under the palms.

"His wife, whom he loved so dearly, died from grief at the loss of her son. The sheik then bought a ship, fitted it out, and induced the Frank physician who lives down there by the fountain, to sail with him to the country of the Franks, to search for young Kairam. They set sail, and had a long passage before reaching the land of those Giaours, those Infidels, who had been in Alessandria. But there every thing was in a horrible tumult. They had just beheaded their sultan; and the pashas and the rich and the poor were now engaged in taking each other's heads off, and there was no order or law in the land Their search for little Kairam was a vain one, and the Frank physician finally advised the sheik to embark for home, as their own heads might be endangered by a longer stay. So they came back again; and since their arrival the sheik has lived just as he does to-day, mourning for his son. And he is in the right. Must he not think, whenever he eats and drinks: 'Perhaps at this moment my poor Kairam hungers and thirsts?' And when he has arranged himself in costly shawls, and holiday suits, as required by his office and rank, must he not think: 'He has probably nothing now with which to cover his nakedness?' And when he is surrounded by singers, dancers, readers, who are all his slaves, does he not think: 'Now my son may be dancing and making

music for his master in the Frank's country, just as he is
ordered?' But what pains him most is the fear lest little Kairam, being so far from the land of his fathers, and
surrounded by Infidels who jest at his religion, may become separated from the faith of his fathers, so that he
will not at the last be able to embrace him in the gardens
of paradise. This is what makes him so mild with his
slaves, and prompts his large gifts to the poor; for he believes that Allah will recompense him by moving the
heart of his son's master to treat Kairam with kindness.
Also, on each anniversary of his son's abduction, he sets
twelve slaves free."

"I have heard of that," said the writer. "One hears
curious stories floating about; but no mention was made
to me of the son. But, on the other hand, it is said that
the sheik is a singular man, and remarkably fond of
stories, and that every year he institutes a story-telling
match between his slaves, and the one who tells the best
story is rewarded with his freedom."

"Don't put any faith in these reports," said the old
man. "It is just as I have told you; it is, however, possible that he seeks the relaxation afforded by a story, on
this day of painful recollections; but still he frees the
slaves on his son's account. But the night is cold, and
I have far to go. *Schalem aleikum* — peace be with you,
young gentlemen, and think better, in the future, of the
good sheik."

The young people thanked the old man for the information he had given them, glanced once more at the sorrowing father, and walked away saying to one another:
"On the whole, I should not care to be the Sheik Ali
Banu."

Not long afterward, it so happened that these same
young men passed down the street at the hour of morning prayers. The old man and his story recurred to their
minds, and they expressed their sympathy for the sheik
as they looked up at his house. But how astonished were

they to find the house and grounds gaily decorated! From the roof, where comely slave women were promenading, banners waved; the porch of the house was covered with costly carpets; silks were laid down over the steps, and beautiful cloth, of a texture so fine that most people would have been glad to have a holiday suit cut from it, was spread well into the street.

"Hey! How the sheik has changed in the last few days!" exclaimed the young writer.. "Is he about to give a banquet? Will he test the powers of his singers and dancers? Only look at this carpet! Is there another as fine in all Alessandria? And this cloth laid right on the ground; really that is too wasteful!"

"Do you know what I think?" said another. "He must be going to receive some guest of high rank; for these are preparations such as are made when a ruler of a great country or a minister of the sultan blesses a house with his presence. Who can possibly be coming today?"

"Look! is not that our old friend below? He would be able to give us some information about this. Ho, there! old gentleman! Can't you come up here a moment?"

The old man noticed their gestures, and approached them, recognizing them as the young men with whom he had conversed some days before. They called his attention to the changes in the sheik's house, and asked him if he knew what distinguished guest was expected.

"You seem to think," replied he, "that Ali Banu has arranged for some festivities, or that he is to be honored by the visit of some great man. Such is not the case; but to-day is the twelfth day of the month of Ramadan, as you know, and is the day on which his son was taken prisoner."

"But by the beard of the Prophet!" exclaimed one of the young fellows; "every thing there has the appearance of a wedding or other festival; and still it is the anniversary of his greatest sorrow. Come, how will you harmonize this discrepancy? Confess that the sheik is somewhat shattered in mind."

"Do you always render such a hasty verdict, my young friend?" asked the old man, smiling. "This time also your arrow was pointed and sharp, and the string of your bow drawn tight; and yet your arrow flew wide of the mark. Know, then, that to-day the sheik expects his son!"

"Then he is found?" shouted the young men joyfully.

"No, and it will probably be a long time before he is found. But listen: Eight or ten years ago, as the sheik was passing this anniversary in sorrow and lamentations, also freeing slaves and giving food and drink to the poor, it so happened that he also gave food and drink to a dervish, who, tired and faint, lay in the shadow of his house. Now the dervish was a holy man, and experienced in prophecies and the signs of the stars. After his refreshment by the kind hand of the sheik, he went up to him and said: 'I know the cause of your sorrow; is not to-day the twelfth of Ramadan, and was it not on this day that you lost your son? But cheer up, for this day of sadness shall be changed to one of joy; know that on this same day your son will sometime return to you.'

"Thus spake the dervish. It would be a sin for a Mussulman to doubt the word of such a man, and although the sorrow of Ali Banu may not have been lessened thereby, yet he continues to look for the return of his son on this day, and adorns his house and porch and steps as though little Kairam might arrive at any moment."

"Wonderful!" exclaimed the writer. "But I should like to see the decorations inside the house, and note how the sheik bears himself amongst all this splendor; but, above all, I should like to listen to the tales that are related to him by his slaves."

"Nothing easier to arrange than that," replied the old man. "The steward of the slaves of that house has been my friend these many years, and would not grudge me a seat in the *salon*, where, among the crowd of servants and friends of the sheik, a single stranger would not be noticed. I will speak to him about letting you in; there are only four of you, and it might be arranged. Come at the ninth hour to this square, and I will give you an answer."

The young men returned their thanks, and went away full of curiosity to see how all this would end.

The young men were on hand at the appointed hour, and on the square before the sheik's house they met the old man, who told them that the steward would admit them. He went before them, not by way of the decorated steps and gate, but through a little side gate, that he closed carefully after them. Then he led them through many passages until they came to the large *salon*. Here there was a great crowd on all sides; there were richly dressed men of rank of the city — friends of the sheik, who had come to console him in his sorrow. There were slaves of every race and nation. But everybody wore a sorrowful expression, for they all loved their master and shared his grief. At one end of the *salon*, on a costly divan, sat the nearest friends of Ali Banu, who were waited upon by slaves. Near them, on the floor, sat the sheik, whose grief would not permit him to sit in state. His head was supported in his hands, and he seemed to be paying little attention to the consolations whispered to him by his friends. Opposite him sat some old and young men in slave costume. The old man informed his young friends that these were the slaves whom Ali Banu would free to-day. Among them were some Franks; and the old man called his friends' special attention to one of them, who was of extraordinary beauty, and was still quite young. The sheik had recently bought him, for an enormous sum, from some slave-dealers of Tunis, and was, notwithstanding his high cost, about to set him free, believing that the more Franks he returned to their fatherland the sooner the Prophet would restore his son.

After refreshments had been handed around, the sheik gave a sign to the steward, who now stood up amid the deep silence that prevailed in the room. He stepped before the slaves who were shortly to be freed, and said in a clear voice: "Men, who will receive your freedom to-day, through the grace of my master Ali Banu, Sheik of Alessandria, conform now to the custom of this house on this day, and begin your narratives."

After much whispering among themselves, an old slave arose and began his story.

THE DWARF NOSEY.

IRE! They are wrong who believe that fairies and magicians existed only at the time of Haroun-al-Raschid, or who assert that the reports of the doings of the genii and their princes, which one hears on the market-place, are untrue. There are fairies to-day, and it is not so long ago that I myself was the witness of an occurrence in which genii were concerned.

In an important city of my dear fatherland, Germany, there lived, some years ago, a poor but honest shoemaker and his wife. In the day time he sat at the corner of the street, repairing shoes and slippers, and even made new ones when he could find a customer, although he had to first purchase the leather, as he was too poor to keep any stock on hand. His wife sold vegetables and fruits, raised by her on a small plat before their door, and many people chose to buy of her because she was clean and neatly dressed, and knew how to make the best display of her vegetables.

These worthy people had a pleasant-faced, handsome boy, well-shaped and quite large for a child of eight years. He was accustomed to sit by his mother's side on the market-place, and to carry home a part of the fruit for the women or cooks who bought largely of his mother; and he rarely returned from these errands without a beautiful flower, or a piece of money, or cakes; — as the masters of these cooks were always pleased to see the little fellow at their houses, and never failed to reward him generously.

One day the shoemaker's wife sat, as usual, in the market-place; while ranged around her were baskets of cabbages and other vegetables, all kinds of herbs and seeds, and also, in a small basket, early pears, apples, and apricots. Little Jacob — this was the boy's name — sat near her and cried her wares in a manly voice: "This way, gentlemen! see what beautiful cabbages! how sweet-smelling are these herbs! early pears, ladies! early apples and apricots! Who buys? My mother offers them cheap." An old woman came to the market, torn and ragged, with a small sharp-featured face, wrinkled with age, and a crooked pointed nose that nearly reached the chin She leaned on a long crutch; and it was not easy to see how she got over the ground, as she limped and slid and staggered along — as if she had wheels on her feet, and was in momentary danger of being tilted over and striking her pointed nose on the pavement.

The shoemaker's wife looked attentively at this old woman. For sixteen years she had been in daily attendance at the market, but had never before seen this singular creature. But she involuntarily shrank back, as the old woman tottered towards her and stopped before her baskets.

"Are you Hannah, the vegetable dealer?" asked the old woman, in a harsh cracked voice, her head shaking from side to side.

U   18°

"Yes, I am she," replied the shoemaker's wife. "Can I do any thing for you?"

"We'll see, we'll see! Look at the herbs, look at the herbs, and see whether you have any thing I want," answered the old woman as she bent down over the baskets, and, pushing her dark skinny hands down among the herbs, seized the bundles that were so tastefully spread out, and raised them one after another to her long nose, snuffing at every part of them. It pressed heavily on the heart of the shoemaker's wife to see her rare herbs handled in such a way, but she did not dare to offer any objections, as purchasers were privileged to examine her goods; and, besides this, she experienced a singular fear of the old woman. When she had rummaged through the basket, the old woman muttered: "Miserable stuff! poor herbs! nothing there that I want; much better fifty years ago; bad stuff — bad stuff!"

These remarks displeased little Jacob. "You are a shameless old woman!" cried he, angrily. "First you put your dirty brown fingers into the beautiful herbs and rumple them, then you put them up to your long nose, so that any one who saw it done will never buy them, and then you abuse our wares by calling them poor stuff, when, let me tell you, the duke's cook buys every thing of us!"

The old woman squinted at the spirited boy, laughed derisively, and said in a husky voice: "Sonny — sonny! So my nose, my beautiful long nose, pleases you? You shall also have one in the middle of your face to hang down to your chin." While speaking, she slid along to another basket containing cabbages. She took the finest white head up in her hands, squeezed them together till they creaked, flung them down again into the basket in disorder, and repeated once more: "Bad wares! poor cabbages!"

"Don't wabble your head about so horribly!" exclaimed the boy, uneasily. "Your neck is as thin as a cabbage-stem; it might break and let your head fall into the basket; who then would buy of us?"

"Don't you like my thin neck?" muttered the old woman, laughing. "You shall have none at all, but your head shall stick into your shoulders, so as not to fall from your little body."

"Don't talk such stuff to the child!" said the shoe-maker's wife, indignant at the continued inspection, fingering and smelling of her wares. "If you want to buy any thing, make haste; you are driving off all my other customers."

"Good! it shall be as you say," cried the old woman, grimly. "I will take these six heads of cabbage. But look here—I have to lean on my crutch and cannot carry any thing; let your little son carry my purchases home; I will reward him."

The child was unwilling to go, and began to cry, as he was afraid of the ugly old woman; but his mother bade him go, as she considered it a sin to burden a weak old woman with so heavy a load. Half crying, he obeyed her; gathered the cabbages together in a towel, and followed the old woman from the market.

She went so slowly that it was three quarters of an hour before she reached a remote part of the city, and finally stopped before a tumble-down house. Then she drew a rusty old hook from her pocket, and inserted it skillfully into a small hole in the door, which sprung open with a bang. But how surprised was little Jacob as he entered! The interior of the house was splendidly fitted up; the ceilings and walls were of marble; the furniture of the finest ebony, inlaid with gold and mother-of-pearl; while the floor was of glass, and so smooth that the boy slipped and fell several times. The old woman then drew a silver whistle from her pocket and whistled a tune that resounded shrilly through the house. In response to this, some Guinea-pigs came down the stairs; but, as seemed strange to Jacob, they walked upright on two legs, wore

nutshells in place of shoes, and had on clothes and even
hats of the latest fashion.

"Where are my slippers, you rabble?" demanded the
old woman, striking at them with her crutch as they
sprang squeaking into the air. "How long must I stand
here waiting?"

The pigs rushed quickly up the stairs, and soon returned, bringing a pair of cocoanut shells lined with
leather, which the old woman put on. Now all her limp-
ing and stumbling disappeared. She threw her staff
away, and glided with great rapidity over the glass floor,
pulling little Jacob along by the hand. At last she
stopped in a room containing all kinds of furniture, that
bore some resemblance to a kitchen, although the tables
were mahogany, and the divans were covered with rich
tapestry, suitable for a room of state.

"Take a seat," said the old woman pleasantly, plac-
ing Jacob in a corner of the divan and moving the table
before him, so that he could not well get out of his seat.
"Sit down; you have had a heavy load to carry. Human
heads are not so light, not so light."

"But, madame, what strange things you say!" cried
the boy. "I am really tired; but then I carried cabbage-
heads that you bought of my mother."

"Eh! you are mistaken," laughed the old woman, as
she lifted the cover of the basket and took out a human
head by the hair. The child was frightened nearly out
of his wits. He could not imagine how this had occurred; but he thought at once of his mother, and that
if any one were to hear of this she would certainly be
arrested.

"I must now give you a reward for being so polite,"
muttered the old woman. "Have patience for a little
while, and I will make you a soup that you will never
forget as long as you live." With this she whistled once
more. Thereupon many Guinea-pigs, all in clothes, came
in; they had kitchen aprons tied around them, and in
their waistbands were ladles and carving-knives. After

these, a lot of squirrels came leaping in, dressed in wide
Turkish trousers, standing upright, and wearing little
velvet caps on their heads. They seemed to be the
scullions, as they raced up and down the walls and
brought pans and dishes, eggs and butter, herbs and meal,
which they placed on the hearth. Then the old woman
glided across the floor in her cocoanut shoes, bustled
about now here and now there, and the boy saw she was
about to cook him something. Now the fire crackled and
blazed up; then the kettle began to smoke and steam; an
agreeable odor was spread through the room; while the
old woman ran back and forth, followed by the squirrels
and Guinea-pigs, and whenever she came to the fire she
stopped to stick her long nose into the pot. Finally the
soup began to bubble and boil, clouds of steam shot up
into the air, and the froth ran over into the fire. Thereupon the old woman took the kettle off, poured some of
its contents into a silver bowl, and placed the same before
little Jacob, saying :

"There, sonny, there, eat some of this soup, and you
shall have those things that so pleased you about me.
You will also become a clever cook; but herbs — no, you
will never find such herbs; why didn't your mother have
them in her basket."

The boy did not understand very well what she said,
but he gave his whole attention to the soup, which was
very much to his taste. His mother had often prepared
him nice food, but never any thing that could equal this.
The fragrance of choice herbs and spices rose from his
soup, which was neither too sweet nor too sour, and very
strong.

While he was swallowing the last drops from the bowl,
the Guinea-pigs burned some Arabic incense, the blue
smoke of which swept through the room. Thicker and
thicker became these clouds, till they filled the room from
floor to ceiling. The odor of the incense had a magical
effect on the boy; for, cry as often as he would that he
must go back to his mother, at every attempt to rouse

himself he sank back sleepily, and finally fell fast asleep
on the old woman's divan. He dreamed strange dreams.
It seemed to him that the old woman was pulling off his
clothes, and giving him in their place the skin of a squirrel. Now he could leap and climb like a squirrel; he
associated with the other squirrels and with the Guinea-
pigs, all of whom were very nice well-bred people, and in
common with them, thought himself in the service of the
old woman. At first his duties were those of a shoe-
black — that is, he had to put oil on the cocoanuts that
served the old woman for slippers, and rub them until
they shone brightly. However, as he had often done
similar work at home, he was quite skillful at it. After
the first year — as it seemed to him in his dream — he
was given more genteel employment; with other squirrels, he was occupied in catching floating particles of dust,
and when they had accumulated enough of these particles, they rubbed them through the finest hair sieve, for
the old woman considered these dust atoms to be something superb, and as she had lost her teeth, she had her
bread made of them. After another year's service, he
thought, he was placed in the ranks of those whose duty
it was to provide the old woman with drinking-water.
You must not suppose that she had had a cistern sunk,
or placed a barrel in the yard to catch rain-water for this
purpose; no, there was much more refinement displayed;
the squirrels — and Jacob among them — had to collect
the dew of the roses in hazelnut shells for the old woman's
drink. And as she was a very thirsty body, the water-
carriers had a hard time of it. In the course of another
year he was given some inside work, such as the position
of floor-cleaner; and as the floor was of glass, on which
even a breath would gather, he had no easy task. They
had to sweep it, and were required to do their feet up in
old cloths, and in that condition step around the room.
In the fourth year he was employed in the kitchen. This
was a position of honor that could be attained only after
a long apprenticeship. Jacob served there, rising from a

scullion to be first pastry-cook, and soon acquired such uncommon cleverness and experience in all arts of the kitchen, that he often wondered at himself. The most difficult dishes — such as pasties seasoned with two hundred different essences, and vegetable soup consisting of all the vegetables on earth — all this he was learned in, and could prepare any thing speedily. Thus had some seven years passed in the service of the old woman, when one day she took off her cocoanut shoes, grasped her crutch, and ordered Jacob to pluck a chicken, stuff it

with herbs, and have it all nicely roasted by the time she came back. He did all this in accordance with the rules of his art. He wrung the chicken's neck, scalded it in hot water, pulled out the feathers, scraped the skin till it was nice and smooth, and, having drawn it, began to collect some herbs for the dressing. In the room where the vegetables were kept he discovered a closet which he had never noticed before, the door of which stood ajar. He went nearer, curious to see what was kept there ; and beheld many baskets, from which a powerful but pleasant odor arose. He opened one of these baskets and found therein herbs of quite peculiar shape and color. The stems and leaves were of a bluish-green, and bore a small flower of brilliant red, bordered with gold. He examined this flower thoughtfully, smelt of it, and discovered that it gave forth the same strong odor that he had inhaled from the soup the old woman had cooked for him so long ago. But so strong was the fragrance that he began to sneeze; he sneezed more and more violently, and at last — woke up, sneezing.

He lay on the divan and looked around him in astonishment. "Really, how true one's dreams do seem!" said he to himself. "Just now I should have been willing to swear that I was a mean little squirrel, the companion of Guinea-pigs and other low creatures, and from them exalted to be a great cook! How my mother will laugh when I tell her all this! But may she not scold me for going to sleep in a strange house, instead of hurrying back to help her at the market-place?"

So thinking, he got up to go away; but found his limbs cramped, and his neck so stiff that he could not move it from side to side. He had to laugh at himself for being so helplessly sleepy; for every moment, before he knew it, he was striking his nose on a clothes-press, or on the wall, or knocked it against the door-frame when he turned around quickly. The squirrels and Guinea-pigs were whining around him, as if they wanted to accompany him, and he actually gave them an invitation to do so, as he stood upon the threshold, for they were nice little creatures; but they rushed quickly back into the house on their nutshells, and he could hear them squeaking from a distance.

It was a remote quarter of the city into which the old woman had led him, and he had difficulty in finding his way out of the narrow alleys; besides, he was in the midst of a crowd who seemed to have discovered a dwarf in the vicinity, for all around him he heard shouts of: "Hey! look at the ugly dwarf! Where does the dwarf come from? Why, what a long nose he has! and look at the way his head sticks into his shoulders, and his ugly brown hands!" At any other time, Jacob would willingly have joined them, as it was one of the delights of his life to see giants or dwarfs, or any rare and strange sights; but now he felt obliged to hurry back to his mother.

He was rather uneasy in his mind when he arrived at the market. His mother still sat there, and had quite a quantity of fruit in the basket; so that he could not have slept very long after all. But still he noticed, before reaching her, that she was very sad, as she did not call on the passers to buy, but supported her head in her hand; and when he came nearer he thought her much paler than usual. He hesitated as to what he should do, but finally mustered up courage to slip up behind her, laid his hand confidingly on her arm and said: "Mother, what is the matter? Are you angry with me?"

His mother turned around, but on perceiving him sprang back with a cry of horror.

"What do you want with me, ugly dwarf?" cried she. "Be off with you! I will not stand such tricks!"

"But, mother, what is the matter with you?" asked Jacob, in a frightened way. "You are certainly not well; why do you chase your son away from you?"

"I have already told you to go your way," replied Hannah, angrily. "You will get no money from me by your jugglery, you hateful monster!"

"Surely, God has taken away her understanding!" said the child, sorrowfully, to himself. "What means shall I take to get her home? Dear mother, only be reasonable now; just look at me once closely; I am really your son, your Jacob."

"This joke is being carried too far," cried Hannah to her neighbor. "Only look at this hateful dwarf, who stands there and keeps away all my customers, besides daring to make a jest of my misfortune. He says to me, 'I am your son, your Jacob,'— the impudent fellow!"

Upon that Hannah's neighbors all got up and began to abuse him as wickedly as they knew how — and mar-

14

ket-women, as you know, understand it pretty well —
ending by accusing him of making sport of the misfortune of poor Hannah, whose son, beautiful as a picture,
had been stolen from her seven years ago: and they
threatened to fall upon him in a body, and scratch his
eyes out, if he did not at once go away.

Poor little Jacob knew not what to make of all this.
Was it not true that he had gone to the market as usual
with his mother, early this morning? that he had helped
her arrange the fruits, and afterwards had gone with the
old woman to her house, had there eaten a little soup,
had indulged in a short nap, and come right back again?
And now his mother and her neighbors talked about seven
years, and called him an ugly dwarf! What, then, had
happened to him?

When he saw that his mother would not hear another
word from him, tears sprang into his eyes, and he went
sadly down the street to the stall where his father mended
shoes. "Now I will see," thought he, "whether my
father will not know me. I will stop in the door-way
and speak to him." On arriving at the shoemaker's
stall, he placed himself in the door-way, and looked in.
The master was so busily occupied with his work, that
he did not notice him at first, but when by chance he
happened to look at the door, he let shoes, thread and
awl drop to the ground, and exclaimed in affright: "In
heaven's name! — what is that? what is that?"

"Good evening, master," said the boy, as he stepped
inside the shop. "How do you do?"

"Poorly, poorly, little master," replied the father, to
Jacob's great surprise; as he also did not seem to recognize him. "My business does not flourish very well, I
have no one to assist me, and am getting old; and yet an
apprentice would be too dear."

"But have you no little son, who could one of these
days assist you in your work?" inquired the boy.

"I had one, whose name was Jacob, and who must
now be a tall active fellow of twenty, who could be a

great support to me were he here. He must lead a
happy life now. When he was only twelve years old he
showed himself to be very clever, and already understood
a good deal about the trade. He was pretty and pleasant too. He would have attracted custom, so that I
should not have to mend any more, but only make new
shoes. But so it goes in the world!"

"Where is your son, then?" asked Jacob, in a trembling voice.

"God only knows," replied the old man. "Seven years
ago,— seven years — he was stolen from us on the
market-place."

"Seven years ago!" exclaimed Jacob in amazement.

"Yes, little master, seven years ago. I remember as
though it were but yesterday how my wife came home
weeping, and crying that the child had been gone the
whole day, that she had inquired and searched every-
where, but could not find him. I had often said that it
would turn out so; for Jacob was a beautiful child, as
everybody said, and my wife was so proud of him, and
was pleased when the people praised him, and she often
sent him to carry vegetables and the like to the best
houses. That was all well enough; he was richly rewarded every time; but I always said: 'Take care! the
city is large, and many bad people live in it. Mind
what I say about little Jacob?' Well, it turned out
as I had predicted. An ugly old woman once came to
the market, haggled over some fruits and vegetables, and
finally bought more than she could carry home. My
wife — compassionate soul — sent the child with her;
and from that hour we saw him no more!"

"And that was seven years ago you say?"

"It will be seven years in the Spring. We had him
cried on the streets, and went from house to house and
inquired for him. Many had known and loved the pretty
youngster, and now searched with us; but all in vain.
Nor did any one know who the woman was that had
bought the vegetables; but a decrepit old woman, some

ninety years of age, said that it was very likely the
wicked witch *Kraeuterweiss*, who comes once in every fifty
years to the city to make purchases."

Such was the story Jacob's father told him; and when
the shoemaker had finished, he pegged away stoutly at
his shoe, drawing the thread out with both fists as far as
his arms could reach.

By and by Jacob comprehended what had happened
to him, namely: that he had not dreamed at all, but that
he must have served the wicked witch as a squirrel for
seven years. Anger and grief so swelled his heart that
it almost broke. The old woman had stolen seven years
of his youth; and what had he received as compensation
therefor? The ability to make cocoanut slippers shine
brightly; to clean a glass floor; and all the mysteries of
cooking that he had learned of the guinea-pigs. He
stood there a long time thinking over his fate, when his
father finally asked him: "Is there any thing in my line
you would like, young master? A pair of new slippers,
or," he added, smiling, "perhaps a covering for your
nose?"

"What's that about my nose?" asked Jacob. "What
do I want of a cover for it?"

"Well," responded the shoemaker, "every one to his
taste; but I must say this much to you: if I had such a
terrible nose, I would make for it a case of rose-colored
patent leather. Look! I have a fine piece of it in my
hand here; it would take at least a yard. But how well
your nose would be protected! As it is now, I know you
can't help striking your nose on every door-post, and
against every wagon that you try to get out of the way
of."

Jacob stood mute with terror. He felt of his nose; it
was thick, and at least two hands long! So, too, had the
old woman changed his figure so that his mother did not
know him, and everybody had called him an ugly dwarf!

"Master," said he, half crying, "have you a mirror
handy, where I can look at myself?"

"Young master," replied his father gravely. "You do not possess a figure that should make you vain, and you can have no reason to look in a glass every hour. Break off the habit; it is an especially silly one for you to indulge in."

"Oh, do but let me look in the glass!" cried Jacob. "I assure you it is not from vanity I ask it."

"Leave me in peace — I have none. My wife has a small one, but I don't know where she keeps it. But if you are bound to look in a glass, across the street lives Urban, the barber, who has a mirror twice as large as your head; look into that; and in the meantime, good morning!"

With these words, his father pushed him gently out of the door, closed it after him, and sat down once more to his work. Jacob, very much cast-down, went across the street to Urban, whom he had known well in the past.

"Good morning, Urban," said he to the barber. "I have come to beg a small favor of you; be so good as to let me look into your glass a moment."

"With pleasure; there it is," laughed the barber, and his customers, who were waiting for a shave, laughed with him. "You are a pretty fellow, tall and slim, with a neck like a swan, hands like a queen, and a stumpy nose that can not be equalled for beauty. You are a little vain of it, to be sure; but keep on looking; it shall not be said of me that I was so jealous I would not let you look in my glass."

The barber's speech was followed by shouts of laughter that fairly shook the shop. Jacob, in the meantime, had approached the mirror and looked at his reflection in the glass. Tears came into his eyes. "Yes, surely you could not recognize your little Jacob, dear mother," thought he. "He did not look thus in those joyful days when you paraded with him before the people!" His eyes had become small, like those of the pigs; his nose was monstrous, and hung down over his mouth and chin;

the neck seemed to have entirely disappeared, as his head sank deeply into his shoulders, and it was only with the greatest effort that he could move it to the right or left. His body was still of the same height as seven years before; but what others gain from the twelfth to the twentieth year in height, he made up in breadth. His back and breast were drawn out rounding, so as to present the appearance of a small but closely-packed sack. This stout, heavy trunk was placed on thin, weak legs that did not seem able to support the weight. But still larger were his arms; they were as large as those of a full-grown man; his hands were rough, and of a yellowish-brown; his fingers long and spindling, and when he stretched them down straight he could touch the ground with their tips without stooping. Such was the appearance of little Jacob, who had grown to be a misshapen dwarf.

He recalled now the morning on which the old woman had come up to his mother's baskets. Every thing that he had criticised about her — the long nose, the ugly fingers, every thing, she had inflicted on him; only the long trembling neck she had left out entirely.

"Well, have you seen enough of yourself, my prince?" said the barber, stepping towards him with a laugh. "Really, if one were to try and dream of any thing like it, it would not be possible. For I will make you a proposal, my little man. My barber shop is certainly well patronized, but not so well as it used to be, which results from the fact that my neighbor, Barber Schaum, has somewhere picked up a giant, who serves to allure customers to his shop. Now, to grow a giant no great art is required; but to produce a little man like you is quite another matter. Enter my service, little man; you shall have food, drink and lodging — every thing; for all which you shall stand outside of my door mornings, and invite the people to come in; you shall make the lather, and hand the customers the towel; and be assured we shall both be benefitted. I shall get more customers than the

man with the giant, while each one of them will cheerfully give you a fee."

Jacob's soul recoiled at the thought of serving as a
sign for a barber. But was he not forced to suffer this
abuse patiently? He therefore quietly told the barber
that he had not the time for such services, and went on
his way.

Although the wicked old woman had changed his
form, she had had no power over his spirit, and of this
fact Jacob was well aware, as he no longer felt and
thought as he had done seven years before. No; he
knew he had grown wiser and more intelligent in this in-
terval; he sorrowed not over his lost beauty, not over
his ugly shape, but only over the fact that he had been
driven like a dog from his father's door. He now resolved
to make one more attempt to convince his mother of his
identity.

He went to her in the market, and begged her to listen to him quietly. He reminded her of the day on
which he had gone home with the old woman, of all the
little details of his childhood, told her of his seven
years' service as a squirrel with the old witch, and how
she transformed him because he had criticised her appearance. The shoemaker's wife did not know what to
think of all this. His stories of his childhood agreed
with her own recollections; but when he told her that he
had been a squirrel for seven years, she exclaimed: "It
is impossible! and there are no witches." And when
she looked at him, she shuddered at the sight of the
ugly dwarf, and did not believe he could be her son.
Finally, she considered it best to lay the matter before
her husband. So she collected her baskets and called
the dwarf to go with her. On reaching the shoemaker's
stall, she said:

"Look here; this person claims to be our lost son,
Jacob. He has told me all how he was stolen from us
seven years ago, and how he was bewitched by an old
hag."

"Indeed!" interrupted the shoemaker, angrily. "Did he tell you that? Wait, you good-for nothing! I told him all this myself, not an hour ago, and now he runs over to jest with you! Enchanted are you, sonny? I will disenchant you again!" With this he picked up a bundle of thongs that he had just cut out, sprang at the dwarf, and lashed him on his back and arms till the dwarf cried out with pain and ran off weeping.

In that city, as in every other, there were but few pitying souls who would assist a poor unfortunate about whom there was any thing ridiculous. Therefore it was that the unfortunate dwarf remained the whole day without food or drink, and at evening was forced to choose the steps of a church for his couch, cold and hard as they were.

But when the rising sun awaked him, he began to think seriously of how he should support himself, now that his parents had cast him off. He was too proud to serve as a sign for a barber's shop; he would not travel round as a mountebank and exhibit himself for money. What should he do? It now occurred to him that as a squirrel he had made great progress in the art of cookery; he believed, not without reason, that he could hold his own with most cooks; and so he resolved to make use of his knowledge.

As soon as the streets began to show signs of life, and the morning was fairly advanced, he entered the church and offered up a prayer. Then he started on his way. The duke, the ruler of the country, was a well-known glutton and high-liver, who loved a good table, and selected his cooks from all parts of the world. To his palace the dwarf betook himself. When he came to the outer gate, the guards asked him what he wanted, and had a little sport with him. He asked to see the master of the kitchen. They laughed, and led him through the court, and at every step servants stopped to look after him, laughed loudly, and fell in behind him, so that by and by a monster procession of servants of all degrees crowded the steps of the palace. The stable-boys threw away their curry-combs, the messengers ran, the carpet-beaters forgot to dust their carpets, everybody pushed and crowded, and there was as much noise and confusion as if the enemy had been before the gates; and the shout —"A dwarf! a dwarf! Have you seen the dwarf!"—filled the air.

The steward of the palace now appeared at the door, with a stern face, and a large whip in his hand. "For heaven's sake, you dogs, why do you make such a noise? Don't you know that the duke still sleeps?" and thereupon he raised the lash and let it fall on the backs of some stable-boys and guards.

"Oh, master!" cried they, "don't you see any thing? We bring here a dwarf — a dwarf such as you have never seen before." The steward was able to control his laughter only with great difficulty, when he saw the dwarf. But it would not do to compromise his dignity by a laugh, so he drove away the crowd with his whip, led the dwarf into the palace, and asked him what he wanted. When he heard that Jacob wanted to see the master of the kitchen, he replied:

"You are mistaken, sonny; it is me, the steward of the palace, whom you wish to see. You would like to become body-dwarf to the duke. Isn't that so?"

"No, master," answered the dwarf; "I am a clever cook, and experienced in all kinds of rare dishes; if you will take me to the master of the kitchen perhaps he can make use of my services."

"Every one to his own way, little man; but you are certainly an ill-advised youth. In the kitchen! Why, as body-dwarf you would have no work to do, and food and drink to your heart's desire, and fine clothes. Still, we will see. Your art will hardly be up to the standard of a cook for the duke, and you are too good for a scullion." With these words the steward took him by the hand and led him to the rooms of the master of the kitchen.

"Gracious master!" said the dwarf, bowing so low

v

that his hands rested on the floor, " have you no use for
a clever cook ? "

The master of the kitchen looked him over from head
to foot, and burst into a loud laugh. " What? You a
cook? Do you think that our hearths are so low that you
can see the top of one by standing on your toes and lift-

ing your head out of your shoulders? Oh dear, little
fellow! Whoever sent you to me for employment as a
cook has made a fool of you." So spoke the master of
the kitchen, laughing loudly ; and the steward and all the
servants in the room joined in the laugh.

But the dwarf did not allow himself to be disconcerted. " An egg or two, a little syrup and wine, and

meal and spices, can be spared in a house where there is such plenty," said he. " Give me some kind of a dainty dish to prepare, furnish me with what I need, and it shall be made quickly before your eyes, and you will have to confess that I am a cook by rule and right."

While the dwarf spoke, it was wonderful to see how his little eyes sparkled, how his long nose swayed from side to side, and his long spider-like fingers gesticulated in unison with his speech. " Come on ! " cried the master of the kitchen, taking the arm of the steward. "Come on; just for a joke, let's go down to the kitchen ! " They went through many passages, and at last reached the kitchen, which was a high roomy building splendidly fitted up. On twenty hearths burned a steady fire ; a stream of clear water, in which fish were darting about, flowed through the middle of the room ; the utensils for immediate use were kept in closets made of marble and costly woods, and to the right and left were ten rooms in which were preserved every thing costly and rare for the palate that could be found in the entire country of the Franks and even in the Levant. Kitchen servants, of all degrees, were running about, rattling kettles and pans, and with forks and ladles in their hands ; but when the master of the kitchen entered, they all stopped and remained so still that one heard only the crackling of the fires and the splashing of the stream.

" What has His Grace ordered for breakfast this morning ? " inquired the master of the kitchen of the breakfast-cook.

" Sir, he has been pleased to order Danish soup and red Hamburg dumplings."

" Very well," said the master of the kitchen. " Did you hear, little man, what His Grace will have to eat ? Do you feel capable of preparing these difficult dishes ? In any event, you will not be able to make the dumplings, for that is a secret."

" Nothing easier," replied the dwarf, to the astonishment of his hearers ; for when a squirrel he had often

made these dishes. " Nothing easier; for the soup, I
shall require this and that vegetable, this and that spice,
the fat of a wild boar, turnip, and eggs; but for the
dumpling," continued he, in a voice so low that only the
master of the kitchen and the breakfast-cook could hear,
"for the dumpling, I shall use four different kinds of
meat, a little wine, the oil of a duck, ginger, and a certain
vegetable called ' stomach's joy.' "

" Ha ! By St. Benedict ! What magician learned you
this ? " cried the cook, in astonishment. " He has given
the receipt to a hair, and the ' stomach's joy ' we did not
know of ourselves. Yes, that would improve the flavor,
no doubt. O you miracle of a cook ! "

" I would not have believed it," said the master of the
kitchen; "but let him make the experiment; give him
what things he wants, and let him prepare the breakfast."

These commands were carried out, and every thing
was laid out near the hearth, when it was discovered that
the dwarf's nose barely came up to the fire-place. Therefore a couple of chairs were placed together, and upon
them a marble slab was laid, and the little magician was
then invited to try his skill. The cooks, scullions, servants, and various other people, formed a large circle
around him, and looked on in astonishment to see how
dexterous were his manipulations and how neatly his
preparations were conducted. When he was through, he
ordered both dishes to be placed on the fire, and to allow
them to cook to the exact moment when he should call
out. Then he began to count *one*, *two*, *three*, and so on,
until he reached five hundred, when he sang out:
"Stop!" The pots were then set to one side, and the
dwarf invited the master of the kitchen to taste of their
contents. The head cook took a gold spoon from one of
the scullions, dipped it in the brook, and handed it to the
master of the kitchen, who stepped up to the hearth with
a solemn air, dipped his spoon into the food, tasted it,
closed his eyes, smacked his lips, and said : " By the life

of the duke, it's superb! Won't you take a spoonful, steward?" The steward bowed, took the spoon, tasted, and was beside himself with pleasure. "With all respect for your art, dear head cook, you have had experience, but have never made either soup or Hamburg dumpling that could equal this!" The cook now took a

taste, shook the dwarf most respectfully by the hand, and said: "Little One! you are a master of the art; really, that 'stomach's joy' makes it perfect."

At this moment the duke's valet came into the kitchen and announced that his grace was ready for his breakfast. The food was now placed on silver plates and sent in to the duke; the master of the kitchen taking the dwarf to his own room, where he entertained him. But they had

not been there long enough to say a pater-noster, (such
is the name of the Franks' prayer, O Sire, and it does not
take half as long to say it as to speak the prayer of the
Faithful,) when there came a message from the duke requesting the presence of the master of the kitchen.   He
dressed himself quickly in his court costume, and followed the messenger.   The duke appeared to be in fine
spirits.   He had eaten all there was on the silver plates,
and was wiping his beard as the master of the kitchen
entered.   "Hear me, master of the kitchen," said he, " I
have always been very well pleased with your cooks up
to the present time; now tell me who it was that prepared my breakfast this morning?   It was never so
delicious since I sat on the throne of my ancestors; tell
me the cook's name that I may send him a present of a
few ducats "

"Sire, it is a strange story," replied the master of the
kitchen; and went on to tell the duke how a dwarf had
been brought to him that morning who wished a place as
cook, and what had occurred afterwards.   The duke was
greatly astonished.   He had the dwarf called, and asked
him who he was, and where he came from.   Now poor
Jacob certainly could not say that he had been enchanted,
and had once taken service as a squirrel; still he kept
to the truth by saying that he had now neither father nor
mother, and had learned how to cook from an old woman.
The duke did not question him further, but examined
the singular shape of his new cook.   "If you will remain
in my service," said the duke, "I will give you fifty ducats
a year, a holiday suit, and two pair of trowsers besides.
You will be expected to prepare my breakfast every
morning with your own hands; must direct the preparation of dinner, and have a general oversight of my kitchen.
As I am in the habit of naming all the people in my
palace, you shall take the name of Nosey, and hold the
office of assistant master of the kitchen."

The dwarf, Nosey, prostrated himself before the

mighty duke of the Franks, kissed his feet, and promised to serve him faithfully.

Thus was the dwarf provided for. And he did his office honor; for it can be said that the duke was quite another man while the dwarf remained in his service. Formerly he had been wont to express his displeasure by throwing the dishes, that were taken in to him, at the heads of the cooks; in fact, once in his anger, he had thrown a roasted calf's foot, that was not tender enough, at the master of the kitchen, and it hit him on the forehead and disabled him for three days. To be sure, the duke made amends for his anger afterwards by distributing handfuls of ducats among his victims; but nevertheless the cooks never took his meals in to him without fear and trembling. Since the dwarf's arrival, however, there was a magical change. Instead of three meals a day, the duke now indulged in five, in order to do justice to the skill of the assistant master of the kitchen; and he never betrayed the least appearance of dissatisfaction. On the contrary, he found every thing new and rare, was sociable and pleasant. and grew fleshier and happier from day to day. He would often send for the master of the kitchen and the dwarf Nosey, in the middle of the meal, and giving them seats on either side of himself, would feed them the choicest morsels with his own fingers; a favor that they both knew how to prize.

The dwarf became the wonder of the city. Permission was constantly sought of the master of the kitchen to see him cook, and a few gentlemen of the highest rank were able to induce the duke to let their cooks take lessons from Nosey, and this brought the dwarf in quite a sum of money, as each pupil had to pay half a ducat daily. And in order to keep the good will of the other cooks, and prevent them from becoming jealous, Nosey distributed this money among them.

Thus lived Nosey, in exceptional comfort and honor, for nearly two years; and only when he thought of his parents did he feel sorrowful. One day, however, a curious incident occurred.

Nosey was especially fortunate in his purchases. For this reason he was in the habit of going to market himself for fowls and fruits, whenever his duties would permit. One morning he went to the goose-market to look for some heavy fat geese, such as his master loved. His form, far from arousing jokes and laughter, commanded respect, for he was known to be the famous chief cook of the duke, and every woman who had geese to sell was happy if he turned his nose towards her. At the further end of a row of stalls, he saw a woman sitting in a corner, who had also geese to sell, but, unlike the other market-women, she did not cry her wares or attempt to attract buyers. To her he went and weighed her geese. They were just what he wanted, and he bought three, together with the cage, shouldered his burden, and started on his way home. It occurred to him as a very strange thing that only two of these geese cackled, as genuine geese are accustomed to do, while the third one sat quite still and reserved, occasionally sighing and sneezing like a human being. "It must be h. lf-sick," said he, as he went along. "I must hurry back so as to kill and dress it." But, to his astonishment, the goose replied, quite plainly :

"If you stick me,
    I will bite ye;
If my neck you do not save,
    You will fill an early grave."

Terribly frightened, Nosey sat the cage down, and the goose looked at him with beautiful intelligent eyes, and sighed. "Good gracious!" exclaimed the dwarf. "Can you speak, Miss Goose? I would not have thought it! Well, now, don't be anxious; one knows how to live without having any designs on such a rare bird. But I would be willing to bet that you have not always had these feathers   I was myself once a contemptible little squirrel."

"You are right," replied the goose, "in saying that I was not born with this ignominious form. Alas! it was never sung to me in my cradle that Mimi, daughter of the great Wetterbock, would meet her death in the kitchen of a duke!"

"Do not be uneasy, dear Miss Mimi," said the dwarf cheerfully. "On my word of honor, and as sure as I am the assistant master of the kitchen of His Grace, no one shall harm you. I will fix you up a coop in my own room, where you shall have plenty of food, and I will devote all my leisure time to your entertainment. The other kitchen servants shall be told that I am fattening a goose with different kinds of vegetables, for the duke; and whenever an opportunity offers, I will set you at liberty."

The goose thanked him with tears, and the dwarf did as he had promised. Nor did he furnish her with common goose food, but with pastry and sweetmeats, and whenever he was at liberty he paid her visits of condolence. They told one another their histories, and in this way Nosey learned that she was a daughter of the magician Wetterbock, who lived on the island of Gothland, and who had begun a quarrel with an old witch, who in turn had vanquished him by a clever stratagem, and had then revenged herself upon him by transforming his daughter into a goose, and bringing her thus far from home   When the dwarf had told her his story, she said:

"I am not inexperienced in these matters. My father gave my sisters and myself instructions in the art, as far as he thought best; your account of the quarrel you had with the old woman over the market baskets, your sudden transformation while inhaling the steam of that vegetable soup, taken in connection with some expressions of the old woman that you told me of, prove conclusively to me that you are bewitched by herbs; that is to say, if you

14*

can find the plant that the old woman used in your transformation, you can be restored to your former shape."

This announcement was not very consoling to the
dwarf, for where was he to find the plant? Still, he
thanked the goose, and strove to be hopeful.

About this time the duke received a visit from a
neighboring prince who was on friendly terms with him.
He sent for the dwarf, and said to him: "Now is the
time when you will have to prove your devotion to me,
and your mastery of the art of cooking. The prince who
visits me is accustomed to the very best, as you know,
and is an excellent judge of fine cooking as well as a
wise man. See to it, therefore, that my table is provided
daily with such dishes as will cause his wonder to increase from day to day. And, on the penalty of my displeasure, you must not make the same dish twice, during
his stay here My treasurer will supply you with all the
money you may want for this purpose. And even though
you be forced to cook gold and diamonds in lard, do it!
I would rather be ruined than put to the blush before
him."

Thus spake the duke; and the dwarf replied with a
low obeisance: "It shall be as you say, my master; God
willing, I will so provide that this prince of epicures
shall be satisfied."

The little cook put forth all his skill. He spared
neither his master's money nor himself. And he might
be seen the livelong day in the midst of clouds of smoke
and flame, while his voice sounded constantly through
the kitchen, as he ordered the under-cooks and scullions
about like a prince. (Sire, I might imitate the camel-
drivers of Aleppo, who, in relating their stories to the
travellers, make their heroes sit down to the most sump-
tuous banquets. They will use a whole hour in their de-
scription of the food with which the table is supplied, and
thereby create such ardent longings and uncontrollable
hunger in their hearers that the caravans are constantly
halting for a meal, and the camel-drivers come in for a

full share of the provisions so involuntarily opened. I say I might imitate them, but I will not.)

The duke's guest had now been fourteen days with him, and had been well entertained. They ate not less than five times a day, and the duke was contented with the skill of his dwarf, for he saw satisfaction on the brow of his guest. But on the fifteenth day, it happened that the duke sent for the dwarf while they sat at table, and presented him to his guest, with the inquiry how the dwarf's cooking had pleased him.

"You are a marvelous cook," replied the prince, "and know what constitutes good cheer. In all the time I have been here, you have not given us the same dish twice, and every thing has been well prepared. But tell me why it is you have let so long a time pass without producing the queen of dishes, the Pastry Souzeraine?"

The dwarf was all of a tremble, for he had never heard of this queen of pastries; but still he recovered himself and replied: "O Sire! I had hoped that the light of your countenance would be shed on this palace for many days yet; therefore I delayed this dish; for what could be a more appropriate compliment from the cook on the day of your departure, than the queen of the pastries?"

"Indeed?" laughed the duke, "and were you waiting for the day of my death, before you should compliment me in the same manner? For you have never placed this pastry before me. But think of some other parting dish: for you must set this pastry on the table to-morrow."

"It shall be as you say, master!" answered the dwarf, as he went out. But he was very much disturbed in mind, for he knew that the day of his disgrace and misfortune was at hand. He had not the slightest idea how to make the pastry. He therefore went to his chamber and wept over his hard fate. Just then the goose, Mimi, who had the run of his chamber, came up to him and inquired the cause of his sorrow. "Cease to weep,"

said she, on learning of the incident of the pastry.
"This *entrée* was a favorite dish of my father's, and I
know about how it is made. You take this and that, so
and so much, and if there should happen to be any little
thing left out, why, the gentlemen will never notice it."
The dwarf, on hearing Mimi's recipe, jumped for joy,
blessed the day on which he had bought the goose, and
ran off to make the queen of the pastries. He first
made a small one by way of experiment, and lo, it tasted
finely, and the master of the kitchen, to whom he gave a
morsel, heartily praised his skill. On the following day,
he baked the pastry in a larger form, and after decorat-
ing it with a wreath of flowers, sent it, hot from the oven,
to the duke's table. He then donned his best suit of
clothes, and followed after it. As he entered the dining-
room, the head carver was in the act of cutting the
pastry and serving it up to the duke and his guest, with
a silver pie-knife. The duke took a large mouthful of
the pastry, cast his eyes up at the ceiling, and said as
soon as he had swallowed it: "Ah! ah! ah! They are
right in calling this the queen of the pastries; but my
dwarf is also king of all cooks — isn't that so, dear
friend?"

The prince helped himself to a small piece, tasted
and examined it attentively, and then, with a scornful
smile, pushed the plate away from him, exclaiming:
"The thing is very cleverly made, but still it isn't the
genuine Souzeraine. I thought it would turn out that
way."

The duke scowled, and reddening with mortification,
cried: "Dog of a dwarf! How dare you bring this disgrace on your master? Shall I have your big head taken
off as a penalty for your bad cookery?"

"Alas, master, I prepared the dish in accordance with
all the rules of art; there certainly can not any thing be
wanting!" cried the dwarf trembling.

"You lie, you knave!" exclaimed the duke, giving
him a kick, "or my guest would not say that some in-

gredient was wanting   I will have you cut up in small pieces and made into a pastry yourself!"

"Have pity!" cried the dwarf, falling on his knees before the guest, and clasping his feet. "Tell me what is wanting in this dish that it does not suit your palate? Do not let me die on account of a handful of meat and meal."

"That wouldn't help you much, dear Nosey," answered the prince, laughing. "I felt pretty sure yesterday that you couldn't make this dish as my cook does. Know, then, that there is an herb wanting, that is not known at all in this country, called *Sneeze-with-pleasure*, and, without this, the pastry is tasteless and your master will never have it as good as mine."

The last words aroused the anger of the duke to the highest pitch. "And yet I will have it!" exclaimed he, with flashing eyes. "For I swear on my princely word, that I will either show you the pastry just as you require it, or —— the head of this fellow impaled on the gate of my palace. Go, dog! Once more I grant you twenty-four hours' time."

The dwarf went back to his own room, and complained to the goose of his fate, for as he had never heard of this plant, he must die. "Is that all that is wanted?" said she. "I can help you in that case, for I learned to know all vegetables from my father. At any other time you might have been doomed; but fortunately now there is a full moon, and at this time the plant blooms. But tell me, are there any old chestnut trees in the vicinity of the palace?"

"Oh, yes," replied the dwarf, with a lighter heart; "by the lake, two hundred steps from the house, there is a large group of them; but what has that to do with it?"

"Well, at the foot of old chestnuts blooms this plant," replied Mimi. "Therefore, let us lose no time in our search. Take me under your arm, and set me down when we are in the garden, and I will assist you."

He did as she said, and went with her to the palace

entrance. But there he was stopped by the guard who extended his weapon, and said: "My good Nosey, it's all up with you; I have received the strictest orders not to let you out of the house."

"But there can't be any objection to my going into the garden," urged the dwarf. "Be so kind as to send one of your comrades to the steward, and ask him

whether I may not be allowed to look for vegetables in the garden." The guard did as requested, and the dwarf received permission to go into the garden, as it was surrounded by high walls and escape was impossible. When Nosey was safely outside, he put the goose down carefully, and she ran on before him to the lake where the chestnut trees stood. He followed her closely, with beating heart, as his last hope was centered on the success of their search, and if they did not find the plant,

he was fully resolved that he would throw himself into
the lake, rather than submit to being beheaded. The
goose wandered about under all the trees, turning aside
every blade of grass with her bill, but all in vain was
her search, and she began to cry from pity and anxiety,
as the night was at hand, and it was difficult to distinguish objects around her.

Just then the dwarf chanced to look across the lake
and he shouted: "Look, look! Across the lake stands
an old chestnut tree; let us go over there and search —
perhaps we shall find my luck blooming there." The
goose took the lead, hopping and flying, and Nosey ran
after as fast as his little legs would carry him. The
chestnut tree cast a large shadow, so that nothing could
be seen under its branches; but the goose suddenly
stopped, clapped her wings with joy, put her head down
into the long grass, and plucked something that she presented with her bill to the astonished dwarf, saying:
"That is the plant, and there are a lot of them growing
there, so that you will never lack for them."

The dwarf examined the plant thoughtfully; it had a
sweet odor, that reminded him involuntarily of the scene
of his transformation. The stems and leaves were of a
bluish-green color, and it bore a brilliant red flower with
a yellowish border.

"God be praised!" exclaimed he at length. "How
wonderful! Do you know that I believe this is the very
plant that changed me from a squirrel to this hateful
form? shall I make an experiment with it?"

"Not yet," replied the goose. "Take a handful of
these plants with you and let us go to your room;
collect what money and other property you have, and
then we will try the virtue of this plant."

Taking some of the plants with them, they went back
to his room, the heart of the dwarf beating so that it
might almost be heard. After packing up his savings,
some fifty or sixty ducats, and his shoes and clothes in
a bundle, he said: "God willing, I will now free myself

of this shape," stuck his nose deep down into the plant and inhaled its fragrance.

Thereupon a stretching and cracking took place in all his limbs; he felt his head being raised from his shoulders; he squinted down at his nose and saw it getting smaller and smaller; his back and breast began to straighten out, and his legs grew longer.

The goose looked on in astonishment. "Ha! how tall, how handsome you are!" exclaimed she. "Thank God! nothing remains of your former shape?" Jacob, greatly rejoiced, folded his hands and prayed. But in his joy he did not forget how much he was indebted to the goose; he longed with all his heart to go at once to his parents, but gratitude caused him to forego this pleasure, and to say: "Whom but you have I to thank for my restoration. Without you I should never have found this plant, and should have forever remained a dwarf, or have died under the ax. Come, I will take you to your father; he, who is so experienced in magic, can easily disenchant you." The goose wept tears of joy, and accepted his offer. Jacob walked safely out of the palace with the goose, without being recognized, and started at once on his way to the coast to reach Mimi's home.

What shall I say further? That they reached their journey's end safely; that Wetterbock disenchanted his daughter, and sent Jacob, loaded down with presents, back to his native city; and that his parents easily recognized their son in the handsome young man; that he bought a shop with the presents given him by Wetterbock; and that he became rich and happy.

To this I will add, that after Jacob's escape from the palace, great trouble ensued; for on the following day, as the duke was about to carry out his threat of taking off the dwarf's head if he did not succeed in finding the plant, that individual was nowhere to be found. But the prince asserted that the duke had connived at his escape, so as not to be compelled to kill his best cook;

and the prince accused the duke of breaking his word. From this a great war broke out between the two rulers, which is known to history as "The Vegetable War." Many battles were fought, but finally peace was restored, and this peace was called "The Pastry Peace," inasmuch as at the peace banquet, the Souzeraine, queen of the pastries, was prepared by the prince's cook, and rejoiced the palate of his grace, the duke.

Thus do the most trivial causes often lead to great results; and this, O Sire, is the story of the *Dwarf Nosey*.

Such was the story of the Frankish slave. When he had finished, Ali Banu had fruits served to him and the other slaves, and conversed, while they were eating, with his friends. The young men who had been introduced into the room so stealthily, were loud in their praises of the sheik, his house, and all his surroundings. "Really," said the young writer, "there is no pleasanter way of passing the time than in hearing stories. I could sit here the livelong day with my legs crossed, and one arm resting on a cushion, with my head supported by my hand, and, if allowable, the sheik's nargileh in my hand, and so situated listen to stories with the greatest zest Something like this, I fancy, will be our existence in the Gardens of Mohammed."

"So long as you are young and able to work," replied the old man, who had conducted the young men into the house, "you can not be in earnest in such an idle wish. At the same time, I admit that there is a peculiar charm about these narratives. Old as I am — and I am now in my seventy-seventh year — and much as I have already heard in my life, still I am not ashamed when I see a large crowd gathered round a story-teller at the corner, to take my place there too and listen to him. The listener dreams that he is an actor in the events that are narrated; he lives for the time being amongst these people, among these wonderful spirits, with fairies and other

W   15

folk, whom one does not meet every day; and has afterwards, when he is alone, the means of entertaining himself, just as does the traveller through the desert, who
has provided well for his wants."

"I had never thought much about wherein the charm
of these stories lay," responded another of the young
men. "But I agree with you. When I was a child, I
could always be quieted with a story. It mattered not,
at first, of what it treated, so long as it was told me, so
long as it was full of incidents and changes. How often
have I, without experiencing the slightest fatigue, listened
to those fables which wise men have devised, and in
which they express a world of wisdom in a sentence:
stories of the fox and the foolish stork, of the fox and the
wolf, and dozens of stories of lions and other animals.
As I grew older, and associated more with men, those
short stories failed to satisfy me; I required longer ones,
which treated too of people and their wonderful for-
tunes "

"Yes, I recall that time very plainly," interrupted one
of the last speaker's friends. "It was you who created
in us the desire for stories of all kinds. One of your
slaves knew as many as a camel-driver could tell on the
trip from Mecca to Medina. And when he was through
with his work, he had to sit down with us on the grass-
plot before the house, and there we would tease until he
began a story; and so it went on and on until night overtook us."

"And was there not then disclosed to us a new, an
undiscovered realm?" said the young writer. "The
land of genii and fairies, containing, too, all the wonders
of the vegetable kingdom, with palaces of emeralds and
rubies, inhabited by giant slaves, who appear when a
ring was turned around on the finger and back again, or
by rubbing a magical lamp, and brought splendid food
in golden shells? We felt that we were transported to
that country; we made those marvelous voyages with
Sinbad, we accompanied Haroun-al-Raschid, the wise

ruler of the Faithful, on his evening walks, and we knew
his vizier as well as we knew each other; in short, we
lived in those stories, as one lives in his nightly dreams,
and for us there was no part of the day so enjoyable as
the evening, when we gathered on the grass-plot, and the
old slave told us stories. But tell us, old man, why it is
that this craving for stories is as strong in us to-day as
it was in our childhood?"

The commotion that had arisen in the room, and the
request of the steward for silence, prevented the old man
from replying. The young men were uncertain whether
they ought to rejoice at the prospect of hearing another
story, or to feel vexed that their entertaining conversation with the old man had been broken off so suddenly.
When silence had been restored, a second slave arose
and began his story.

ABNER, THE JEW,

WHO HAD SEEN NOTHING.

IRE, I am from Mogadore, on the coast of the Atlantic, and during the time that the powerful Emperor Muley Ismael reigned over Fez and Morocco, the following incident occurred, the recital of which may perhaps amuse you. It is the story of Abner, the Jew, who had seen nothing.

Jews, as you know, are to be found every-where, and every-where they are Jews — sharp, with the eye of a hawk for the slightest advantage to be gained ; and the more they are oppressed the more do they exhibit the craft on which they pride themselves. That a Jew may sometimes, however, come to harm through an exhibition of his smartness, is sufficiently shown by what befel Abner, one afternoon, as he took his way through the gates of Morocco for a walk.

He strode along with a pointed hat on his head, his form enveloped in a plain and not excessively clean mantle, taking from time to time a stolen pinch from a gold box that he took special pains to conceal. He stroked his mustaches, and in spite of the restless eyes that expressed fear, watchfulness, and the desire to discover something that could be turned to account, a certain satisfaction was apparent in his shifting countenance, which plainly denoted he must have recently concluded some very good bargains. He was doctor, merchant, and every thing else that brought in money. He had this day sold a slave with a secret defect, had bought a camel-load of gum very cheap, and had prepared the last dose for a wealthy patient—not the last before his recovery, but the last before his death.

He had just emerged from a small thicket of palm and date trees, when he heard the shouts of a number of

people running after him. They were a crowd of the emperor's grooms, headed by the master of the horse, looking about them on all sides as they ran, as if in search of something.

"Philistine!" panted the master of the horse. "Have you not seen one of the emperor's horses, with saddle and bridle on, run by?"

"The best racer to be seen anywhere — a small neat hoof, shoes of fourteen carat silver, a golden mane, fifteen hands high, a tail three and a half feet long, and the bit of his bridle of twenty-three carat gold?"

" That's he ! " cried the master of the horse. " That's he ! " echoed the grooms. "It is Emir," said an old riding-master. " I have warned the Prince Abdallah not to ride Emir without a snaffle. I know Emir, and said beforehand he would throw the prince, and though his bruises should cost me my head, I warned him beforehand. But quick ! which way did he go ? "

" I haven't seen a horse at all ! " returned Abner, smiling. " How then can I tell you where the emperor's horse ran ? "

Astonished at this contradiction, the gentlemen of the royal stables were about to press Abner further, when another event occurred, that interfered with their purpose.

By one of those singular chances of which there are numerous examples, the empress's lap-dog had turned up missing; and a number of black slaves came running up, calling at the top of their voices : " Have you seen the empress's lap-dog ? "

"A small spaniel," said Abner, " that has recently had a litter, with hanging ears, bushy tail, and lame in the right fore-leg ? "

" That's she — her own self ! " chorused the slaves. " That's Aline ; the empress went into fits as soon as her pet was missed. Aline, where are you ? What would become of us if we were to return to the harem without you ? Tell us quickly, where did you see her run to ? "

" I have not seen any dog, and never knew that my empress — God preserve her — owned a spaniel ! "

The men from the stable and harem grew furious at Abner's insolence, as they termed it, in making jests over the loss of imperial property ; and did not doubt for a moment that Abner had stolen both dog and horse. While the others continued the search, the master of the horse and the chief eunuch seized the Jew, and hurried him, with his half-sly and half-terrified expression, before the presence of the emperor.

Muley Ismael, as soon as he heard the charge against

Abner, sent for his privy-counsellor, and, in view of the importance of the subject, presided over the investigation himself. To begin with, fifty lashes on the soles of the feet were awarded the accused. Abner might whine or shriek, protest his innocence or promise to tell every thing just as it had happened, recite passages from the Scripture or from the Talmud; he might cry: " The displeasure of the king is like the roar of a young lion, but his mercy is like dew on the grass," or " Let not thy hand strike when thy eyes and ears are closed." Muley Ismael made a sign to his slaves, and swore by the beard of the Prophet, and his own, that the Philistine should pay with his head for the pains of the Prince Abdallah and the convulsions of the empress, if the runaways were not restored.

The palace of the emperor was still resounding with the shrieks of the Jew, as the news was brought that both dog and horse had been found. Aline was surprised in the company of some pug dogs, quite respectable curs, but not fit associates for a court lady ; while Emir, after tiring himself out with running, had found the fragrant grass on the green meadows by the Tara brook suited his taste better than the imperial oats — like the wearied royal huntsman who, having lost his way on the chase, forgot all the delicacies of his own table as he ate the black bread and butter in a peasant's hut.

Muley Ismael now requested of Abner an explanation of his behavior, and the Jew saw that the time had come, although somewhat late, when he could answer ; which, after prostrating himself three times before his highness's throne, he proceeded to do in the following words:

"Most high and mighty Emperor, King of Kings, Sovereign of the West, Star of Justice, Mirror of Truth, Abyss of Wisdom, you who gleam like gold, sparkle like a diamond, and are as inflexible as iron! Hear me, as it is permitted your slave to lift his voice in your august presence. I swear by the God of my fathers, by Moses and the Prophets, that I never saw your sacred horse, and the amiable dog of my gracious empress, with the eyes of my body. But listen to my explanation.

"I walked out to refresh myself after the fatigues of the day, and in the small wood where I had the honor to meet his excellency, the master of the horse, and his vigilancy, the black overseer of your blessed harem, I perceived the trail of an animal in the fine sand between the palms. As I am well acquainted with the tracks of various animals, I at once recognized these as the foot-prints of a small dog; other traces near the prints of the fore-paws where the sand seemed to be lightly brushed away, assured me that the animal must have had beauti-ful pendant ears; and as I noticed how, at long intervals, the sand was brushed up, I thought: the little creature has a fine bushy tail that must look something like a tuft of feathers, and it has pleased her now and then to whip up the sand with it. Nor did it escape my obser-vation that one paw had not made as deep an imprint on the sand as the others; unfortunately, therefore, it could not be concealed from me that the dog of my most gracious empress — if it is permitted me to say it aloud —limped a little.

"Concerning your highness's horse, I would say that on turning into a path in the wood I came upon the tracks of a horse. I had no sooner caught sight of the small noble hoof-print of the fine yet strong frog of the foot, than I said in my heart; a horse of the Tschenner stock, of which this must have been one of the noblest specimens, has passed by here It is not quite four months since my most gracious emperor sold a pair of this breed to a prince in the land of the Franks, and my brother Ruder was there when they agreed on the price, and my most gracious emperor made so and so much by the transaction. When I saw how far apart these hoof-prints were, and how regular were the distances between them, I thought: that horse galloped beautifully and gently and could only be owned by my emperor; and I thought of the war horse described by Job —'He paweth

in the valley, and rejoiceth in his strength; he goeth on
to meet the armed men. He mocketh at fear, and is not
affrighted: neither turneth he back from the sword.
The quiver rattleth against him, the glittering spear and
the shield.' And as I saw something glistening on the
ground, I stooped down, as I always do in such cases,
and lo, it was a marble stone in which the hoof of the
running horse had cut a groove, from which I perceived
that the shoe must have been of fourteen carat silver,
as I have learned the mark each metal makes, be it pure
or alloyed. The path in which I walked was seven feet
wide, and here and there I noticed that the dust had
been brushed from the palms; the horse switched it off
with his tail, thought I, which must therefore be three
and a half feet long. Under trees that began to branch
about five feet from the ground, I saw freshly-fallen
leaves, that must have been knocked off by the horse
in his swift flight; hence he was fully fifteen hands
high; and behold, under the same trees were small tufts
of hair of a golden lustre, hence his hide would have
been a yellow-dun! Just as I emerged from the copse,
my eye was caught by a deep scratch on a wall of rock.
I ought to know what caused this, thought I, and what
do you think it was? I put a touch-stone, dusted over,
on the scratch, and got an impression of some fine hair-
lines such as for fineness and precision could not be ex-
celled in the seven provinces of Holland. The scratch
must have been caused by the stem of the horse's bit
grazing the rock, as he ran close by it. Your love of
splendor is well-known, King of Kings; and one should
know that the most common of your horses would be
ashamed to champ any thing less fine than a golden bit.
Such was the result of my observations, and if——"

"Well, by the cities of the Prophet!" cried Muley
Ismael, "I call that a pair of eyes! Such eyes would not
harm you, master of the huntsmen; they would save you
the expense of a pack of hounds; you, minister of the
police, could see further than all your bailiffs and spies.

Well, Philistine, in view of your uncommon acuteness, that has pleased us so well, we will show you clemency; the fifty lashes that you justly received are worth fifty zecchini, as they will save you fifty more; so draw your purse and count out fifty in cash, and refrain in the future from joking over our imperial property; as for the rest, you have our royal pardon."

The whole court were astonished at Abner's sagacity, and his majesty, too, had declared him to be a clever fellow; but all this did not recompense him for the anguish he suffered, nor console him for the loss of his dear ducats. While groaning and sighing, he took one coin after another from his purse, aud before parting with it weighed it on the tip of his finger. Schnuri, the king's jester, asked him jeeringly whether all his zecchini were tested on the stone by which the bit of Prince Abdallah's dun horse was proved. "Your wisdom to-day has brought you fame," said the jester; "but I would bet you another fifty ducats that you wish you had kept silent. But what says the Prophet? 'A word once spoken can not be overtaken by a wagon, though four fleet horses were harnessed to it.' Neither will a greyhound overtake it, Mr. Abner, even if it did not *limp.*"

Not long after this (to Abner) painful event, he took another walk in one of the green valleys between the foot-hills of the Atlas range of mountains. And on this occasion, just as before, he was overtaken by a company of armed men, the leader of whom called out:

"Hi! my good friend! have you not seen Goro, the emperor's black body-guard, run by? He has run away, and must have taken this course into the mountains."

"I can not inform you, General," answered Abner.

"Oh! Are you not that cunning Jew who had seen neither the dog nor the horse? Don't stand on ceremony; the slave must have passed this way; can you not scent him in the air? or can you not discover the print of his flying feet in the long grass? Speak! the slave must have passed here; he is unequalled in killing sparrows with a pea-shooter, and this is his majesty's greatest diversion. Speak up! or I will put you in chains!"

"I can not say I have seen what I have yet not seen."

"Jew, for the last time I ask, where is the slave? Think on the soles of your feet; think on your zecchini!"

"Oh, woe is me! Well, if you will have it that I have seen the sparrow-shooter, then run that way; if he is not there, then he is somewhere else."

"You saw him, then?" roared the general.

"Well, yes, Mr. Officer, if you will have it so."

The soldiers hastened off in the direction he had indicated; while Abner went home chuckling over his cunning. Before he was twenty-four hours older, however, a company of the palace guards defiled his house by entering it on the Sabbath, and dragged him into the presence of the Emperor of Morocco.

"Dog of a Jew!" shouted the emperor. "You dare to send the imperial servants, who were pursuing a fugitive, on a false scent into the mountains, while the slave was fleeing towards the coast, and very nearly escaped on a Spanish ship. Seize him, soldiers! A hundred on his soles, and a hundred zecchini from his purse! The more his feet swell under the lash, the more his purse will collapse."

You know, O Sire, that in the kingdom of Fez and Morocco the people love swift justice; and so the poor Abner was whipped and taxed without consulting his own inclinations beforehand. He cursed his fate, that condemned his feet and his purse to suffer every time it pleased his majesty to lose any thing. As he limped out of the room, bellowing and groaning, amidst the laughter of the rough court people, Schnuri, the jester, said to him:

"You ought to be contented, Abner, ungrateful Abner; is it not honor enough for you that every loss that our gracious emperor—whom God preserve—suffers, likewise arouses in your bosom the profoundest grief? But if you will promise me a good fee, I will come to your shop in Jews Alley an hour before the Sovereign of the West is

to lose any thing, and say : ' Don't go out of your house,
Abner; you know why; shut yourself up in your bed-
room under lock and key until sunset.' "

This, O Sire, is the story of *Abner, the Jew, Who
had seen Nothing*.

When the slave had finished, and every thing was
quiet in the *salon*, the young writer reminded the old man
that the thread of their discourse had been broken, and
requested him to declare wherein lay the captivating
power of tales.

" I will reply to your question," returned the old man.
"The human spirit is lighter and more easily moved than
water, although that is tossed into all kinds of shapes, and
by degrees, too, bores through the thickest objects. It is
light and free as the air, and, like that element, the
higher it is lifted from earth, the lighter and purer it is.
Therefore is there an inclination in humanity to lift itself
above the common events of life, in order to give itself
the freer play accorded in more lofty domains, even if
it be only in dreams. You yourself, my young friend, said
to me: ' We lived in those stories, we thought and felt
with those beings,' and hence the charm they had for you.
While you listened to the stories of yonder slaves, that
were only fictions invented by another, did you also use
your imagination? You did not remain in spirit with the
objects around you, nor were you engrossed by your
every-day thoughts; no, you experienced in your own
person all that was told; it was you yourself to whom this
and that adventure occurred, so strongly were you interested in the hero of the tale. Thus your spirit raised
itself, on the thread of such a story, over and away from
the present, which does not appear so fair or have such
charms for you.   Thus this spirit moved about, free and
unconfined in a strange and higher atmosphere; fiction
became reality to you — or, if you prefer, reality became
fiction — because your imagination and being were absorbed into fiction."

"I do not quite comprehend you," returned the young merchant; "but you are right in saying that we live in fiction, or fiction lives in us. I remember clearly that beautiful time when we had nothing to do. Waking, we dreamed; we pretended that we were wrecked on desert islands, and took counsel with one another as to what we should do to prolong our lives; and often we built ourselves huts in a willow copse, made scanty meals of miserable fruits, although we could have procured the very best at the house not a hundred paces distant; yes, there were even times when we waited for the appearance of a kind fairy, or a wonderful dwarf, who should step up to us and say: 'The earth is about to open—will it please you to descend with me down to my palace of rock-crystal, and take your choice of what my servants, the baboons, can serve up?'"

The young men laughed, but confessed to their friend that he had spoken truth. "To this day," continued another, "this enchantment creeps over me now and then. I became, for instance, somewhat vexed at the stupid fable with which my brother would come rushing up to the door: 'Have you heard of the misfortune of our neighbor, the stout baker? He had dealings with a magician, who, out of revenge, transformed him into a bear, and now he lies within his chamber growling fearfully.' I would get angry, and call him a liar. But what a different aspect the case took on when I was told that the stout neighbor had made a journey into a far-distant and unknown land, and there fell into the hands of a magician who transformed him into a bear! I would after a while find myself absorbed in the story; would take the trip with my stout neighbor; experience wonderful adventures, and it would not have astonished me very much if he had actually been stuck into a bear-skin and forced to go on all fours."

"And yet," said the old man, "there is a very delightful form of narrative, in which neither fairies nor magicians figure, no palace of crystal and no genii who bring the most delicious food, no magic horse, but a kind that differs materially from those usually designated as tales.''

"Another kind?" exclaimed the young men. "Please explain to us more clearly what you mean.''

"I am of the opinion that a certain distinction should be made between fairy tales and narratives which are commonly called stories. When I tell you that I will relate a fairy tale, you would at the outset count upon its treating of events outside of the usual course of life and of its being located in a kingdom entirely different from any thing on earth. Or, to make my meaning plain, in a fairy tale you would look for other people as well as mortals to appear; strange powers, such as fairies and magicians, genii and ruling spirits, are concerned in the fate of the person of whom the tale treats; the whole fabric of the story takes on an extraordinary and wonderful shape, and has somewhat the appearance of the texture of our carpets, or many pictures of our best masters which the Franks call arabesques. It is forbidden the true Mussulman to represent human beings, the creatures of Allah, in colors and paintings, as a sin; therefore one sees in this texture wonderful tortuous trees, and twigs with human heads; human beings drawn out into a bush or fish; in short, forms that remind one of the life around him, and are yet unlike that life. Do you follow me?"

"I believe I perceive your meaning," said the young writer; "but continue."

"After this fashion then is a fairy tale; fabulous, unusual, astonishing; and because it is untrue to the usual course of life, it is often located in foreign lands or referred to a period long since passed away. Every land, every tribe, has such tales; the Turks as well as the Persians, the Chinese as well as the Mongolians; and even in the country of the Franks there are many, at least so I was told by a learned Giaour; still they are not as fine as ours, for instead of beautiful fairies who live in splendid palaces, they have decrepit old women, whom they name witches — an ugly, artful folk, who dwell in miserable huts, and instead of riding in a shell wagon, drawn by griffins, through the blue skies, they ride through the mist astride of a broomstick. They also have gnomes and spirits of the earth, who are small, undersized people, and cause all kinds of apparitions. Such are the fairy tales; but of far different composition are the narratives commonly called stories. These are located in an orderly way on the earth, treat of the usual affairs of life, the wonderful part mostly made up of the links of fate drawn about a human being, who is made rich or poor, happy or unhappy, not by magic or the displeasure of fairies, as in the tale, but by his own action, or by a singular combination of circumstances."

"Most true!" responded one of the young men; "and such stories are also to be found in the glorious tales of Scheherazade called 'The Thousand and One Nights.' Most of the events that befel King Haroun-al-Raschid and his vizier were of that nature. They go out disguised and see this and that very singular incident, which is afterwards solved in a natural manner."

"And yet you must admit," continued the old man "that those stories did not constitute the least interesting part of 'The Thousand and One Nights.' And still, how they differ in their motive, in their development and in their whole nature from the tales of a Prince Biribinker, or the three dervishes with one eye, or the fisher who drew from the sea the chest fastened with the seal of Salomo! But after all there is an original cause for the distinctive charms possessed by both styles — namely, that we live to experience many things striking and unusual. In the fairy tales, this element of the unusual is supplied by the introduction of a fabulous magic into the ordinary life of mortals; while in the stories something happens that, although in keeping with the natural laws, is totally unexpected and out of the usual course of events."

"Strange!" cried the writer, "strange, that this natural course of events proves quite as attractive to us as the supernatural in the tales. What is the explanation of that?"

"That lies in the delineation of the individual mortal," replied the old man. "In the tales, the miraculous forms the chief feature, while the mortal is deprived of the power of shaping his course; so that the individual figures and their character can only be drawn hastily. It is otherwise with the simple narrative, where the manner in which each one speaks and acts his character, in due proportion, is the main point and the most attractive one."

"Really, you are right!" exclaimed the young merchant. "I never took time to give the matter much thought. I looked at every thing, and then let it pass by me. I was amused with one, found another wearisome, without knowing exactly why; but you have given us the key that unlocks the secret, a touch-stone with which we can make the test and decide properly."

"Make a practice of doing that," answered the old man, "and your enjoyment will constantly increase, as you learn to think over what you have heard. But see, another slave has risen to tell his story."

THE YOUNG ENGLISHMAN.

IRE, I am a German by birth, and have been in your country too short a time to be able to entertain you with a Persian tale or an amusing story of sultans and viziers. You must, therefore, permit me to tell you a story of my native land. Sad to say, our stories are not always as elevated as yours — that is, they do not deal with sultans or kings, nor with viziers and pashas, that are called ministers of justice or finance, privy-counsellors, and the like, but they treat very modestly (soldiers sometimes excepted) of persons outside of official life.

In the southern part of Germany lies the town of Gruenwiesel, where I was born and bred. It is a town identical with its neighbors; in its centre a small market-place with a town-pump, on one corner a small old town-hall, while built around the square were the houses of the justice of the peace and the well-to-do merchants, and, in a few narrow streets that opened out of the square, lived the rest of the citizens. Everybody knew everybody else; every one knew all that was going on; and if the minister, or the mayor, or the doctor had an extra dish on the table, the whole town would know of it before dinner was over. On afternoons, the wives went out to coffee parties, as we call them, where, over strong coffee and sweet cakes, they gossiped of the great events of the day, coming to the conclusion that the minister must have invested in a lottery ticket and won an unchristian

X   15*

amount of money, that the mayor was open to a bribe, and that the apothecary paid the doctor well to write costly prescriptions.   You may therefore imagine, Sire, how unpleasant it was for an orderly town like Gruenwiesel, when a man came there of whom nothing was known — not even where he came from, what he wanted there, or on what he lived.   The mayor, to be sure, had seen his passport, a paper that every one is compelled to have in our country ——

"Is it, then, so unsafe on the street," interrupted the sheik, "that you must have a firman from your sultan in order to protect yourselves from robbers?"

No, Sire, (replied the slave); these passports do not protect us from thieves, but are only a regulation by which the identity of the holder is every-where established. Well, the mayor had investigated this strange man's passport and at a gathering at the doctor's house had said that it had been found all right from Berlin to Gruenwiesel, but there must be some cheat in it, as the man was a suspicious-looking character.   The mayor's opinion being entitled to great weight in Gruenwiesel, it is no wonder that from that time forth the stranger was looked upon with suspicion.   And his course of life was not adapted to change this opinion of my countrymen.   The stranger rented an entire house that had formerly been unoccupied, had a whole wagon full of singular furniture — such as stoves, ranges, frying-pans, and the like — put in there, and lived there alone by himself.   Yes, he even cooked for himself; and not a single soul entered his house, with the exception of an old man living in Gruenwiesel, who made purchases for him of bread, meat, and vegetables.   Still, even this old man was only allowed to step inside the door, where he was always met by the stranger, who relieved him of his bundles.

I was ten years of age when this man came to our town, and I can to-day recall the uneasiness which his presence caused, as clearly as though it had all happened yesterday.   He did not come in the afternoon, like the

other men, to the bowling alley; nor did he visit the inn
in the evening, to discuss the news over a pipe of tobacco.
It was in vain that, one after another, the mayor, the
'squire, the doctor, and the minister invited him to dinner
or to lunch; he always excused himself. Thus it was
that some believed him crazy; others took him to be a
Jew; while a third party firmly insisted that he was a
magician or sorcerer.

I grew to be eighteen, twenty years old, and still this
man passed under the name of "the strange gentleman."
There came a day, however, on which some fellows came
to our town leading a number of strange animals. They
were a rough lot of vagrants, who had a camel that would
kneel, a bear that danced, some dogs and monkeys looking very comical in clothes and playing all sorts of tricks.
These vagrants generally go through the town, stopping
at all the cross streets and squares, making a horrible
tumult with a small drum and fife, compelling their animals to dance and perform tricks, and then collect money
in the houses. But the band, which was now exhibiting
in Gruenwiesel, was distinguished above others of its
class by the presence of a monster orang-outang, nearly
as large as a human being, which walked on two legs, and
could perform all manner of clever tricks. This dog-and-
ape-troupe stopped before the house of the strange gentleman. At the sound of the fife and drum, the latter appeared at the dust-dimmed window, looking rather displeased; but after a time his face lighted up, and, to
everybody's surprise, he opened the window, looked out,
and laughed heartily at the tricks of the orang-outang,
and even gave such a large silver coin to the show that
the whole town spoke of it.

On the following day these vagrants left the place.
The camel carried a large number of baskets in which
the dogs and monkies sat demurely, while the men and
the big ape walked behind the camel. They had hardly
been gone an hour, however, when the strange gentleman
sent to the post, and ordered, to the astonishment of the

postmaster, a carriage with post-horses, and shortly drove through the same gate, out on the same road that had been taken by the band of men and monkeys. The whole town was vexed because it could not be learned where he was bound. Night had set in before the strange gentleman returned to the gate But another person sat in the wagon with him, who pressed his hat down over his face, and had bound up his mouth and ears in a silk handkerchief. The gate-keeper held it to be his duty to question the other stranger, and to ask him for his passport; he answered, however, very roughly, muttering away in a quite unintelligible language.

"It is my nephew," said the strange gentleman, pleasantly, to the gate-keeper, as he pressed some silver coin into his hand; "it is my nephew, who does not at present understand very much German. He was just now cursing in his own dialect at our being stopped here."

"Well, if he is your nephew," replied the gate-keeper, "of course a pass is not necessary. He will probably lodge with you?"

"Certainly," said the strange gentleman, "and will most likely remain here some time."

The gate-keeper had no further objections to make, so the strange gentleman and his nephew drove into the town. The mayor and citizens, however, were not very well pleased with the action of the gate-keeper. He might at least have taken notice of a few words of the nephew's dialect, so that thereby it might have been easily ascertained from what country he and his uncle originally came. On this the gate-keeper asserted that his dialect was neither French nor Italian, but it sounded broad enough to be English.

Thus did the gate-keeper help himself out of disgrace, and at the same time supply the young man with a name. For every body now was talking about the young Englishman.

But, like his uncle, the young Englishman did not show himself either at the bowling alley or the beer

table; but yet he gave the people much to busy themselves about in another way. For instance, it often happened that, in the formerly quiet house of the strange
gentleman, such fearful cries and noises were heard, that
the people would crowd together before the house and
look up at the windows. They would then see the young
Englishman, clad in a red coat and green knee-breeches,
with bristly hair, and a frightened expression, run by the
windows, and through all the rooms, with inconceivable
rapidity, chased by his uncle, wearing a red dressing-
gown, with a hunting whip in his hand; he often missed
hitting him, but after a time the crowd felt sure that the
young man had been caught, as the most pitiable cries
and whip-lashings were heard. The ladies of the town
now felt such a lively sympathy for the young man who
was treated so cruelly that they finally prevailed on the
mayor to take some steps in the matter. He wrote the
strange gentleman a note, in which he expressed his
opinion very emphatically about the way the young Englishman had been treated, and threatened that if any
more such scenes occurred he would take the young man
under his own protection.

But who could have been more astonished than was
the mayor, when, for the first time in ten years, he saw
the strange gentleman enter his house! The old gentleman excused his conduct, on the ground that it was in
accordance with the expressed charge of the young man's
parents, who had sent their son to him to be educated.
This youth was in other respects wise and forward for his
years, but he did not learn languages easily ; and he was
very anxious to teach his nephew to speak German fluent-
ly, that he might take the liberty of introducing him to
the society of Gruenwiesel. And yet this language
seemed so hard for him to acquire, that often there was
nothing left to do but to whip it into him. The mayor
expressed himself well satisfied with these explanations,
only advising moderation on the old man's part; and he
said that evening, over his beer, that he had seldom seen

so intelligent and clever a man as the strange gentleman.
" It is a pity," added he, in conclusion, " that he comes so
little into society; still, I think that when the nephew is
a little further advanced in German, he will visit my circle oftener."

Through this single circumstance, the public opinion
of the town was completely changed. The stranger was

looked upon as a clever man, wishes for his better acquaintance were freely expressed, and when, now and
then, a terrible shriek was heard to come from the house,
the Gruenwiesel people simply said: " He is giving his
nephew lessons in the German language," and ceased to
block up the street before his house, as they had been
wont to do on hearing those cries. In the course of three
months the German exercises seemed to be finished, as

the old gentleman took another step in the education of his nephew. There lived a feeble old Frenchman in the town, who gave the young people lessons in dancing. The old gentleman sent for him one day, and told him that he wished his nephew to be instructed in dancing. He gave him to understand that while the young man was quite docile, yet where dancing was concerned he was rather peculiar; he had, for instance, once learned how to dance from another master, but so singular were the figures taught him, that he could not be taken out into society. But then his nephew believed himself to be a great dancer, notwithstanding the fact that his dancing did not bear the slightest resemblance to a waltz or a gallopade. As for the rest, he promised the dancing-master a thaler a lesson; and the Frenchman announced himself as ready to begin the instruction of this peculiar pupil. Never in the world, as the Frenchman privately asserted, was there anything so extraordinary as these dancing-lessons. The nephew, quite a tall, slim young man, whose legs were still much too short, would make his appearance, finely dressed in a red coat, loose green trousers, and kid gloves. He spoke but little, and with a foreign accent, was at the beginning fairly clever and well-behaved, but would suddenly break into the wildest leaps, danced the boldest figures that took away the master's sight and speech; and if he attempted to set him right again, the young man would draw off his dancing-shoes, and throw them at the master's head, and then get down on the floor and run about on all fours. Summoned by the noise, the old gentleman would then rush out of his room, attired in a loose red dressing-gown, with a gold-paper cap on his head, and lay the hunting whip on the back of the young man without mercy. The nephew would thereupon scream frightfully, spring upon tables and bureaus, and cry out in an odd foreign tongue. The old man in the red dressing-gown would at length catch him by the leg, drag him down from a table, beat him black and blue, and choked him by twisting his cravat, whereupon he would become clever and decent again, and the dancing-exercise would continue without further interruption.

But when the Frenchman had advanced his pupil so far that music could be used during the lesson, there was a magical change in the nephew's behavior. A town musician was called in, and given a seat on the table in the *salon* of the desolate house. The dancing-master would then represent a lady, the old gentleman furnishing him with a silk dress and an Indian shawl; and the nephew would request the lady to dance with him. The young Englishman was a tireless dancer, and would not let the Frenchman escape out of his long arms, but forced him to dance, in spite of his groans and cries, till he fell down from fatigue, or until the fiddler's arm became too lame to keep up the music.

The dancing-master was nearly brought to his grave by these lessons, but the thaler that he received regularly every day, and the good wine that the old man set out for him, caused him to keep on, even though he firmly resolved each day not to enter the desolate house again.

But the inhabitants of Gruenwiesel took an altogether different view of the matter. They found that the young man must have sociable qualities; while the young ladies rejoiced that, in the great scarcity of young men, they should have so nimble a dancer for the forthcoming winter.

One morning the maids, on returning from market, reported to their mistresses a wonderful occurrence Before the desolate house, a splendid coach, with beautiful horses, was drawn up, with a footman in rich livery holding open the door. Thereupon the door of the desolate house was opened, and two richly dressed gentlemen stepped out, one of whom was the old gentleman and the other probably the young Englishman, who had had such a hard time in learning German, and who danced so actively. Both men took seats in the coach, the footman sprang up on the rack at the back, and the coach—

just think of it! — had been driven up to the mayor's door.

As soon as the ladies had heard these stories from their servants, they tore off their kitchen aprons and caps, and dressed themselves in state. "Nothing is more certain," they exclaimed to their families, while all were running about to set the parlor in order, "nothing is more certain than that the stranger is about to bring his nephew out. The old fool has not had the decency to set his foot in our house for ten years; but we will pardon him on account of the nephew, who must be a charming fellow." Thus said the ladies, and admonished their sons and daughters to appear polite if the strangers came — to stand up straight, and also to take more pains than usual in their speech. And the wise women of the town were not wrong in their calculations, as the old gentleman went the rounds with his nephew, to recommend himself and the young Englishman to the favor of the Gruenwiesel families.

Every-where the people were quite charmed with the appearance of the two strangers, and felt sorry that they had not made the acquaintance of these agreeable gentlemen earlier. The old gentleman showed himself to be a worthy, sensible man, who, to be sure, smiled a little over all he said, so that one was not quite sure whether he was in earnest or not; but he spoke of the weather, of the suburbs, and of the Summer pleasures in the cave on the mountain side, so wisely and elaborately that every one was charmed with him. But the nephew! He bewitched everybody; he took all hearts by storm. Certainly, so far as his exterior was concerned, his face could not be called handsome; the under part, the chin especially, protruded too far, and his complexion was exceedingly dark; then, too, he frequently made all sorts of singular grimaces, closing his eyes and gnashing his teeth; but in spite of all this, the contour of his face was found to be unusually interesting. Nothing could be more athletic than his figure. His clothes, it is true,

16

hung somewhat loosely and unevenly on his body; but he was pleased with every thing; he flew about the room with uncommon activity, threw himself here on a sofa and then in an arm-chair, and stretched out his legs before him. But what in another young man would have been considered vulgar and unseemly, passed in the case of the nephew for agreeableness. "He is an Englishman," they would say, "they are all like that; an Englishman can lie down on a sofa and go to sleep while ten

ladies stand up for lack of a seat; we shouldn't take it amiss in an Englishman." He was very watchful, however, of the old gentleman, his uncle; and when he began to spring about the room, or, as he seemed constantly inclined to do, put his feet up in a chair, a serious look served to make him behave himself a little better. And then, how could any one take any thing amiss, when the uncle on entering would say to the lady of the house: "My nephew is still somewhat coarse and uncultured, but I am sanguine that a little society will do much to polish his manners, and I therefore recommend him to you with my whole heart."

Thus was the nephew brought into society, and all Gruenwiesel spoke of nothing else for two whole days. The old gentleman did not stop with this, however, but set about changing his entire course of life. In the afternoon, in company with his nephew, he would go out to the cave on the mountain, where the most respectable gentlemen of Gruenwiesel drank beer and played at bowls. The nephew there showed himself to be an accomplished master of the sport, as he never bowled down less than five or six pins. Now and then, it is true, a singular spirit seemed to control him. He would, for instance, often chase a ball with the speed of an arrow, right down among the pins, and there set up all kinds of strange noises; or when he had knocked down the king, or made a strike, he would stand on his beautifully curled head, and throw his feet into the air; or when a wagon rattled by, he would be found, before he was fairly missed from the room, on the driver's seat, would ride a short distance, and then come back.

On these occasions, the old gentleman was accustomed to beg pardon of the mayor and the other gentlemen, for the antics of his nephew; but they laughed, charged it all to the account of his youth, asserted that at his age they were also as nimble, and loved the harum-scarum chap, as they called him, uncommonly well.

But there were also times when they were not a little vexed with him, and yet they did not venture to make any complaints, because the young Englishman passed every-where as a model of culture and intelligence. The old gentleman was accustomed to take his nephew with him every evening to the "Golden Hirsch," an inn of the town. Although the nephew was quite a young man, he did all that his elders did, placed his glass before him, put on an enormous pair of spectacles, produced a mighty pipe, lighted it, and blew his smoke among them mischievously. If the papers, or war, or peace, were spoken of, and the doctor and the mayor fell into a discussion on these subjects, surprising all the other gentlemen by their deep political knowledge, the nephew was quite liable to interpose very forcible objections; he would strike the table with his hand, from which he never drew the glove, and gave the doctor and the mayor very plainly to understand that they had not any correct information on these subjects; that he had heard all about them himself, and possessed a deeper insight into them. He then gave expression to his own views, in singular broken German, which received, much to the disgust of the mayor, the approval of all the other gentlemen; for he must, naturally, as an Englishman, understand all this much better than they.

Then when the mayor and doctor, to conceal the anger they did not dare express, sat down to a game of chess, the nephew would come up, look over the mayor's shoulders with his great goggles, and find fault with this and that move, and tell the doctor he must move thus and so, until both men were secretly burning with anger. If then the mayor challenged him to play a game, with the design of mating him speedily — as he held himself to be a second Philidor — the old gentleman would grasp his nephew by the cravat, whereupon the young man at once became quiet and polite, and gave mate to the mayor.

They had been accustomed to play cards of an evening at Gruenwiesel, at half a kreuzer a game for each player; this the nephew thought was a miserable stake, and laid down crown-thalers and ducats himself, asserting that not one of them could play as well as he, but generally consoled the insulted gentlemen by losing large sums of money to them. They suffered no twinges of conscience in this taking of his money. "He is an Englishman, and inherits his wealth," said they, as they shoved the ducats into their pockets.

Thus did the nephew of the strange gentleman establish his respectability in the town in a very short time.

The oldest inhabitants could not remember having ever seen a young man of this style in Gruenwiesel, and he created the greatest sensation that had ever been known there. It could not be said that the nephew had learned any thing more than the art of dancing; Latin and Greek were to him, as we were wont to express it, "Bohemian villages." In a game at the mayor's house he was called upon to write something, and it was discovered that he could not even write his own name. In geography, he made the most egregious blunders — as he would place a German city in France, or a Danish town in Poland; he had not read any thing, had not studied any thing, and the minister often shook his head seriously over the utter ignorance of the young man. Yet, in spite of all these defects, every thing he said or did was considered excellent; for he was so impudent as to claim that he was always right, and the close of every one of his speeches was, "I know better than you!"

Winter came, and now the young Englishman appeared in still greater glory. Every party was voted wearisome where he was not a guest. People yawned when a wise man began to speak; but when the young Englishman uttered the veriest nonsense in broken German, all was attention. It was now discovered that the young man was also a poet, for rarely did an evening go by that he did not pull out a piece of paper from his pocket and read some sonnets to the company. There were, to be sure, some people who maintained that some of these poems were poor and without sense, and that others they had read somewhere in print; but the nephew did not permit himself to be put down in any such manner. He read, and read, directed the attention of his hearers to the beauties of his verses, and was applauded to the echo.

His great triumph, however, was at the Gruenwiesel ball. No one could dance more gracefully and rapidly than he. None could execute such uncommonly difficult steps. His uncle dressed him in the greatest splen-

dor, after the latest fashion; and although the clothes
did not fit his body very well, yet every one thought
him charmingly dressed. The men, to be sure, thought
themselves somewhat insulted by the new fashion which
he introduced. The mayor had always been accustomed
to open the ball in his own person, while the leading
young people had the right to arrange the other dances;
but since the appearance of the young Englishman, all
this was changed. Without much ceremony, he took the
next best lady by the hand and led her out on the floor,
arranged every thing to suit himself, and was lord and
master and king of the ball. But because these innova-
tions were acceptable to the ladies, the men did not venture to make any objections, and the nephew held firmly
to his self-appointed office.

This ball seemed to furnish great entertainment for
the old gentleman; he never once took his eyes off his
nephew, wore a smiling face, and when all the world of
Gruenwiesel moved up to him to sound the praises of the
noble well-bred youth, he could no longer contain himself from very joy, but broke out into a hearty laugh,
and conducted himself almost foolishly. The Gruenwiesel people attributed these singular manifestations of
pleasure to his great love for his nephew, and did not
think them unnatural. Still, every now and then he had
to turn his fatherly attention to his nephew, for, in the
middle of an elegant dance, the young man would leap
up to the platform where the town musicians sat, take
away the bass-viol from its owner, and scrape out a horrible medley; or for a change he would throw his heels
up into the air and dance about on his hands. At such
times, the old gentleman would take him aside, would
talk to him very seriously, and tighten his neck-tie, until
he once more was tractable.

Thus did the nephew conduct himself in society. It
is usually the case with social customs, that the objec-
tionable ones spread much more rapidly than the good
ones; and a new and striking fashion, even though ludi-

crous in itself, may have something attractive in it for young people who have not thought very deeply about themselves and the world. Thus it was in Gruenwiesel, over the young Englishman and his singular manners. When the young people saw how he, with his perverse disposition, with his coarse laughs and jests, with his rude answers to elderly people, was more praised than blamed, that all this was considered spirited, they said to themselves, " It would be very easy for me to become such a spirited fellow." They had formerly been industrious and clever young people ; now they thought, " Of what use is study, when ignorance is more highly rewarded ?" They let books alone, and spent their time on the square and in the streets. Formerly they were well-behaved and polite towards every one — had waited until they were spoken to, and then replied modestly; but now they placed themselves in the company of their elders, gossiped with them, gave expression to their opinions, and even laughed in the mayor's face when he spoke, and affirmed that they knew better than he Formerly the young men of Gruenwiesel had had a horror of a coarse and vulgar life; but now they sang all kinds of low songs, smoked tobacco in enormous pipes, and frequented the worst saloons. They also bought large goggles, although their sight was not impaired, set them on their nose, and thought that they were now made, as they looked just like the celebrated young Englishman. At home, or when they were visiting, they would lie down on the lounge with their boots and spurs on ; they tilted back their chairs in company, or put their elbows on the table and rested their cheeks on their fists — a posture that was in the highest degree charming to look at. All in vain did their mothers and friends tell them how foolish and disgraceful these actions were; they quoted the shining example of the nephew in defence of their behavior. All in vain was it represented to them that one should overlook in the nephew, as a young Englishman, a certain national rudeness;—the young men

of Gruenwiesel would assert that they had just as good
a right as the best Englishman living, to be rude in
a spirited way; in short, it was a pity to see how the
evil example of the nephew had completely destroyed
the customs and good manners of Gruenwiesel.

But the joy of the young men, in their rude unre-
strained life did not last long, as the following event
wrought a complete change in the scene. The Winter
amusements were to close with a concert, that was to be
given, partly by the town musicians, and partly by the
lovers of music in Gruenwiesel. The mayor played the
violoncello, the doctor the bassoon, extremely well; the
apothecary, although he had a very poor talent for it,
blew the flute; the young ladies of Gruenwiesel had
learned some songs, and every thing was all nicely arranged. But the strange gentleman gave out that while
the concert would undoubtedly be a success, yet it was
a mistake not to introduce a duet, as a duet was a recognized feature of every concert. The old gentleman's
declaration proved quite an embarrassment to the man-
agers. It was true that the mayor's daughter sang like
a nightingale; but where should they find a gentleman
who could sing a duet with her? In their perplexity,
they at last hit upon the old organist who had once possessed an excellent bass voice; but the strange gentleman asserted that they need have no uneasiness on that
score, as his nephew was an exceptionally fine singer.
They were not a little surprised over this new accomplishment of the young man, and requested him to sing
something, that they might judge of his acquirements.
He sang for them, and, barring a few outlandish affecta-
tions which were supposed to be the English style, he
sang like an angel. The duet was therefore decided on
and hurriedly practiced, and the evening finally came on
which the ears of the Gruenwiesel people were to be
refreshed with a concert.

The old gentleman, sad to say, was sick and could not
attend the concert; but he gave the mayor, who called

on him just before the hour of opening the concert, some directions regarding his nephew. "He is a good soul, my nephew," said he, "but now and then he is overtaken by all sorts of singular fancies, and does many stupid things; it is, therefore, a great misfortune that I can not be present at your concert, as in my presence he always behaves himself—he well knows why! I must say, in his favor, that he does not commit these actions in a spirit of wantonness, but they are a fault of his constitution, deeply implanted in his nature. If then, Mr. Mayor, he should sit down on the music-desk, or attempt to play the bass-viol, just loosen his neck-tie a little; or, if that does not help matters, pull it off entirely, and you will see how quiet and well-behaved he will become." The mayor thanked the sick man for his confidence, and promised that if it should be necessary he would carry out his instructions.

The concert-hall was crowded; all Gruenwiesel and the surrounding country were there. All the royal gamekeepers, the ministers, officials, landlords, and others, within a circumference of ten miles, came with their numerous families to share the rare enjoyment of the concert with the Gruenwiesel people. The town musicians did themselves honor. After them, the mayor appeared with his violoncello, accompanied by the apothecary with his flute; after these, the organist sang, amid universal applause; and the doctor, too, was cheered not a little when he appeared with his bassoon.

The first part of the concert was over, and every one was impatiently awaiting the second part, in which the young stranger was to sing a duet with the mayor's daughter. The nephew was present, in a brilliant costume, and had already attracted the attention of all present. He had, with the greatest composure, laid himself back in an easy chair, which had been reserved for a countess of the neighborhood, stretched his legs out before him, and stared at everybody through a large spyglass, stopping occasionally to play with a large mastiff

Y

which he, in spite of the rule excluding dogs, had
brought with him into this goodly company. The countess
for whom the chair had been reserved, put in an appearance; but he showed no disposition to vacate the
seat,—on the contrary, he settled himself down in it more
comfortably, and as no one dared say any thing to the
young man about it, the noble lady was forced to take a
common straw-bottomed chair in the midst of the other
ladies; a proceeding that vexed her not a little.

During the excellent playing of the mayor, during the
fine singing of the organist, yes, even while the doctor
was performing some fantasias on the bassoon, and
all were breathlessly listening, the young Englishman
amused himself by having the dog fetch his handkerchief, or chatted aloud with his neighbors, so that every
one who was not acquainted with him wondered at
the extraordinary conduct of the young man.

It was no wonder, therefore, that there was great
curiosity to hear him in the duet. The second part began; the town musicians had opened with a short
piece of music, and now the mayor, with his daughter,
stepped up to the young man, handed him a sheet of
music, and said: "Mosjoh! Will it please you to sing
the duet now?" The young man laughed, gnashed his
teeth, sprang up, and the others followed him to the
music-stand, while the entire company were in full expectation. The organist began the accompaniment and
beckoned the nephew to begin. The young Englishman looked through his goggles at the music, and broke
out into the most discordant tones. The organist called
out to him, "Two tones deeper, your honor! You
must sing in C, C!"

Instead of singing in C, however, the nephew took off
his shoe, and struck the organist such a blow on the head
that the powder flew in all directions. As the mayor
saw this, he thought: "Ha! he has another attack!"
and sprang forward, seized him by the throat, and
loosened his neck-tie; but this only increased the young

man's violence; he no longer spoke German, but a strange language instead, that no one understood, and began to leap about in an extraordinary manner. The mayor was very much annoyed by this unpleasant disturbance; he therefore resolved, inasmuch as the young man must have been attacked by some very unusual symptoms, to remove the cravat entirely. But he had no sooner done this, than he stood motionless with horror, for instead of a human skin and complexion, the neck of the young man was covered with a dark-brown fur. The young man took some higher leaps, grasped his hair with his gloved hands, pulled it, and, oh, wonder! this beautiful hair was simply a wig, which he flung into the mayor's face; and his head now appeared, covered with the same brown fur.

He jumped over tables and benches, threw down the music-stands, stamped on the fiddles and clarionet, and appeared to have gone mad. "Catch him! catch him!" shouted the mayor, quite beside himself. "He is out of his senses, catch him!" That was, however, a difficult thing to do, as the Englishman had pulled off his gloves, disclosing nails on his fingers, with which he scratched the faces of those who attempted to hold him. Finally an experienced hunter succeeded in holding him. He bound his long arms down by his side so that he could only move his feet. The people gathered round and stared at the singular young gentleman, who no longer resembled a human being.

Just then a scientific gentleman of the neighborhood who had a large cabinet full of specimens of natural history, and possessed all kinds of stuffed animals, approached nearer, examined him closely, and then exclaimed, in tones of surprise: "Good gracious! ladies and gentlemen, how is it you bring this animal into genteel company? That is an ape, of the *Homo Troglodytes* species. I will give six thalers for him on the spot, if you will let me have him, for my cabinet."

Who could describe the astonishment of the Gruenwiesel people as they heard this! "What! an ape, an orang-outang in our society? The young stranger a common ape?" cried they, and looked at one another in a stupefied way. They could not believe it; they could not trust their ears. The men examined the animal more closely, but it was beyond all doubt a quite natural ape.

"But how is this possible," cried the mayor's wife. "Has he not often read his poems to me? Has he not eaten at my table, just like any other man?"

"What?" exclaimed the doctor's wife. "Has he not often drank coffee with me, and a great deal of it? And has he not talked learnedly with my husband, and smoked with him?"

"What! is it possible!" cried the men; "has he not bowled nine-pins with us at the cave? and discussed politics like one of us?"

"And how can it be?" lamented they all; "has he not danced at our balls? An ape! an ape? It is a miracle! It is witchcraft!"

"Yes, it is witchcraft, and a satanic spook!" echoed the mayor, exhibiting the cravat of the nephew, or ape. "See, this cloth contains the magic that made him so acceptable to our eyes. There is a broad strip of elastic parchment covered with all manner of singular characters. I think it must be Latin. Can any one read it?"

The minister, a scholarly gentleman who had lost many a game of chess to the young Englishman, walked up, examined the parchment, and said: "By no means! They are only Latin letters," and read:

> "THE APE CAN DO MOST COMIC FEATS,
> WHEN OF THE APPLE FRUIT HE EATS."

"Yes, it is a wicked fraud, a kind of sorcery; and the perpetrator of it should be made an example of."

The mayor was of the same opinion, and started to go to the house of the stranger, who must be a sorcerer; while six militia-men took the ape along, as the stranger would be immediately put on trial.

They arrived at the desolate house, accompanied by a

large crowd of people, as every one was anxious to see the outcome of the affair. They knocked on the door and pulled the bell, but no one responded. The mayor, in his wrath, had the door beaten in, and went up to the room of the stranger. But nothing was to be seen there save various kinds of old furniture. The strange gentleman was not to be found; but on his work-table lay a large sealed letter, directed to the mayor, who immediately opened it. He read:

"MY DEAR GRUENWIESEL FRIENDS:—When you read this I shall be far away from your town, and you will have discovered of what rank and country my dear nephew is. Take this joke, which I have allowed myself to indulge in at your expense, as a lesson not to seek the society of a stranger who prefers to live quietly by himself. I felt above sharing in your eternal clack, in your miserable customs, and your ridiculous manners. Therefore, I educated a young orang-outang, which, as my deputy, won such a warm place in your affections. Farewell; make the best use of this lesson."

The people of Gruenwiesel were not a little ashamed at the position they were in before the whole country. They had hoped that all this could be shown to have some connection with supernatural things. But the young people experienced the deepest sense of shame, because they had copied the bad customs and manners of an ape. They ceased to prop their elbows on the table; they no longer tilted back their chairs; they were silent until spoken to; they laid aside their spectacles, and were good and obedient; and if any one of them chanced to slip back into the old ways, the Gruenwiesel people would say, "It is an ape!" But the ape, that had so long played the *rôle* of a young gentleman, was surrendered to the learned man who possessed a cabinet of natural curiosities. He allowed the ape to have the run of his yard, fed it well, and showed it as a curiosity to strangers, where it can be seen to this day.

There was loud laughter in the *salon*, when the slave
had concluded, in which the young men joined. " There
must be singular people among these Franks ; and, of a
truth, I would rather be here with the sheik and mufti in
Alessandria, than in the company of the minister, the
mayor, and their silly wives in Gruenwiesel ! "

" You speak the truth there," replied the young merchant, " I should not care to die in the Frank's country.
They are a coarse, wild, barbaric people, and it must be
terrible for a cultivated Turk or Persian to live there."

" You will hear all about that presently," promised
the old man. " From what the steward told me, the fine-
looking young man yonder will have something to say
about the Franks, as he was among them for a long time,
and is by birth a Mussulman."

" What, the last one in the row? Really, it is a sin
for the sheik to free him! He is the handsomest slave
in the whole country. Only look at his courageous face,
his sharp eye, his noble form! He might give him some
light duties, such as fan or pipe-bearing. It would be an
easy matter to provide such an office for him, and truly
such a slave as he would be an ornament to the palace.
And the sheik has only had him three days, and now
gives him away? It is folly! It is a sin!"

" Do not blame him—he, who is wiser than all Egypt;"
said the old man, impressively. "I have already told
you that he gives this slave his freedom, believing that
he will thereby deserve the blessing of Allah. You say
the slave is handsome and well-formed; and you say the
truth. But the son of the sheik—whom may the Prophet
restore to his father's house—was also a beautiful boy,
and must be now tall and well-formed. Shall the sheik
then save his money, and set a less expensive slave free,
in the hope to receive his son therefor? He who wishes
to do anything in the world had far better not do it at all,
than not do it well."

" And see how the sheik's eyes are fastened on this
slave! I have noticed it the whole evening. During the

recital of the stories, his look was fixed on the young slave's face. It evidently pains him to part with him."

"Do not think that of the sheik. Do you think the loss of a thousand tomans would pain him who every day receives three times that sum?" asked the old man. "But when his glance falls sorrowfully on the young slave, he is doubtless thinking of his son, who languishes in a strange land, and whether a merciful man lives there who will buy his freedom and send him back to his father."

"You may be right," responded the young merchant, "and I am ashamed that I have been looking at only the darker and ignobler traits of people, while you prefer to see a nobler meaning underlying their actions. And yet, taken as a whole, mankind are bad; have you not found it so, old man?"

"It is precisely because I have not found it so, that I love to think well of people. I used to feel as you do. I lived so thoughtlessly, heard much that was bad about people, experienced much that was wicked in myself, and so readily began to look upon humanity as made up of a poor lot of creatures. Still, I chanced to think that Allah, who is as just as wise, would not suffer so abandoned a race to people this fair earth. I thought over again what I had seen and what I had experienced in my own person, and behold! I had taken account only of the evil and had forgotten the good. I had paid no attention when one had performed a deed of charity; it seemed quite natural when whole families lived virtuous and orderly lives; but whenever I heard of something wicked or criminal, I stored it away in my memory. Thus did I begin to look about me with clearer eyes. I rejoiced when I found that the good was not so rare a quality as I had at first thought it. I noticed the evil less, or it made less impression on my mind; and so I learned to love humanity, learned to think well of people. And in my long life, I have made fewer mistakes in speaking and thinking well of people, than I should have made if I had looked upon them as avaricious or ignoble or ungodly."

The old man was interrupted here by the steward, who said: "Sir, the Sheik of Alessandria, Ali Banu, has remarked your presence here with pleasure, and invites you to step forward and take a seat near him."

The young men were not a little astonished at the honor shown the old man whom they had taken for a beggar; and when he had left them to sit with the sheik, they held the steward back and the young writer asked him: "By the beard of the Prophet! I implore you to tell us who this old man is with whom we have been conversing, and whom the sheik so honors?"

"What!" cried the steward clasping his hands in surprise, "do you not know this man?"

"No."

"But I have seen you speaking with him several times on the street, and my master has also noticed this and only recently said, 'They must be valiant young people with whom this man grants a conversation.'"

"But tell us who he is!" cried the young merchant impatiently.

"Go away; you are trying to make a fool of me," answered the steward. "No one enters this *salon* without special permission, and to-day the old gentleman sent word to the sheik that he would bring some young men with him into the *salon*, if it were not disagreeable to the sheik, and the sheik sent back the reply that his house was at his service."

"Do not leave us longer in ignorance. As true as I live, I do not know who the man is. We got acquainted with him by chance, and fell to talking with him."

"Well, you may consider yourselves fortunate, for you have conversed with a famous and learned man, and all present honor you and wonder at you accordingly. He is none other than Mustapha, the learned dervish."

"Mustapha! the wise Mustapha, who educated the sheik's son, who has written many learned books, and

travelled to all parts of the world? Have we spoken with
Mustapha? And spoken, too, as though he were one of
us, without the least respect!"

While the young men were talking about the dervish,
Mustapha, and the honor they felt had been done them
by his condescension, the steward came to them again,
and invited them to follow him, as the sheik wished to
speak with them. The hearts of the young men beat
excitedly. Never yet had they spoken with a man of
such high rank. But they collected their wits, so as not
to appear like fools, and followed the steward to the
sheik. Ali Banu sat upon a rich cushion, and refreshed
himself with sherbet. At his right sat the old man, his
shabby clothes resting on splendid cushions, while his
well-worn sandals were placed on a rich rug; but his
well-shaped head, and his eye, expressive of dignity and
wisdom, indicated that he was a man worthy to be seated
near the sheik.

The sheik was very grave, and the old man appeared
to be speaking words of consolation and of hope to him.
The young men also feared that their summons to the
sheik had been caused by a stratagem on the part of the
old man, who very likely would now ruin them by a word
to the sorrowing father.

"Welcome, young men," said the sheik. "Welcome
to the house of Ali Banu! My old friend here deserves
my thanks for bringing you with him; still I am a little
inclined to quarrel with him that he did not make me
acquainted with you before this. Which of you is the
young writer?"

"I, O Sire! and at your service!" replied the writer,
crossing his arms on his breast and making a low obeisance.

"You are pleased with stories, and also love to read
books with beautiful verses and wise sayings?"

The young man blushed, and answered: "O Sire!
for my part, I know of no pleasanter way of passing the
day. It cultivates the mind and whiles away the time.

16*

But every one to his taste; I do not quarrel with any one who does not ———"

"Very well, very well," interrupted the sheik, with a laugh, as he beckoned the second young man forward. "And now who may you be?"

"Sire, my duties are those of an assistant to a physician, and I have cured some patients myself."

"Just so," replied the sheik. "And you are one who loves high-living. You would like to sit down to a good table with your friends. Isn't that so? Have I not guessed right?"

The young man was much abashed; he felt that the old man had betrayed him also; but he plucked up courage to say: "Oh yes, Sire, I reckon it as one of the great enjoyments of life to be able to make merry now and then with one's friends. My purse does not permit me to entertain my friends with much besides watermelons, and other cheap things; but still we contrive to be merry even with these — so that it stands to reason that if my purse was longer our enjoyment would be proportionately increased."

This spirited answer pleased the sheik so well that he could not refrain from laughing. "Which of you is the young merchant?" was his next inquiry.

The young merchant made his obeisance to the sheik with an easy grace, for he was a man of good breeding; and the sheik said to him:

"And you? Do you not take pleasure in music and dancing? Are you not charmed to hear good artists sing and play, and to see dancers perform ingenious dances?"

The young merchant replied: "I see clearly, O Sire, that this old gentleman, in order to amuse you, has told you of all our follies. If he thereby succeeded in cheering you up, I shall not regret having been made the object of your sport. As concerns music and dancing, however, I will confess that it would be difficult to find any thing that so cheers my heart. But yet, do not sup-

pose that I blame you, O Sire, that you do not likewise————"

"Enough! not another word!" cried the sheik, smiling, and waving his hand. "Every one to his taste, you
were about to say. But there stands another: that must
be the young man who is so fond of travelling. Who,
then, are you, young gentleman?"

"I am a painter, O Sire," answered the young man.
"I paint landscapes, sometimes on the walls of *salons*,
and sometimes on canvas. To see foreign lands is,
above all things, my wish, for one sees there a great
variety of beautiful regions that can be reproduced, and
what one sees and sketches is as a rule much finer than
that which is evolved from one's fancy."

The sheik surveyed the group of handsome young
men with an earnest look. "I once had a dear son,"
said he, "and he must by this time be grown up like you.
You should be his companions, and every one of your
wishes should be satisfied. With that one he would read,
hear music with this, with the other he would invite good
friends and make merry, and I would send him with the
painter to beautiful regions and would then feel sure of
his safe return. But Allah has ordained otherwise, and
I bow uncomplainingly to his will. Still, it is within my
power to fulfill your wishes, and you shall leave Ali Banu
with happy hearts. You, my learned friend," continued
he, turning to the young writer, "will take up your residence in my house, and take charge of my books. You
will be at liberty to do as you think best, and your only
duty will be, when you have read some very fine story, to
come and relate it to me. You, who love to sit at a
good table with your friends, shall have the oversight of
my entertainments. I myself live alone and take no
pleasures; but it is a duty that attaches to my office to
now and then invite guests. Now you shall prepare
every thing in my place, and can also invite your friends
whenever you please to sit down with you — and, let it
be understood, to something better than watermelons. I

certainly can not take the young merchant away from his business, which brings him in money and honor; but every evening, my young friend, dancers, singers, and musicians will be at your service, and will play and dance for you to your heart's content. And you," turning to the painter, " shall see foreign lands, and educate your tastes by travel. My treasurer will give you for your first journey, that you can start on to-morrow, a thousand gold pieces, together with two horses and a slave. Travel wherever you desire; and when you see anything beautiful, paint it for me."

The young men were beside themselves with astonishment, speechless with joy and gratitude. They would have kissed the ground at the feet of the kind man, but he prevented them. "If you are indebted to any one, it is to this wise old gentleman who told me about you. He has also given me pleasure in this matter by making me acquainted with four such worthy young gentlemen."

The dervish, Mustapha, however, checked the thanks of the young men. "See," said he, "how one should never judge too hastily. Did I exaggerate the goodness of this noble man?"

"Let us hear from another of the slaves, who is to be liberated to-day," interrupted Ali Banu; and the young gentlemen took their seats.

The young slave who had attracted general attention by reason of his beautiful form and features and his bright look, now arose, and in a melodious voice began his story.

THE STORY OF ALMANSOR.

IRE, the men who have preceded me have told wonderful stories which they had heard in strange lands; whilst I must confess with shame that I do not know a single tale that is worthy of your attention. Nevertheless if it will not weary you, I will relate the strange history of one of my friends.

On the Algerian privateer, from which your generous hand set me free, was a young man of my own age who did not seem to have been born to the slave-costume that he wore. The other unfortunates on the ship were either rough, coarse people, with whom I did not care to associate or people whose language I did not understand; therefore, every moment that I had to myself was spent in the company of this young man. He called himself Almansor, and, judging from his speech, was an Egyptian. We were well pleased to be in each other's society, and one day we chanced to tell our stories to one another; and I discovered that my friend's story was far more remarkable than my own. Almansor's father was a prominent man in an Egyptian city, whose name he failed to give me. The days of his childhood passed pleasantly, surrounded by all the splendor and comfort earth could give. At the same time, he was not too tenderly nurtured, and his mind was early cultivated: for his father was a wise man who taught him the value of virtue, and provided him with a teacher who was a famous scholar, and who instructed him in all that a young man should know. Almansor was about ten years old when the Franks came over the sea to invade his country and wage war upon his people.

The father of this boy could not have been very favorably regarded by the Franks, for one day, as he was about to go to morning prayers, they came and demanded first his wife as a pledge of his faithful adherence to the Franks, and when he would not give her up, they seized his son and carried him off to their camp.

When the young slave had got this far in his story, the sheik hid his face in his hands, and there arose a murmur of indignation in the *salon.* "How can the young man there be so indiscreet?" cried the friends of the sheik, "and tear open the wounds of Ali Banu by such stories, instead of trying to heal them? How can he recall his anguish, instead of trying to dissipate it?" The steward, too, was very angry with the shameless youth, and commanded him to be silent. But the young slave was very much astonished at all this, and asked the sheik whether there was any thing in what he had related that had aroused his displeasure. At this inquiry, the sheik lifted his head, and said: "Peace, my friends; how can this young man know any thing about my sad misfortune, when he has not been under this roof three days! might there not be a case similar to mine in all the cruelties the Franks committed? May not perhaps this Almansor himself ——— but proceed, my young friend!" The young slave bowed, and continued:

The young Almansor was taken to the enemy's camp. On the whole, he was well treated there, as one of the generals took him into his tent, and being pleased with the answers of the boy that were interpreted to him, took care to see that he wanted for nothing in the way of food and clothes. But the homesickness of the boy made him very unhappy. He wept for many days; but his tears did not move the hearts of these men to pity. The camp was broken, and Almansor believed that he was now about to be returned to his home; but it was not so. The army moved here and there, waged war with the Mamelukes, and took the young Almansor with them wherever they went. When he begged the generals to let him return home, they would refuse, and tell him that he would have to remain with them as a hostage for his father's neutrality. Thus was he for many days on the march.

One day, however, there was a great stir in camp, and it did not escape the attention of the boy. There was talk about breaking camp, or withdrawing the troops, of embarking on ships; and Almansor was beside himself with joy. "For now," he reasoned, "when the Franks are about to return to their own country, they will surely set me at liberty." They all marched back towards the coast, and at last reached a point from which they could see their ships riding at anchor. The soldiers began to embark, but it was night before many of them were on the vessels. Anxious as Almansor was to keep awake — for he believed he would soon be set at liberty — he finally sank into a deep sleep. When he awoke, he found himself in a very small room, not the one in which he had gone to sleep in. He sprang from his couch; but when he struck the floor, he fell over, as the floor reeled back and forth, and every thing seemed to be moving and dancing around him. He at last got up, steadied himself against the walls, and attempted to make his way out of the room.

A strange roaring and rushing was to be heard all about him. He knew not whether he waked or dreamed; for he had never heard anything at all like it. Finally he reached a small stair-case, which he climbed with much difficulty, and what a sensation of terror crept over him! For all around nothing was to be seen but sea and sky; he was on board a ship! He began to weep bitterly. He wanted to be taken back, and would have thrown himself into the sea with the purpose of swimming to land if the Franks had not held him fast. One of the officers called him up, and promised that he should soon be sent home if he would be obedient, and represented to him that it would not have been possible to send him home across the country, and that if they had left him behind he would have perished miserably.

But the Franks did not keep faith with him; for the ship sailed on for many days, and when it finally reached land, it was not the Egyptian, but the Frankish coast. During the long voyage, and in their camp too, Almansor had learned to understand and to speak the language of the Franks; and this was of great service to him now, in a country where nobody knew his own language. He was taken a long journey through the country, and everywhere the people turned out in crowds to see him; for his conductors announced that he was the son of the King of Egypt, who was sending him to their country to be educated. The soldiers told this story to make the people believe that they had conquered Egypt, and had concluded a peace with that country. After his journey had continued several days, they came to a large city, the end of their journey. There he was handed over to a physician, who took him into his home and instructed him in all the customs and manners of the Franks.

First of all, he was required to put on Frankish clothes, which he found very tight, and not nearly as beautiful as his Egyptian costume. Then he had to abstain from making an obeisance with crossed arms, but when he wished to greet any one politely, he must, with one hand, lift from his head the monstrous black felt hat that had been given him to wear, let the other hand hang at his side, and give a scrape with his right foot. He could no longer sit down on his crossed legs, as is the proper custom in the Levant, but he had to seat himself on a high-legged chair, and let his feet hang down to the floor. Eating also caused him not a little difficulty; for every thing that he wished to put in his mouth he had to first stick on a metal fork.

The doctor was a very harsh, wicked man, given to teasing the boy; for when the lad would forget himself and say to an acquaintance, "*Salem aleicum!*" the doctor would beat him with his cane telling him he should have said, "*Votre serviteur!*" Nor was he allowed to think, or speak, or write in his native tongue; at the very most, he could only dream in it; and he would doubtless have entirely forgotten his own language, had it not been for a man living in that city, who was of the greatest service to him.

This was an old but very learned man, who knew a little of every Oriental language — Arabic, Persian, Coptic, and even Chinese. He was held in that country to be a miracle of learning, and he received large sums of money for giving lessons in these languages. This man sent for Almansor several times a week, treated him to rare fruits and the like; and on these occasions the boy felt as if he were at home once more in his own country. The old gentleman was a very singular man. He had some clothes made for Almansor, such as Egyptian people of rank wore. These clothes he kept in a particular room in his house, and whenever Almansor came, he sent him with a servant to this room and had the boy dressed after the fashion of his own country. From there the boy was taken to a *salon* called "Little Arabia." This *salon* was adorned with all kinds of artificially-grown trees — such as palms, bamboos, young cedars, and the like; and also with flowers that grew only in the Levant. Persian carpets lay on the floor, and along the walls were cushions, but nowhere Frankish tables or chairs. Upon one of these cushions the old professor would be found seated, but presenting quite a different appearance from common. He had wound a fine Turkish shawl about his head for a turban, and had fastened on a gray beard, that reached to his sash, and looked for

all the world, like the genuine beard of an important
man. With these he wore a robe that he had had made
from a brocaded dressing-gown, baggy Turkish trowsers,
yellow slippers, and, peaceful as he generally was, on

these days he had buckled on a Turkish sword, while in
his sash stuck a dagger set with false stones.   He smoked
from a pipe two yards long, and was waited on by his
servants, who were likewise in Persian costumes, and one

half of whom had been required to color their hands and face black.

At first all this seemed very strange to the youthful Almansor; but he soon found that these hours could be made very useful to him, were he to join in the mood of the old man. While at the doctor's he was not allowed to speak an Egyptian word, here the Frankish language was forbidden. On entering, Almansor was required to give the peace-greeting, to which the old Persian responded spiritedly, and then he would beckon the boy to sit down near him, and began to speak Persian, Arabic, Coptic, and all languages, one after another, and considered this a learned Oriental entertainment. Near him stood a servant — or, as he was supposed to be on these days, a slave — who held a large book. This book was a dictionary; and when the old man stumbled in his words, he beckoned to the slave, looked up what he wanted to say, and then continued his speech.

The slaves brought in sherbet in Turkish vessels and to put the old man in the best of humors, Almansor had only to say that every thing here was just as it was in the Levant. Almansor read Persian beautifully, and it was the chief delight of the old man to hear him. He had many Persian manuscripts, from which the boy read to him, then the old man would read attentively after him, and in this way acquired the right pronunciation. These were holidays for little Almansor, as the professor never let him go away unrewarded, and he often carried back with him costly gifts of money or linen, or other useful things which the doctor would not give him.

So lived Almansor for some years in the capital of the Franks; but never did his longing for home diminish. When he was about fifteen years old, an incident occurred that had great influence on his destiny. The Franks chose their leading general — the same with whom Almansor had often spoken in Egypt — to be their king. Almansor could see by the unusual appearance of the streets and the great festivities that were taking place, that something of the kind had happened; but he never once dreamed that this king was the same man whom he had seen in Egypt, for that general was quite a young man. But one day Almansor went to one of the bridges that led over the wide river which flowed through the city, and there he perceived a man dressed in the simple uniform of a soldier, leaning over the parapet and looking down into the water. The features of the man impressed him as being familiar, and he felt sure of having seen him before. He tried to recall him to memory; and presently it flashed upon him that this man was the general of the Franks with whom he had often spoken in camp, and who had always cared kindly for him. He did not know his right name, but he mustered up his courage, stepped up to him, and, crossing his arms on his breast and making an obeisance, addressed him as he had heard the soldiers speak of him among themselves: " *Salem aleicum*, Little Corporal! "

The man looked up in surprise, cast a sharp look at the boy before him, recalled him after a moment's pause, and exclaimed: " Is it possible! you here, Almansor? How is your father? How are things in Egypt? What brings you here to us? "

Almansor could not contain himself longer; he began to weep, and said to the man: " Then you do not know what your countrymen — the dogs — have done to me, Little Corporal? You do not know that in all this time I have not seen the land of my ancestors? "

" I cannot think," said the man, with darkening brow, " I cannot think that they would have kidnapped you."

" Alas," answered Almansor," it is too true. On the day that your soldiers embarked, I saw my fatherland for the last time. They took me away with them, and one general, who pitied my misery, paid for my living with a hateful doctor, who beats and half starves me. But listen, Little Corporal," continued he confidentially, " it is well that I met you here; you must help me."

The man whom he thus addressed, smiled, and asked in what way he should help him.

"See," said Almansor, "it would be unfair for me to ask much from you; you were very kind to me, but still

I know that you are a poor man, and when you were general you were not as well-dressed as the others, and now, judging from your coat and hat, you cannot be in very good circumstances. But the Franks have recently

chosen a sultan, and beyond doubt you know people who
can approach him — the minister of war, maybe, or of
foreign affairs, or his admiral; do you?"

"Well, yes," answered the man; "but what more?"

"You might speak a good word for me to these people,
Little Corporal, so that they would beg the sultan to let
me go. Then I should need some money for the journey
over the sea; but, above all, you must promise me not to
say a word about this to either the doctor or the Arabic
professor!"

"Who is the Arabic professor?"

"Oh, he is a very strange man; but I will tell you
about him some other time. If these two men should
hear of this, I should not be able to get away. But will
you speak to the minister about me? Tell me honestly!"

"Come with me," said the man; "perhaps I can be
of some use to you now."

"Now?" cried the boy, in a fright. "Not for any consideration now; the doctor would whip me for being gone
so long. I must hurry back!"

"What have you in your basket?" asked the soldier,
as he detained him. Almansor blushed, and at first was
not inclined to show the contents of his basket; but
finally he said: "See, Little Corporal, I must do such
services as would be given to my father's meanest slave.
The doctor is a miserly man, and sends me every day an
hour's distance from our house to the vegetable and fish-
market. There I must make my purchases among the
dirty market-women, because things may be had of them
for a few coppers less than in our quarter of the city.
Look! on account of this miserable herring, and this
handful of lettuce, and this piece of butter, I am forced
to take a two hours' walk every day. Oh, if my father
only knew of it!"

The man whom Almansor addressed was much moved
by the boy's distress, and answered: "Only come with
me, and don't be afraid. The doctor shall not harm you,
even if he has to go without his herring and salad to-day.

Cheer up, and come along." So saying, he took Almansor by the hand and led him away with him; and although the boy's heart beat fast when he thought of the doctor, yet there was so much assurance in the man's words and manner, that he resolved to go with him. He therefore walked along by the side of the man, with his basket on his arm, through many streets; and it struck him as very wonderful that all the people took off their hats as they passed along and paused to look after them. He expressed his surprise at this to his companion, but he only laughed and made no reply.

Finally they came to a magnificent palace. "Do you live here, Little Corporal?" asked Almansor.

"This is my house, and I will take you in to see my wife," replied the soldier.

"Hey! how finely you live! The sultan must have given you the right to live here free."

"You are right; I have this house from the emperor," answered his companion, and led him into the palace. They ascended a broad stair-case, and on coming into a splendid *salon*, the man told the boy to set down his basket, and he then led him into an elegant room where a lady was sitting on a divan. The man talked with her in a strange language, whereupon they both began to laugh, and the lady then questioned the boy in the Frankish language about Egypt. Finally the Little Corporal said to the boy: "Do you know what would be the best thing to do? I will lead you myself to the emperor, and speak to him for you!"

Almansor shrank back at this proposal, but he thought of his misery and his home. "To the unfortunate," said he, addressing them both, "to the unfortunate, Allah gives fresh courage in the hour of need. He will not desert a poor boy like me. I will do it; I will go to the emperor. But tell me, Little Corporal, must I prostrate myself before him? must I touch the ground with my forehead? What shall I do?"

They both laughed again at this, and assured him
that all this was unnecessary.

" Does he look terrible and majestic ? " inquired he
further. " Tell me, how does he look ? "

His companion laughed once more, and said: " I
would rather not describe him to you, Almansor. You
shall see for yourself what manner of man he is. But
I will tell you how you may know him. All who are in
the *salon* will, when the emperor is there, respectfully
remove their hats. He who retains his hat on his head
is the emperor."

So saying, he took the boy by the hand and went with
him towards the *salon* The nearer they came, the faster
beat the boy's heart, and his knees began to tremble. A
servant flung open the door, and revealed some thirty
men standing in a half-circle, all splendidly dressed and
covered with gold and stars (as is the custom in the land
of the Franks for the chief ministers of the king). And
Almansor thought that his plainly-dressed companion
must be the least among these. They had all uncovered
their heads, and Almansor now looked around to see who
retained his hat; for that one would be the king. But
his search was in vain; all held their hats in their hands,
and the emperor could not be among them. Then, quite
by chance, his eye fell upon his companion, and behold
———— he still had his hat on his head !

The boy was utterly confounded. He looked for a
long time at his companion, and then said, as he took off
his own hat : "*Salem aleicum*, Little Corporal ! This much
I know, that I am not the Sultan of the Franks, nor is
it my place to keep my head covered. But you are the
one who wears a hat; Little Corporal, are you the emperor ? "

" You have guessed right," was the answer; " and,
more than that, I am your friend. Do not blame me for
your misfortune, but ascribe it to an unfortunate compli-
cation of circumstances, and be assured that you shall
return to your fatherland in the first ship that sails. Go

back now to my wife, and tell her about the Arabic professor and your other adventures. I will send the herrings and lettuce to the doctor, and you will, during your stay here, remain in my palace."

Thus spake the emperor. Almansor dropped on his knees before him, kissed his hand, and begged his forgiveness, as he had not known him to be the emperor.

"You are right," answered the emperor, laughing. "When one has been an emperor for only a few days, he cannot be expected to have the seal of royalty stamped on his forehead." Thus spake the emperor, and motioned the boy to leave the *salon.*

After this Almansor lived happily. He was permitted to visit the Arabic professor occasionally, but never saw the doctor again. In the course of some weeks, the emperor sent for him, and informed him that a ship was lying at anchor in which he would send him back to Egypt. Almansor was beside himself with joy. But a few days were required in which to make his preparations; and with a heart full of thanks, and loaded down with costly presents, he left the emperor's palace, and travelled to the seashore, where he embarked.

But Allah chose to try him still more, chose to temper his spirit by still further misfortune, and would not yet let him see the coast of his fatherland. Another race of Franks, the English, were carrying on a naval warfare with the emperor. They took away all of his ships that they could capture; and so it happened that on the sixth day of Almansor's voyage, his ship was surrounded by English vessels, and fired into. The ship was forced to surrender, and all her people were placed in a smaller ship that sailed away in company with the others. Still it is fully as unsafe on the sea as in the desert, where the robbers unexpectedly fall on caravans, and plunder and kill. A Tunisian privateer attacked the small ship, that had been separated from the larger ships by a storm, and captured it, and all the people on board were taken to Algiers and sold.

Almansor was treated much better in slavery than were the Christians who were captured with him, for he was a Mussulman; but still he had lost all hopes of ever seeing his father again. He lived as the slave of a rich man for five years, and did the work of a gardener. At the end of that time, his rich master died without leaving any near heirs; his possessions were broken up, his slaves were divided, and Almansor fell into the hands of a slave-dealer, who had just fitted up a ship to carry his slaves to another market, where he might sell them to advantage. By chance I was also a slave of this dealer, and was put on this ship together with Almansor. There we got acquainted with each other, and there it was that he related to me his strange adventures. But as we landed I was a witness of a most wonderful dispensation of Allah. We had landed on the coast of Almansor's fatherland; it was the market-place of his native city where we were put up for sale; and O, Sire! to crown all this, it was his own, his dear father who bought him!

The sheik, Ali Banu, was lost in deep thought over this story, which had carried him along on the current of its events. His breast swelled, his eye sparkled, and he was often on the point of interrupting his young slave; but the end of the story disappointed him.

"He would be about twenty-one years old, you said?" began the sheik.

"Sire, he is of my age, from twenty-one to twenty-two years old."

"And what did he call the name of his native city? You did not tell us that."

"If I am not mistaken, it was Alessandria!"

"Alessandria!" cried the sheik. "It was my son! Where is he living? Did you not say that he was called Kairam? Has he dark eyes and brown hair?"

"He has, and in confidential moods he called himself Kairam, and not Almansor."

"But, Allah! Allah! Yet, tell me: his father bought him before your eyes, you said. Did he say it was his father? Is he not my son!"

The slave answered: "He said to me: 'Allah be praised; after so long a period of misfortune, there is the market-place of my native city.' After a while, a distinguished-looking man came around the corner, at whose appearance Almansor cried: 'Oh, what a blessed gift of heaven are one's eyes! I see once more my revered father!' The man walked up to us, examined this and that one, and finally bought him to whom all this had happened; whereupon he praised Allah, and whispered to me. 'Now I shall return to the halls of fortune; it is my own father that has bought me.'"

"Then it was not my son, my Kairam!" exclaimed the sheik in a tone of anguish.

The young slave could no longer restrain himself. Tears of joy sprang into his eyes; he prostrated himself before the sheik, and said: "And yet it is your son, Kairam Almansor; for you are the one who bought him!"

"Allah! Allah! A wonder, a miracle!" cried those present, as they crowded closer. But the sheik stood speechless, staring at the young man, who turned his handsome face up to him. "My friend Mustapha!" said the sheik at last to the old man, "before my eyes hangs a veil of tears so that I cannot see whether the features of his mother, which my Kairam bare, are graven on the face of this young man. Come closer and look at him!"

The old dervish stepped up, examined the features of the young man carefully, and laying his hand on the forehead of the youth, said: "Kairam, what was the proverb I taught you on that sad day in the camp of the Franks?"

"My dear master!" answered the young man, as he drew the hand of the dervish to his lips, "it ran thus: *So that one loves Allah, and has a clear conscience, he will not be alone in the wilderness of woe, but will have two companions to comfort him constantly at his side."*

The old man raised his eyes gratefully to heaven, drew the young man to his breast, and then gave him to the sheik, saying: "Take him to your bosom; as surely as you have sorrowed for him these ten years, so surely is he your son!"

The sheik was beside himself with joy; he scanned the features of his newly-found son again and again, until he found there the unmistakable picture of his boy as he was before he had lost him. And all present shared in his joy, for they loved the sheik, and to each one of them it was as if a son had that day been sent to him.

Now once more did music and song fill these halls, as in the days of fortune and of joy. Once more must the young man tell his story, and all were loud in their praises of the Arabic professor, and the emperor, and all who had been kind to Kairam. They sat together until far into the night; and when the assembly broke up, the sheik presented each one with valuable gifts that they might never forget this day of joy.

But the four young men, he introduced to his son, and invited them to be his constant companions; and it was arranged that the son should read with the young writer, make short journeys with the painter, that the merchant should share in his songs and dances, and the other young man should arrange all the entertainments. They too received presents, and left the house of the sheik with light hearts.

"Whom have we to thank for all this?" said they to one another; "whom but the old man? Who could have foreseen all this, when we stood before this house and declaimed against the sheik?"

"And how easily we might have been led into turning a deaf ear to the discourses of the old man, or even into making sport of him? For he looked so ragged and poor, who would have suspected that he was the wise Mustapha?"

"And — wonderful coincidence — was it not here that we gave expression to our wishes?" said the writer. "One would travel, another see singing and dancing, the third have good company, and I —— read and hear stories; and are not all our wishes fulfilled? May I not read all the sheik's books, and buy as many more as I choose?"

"And may not I arrange the banquets and superintend all his entertainments, and be present at them myself?" said the other.

"And I, whenever my heart is desirous of hearing songs and stringed instruments, may I not go and ask for his slaves?"

"And I," cried the painter; "until to-day I was poor, and could not set foot outside the town; and now I can travel where I choose."

"Yes," repeated they all, "it was fortunate that we accompanied the old man, else who knows what would have become of us?"

So they spoke and went cheerful and happy to their homes.